LOVE AND SACRIFICE

Danielle Shaw

ISBN: 978-1-911445-02-9

First published in 1997 by London Bridge.

This edition published in 2015 by Endeavour Press Ltd.

Printed and bound in Great Britain by Clays Ltd, St Ives plc.

Endeavour Press is the UK's leading independent publisher.

We publish a wide range of genres including history, crime, romance, historical fiction and thrillers.

Every week, we give away free e-books.

For more information about our titles, go to our website:
www.endeavourpress.com/our-books/

Or sign up for our newsletter at:
www.endeavourpress.com

The Secret Affair

Secrets From the Past

The Secret Affair

Sunflower Morning

When Summer Fades

A Fabric of Dreams

For Kjell with love,
Also grateful thanks to Margaret, Judith and Gill for their friendship,
love and support throughout a very difficult year.

Table of Contents

CHAPTER ONE   1
CHAPTER TWO   8
CHAPTER THREE   15
CHAPTER FOUR   23
CHAPTER FIVE   30
CHAPTER SIX   36
CHAPTER SEVEN   43
CHAPTER EIGHT   52
CHAPTER NINE   59
CHAPTER TEN   65
CHAPTER ELEVEN   75
CHAPTER TWELVE   82
CHAPTER THIRTEEN   94
CHAPTER FOURTEEN   101
CHAPTER FIFTEEN   110
CHAPTER SIXTEEN   118
CHAPTER SEVENTEEN   132
CHAPTER EIGHTEEN   141
CHAPTER NINETEEN   151
CHAPTER TWENTY   159
CHAPTER TWENTY ONE   164
CHAPTER TWENTY TWO   173
CHAPTER TWENTY THREE   184
CHAPTER TWENTY FOUR   197
CHAPTER TWENTY FIVE   206
CHAPTER TWENTY SIX   221

CHAPTER TWENTY SEVEN 234
CHAPTER TWENTY EIGHT 240
CHAPTER TWENTY NINE 252
CHAPTER THIRTY 264
CHAPTER THIRTY ONE 273
CHAPTER THIRTY TWO 286
CHAPTER THIRTY THREE 295
CHAPTER THIRTY FOUR 304

CHAPTER ONE

'Two weeks, Andrew! *You* are going away for two weeks! We've only just celebrated Christmas and New Year. Isn't the snow enough for you in Scotland?' Jenny Sinclair's eyes blazed with anger. Her cheeks flushed scarlet as she regarded her brother.

Half expecting his sister's disapproval, Andrew Sinclair uneasily busied himself with the open files on his desk, while Stevie, who was taking the minutes of the meeting, anticipated a further verbal explosion.

'Well?' demanded Jenny.

Andrew opened his mouth to speak, only to be silenced by the ringing of the phone. Saved by the bell, he thought, grabbing the receiver and holding it like a lifeline. Jenny had every right to protest about his imminent absence from the family firm, yet there was also his wife to consider… The relief on Andrew's face soon gave way to concern. Replacing the receiver, he headed swiftly for the door.

'Andrew?' Jenny asked, her voice losing its earlier sharpness. 'Is there anything wrong?'

'It's Fiona,' Andrew said, all colour draining from his usually florid cheeks. 'She has a temperature. Mary's rung the doctor; she thinks it could be meningitis.'

Meningitis! Children died of that, didn't they? Only last week there'd been a case in the paper. Alarmed, Jenny thought anxiously of her niece. At six years old, Fiona was the youngest of Andrew's three children and the adored baby of the entire family. She and Cameron had been godparents and Jenny loved her dearly. Nothing must happen to Fiona!

Closing her notebook, Stevie turned her wheelchair to face Jenny. 'At any other time I'd say he was saved by the bell, but not today.'

Jenny poured two cups of coffee and handed one to Stevie, her PA. The two women worked well together, although hiring Stevie had been another occasion when brother and sister had done battle.

'You can't be serious about employing a cripple!' Andrew had demanded.

'I don't need Stevie's legs, I need her mind and her business acumen. Have you seen her CV?'

Forced to admit that he hadn't, Jenny had ignored her brother's disapproving looks and Stevie had joined the Sinclair team. There could be no excuses with regard to disabilities or wheelchair access, either. Their late father, William Sinclair, had himself spent his last years at the family business wheelchair-bound. As a result the offices and corridors of Sinclair Tartans were more than able to cope with Stevie's streamlined machine.

To Jenny's satisfaction and Andrew's despair, Stevie negotiated each obstacle with ease and dexterity. Even now it still amused Jenny to watch Andrew's face as the wheelchair ploughed tracks into his office carpet. The expanse of deep pile in Sinclair colours was Andrew's pride and joy. He never said anything, just glowered with annoyance.

Rubbing at the flattened pile with the toe of her shoe, Jenny watched as the bright-coloured tufts sprang up once more. Perhaps she had been a bit sharp with Andrew. His sheer hard work and determination had certainly helped Sinclair's through the recent recession. However, the start of a new year meant they must continue to make similar progress. Sauntering off on holiday was hardly conducive to that!

Jenny sighed and tugged at her strawberry blonde hair where it was tied at the nape of her neck with a black velvet bow. Determinedly she turned to face Stevie.

'If Andrew goes away we run the risk of losing valuable business.

Can't he see it's vital that we keep ahead of the market? I refuse to let Sinclair's lag behind its competitors. Anyway,' she said, taking Stevie's cup, 'I doubt if he'll go now… if Fiona is ill.'

Andrew's absence from the office left Jenny with a heavy workload. By the end of the afternoon she was both surprised and delighted when her sister-in-law rang inviting her for supper. Mary was an excellent cook; her ample proportions bore witness to the fact. Yet despite her size, she was always elegant and well dressed.

Tonight was no exception as Mary, in fine cashmere skirt and silk blouse, met her at the door, along with a wonderful smell of herbs and spices. Fiona, to Jenny's surprise, came bouncing along the hallway to meet her.

'Fiona! I thought you were poorly. Why aren't you in bed?'

'She should be but she wanted to wait up to see you. Hurry away to your room now Fiona, we grownups want our supper.'

Before obeying her mother, Fiona gave Jenny a warm hug.

Jenny smiled, watching her niece run to the top of the stairs. 'Well, what's wrong with you? You don't look too bad to me.'

From the landing, Fiona called down, 'I've got chicken spots, look!' With her words whistling through the gaps in her missing front teeth, Fiona lifted up her nightdress to reveal a mass of tiny red blisters.

'Thank heavens it wasn't meningitis,' Mary said as an aside. 'Have you had chicken pox, Jennifer?'

'Yes, I had it when I was small. It was awful, all that dreadful scratching and cold calamine lotion dabbed everywhere.' She shuddered at the memory and was grateful for the drink Andrew handed her when she entered the dining room.

'You look as if you could do with this. Sorry to have left you holding the fort, especially when there's so much going on.'

Relieved to find no hint in Andrew's voice of their earlier

3

disagreement, Jenny took a generous gulp of the refreshing Sancerre. She might have the quick temper associated with people of her colouring but she also hated atmospheres. Life was too short. She'd often heard of families having rows followed by long silences only to be brought together by unforeseen tragedies.

By inevitable association the most recent tragedies in Jenny Sinclair's life came to mind: the death of her beloved father – the result of a wasting and debilitating illness – and the sudden departure at Christmas of her fiancé. After six years, and without warning, Cameron Ross had ended their engagement. It had been so sudden, in fact, that Jenny was still recovering from the shock. Even her family were unaware of the circumstances. Blinking back tears, she was glad of the diversion when Mary called them to the table and Catriona and Iain, the two elder Sinclair children, joined their parents for supper.

Feeling more relaxed as a genial atmosphere pervaded the room, Jenny enquired after Catriona and Iain's studies before turning the conversation to the matriarch of the family; Morag Sinclair and her companion, Flora Tandy.

'Mother and Miss Tandy have had the most dreadful colds,' Jenny began.

'I'm not surprised,' Mary retorted, 'Why Mother-in-law insists on remaining in that cold, grey house with only an electric fire for heat, is beyond me! Goodness knows why Tandy has put up with her for so long. It's always raining on the west coast, too.'

'That's a bit of an exaggeration, Mary. The summers can be wonderful at Conasg. Besides,' Andrew said tersely, running his hands through his thick sandy hair. 'Aren't you forgetting something? Conasg House is the Sinclair family home and has been for years. It can't have been easy for Mother when…'

Jenny thought he was going to say, when father died. Instead he continued softly 'when she had to keep the mill running. It was only her canny head for business that kept Sinclair's going.'

Nodding in silent agreement, Jenny wondered what her mother would make of the blazing log fire that burnt in the grate, in addition to the central heating. Not for Mary were there layers of thermal underwear and thick sweaters. No wonder she could wear silk on such a cold evening.

'Jenny – more wine, or perhaps a brandy?' Andrew stood by her side, for once his stomach not hidden behind his desk. Like his wife, he was putting on weight from too much rich food and too little exercise.

'No thanks, Andrew, but if you'd just add a little soda water to this drink? Don't forget I'm driving and I must be going soon. I had some fresh ideas for Sinclair's this afternoon and I'd like to work on them before going to bed. Perhaps we could discuss them next week?'

Going to fetch her coat, Jenny was unaware of the furtive glances in Andrew's direction, both from his wife and his two older children. In the hall, however, she was startled to find Fiona sitting on the stairs.

'Have they asked you yet?' Fiona whispered. '*Please*, will you say yes?'

'Asked me what?' Jenny turned to find Andrew and family all hovering behind her.

Andrew and Mary looked shamefaced. It was Iain who broke the silence.

'We – er – were wondering if you'd look after Fiona… while we're away.'

Jenny surveyed them in utter disbelief. 'Are you saying you still intend to go – even if it means leaving Fiona behind?'

'Please Auntie Jen,' begged Catriona. 'We've been looking forward to this holiday for ages… especially as Dad's booked for two weeks!'

Andrew flinched visibly, recalling Jenny's earlier outburst.

'You see, you've already had chicken pox, Jennifer,' Mary continued, taking up the cause, 'and Dr McAllister said she won't be infectious for long. Andrew thought you could take her into the office with you. Apart from Stevie, there'll be no one else there...'

Jenny thought of Andrew's palatial office and felt a small hot hand, clutch tightly onto hers. She studied Fiona's round freckled face, curtained by two thick auburn plaits, and became transfixed by the intensity of the child's pleading dark brown eyes. Cameron's eyes had held that same intensity when he'd... Jenny shuddered, and turned towards her brother.

'What about the backlog from this morning's meeting? Isn't there a trade fair, too? You know you *never* miss those, Andrew.'

These were questions Mary couldn't answer. Andrew's reply left Jenny speechless.

'Well, you've got Stevie, haven't you? You of all people must realize how efficient she is!'

Unable to believe her ears, Jenny found herself sitting at the foot of the stairs with a warm, spotty body curled on her lap. Surrounded on all sides by Sinclairs, there was nothing for it but to concede. She would, however, make one condition.

'Very well,' she said flatly, 'but if I'm to look after Fiona *and* take responsibility for the office and the trade fair, Andrew must promise to consider my proposals for Sinclair's on his return.'

It was Andrew's turn to feel the focus of five pairs of eyes. They turned towards him with an air of expectancy.

'OK, I agree,' he said, his voice tinged with reluctance, thinking more of the respite from family pressure and the prospect of two weeks' skiing ahead.

There were whoops of joy from Catriona and Iain and a wet kiss planted firmly on Jenny's cheek by Fiona, with a request for Auntie Jen to take her to bed. At the top of the stairs Jenny surveyed the delighted quartet still standing in the hallway. It annoyed her to see Mary's smug look of satisfaction as she said to Andrew, 'There you are, I told you Jennifer wouldn't mind.' The problem was, however, that Jennifer minded very much indeed!

A jumble of thoughts raced through her head on the journey home: the first being would she be able to cope? But as Fiona was usually such a well-behaved child and as Andrew had been at pains to point out, she would also have Stevie to lend a hand… Jenny smiled quietly to herself within the confines of her car. She couldn't wait to tell Stevie of Andrew's compliment.

Leaving the bright lights of Edinburgh and its busy city streets, Jenny knew the main problem would be her business plan. That would require her immediate attention. Now, with little more than two weeks to complete it - before Andrew's return, she was determined he kept to his side of the bargain.

After what seemed like an eternity Jenny pulled into her driveway, where the day's anxieties and flashes of inspiration gave way to tiredness and contentment. Mary, she thought, could keep her large city house where theatres and shops compensated for the long hours Andrew spent at the office. Jenny, on the other hand, was far happier here in East Lothian. Her pretty cottage with its pantiled roof and tiny windows always seemed to welcome her home.

'Yes, I will cope,' she murmured sleepily. 'I'll make a list before going to bed.' At the top she wrote 'calamine lotion' and 'cotton wool' and at the bottom 'MOTHER'. By the words 'Sinclair business plan', there was simply a row of question marks.

CHAPTER TWO

An air of expectancy filled the large Edinburgh house. Mary and Catriona rushed back and forth with assorted piles of ski wear. Their baggage allowance already exceeded, as Andrew paced the floor, refusing point-blank to pay for any excess. Iain meanwhile tried on his new ski boots for the umpteenth time and, taking up his batons, practiced slalom manoeuvres along the hallway.

'Iain! Will you not do that, you'll ruin the carpet!' Andrew's tone was one of exasperation. 'Mary, where's Fiona? Is she ready yet? I told Jennifer I would be there half an hour ago.'

'Coming, Daddy,' called a voice and Fiona came bouncing down the stairs, auburn plaits swinging and chicken pox glowing.

Seeing his *baby* minus her front teeth and face full of spots, Andrew was overcome by a sudden pang of guilt. Fiona certainly looked a picture, but none any artist of merit would care to paint. 'Ready then?' he asked, hugging her warmly.

Fiona nodded and gave her father a small holdall. It was open and inside he recognized her most treasured possessions. Despite constant teasing from her brother and sister, Fiona would go nowhere without them.

'I only hope Auntie Jennifer's going to have room for all this,' Andrew said, taking his youngest child and her luggage to the car.

'And I only hope Jennifer's cottage is going to be warm enough,' Mary called, appearing with an armful of apres-ski wear. 'You will remind her to keep the child warm.'

Andrew remained tight lipped and silent. His sister's cottage was not Conasg House.

*

Sitting by the fire, Jenny watched as flames enveloped logs of apple wood and fir. The apple was from the gnarled old tree that had once stood at the bottom of the garden, and the fir was the remains of her Christmas tree. She felt strangely melancholy. It was like setting fire to part of her life; soon there would be nothing left but ashes.

Since Christmas she'd spent many long hours thinking of Cameron and wondering what might have happened if only he hadn't broken off their engagement. But 'what if' and 'if only' were such futile words. She and Cameron were no longer an item and she only had herself – or according to Cameron, Sinclair's – to blame for that.

Stabbing angrily at a glowing log with a brass-handled poker, Jenny relived Christmas and New Year. Christmas had been spent with Cameron's sister Isla and her husband at their rambling old vicarage. There the crumbling masonry had echoed to the sounds of gurgling babies and jovial adults, interspersed with the constant monotonous thump of bass from teenage bedrooms. And, while appreciative of Isla's hospitality, Jenny had been mildly relieved when the time came to depart.

Standing on the doorstep, clutching the youngest of her brood, Isla had smiled broadly as the baby's chubby hands reached eagerly for Jenny.

'See how she adores you, Jenny; she doesn't want you to go. You've been such a help this Christmas. I don't know how I would have managed without you.'

Disentangling tiny fingers from her hair, Jenny had noticed Cameron's aggrieved look and heard his disgruntled mutterings.

'And what's got into you, little brother?' Isla teased. 'You look as if someone's taken away your favourite toy.'

'Hasn't it occurred to you, that it would have been nice to have had

9

Jenny to myself, instead of finding her constantly monopolized by endless streams of children?'

'But Cameron,' Jenny broke in, 'we've only been here three days.'

'Och. Take no notice of him,' Isla said. 'Being the youngest of the family, Cameron was always spoilt – and when he couldn't get his own way he sulked, just like he's doing now. I'd advise you to take heed, Jenny. Remember that when you've wee ones of your own.'

'Hmph! Chance would be a fine thing,' Cameron flung back at his sister, taking Jenny's bags to the car.

'And what was that supposed to mean?' Jenny asked, watching him switch on the ignition and clumsily engage first gear.

'Exactly what it implies. How can we have children when we're not even married? I take it you still want children?'

'Of course. We both do. We've talked about it often enough, haven't we? Ever since we became Fiona's godparents.'

Cameron threw her a sideways glance. 'And how long ago was that?'

'Six years. What's that got to do with it?'

'That's how long you've been saying you're going to marry me.'

'Well, I will; and we'd even set a date, remember? But it wasn't easy for my mother when my father died…'

'Your father's been dead for three years…'

'And you were away at sea for so long that we simply didn't see each other…'

'That's right, blame it on the Royal Navy!'

'I'm not. I'm simply trying to point out that things haven't been easy. There's also Sinclair's…'

Cameron laughed bitterly. 'Ah, that's more like it. Sinclair's! I wondered when that was going to come into the argument.'

'I wasn't aware we were having an argument.'

Ten minutes later, having ignored Jenny's last remark, Cameron turned the car precariously into the graveled driveway of her cottage, narrowly missing the gatepost.

'For goodness' sake, Cameron! Be careful. Do you realize you nearly broke the…?'

'Oh, yes,' he sighed sarcastically, 'I realize only to well. And, speaking of breaking, I am breaking off our engagement.'

Stepping from the car, Jenny stared at him in disbelief.

'But only moments ago you were talking about getting married…'

Cameron walked with her to the front door, then, putting her bags in the porch turned and cupped her face in his hands. For once the familiar, warm brown eyes were cold. 'Jenny,' he whispered, kissing her forehead with icy lips, 'aren't you forgetting something? You are already married… You, my dear, are married to Sinclair's!'

Numbed, Jenny watched him walk back to the car. 'What about Conasg? You were supposed to be coming with me to Conasg House for New Year. You even said you were looking forward to the peace and quiet of a Sinclair gathering.'

Cameron nodded ruefully, climbing back into his car. 'Yes, I did. However, that's something else you've forgotten, I'm not a Sinclair and never shall be!'

*

Through misted eyes, Jenny sat up with a jolt as a sudden noise broke the melancholy silence. This time it was not the sound of Cameron's sporty hatchback departing angrily but the smooth purr of Andrew's BMW drawing up outside.

The car door slammed and Fiona went running down the path before Andrew had time to stop her. He'd fully intended to carry her indoors wrapped in the blanket as instructed by Mary. Now it lay on the cream leather seat with the array of Fiona's treasures that had spilled from the holdall as he's negotiated the twists and turns in the road. Gathering the contents together, Andrew looked about him in the darkness. This place was so remote, and it still bothered him that Jenny chose to live here.

'Come along, Daddy, I need my slippers,' Fiona called, already sitting by the fire.

'Hmm. I see you've got yourself nicely installed,' Andrew said, producing slippers like rabbits with large floppy ears. He was pleased to see the blazing log fire – he could at least report back to his wife on the question of warmth.

'Jennifer - um - Mary and I... we're really grateful to you for helping us out. I think Fiona's actually delighted she's got chicken pox and isn't coming with us.'

Fiona, who'd already said goodbye to her father, was rummaging in her bag for a book. She looked up in her aunt's direction. Yes, her Daddy was right. 'We're going to have a lovely time together, aren't we Auntie Jenny?' she said brightly. 'I can be *your* little girl while Mummy and Daddy are on holiday, 'cos you haven't got one and Uncle Cameron's gone away and left you...'

Andrew froze as he walked towards the door. 'Jennifer... I'm so sorry... I'm sure Fiona didn't mean to...'

'It's all right, Andrew. Don't worry. Out of the mouths of babes, as they say.' Jenny watched as Andrew's gaze fell on the photograph of Cameron, still gracing the mantelpiece. 'Besides... Fiona's company is probably just what I need at the moment.'

*

The scene at the airport was one of chaos, to the extent Andrew thought half of Scotland was going away. Mary groaned at the lengthening check-in queues sprouting skis from every angle. They weren't the easiest things to manage at the best of times. She watched Andrew and Iain perch theirs precariously on suitcases. Pausing for a moment to survey the snake-like meanderings across the terminal, Mary was thankful that Fiona had been spared this ordeal.

In an adjoining queue a younger man stood with two small girls, one fair-haired and blue-eyed and the other with olive skin, deep brown eyes and even darker curls. Distressed by the swirling mass of impatient bodies, noise and luggage, the children cried and clung to their father. Then, recognizing a familiar face, walking down the line towards them, they relaxed and released their grasp. An elegant woman dressed in black and scarlet ignored their outstretched arms.

'Now what's all this fuss? Don't cry, darlings, Mummy will be back soon. She's only going for a *leetle* holiday.'

The accent was strong and Mary, recognizing it as Italian, studied the woman discreetly. Numerous heads turned in the same direction, including that of Mary's immediate neighbour, who voiced her thoughts openly.

'Poor wee things! Fancy leaving them behind like that. She might be a stunner to look at... but anyone can see she's no good as a mother!'

Filled with a sudden pang of guilt, Mary turned towards her husband. 'Andrew, ring Jennifer and see if Fiona's all right. There's still time. We will be in this queue for ages.'

Hesitating for a moment, Andrew knew he'd get no peace until he did. Moving to one side, he found a less noisy corner and reached for his mobile.

'Fiona's perfectly OK', he said five minutes later. 'She's had a good night's sleep and Jennifer's giving her breakfast in bed.'

Catriona looked towards the two small girls and retorted angrily. 'I bet they don't get breakfast in bed. In fact they look as if they've been dragged from theirs. Do you think that man is their father? Poor thing,' she continued, startling her mother with her vehemence, 'no wonder he looks so embarrassed, with everyone staring at *her!*'

At just sixteen, Catriona was constantly bemoaning the fact that she thought her parents old-fashioned, yet deep down she was glad her own mother would never embarrass her by posturing and parading like the woman in scarlet and black.

Her brother, on the other hand, couldn't take his eyes off the striking Italian. At seventeen and a half, Iain Sinclair was beginning to take a keen interest in the opposite sex. When eyes the colour of dark chocolate flashed in his direction, he simply melted.

'What a stunner!' he whispered to his father. 'Pity we don't have any like that at the academy. I wouldn't mind studying for my highers then.'

Andrew merely nodded, conscious of Mary's penetrating look of disapproval. The woman was indeed beautiful and she knew it. She also knew, as she shook a mass of jet-black hair about her shoulders, that she was playing to a full house.

'Gosh, Dad! Do you see she's boarding the same flight as us?'

'Quiet, Iain!' Mary hissed. 'People will hear you!'

Nearing the departure gates, Gina Hadley bade an over-dramatic goodbye to her two children and fluttered her eyelashes at her audience.

' *Ciao*, Celestina. *Ciao*, Emily. Be good, my darlings.'

Her attempt at a loving farewell to her husband, however, was less convincing when she kissed the air on both sides of his cheeks. In response, Paul Hadley replied softly, 'Goodbye, Gina. I hope you have a good time.'

Fortunately, both he and his daughters were out of earshot when Mary's neighbour added to her earlier caustic remark. 'Hmph! There's no doubt about the sort of time, *she'll* be having. Those poor wee things are probably better off without her!'

CHAPTER THREE

To Jenny's surprise the weekend went all too quickly. She delighted in Fiona's company, playing games, reading books and eating toasted teacakes by the fire.

'It's like a picnic indoors,' gasped Fiona when Jenny produced the old-fashioned toasting fork that had once belonged to her grandmother.

Later, freshly bathed and dabbed with calamine lotion, like a giant marshmallow dusted with sugar, Fiona snuggled next to Jenny in the big double bed. Quietly she watched her aunt study the trade fair catalogue and then looked at her picture book until overcome by a fit of scratching.

Anxious that Andrew and Mary shouldn't return to find Fiona covered in chicken pox scars, Jenny said thoughtfully, 'Fiona, if you promise not to scratch, I'll give you a special treat. Now… what would you like?'

The child thought long and hard. Toys, books, dolls? No, she had all those. What could she think of as a special treat? Her eyes widened excitedly. 'I've got it, Auntie Jenny, I know what I want! A picnic, a proper outdoor picnic like the one in the book.' Fiona pointed to the pages in front of her. It had been that evening's bedtime story: a mouse was having a picnic with all her friends in a woodland glade.

'Very well, you shall have your picnic, but later in the year, when the weather is warmer. Now you must try to stop scratching and go to sleep.'

'Will there be *mices* and will there be *pwimwoses*?'

'Yes, I expect we'll find mice and primroses, but you'll have to be very good and very quiet.'

Kissing Fiona on the forehead, Jenny switched off the light. She was also tired. The trade fair catalogue and her plans for Sinclair's would simply have to wait until morning.

With aunt and niece sleeping through the alarm, Monday morning began badly. To Jenny's despair Fiona refused to leave for the office without all her treasured possessions, and from the moment she arrived at Sinclair's the phones barely stopped ringing. It was late morning before she noticed the thank-you gift of flowers and champagne sent by Andrew.

That's all very well, she told herself, examining the bottle of Bollinger, but it wasn't going to help her get through the backlog of paperwork, even if it did ease Andrew's conscience.

After lunch Fiona came in search of attention. She'd played quietly in her father's office during the morning but now wanted Jenny to read to her. Reaching for the book, Jenny dislodged the trade fair catalogue and gasped. The trade fair! It had completely slipped her mind. Partly because Andrew had left a note saying not to bother, if there wasn't time - he knew how she hated these gatherings - and also because he would see Bill Freeman himself on his return.

The difficulty was, Jenny told herself, her brother had been at school with Bill Freeman. It was the old boy network in operation and Andrew was more than happy to let things continue as before.

'Whereas I'm not!' she declared, flicking through the lists of exhibitors, 'So... sorry Bill, but as I'm in charge of this one...'

Switching off her laptop, Jenny called through to Stevie. 'Fancy reading a story about a mouse having a picnic? Only I really must be going if I'm to get to this extravaganza before they all pack up for the night and go home.'

Stevie smiled and re-positioned her wheelchair. Fiona, still clutching her favourite book, climbed onto her lap and giggled. Jenny, meanwhile, grabbed her phone, ipad and handbag and hurried to the door.

'Call me if you need me,' she said.

*

At that precise moment Paul Hadley needed something or someone, only he wasn't quite sure which. Like Jenny, his day had also begun badly. The frantic search for Celestina's uniform, hampered by the debris left in the wake of Gina's departure, was swiftly followed by Emily bursting into tears when she couldn't find her nursery school apron. Now his thoughts turned to more urgent matters... work! He desperately needed to find some.

With Gina flitting all over the place, both for work and pleasure, Paul had been forced into taking drastic action. Someone had to look after the girls and that someone was him! Unfortunately things had happened far too quickly and, declining his last assignment and parting company with Baynham's, his only option was to work from home.

Working from home was one thing, Paul concluded with a wry smile, studying his reflection in the hall mirror before he left to fetch the girls from school and nursery, as for convincing someone to employ him...

With Cele and Emily skipping merrily along, posters from the trade fair caught Paul's attention. If the neighbour could have the girls for an hour, perhaps he could put in an appearance. Just one contract would make all the difference...

'Thanks, Helen, you're an angel,' Paul shouted across as he ran back indoors.

Confronted once more by the hall mirror, he was reminded again of his crumpled appearance. His long blond hair flopped untidily across his forehead and troubled blue eyes stared back at him, expressing their deep concern.

'Well, Paul Hadley, a change of shirt and a comb through your hair won't come amiss, will it?' he muttered. No wonder people had been staring at the airport: Gina all done up like a dog's dinner and her husband looking like something the cat dragged in! Now... where to find a clean shirt?

Long before he reached the wardrobe, realization dawned. Knowing Gina, there would be none ironed. His only hope was the utility room. There, greeted by a pile of clothes strewn across the muddied quarry tiled floor, he emitted an exasperated groan. Even the door of the tumble drier gaped open, its mouth seeming to spew forth a tangle of shirts, blouses and socks. The dilemma now was what was clean and what was dirty, particularly as the whites were all the same dingy grey. As for the coloureds... Paul with his expert designer's eye was at a loss to describe them.

From the dark cavernous interior of the tumble drier, he tugged at a bundle of fiendishly entwined sleeves and grabbed the first available shirt. Plugging in the iron, he smoothed the stubborn creases and watched in horror as rusty brown water leaked from holes not clogged with melted fabric.

'Damn you, Gina! Damn you!' he cried in desperation.

Like sludge on a clear blue sea, a dirty brown stain seeped slowly across the back of his shirt.

With time at a premium Paul had little choice other than to iron the collar and front panels and fetch his jacket. The result was far from satisfactory and the fabric felt warm and moist against his back. Making his way to the only room in any semblance of order - his bedroom/come study - he took stock of the current situation.

He knew only too well what he wanted; security for his wife and children, but what did Gina want? From the surrounding chaos it would appear she didn't want motherhood and domesticity. Yet, before they'd married, Gina had declared that was all she'd ever wanted. Was it, he wondered, or had she just chosen him as a ticket to freedom? Reflecting on their very first meeting at the local *trattoria*, Paul's mood changed from anger to sadness.

Theirs had been a whirlwind courtship, beginning with the photos he'd taken of Gina and her friends on their day off and ending with marriage and the subsequent birth of Celestina twelve months later. Life had been idyllic until Emily was born. Then, quite by chance, when Baynham's offered Gina a modelling assignment, everything had changed.

Reversing into the parking bay, Paul recalled how that first job for Baynham's had heralded disaster. From that moment a life of glamour had beckoned and Gina had followed it, ever eager and hungry for more, leaving behind all thoughts of her husband and children. Paul's concern for Cele and Emily was of little consequence. Gina refused to co-operate. The end, when it came, was inevitable. Paul had no choice but to hand in his notice. The welfare of his children was paramount and his only hope now was the trade fair. He paused, scanning the list of exhibitors displayed in the foyer.

'Paul? Paul Hadley! How are you? I haven't seen you in ages. How's that gorgeous wife of yours?'

Turning, Paul felt a firm hand clasp his in greeting. Though he had no desire to discuss his private life at present, he was nevertheless pleased to see Alistair Jennings. They'd worked together several years ago.

'So what's brought you here this afternoon?' Alistair enquired.

Five minutes later, having chosen deliberately to be economical with the truth, Paul sought Alistair's advice.

'Hmm. Well… I suppose you could try Sinclair's. I overheard Jenny Sinclair making some enquiries a short while ago.'

Paul frowned. 'Sinclair's? I don't think I know them, do I?'

'You must do… Sinclair Tartans… old family firm? A bit old fashioned if you ask me, but weathering the storm reasonably well.'

The funny thing is,' Alistair continued, 'it's usually Andrew Sinclair who attends these jaunts but I gather he's not here... Besides, he always uses Freeman's.'

Paul looked dejected, Freeman's were strong opposition. 'How do I get to meet Andrew Sinclair, then? Can you introduce me some time?'

'Not unless you want to wait another two weeks, and if you don't mind my saying so, just from looking at you, I'd say your situation is pretty desperate at the moment.'

Feeling distinctly uncomfortable, Paul raked a hand through his unruly hair. He knew his clothes were shabby and alongside Alistair, who was always immaculately turned out, the contrast was even more pronounced. He was anxious to get away. 'So... if you can't introduce me to Andrew Sinclair, can you point out this – er – Jenny that you mentioned earlier?'

Paul followed Alistair's gaze as he scanned the crowds, stopping on two women deep in conversation. The taller of the two, with dark hair and eyes, made him think automatically of Gina. His heart sank.

'There you are, Jenny Sinclair – the one in the black skirt and tartan jacket. Have a word with her. I'm sure you'll find her a real soft touch compared to Andrew. Now, if you'll excuse me, I'm meeting a client.'

Patting Paul's arm, Alistair turned and reached for his brief case.

'By the way,' he called back, 'we must get together for a drink sometime. Don't forget to give my love to Gina.'

Alistair's words were lost on Paul as he studied the slight, trim figure with hair like burnished copper. His relief was palpable. The last person he wanted to think about was Gina. His main concern now was not to lose sight of Jenny Sinclair in the crowds.

'Mrs Sinclair?'

Heading for the door, Jenny stopped in her tracks. Her head ached and her feet were sore from the constant trampling of male footwear. It was also getting late and there was still the prospect of Fiona for almost another two weeks. The last thing she needed was to be confronted by yet another smooth-talking salesman. She turned sharply.

'Actually, it's *Miss* Sinclair!'

Paul stood in embarrassment, duly corrected. 'Miss Sinclair, I apologize. I wondered if you could spare me half an hour of your time? My name is Paul Hadley – I'm a designer... and Alistair Jennings suggested I might be able to help you.'

At that precise moment Paul didn't have a clue if he could help Sinclair Tartans but, deciding it was worth a damned good try, he extended his hand in greeting.

Accepting Paul's hand it was Jenny's turn to feel embarrassed. Cautiously she studied the man who gave the appearance of having slept on a park bench. He was certainly no smarmy sales rep, so what had she to lose?

'Ten-thirty sharp, tomorrow morning, Mr Hadley,' she said, giving him her business card. 'I'll tell my assistant to expect you.'

Paul watched her go in disbelief, then realized the time. He would be late fetching the girls from the neighbour and they'd be wanting their tea.

'We'll go for a pizza,' he told himself, walking to the car park, 'and I'll cook us a proper supper tomorrow. Tonight, Paul Hadley, you have shirts to wash and iron and a suit to press!'

*

Jenny found Fiona pushing Stevie around the boardroom in her wheelchair.

'It's role reversal,' Stevie whispered, clutching a lop-eared toy rabbit. 'I'm the baby, she's the mummy.'

Jenny smiled and gathered up Fiona's belongings. What would Andrew say? Endless rows of wheel marks criss-crossed the magnificent red, green and blue plaid. The carpet had never seen so much traffic.

'Well, Stevie, I think it's going to be poached eggs, Marmite soldiers and bed by eight tonight. I'm exhausted. Andrew can keep his trade fairs.'

'No luck, then?' Stevie asked. 'I take it was all a complete waste of time.'

'Not exactly, because I met the scarecrow from The Wizard of Oz and he's coming here at ten-thirty tomorrow. Actually… I think he said his name was Paul Hadley, so you'd better put it in the diary.'

Listening intently to this conversation, Fiona's eyes opened in wonderment. Had her aunt really met the scarecrow who'd featured in one of her favourite films? And was he also coming to the office tomorrow? Amazed and delighted, she couldn't wait to see!

CHAPTER FOUR

The next day found Paul in control, with no intention of being late for his appointment. He found his one decent suit, still in its polythene wrapper from its visit to the cleaners, and washed and ironed a shirt without mishap. Thinking back to the previous day's disasters, Jenny Sinclair had clearly noticed his crumpled appearance. Today he'd show her he could at least look presentable. To complement the dark navy-blue suit he selected an Italian silk tie; one of Gina's many peace offerings. There, he had to admit she had good taste.

Stopping in front of the hall mirror, Paul pushed his hair away from his forehead. Perhaps he should have had a haircut but as he chose to wear his hair longer… He shrugged his shoulders; it was too risky at this late stage. No, he would face Jenny Sinclair as he was. Though still unsure what he could offer her by way of constructive advice, his main objectives were to arrive on time and remember to call her Miss Sinclair.

If Paul was surprised to find Jenny's PA in a wheelchair he didn't show it. He was too engrossed in the photos and brochures that surrounded him as he sat in the outer office. His first impression was of an old-established family firm – with good marketable products – in need of a little updating. The difficulty was, some of these families were so set in their ways and resented change. Paul studied the portrait of three people (two women and a man), hanging on the wall and decided to gauge the situation carefully. Jennifer he recognized, so presumably the man by her side was her brother. As for the elderly lady sitting between them, he had no idea, though together they appeared a truly formidable trio.

At ten-thirty precisely Stevie directed Paul to Jenny's office, where she stood waiting to greet him. Yesterday evening having agreed to this meeting, she'd been strangely apprehensive. Now, if Paul had been astute enough to mask his surprise at Stevie's wheelchair, Jenny did likewise at the change in Mr Hadley's appearance. Today there was no sign of the scarecrow that had so intrigued Fiona on their way home; nor could she fail to notice the particular emphasis he'd placed on calling her *Miss* Sinclair when he'd arrived.

Sitting opposite Jenny, Paul in turn studied her discreetly. Her suit was neat and elegant and his artist's eye recalled the two-piece she'd worn yesterday: the black skirt and subdued tartan jacket. Today her jacket was black but her skirt and the velvet trimmed revers on the collar were tartan. A clever idea of combining two suits to create four different outfits. Gina would never consider such a combination. She much preferred the outrageous, and to draw attention to herself.

Dispensing with preliminaries, Jenny came straight to the point.

'Sinclair's are an old family firm, Mr Hadley, and we have some excellent products; however, I do think it's time to move forward and look to different markets. So... do you think you can help us make that move?'

Taken aback by her forthright request, Paul hesitated for a moment. This wasn't at all what he was expecting... but offered this opportunity... 'I'm sure I can Miss Sinclair, given some time and research, plus of course details of past products manufactured under the Sinclair label and...'

'Good! I can give you all those,' Jenny said, leaving her desk. Calling through to Stevie for coffee, she motioned for Paul to follow her through to the boardroom. 'I think you'll find all the information you'll need is in here.'

Looking to where shelves were lined neatly with books, files and samples, one book in particular caught Paul's eye; an embossed tartan volume of considerable size.

'Take whatever information you require, Mr Hadley, as long as you return everything by Friday. Then… perhaps you can come back a week today with your ideas?'

A week! In stunned silence Paul took the coffee Jenny handed him and watched the steam rise from the gold-rimmed green cups. A week! He'd never been asked to produce anything so quickly. It would be impossible to complete a thorough project in such a short time. His mouth went dry. How could he explain the difficulties involved? He needed this job but he also needed more than a week if he was to do it successfully.

Sipping her coffee, Jenny added thoughtfully, 'Of course I'm not expecting a complete project, merely a rough proposal. I'm sorry, Mr Hadley, I should have explained at the beginning… Andrew - my brother - and I have opposing views on which paths Sinclair's should be taking at present. With Andrew and his wife on holiday, I see this as my opportunity to change our designs and hopefully get my mother on my side before his return.'

Deeply intrigued, Paul recalled the portrait of the formidable trio in Reception. So the elderly woman who had looked so dour was Jennifer Sinclair's mother, and no doubt the family's matriarch. While the cat's away the mice will play, he mused. In this instance the mice being Mrs Sinclair senior and her daughter.

Finishing his coffee, Paul studied Jenny cautiously. This petite and feisty-looking young woman was offering him the chance of a lifetime, yet it could also mean becoming embroiled in a battle between brother and sister. He suppressed a smile, what the hell? It was a chance he simply had to take.

While Paul contemplated family feuds, Jenny placed brochures and books on the table for his perusal. Picking up the embossed tartan volume that had earlier caught his eye, he opened the pages carefully.

'Would it,' he asked softly, 'be OK if I borrowed this? I can tell it's a very special edition...'

Jenny hesitated. It was one of Andrew's prized possessions. The book told of Scottish clans and their descendants, giving in minute detail the history of each family. It was always Andrew's intention to study it from cover to cover, in the hope of finding direct connections to the present lairds. To date, not having much time for reading, he hadn't, but Andrew – and Mary, were certain he would, one day.

'Yes, take it,' Jenny said, before considering a change of mind. She pushed a large manila envelope towards him. 'Only do please take special care of it and return it by Friday.'

Sliding the book carefully into the envelope, Paul placed it in his briefcase, and from the corner of his eye saw the door to the boardroom opening slowly. Jenny looked up, fully expecting it to be Stevie. Instead, it was Fiona who peeped round the door. Her face, initially a picture of wide-eyed curiosity, altered to one of complete disappointment.

'Oh!' she faltered. 'Are you really the scarecrow who went with Dorothy and the tin man to find...?'

'Fiona!' broke in Jenny, desperate to silence her niece.

Paul smiled kindly and walked to where Fiona stood transfixed in the doorway. 'No, I'm not,' he said. 'Why... did you think I was?'

'Um – well, you don't look him,' whispered Fiona, casting a furtive glance at her aunt, 'but Auntie Jen said she met him yesterday and he was coming to see her at half-past ten. Wasn't that when you arrived?'

Paul and Fiona turned in Jenny's direction as a rush of colour flooded her face. Her once pale cheeks were suffused with embarrassment. What could she say? Fiona, sensing something was horribly wrong, hurried away to the sanctuary of her father's office.

'I'm sorry about that… Fiona's my niece, I'm looking after her while Andrew and his family are away.'

Paul ran a hand over his hair and fixed Jenny with a curious smile, as if awaiting further explanation. When none was forthcoming, he said softly, 'Don't worry, I have two girls of my own. They're both blessed with a wonderful sense of imagination and never fail to amaze me. Anyway,' he said, closing his briefcase and holding out his hand. 'Don't worry about the books, I'll take good care of them and return them on Friday. Goodbye, *Miss* Sinclair and thank you for your time.'

Numbed to the quick, Jenny could only watch after him in silence. He must have realized she'd referred to him as looking like a scarecrow following yesterday's meeting. He'd certainly looked unkempt then, but today… well, he was certainly looking smarter.

'But not smart as in naval-smart,' she murmured, walking back to her desk. There, opening the top left-hand drawer, she removed the silver-framed photo of Cameron in full naval-officer's uniform. At one time she'd always thought his dark chocolate brown eyes had been smiling at her. Now she wasn't so sure; they appeared almost mocking and cruel. Feeling a shiver run down her spine, she replaced the photo and closed the drawer just as Stevie appeared in the doorway.

'Hmm, so that was Dorothy's companion on the yellow brick road, was it? A dishy sort of scarecrow if you ask me.'

'I'm not! And don't you start, Stevie! I've already had enough from Fiona. Can you believe she actually asked him if he…'

Explaining the whole embarrassing scenario, Jenny continued, 'I honestly don't mind confessing, I just wanted that enormous carpet of Andrew's to swallow me up and take me out of here. Goodness knows what Mr Hadley must have thought.' She cast her gaze to the vast expanse of tartan carpet as if willing the edges to curl up and whisk her away. Instead it was only Stevie's lips that curled as they broke into a smile.

'I'm so sorry, Jenny,' she laughed, 'but I think it's hilarious.'

Jenny's face remained flushed and confused.

'Oh, come on,' said Stevie, 'it's not that bad, is it? Besides, Mr Hadley looks as if he's got a sense of humour. He has what my mum calls "lovely smiling eyes".'

Jenny sighed. She hadn't really noticed but assumed they were probably blue. She usually only noticed brown eyes, and then simply to compare them with Cameron's. She felt a lump in her throat as tears pricked her eyelids. She'd begun this week determined to forget Cameron and stand up to Andrew. Now everything seemed to be crumbling about her.

Desperate to reassure, Stevie spun her wheelchair to face Jenny head on. 'I think you're worrying unduly; he probably doesn't even remember Judy Garland and the Wizard of Oz.'

'Hmm, I wouldn't bank on it. During the short time he was here, Mr Hadley just happened to mention he has two little girls of his own. I expect that just like Fiona, they sat and watched the film over the Christmas holidays. And also like Fiona, they too would like red shoes!'

Prompted by thoughts of bedtime stories, Jenny was reminded that she hadn't seen her niece since the child fled the boardroom. Poor Fiona! It couldn't be easy for her with her parents away and the chicken pox still causing discomfort. She was also probably hungry and no doubt wanting her lunch.

Fiona sat on the floor of Andrew's office surrounded by her toys and books. She hung her head when her aunt entered the room, and Jenny could see that she'd been crying.

'I'm s-sorry, Auntie Jenny, was I rude to the man? Mummy says it's not nice to be rude... but you did say the scarecrow from the film was coming to see you and I thought...'

Jenny sat on the floor cradling Fiona in her arms as her niece's eyes filled with tears once more. 'If you're c-cross with me,' Fiona sobbed, 'does that mean we won't have our picnic?'

Stroking the thick amber hair they'd plaited so carefully that morning, Jenny whispered soothing words of comfort. No, she wasn't cross with Fiona. It was just a simple misunderstanding. Grown-ups often said one thing and meant another. She would explain to Mr Hadley when he returned on Friday. 'As for our picnic,' she concluded, 'Yes, of course we'll still have it. Though summer is really the best time for picnics, I promise we'll go in the spring when the primroses are in bloom. Now, speaking of food, what about some lunch?'

CHAPTER FIVE

For the rest of the week, Jenny chose to forget about Paul and the embarrassing scarecrow incident. It was Fiona who reminded her as they drove into work on Friday morning.

'Isn't the man coming today?'

'The man?' Jenny queried while negotiating the bend in the road. There had been snow in the night, leaving large drifts. 'What man?'

'The man who borrowed Daddy's books.'

The car swerved slightly, Jenny's concentration interrupted. Fiona had missed nothing. She'd presumably seen Paul with the books and brochures. Fiona was right, Paul Hadley had promised to return everything today. More importantly, Jenny wondered, would he also be bringing some ideas to keep Sinclair's operating in a very competitive market?

By lunchtime, with no sign him and still with her shopping to do, Jenny left strict instructions for Stevie to check the books, particularly Andrew's prized volume, should Paul arrive in her absence. As yet there was no need to panic – after all, the office didn't close until five o'clock.

Returning to find Fiona and Stevie having lunch, Jenny's enquiring look was met with a definite shake of the head. Anxious not to draw attention to the situation, she took a parcel from her shopping bag.

'Here you are, Fiona, as you've been so good this week, and I've hardly seen you scratching, I've bought you a present. It's to use indoors until we can have the real thing.'

Fiona's eyes opened wide in excitement. She tore open the paper to reveal a blue and white doll's tea set.

'Oh, Auntie Jen, it's lovely,' she cried, and ran to give her aunt a hug.

'Don't I get a hug for giving you lunch?' Stevie asked, and was promptly rewarded with a wet kiss on the cheek.

'P'raps we can have a tea party this afternoon?' Fiona asked, fixing the two women with pleading eyes.

Desperate to get Stevie alone to enquire if there had been any news from Paul, Jenny realized that with Fiona around it wasn't going to be easy. Quickly she removed her Paisley shawl from about her shoulders and handed it to her niece, then she took a packet of shortbread from her shopping.

'Here,' she said, 'take these. You can use my shawl as a picnic rug and we'll have the shortbread with our tea. Run along now and get it ready for us. Stevie and I have a great deal of work to. We'll come in at four o'clock.'

Relieved to see Fiona disappear with a mission in mind, Jenny turned to Stevie. 'Well?'

'No sign of him, I'm afraid. No telephone call, nothing.'

'Nothing! OK. Call me the minute you hear anything... anything at all.'

During the afternoon, Jenny found it hard to concentrate. Her thoughts kept returning to Andrew's precious book. To think she'd allowed Paul to take it, when she knew so little about him. Yes, she'd given him her business card, but in return she'd received nothing. She's even been foolish enough not to ask for a contact number – let alone an address! How stupid of her! What if he didn't bring the book back? How could she find him? More worryingly, what would Andrew say if he returned to find empty spaces on his bookshelves?

Jenny stood anxiously at the office window. It was already dark outside and there were few people in the square below. No one stopped or spoke, looking so miserable, pinched and drawn, wrapped up against the icy chill. Seemingly they had only one thought in their minds, that of going home. Jenny too would soon have to think about going. Worrying about Paul's non-appearance, she'd even forgotten Fiona's tea party.

A screech of brakes in the car park below caused her to peer through the enveloping gloom. At that moment no one could have been more relieved to see Paul emerge from the car, with the same briefcase that had carried away Andrew's books. Not only did he appear harassed, but also there seemed to be some confusion coming from the back seat of the car.

Two small girls sat in obvious distress and Paul was trying to reason with them. Looking first at his watch and then in the direction of Jenny's office, he hesitated before helping his daughters from the car.

'Miss Sinclair, I do apologize for being so late. My neighbour was due to fetch the girls from school for me, but she had a call to say that her mother had been rushed to hospital. I then offered to take her there, it being the least I could do as she often helps me and...'

Relief flooded Jenny's face. 'Please don't concern yourself, Mr Hadley. You're here now. That's all that matters. I'm sure you could do with a cup of tea after all that rushing around. Do sit down.'

Paul nodded and sank into a chair. He'd been dreading her reaction to his tardiness. So far their business relationship – brief though it was, had been somewhat bizarre. Unlocking his briefcase, he was aware of Jenny watching his every move as one by one he placed every book, brochure and file upon her desk.

Making a mental check of everything, Jenny observed that each borrowed item was now carefully wrapped in tissue paper. She was duly impressed.

'Did you find them of any help?' she asked, and was further amazed to hear his response.

'Yes. Very much so! I intend to prepare a file for you this weekend, ready for next Tuesday… as you requested.'

His statement was almost questioning, as if he half expected her to say she'd changed her mind. To his relief she voiced no such objection, making only some comment about Stevie and tea. Puzzled by Stevie's non-appearance, Jenny walked to the door and looked into the corridor.

'Um - I think she may have taken my girls to the cloakroom. Coming straight from school in such a rush and taking Helen to the hospital, I'm afraid there wasn't time.' Paul gave an embarrassed cough. Already this week there had been more than one occasion when he'd realized it wasn't going to be easy trying to look after his daughters and work from home at the same time. To his surprise Jenny seemed unperturbed. She'd had Fiona with her all week at the office and was becoming quite used to the ways of little girls. Besides, she announced, she was perfectly capable of making tea herself.

Paul looked up when Jenny reappeared with the tray. There was no sign of tartan today. Instead, she wore a plain woollen suit of bottle green with a contrasting patterned blouse. The subtle colours reminded him of autumn heather. How well they complimented her colouring. She also looked far less flustered than at their first meeting. Perhaps it had something to do with the quiet calm in her orderly and spacious office, which was quite unlike his own.

That, Paul had already decided, was to be his next task: organizing the corner of his bedroom where he had his study, a must if he was to produce something worthwhile for Sinclair's. Gina had long since taken over the master bedroom; she claimed she slept better on her own and only occasionally wanted his company. He'd been deeply hurt at first but as Gina became increasingly volatile, craving more clothes, more holidays and more excitement, in what she constantly referred to as her *boring life* – he became thankful for the separation.

While Jenny replaced Andrew's books and assorted brochures back on the shelves, and Paul drank his tea, the moment's silence was broken by children's excited laughter.

Alarmed, Paul stood up, almost spilling his tea. 'The girls! I hope they haven't got into mischief.'

Jenny, recognizing Fiona's delightful, gurgling laughter, headed in the direction of Andrew's office with Paul following closely behind, his face etched with concern. They opened the door to find three small girls sitting on the floor, with Fiona's new tea-set neatly laid out on Jenny's shawl. On the small plates were shortbread biscuits and in the cups, orange juice.

'I waited for you but you never came!' said Fiona, scolding Jenny for her non-appearance. 'So Cele and Emily are having tea with me instead!'

Jenny and Paul stood in silence, while Celestina and Emily glanced nervously towards their father. Paul looked worried, his gaze searching the room for damage. The girls were usually very well behaved but the furnishings and accessories in this office must have cost a small fortune.

'You really shouldn't be in here, you know,' he began, addressing his daughters.

Fiona broke in defiantly and in one breath announced, 'I invited them and this is *my* daddy's office and *we* are having an indoor picnic 'cos Auntie Jen is going to take me on a proper picnic later.'

Not knowing what to say, Paul looked to Jenny for support. Was Fiona being precocious or was she simply protecting Cele and Emily? Something about the youngest child touched Jenny immediately. The poor thing looked terrified seeing this unknown woman standing there with her father. Her lower lip trembled as if she was going to cry.

'Well, I'm sure that's very kind of you, Fiona,' Jenny said, fixing the trio with a warm smile, 'but it is getting a little late for a picnic today. Another time perhaps? I'm sure Mr Hadley is waiting to take the girls home. I expect their mummy is waiting to give them their tea.'

All three girls looked at Paul but he said nothing. It was far too complicated to explain. Instead he helped them gather Fiona's tea things together and led them to the door.

'Until next Tuesday, then, Miss Sinclair. Have a good weekend. Goodbye, Fiona, and thank you for looking after my girls.'

As they reached the end of the corridor Fiona ran after them. Jenny watched as she handed over the remains of the shortbread but was unable to hear any of her niece's whispered conversation with Paul. He simply looked back at Jenny and smiled.

'What did you say to Mr Hadley?'

'Oh, I just said you didn't really think he looked like a scarecrow and perhaps he'd also like to come on our picnic.'

Conscious that she was blushing, Jenny was glad there was no one to see the colour spread across her cheeks. To save further embarrassment, she determined to keep Fiona tucked safely away when Paul Hadley returned the following Tuesday.

CHAPTER SIX

'Grannie is on the phone,' Fiona's voice called into the garden.

Jenny was kneeling beneath her new apple tree, planted last autumn. She was clearing away dead leaves from small green shoots that pierced the rich brown earth. Kicking off her wellingtons, she ran to the phone. The contrast between the crisp morning air and the warmth of her kitchen caught at her throat.

'Jennifer, are you all right? Your voice sounds quite dreadful.'

'Yes, I'm fine, thank you Mother, I've just run in from the garden. I wasn't sure how long Fiona had kept you waiting on the end of the line.'

Morag chuckled and waited for her daughter to catch her breath. 'Oh, I've not been waiting long at all. In fact I've been having a *most* interesting chat with my youngest granddaughter. I gather you've been having quite an eventful time together. By the way… how is the chicken pox?'

'Oh, coming along nicely, hardly any scabs left at all now. Fiona was really quite poorly at first, but she's been so good about everything.'

Jenny felt it inappropriate to criticize Andrew and Mary for going away; Morag on the other hand had no such compunction. In her book, business and family came before holidays.

'I think Andrew and Mary should be grateful they have you to call on, Jennifer, particularly as Fiona says it's been a *very* busy week at the office.'

Jenny, wondering what Fiona had been telling her Grannie, preferred to change the subject.

'Mother, I thought I might drive over and see you on Friday evening and bring Fiona too, if that's all right? I've been working on some ideas for Sinclair's that might interest you.'

Morag's voice brightened. 'That would be lovely, Jennifer. It all sounds so intriguing. I'll ask Tandy to make some of her special gingerbread men for Fiona.'

To Morag it seemed an age since she'd seen Jennifer and Fiona, yet it had only been New Year. Since then she'd found the endless rain and short daylight hours of early January particularly depressing. Followed by colds that had been difficult to shake off, she and Tandy had lately been getting on each other's nerves. It would be nice to think of Conasg House ringing to the sound of voices next weekend - especially younger ones.

Fiona, who had been listening in on the conversation, danced excitedly about the kitchen. She loved going to Conasg. The large, grey stone house with its antiquated furnishings and dark passages meant adventure. It was also totally removed from her parents' house in Edinburgh. For Jenny, further coherent conversation with her mother was out of the question. There was only time for Morag to enquire if Andrew had telephoned.

'I've had one very quick call,' Jenny said, 'but the line was poor and Andrew didn't say much, other than that they were having a great time and there was plenty of snow.' With Fiona's excited chattering she couldn't quite catch Morag's comment but was sure she'd said something about all the snow that had fallen in Scotland in recent weeks.

*

Andrew and his children were indeed having a great time. The same, however, could not be said of his wife. On their very first day, misjudging a ski-tow, Mary had landed badly and sprained her wrist. The sprain, though only slight, meant being confined to the hotel. There, in the combined pool, sports and spa complex, Mary had to make do with indoor exercise.

The only other occupant of the pool, she discovered, was an elderly widow on holiday with her middle-aged son. With no intention of skiing she made no secret of the fact that she was here merely to keep an eye on him. To date, Phyllis King had done her utmost to protect her son from the clutches of undesirable females, and she fully intended to see it remain that way.

'The trouble with Gordon,' Mrs King confided, as she and Mary shared a table for tea on the second afternoon, 'is that he's too vulnerable as far as the opposite sex is concerned. It's not Gordon they're interested in, you know, it's his money. My late husband left him a great deal. Anyway... as I said to him, at fifty-four, what does he want with a wife? Surely his mother should be all the company he needs?'

Mary, not knowing how to respond, poured milk into her tea.

'Goodness,' she gasped, 'doesn't that look disgusting! The staff here might call it tea, my mother-in-law, however, would call that thin!'

Mrs King snorted in agreement and stirred aggressively at her tea in the tall glass mug. Her attempt at drawing more flavour from the depleted tea bag was in vain.

'I told Gordon to pack some tea bags,' she said, 'we always have this problem wherever we travel. Of course I should have known better... he never listens to me! And why they can't use cups instead of glass mugs...'

'Don't worry, Mrs King, Andrew and I always come prepared. I'm afraid I don't have any china cups but I do have some teabags. I'll bring some to your room later.'

'That's very kind of you, I must say. Now I insist you call me Pyhllis. I feel sure we shall become great friends if we are to spend our afternoons together.'

Mary shuddered at the prospect and eyed the twisted arthritic fingers placed upon her hand in a gesture of friendship. Please God, she thought to herself, that my wrist heals soon.

The quiet of the tea discussion was shattered by a woman's shrill laughter. Mary recognized it instantly. She and Phyllis turned to see Gordon walking through the doorway with Gina. Withdrawing her hand from Mary's, Gordon's mother clutched at the arms of her chair until her knuckles grew white. Dumbstruck, she watched her son struggle with Gina's skis.

'Gordon, you are a *perfect* darling,' Gina pronounced loudly. 'Perhaps I shall see you later, yes?'

Not if your mother has anything to do with it, Gordon, Mary wanted to add.

Over dinner, describing their day's activities – or lack of them, Mary made special reference to Gordon's return with Gina and his mother's subsequent disapproval.

'But you have to admit Mum, she is a bit of a stunner; even Dad couldn't take his eyes off her today!'

Iain winced as Catriona kicked him under the table and Mary cast a withering look in Andrew's direction. Nursing a bruised shin, Iain determined to get his own back. 'Well, I think Gina's a bit of all right! Anyway, what about Phillipe, your ski-instructor fellow?' he said, turning to his sister, 'You can't pretend you haven't got the hots for him!'

'Iain, please! What will people think?' Mary looked anxiously about the dining room. Her worries were unjustified. No one had heard their conversation as all eyes were on the door. Gina was making her entrance.

Gone was the bright turquoise and pink ski-wear of the afternoon, and in its place were exquisitely cut black velvet trousers and a black and gold top. Gina resembled a tigress on the prowl. Phyllis King watched with gimlet eyes, as this brazen creature slunk across the floor in search of her prey. Where would she pounce?

Gordon made as if to stand, ready to offer Gina a chair, but bony fingers dug into his wrist. 'Sit down!' Phyllis hissed. 'Don't make a fool of yourself.'

Gina's cat-like eyes fluttered only briefly in Gordon's direction. There would be no kill at that table this evening. Instead, hearing someone call her name, she headed for the corner of the dining room.

'Phillipe,' she purred. 'Where have you been today? I'm quite cross with you, my darling. Have you been making all those poor little English girls fall in love with you?'

'Can I help it if they do, Gina? Anyway, they are nothing compared to you.' Phillipe laughed and raised his glass to her with a knowing wink.

Watching the hurt and disappointment register in her daughter's face, Mary realized that this dark, swarthy Romeo must be Catriona's ski-instructor.

'There you are, you've lost him now,' sneered Iain, only adding to the pain and humiliation, 'He doesn't like pale English girls, he prefers hot-blooded Italian ones!'

'I'm not English, I'm Scottish!' Catriona cried, pushing back her chair and hurrying from the room.

'Andrew, I suggest you have a firm word with your son!' Mary said, following close on the heels of her daughter.

After some persuasion, Catriona emerged red-eyed from the bathroom. Mary put a comforting arm about her shoulders and sat with her on the bed. 'My dear, you really mustn't get so upset. You know what they say about ski-instructors. Oh, I know they all look gorgeous in their red sweaters, with their golden tans, but they're all Romeos, ready to break the hearts of innocent girls like yourself.'

Catriona blew her nose on a tissue and reached for yet another from the box beside her. Deep down she knew her mother was right, but this was to be her first holiday with no small sister tagging along. A holiday where perhaps romance would blossom and flourish. Her friends at the academy had been so jealous when she'd told them of the forthcoming holiday. She'd already confided in her diary how attentive Phillipe had been: how he'd whispered gentle words of encouragement when she'd stumbled and how he'd held out his arms to help her. Gazing into his eyes, Catriona's heart was lost. No matter what anyone said, she was in love with Phillipe!

'It's not fair,' Catriona sighed. 'She's so beautiful, I don't stand a chance, and Iain's being such a pig! Still it's only because Gina ignored him at lunchtime. She was more interested in Dad and Mr King. It's obvious why she fancies older men; they're the ones with the money!'

'Catriona!' Mary gasped, wondering what had taken place at lunchtime. She was certainly keen to find out. She'd been so looking forward to this holiday, yet somehow it seemed doomed from the onset.

First there had been Fiona's chicken pox, then the sprained wrist and now… Well, what was there now? A love-struck sixteen-year-old and her husband and son – and no doubt most of the other male guests in the hotel – infatuated by Gina Dintino. They'd hardly been here five minutes and Mary was already sick of the name. No matter how she felt tomorrow, sprained wrist or not, Mary was determined to join her family skiing. Before then however, she must take the promised teabags to Phyllis King.

Approaching the room, Mary heard raised voices, or at least that of Gordon's mother. 'Did you hear what I said, Gordon? I absolutely forbid you to have anything more to do with that woman. She's nothing but a trollop! Think of your reputation and the business.'

Mary didn't wait for Gordon's reply. Instead she crept silently away to rejoin Andrew and make a few suggestions of her own.

*

The next morning, cloudless blue skies and sunlight glistening on dazzling white snow dispelled all the previous night's upsets. Mary, passing the tea bags to Phyllis King at breakfast, whispered in her ear, 'Don't worry, I'll keep a discreet eye on Gordon for you.'

'Thank you, my dear... thank you in more ways than one,' the old lady replied, her twisted fingers accepting the welcome package.

Walking away to complete the Sinclair quartet, Mary wondered if it wasn't perhaps a little unfair even to think of spying on Gordon. With such a domineering mother, the poor man deserved a bit of fun and freedom. In her mind's eye Mary pictured Gordon with his mother on one side and Gina on the other. What a dreadful combination, although Gina was quite possibly the more dangerous of the two.

Joining the queue for the ski-lift Mary determined to find a more suitable companion for Gordon. She scanned the most likely-looking candidates and, lost in thought as the agony aunt of the ski slopes, missed the arrival of Gina and her entourage. A mixed party of glitterati, dressed more for a fashion shoot than a day's skiing, gathered to one side.

They talked excitedly together in a mixture of languages. Mary discerned French, German and Italian. It was only when they joined the queue it became clear that Gina's party would not be accompanying them today. From what little French and Italian Mary remembered from her school days, she realized the group would be skiing off-piste instead; it would be far more exciting. Mary breathed a huge sigh of relief. Today Gordon and her husband would be quite safe.

CHAPTER SEVEN

Hoping he'd taken all the necessary information from Andrew Sinclair's books, Paul sat at his desk, surrounded by rough sketches and scribbled notes. Only time would tell and he recalled the anxious look on Miss Sinclair's face when he'd arrived late, not to mention the conversation with Fiona.

The Wizard of Oz... Dorothy's scarecrow. 'Poor Fiona,' he chuckled, reaching for a pencil. With her missing front teeth and subsequent lisp, not only had she rushed to hand over the last of her shortbread, but also extended an invitation to join them on their picnic. He hoped she hadn't got into trouble with her aunt. Thinking of how defiant she'd been in defence of Celestina and Emily, Paul wished his daughters could be half so confident. He hadn't been cross with them at all, merely concerned that they'd gone into Mr Sinclair's office uninvited.

Today the girls were installed in the dining room. Seeing their father busily sketching, they'd asked if they could draw too. Paul gave them some of his special paper and found pencils and crayons before explaining the importance of his own work. He knew from experience they would remain quietly occupied until lunchtime.

After lunch the girls chatted and showed Paul their drawings. He was encouraged to see that he appeared in most of them. There were pictures of him taking his daughters to school, swimming and dancing, plus their recent walk in the park. Admiring their efforts, Paul saw Cele push a picture to the bottom of the pile. 'What's that one, Cele? Let me have a look.'

Cele's face became troubled as she reluctantly pushed the drawing towards him. Paul studied the picture but made no comment. On the white sheet of paper were several triangles – presumably mountains – with a female form standing between two peaks.

The mass of black hair and blood red mouth could only be Gina. Stick-like objects protruded from her hands and feet - Cele's attempt at drawing skis. What concerned Paul most however, was that the entire drawing had been scribbled on. Doubtless this was why Celestina had looked so worried. It was Emily who broke the silence.

'We didn't like it so we drawed all over it! Mummies shouldn't go away and leave their little girls. Fiona's mummy left her too, which wasn't nice 'cos she had spots.'

Paul had indeed noticed Fiona's spots, but thought little of it as Cele continued the conversation. 'Yes – but Fiona said we can go on her picnic when she's better. You will let us go, won't you Daddy?'

Grateful for the diversion from the disturbing picture of Gina, Paul was hesitant. 'I don't know, it's not up to me. It would appear it's Fiona's auntie who is arranging the picnic. We can't simply invite ourselves.'

'But we're not!' echoed the girls. 'Fiona invited us and you too, when she gave you the biscuits.'

Knowing Fiona had been most insistent with her invitation, Paul couldn't possibly disagree. Added to which she'd also assured him that he didn't really look like a scarecrow, though her aunt had thought his hair was 'a wee bit long and untidy.'

Smiling ruefully, Paul concluded that whatever else happened to Sinclair's, they need not worry about their survival. If Fiona Sinclair joined the firm in later years, their success would be guaranteed! 'Come along, you two,' he said, turning to the girls. 'Let's get our coats. We could do with some fresh air and exercise.'

Wrapped up against the cold January weather, Paul led the girls through the main shopping centre to the park. There they ran in and out of the bare tree-lined avenue to the swings. Paul pushed them both, watching their brightly coloured scarves billow behind them as they soared higher and higher, their laughter filling the air.

'Stop now, Daddy! I don't want to go higher. I might go over the treetops into heaven.'

Deeply puzzled, Paul reigned in Emily's swing. 'Whoever gave you that idea?'

'My friend Gemma at nursery. Her grannie has just died and she's gone to heaven – that's in the sky, isn't it?'

'I don't think you need worry about that.'

'Is Helen's mummy going to die?'

'No! Certainly not!' Paul replied, this time in answer to Cele's question concerning their next-door neighbour. 'Helen's mummy has only broken her leg, but I expect she'll be in hospital for quite a while.'

'P'raps we can draw her a get well picture?'

Paul helped the girls from the swings. 'That sounds like a good idea. Now, I think we should head back home for some tea and Fiona's shortbread, don't you?'

On the way Cele and Emily chattered excitedly about the pictures they would like to draw. They liked Helen Craig, the retired schoolteacher who had knitted their bright woollen hats, scarves and mittens. Helen's house was cosy and welcoming and she never shouted at them, not like their mummy. That night the girls prayed for Helen's mother to make a speedy recovery, partly from genuine concern and also because if Helen was at the hospital, they couldn't go to her house!

With the girls bathed and tucked up in bed, Paul sat alone with his thoughts. As on so many previous occasions, the hurt was still there. Gina had been gone a week and hadn't telephoned once. At bedtime there had been the familiar awkward questions about mummy coming home. He could only reply that he didn't know. He never knew when Gina was coming home, yet she always rang the moment she became bored.

The Sinclair file lay open on his desk. Paul picked up a pen and jotted down some more ideas. They were all sound possibilities but nevertheless lacked that something special he was looking for. Jenny Sinclair would be expecting that same 'something special' from him. He could hardly return to her office with the usual run-of-the-mill ideas he'd seen in the shops on the way home with the girls. Ties, rugs, scarves, purses and handbags had been done a hundred times before; Sinclair's deserved better than that. For a moment he thought of ringing Jenny, but realized it was Saturday evening. Besides, remembering the engagement ring on her finger, he assumed she would be spending a romantic evening with her fiancé.

Numerous sketches later, Paul succumbed to tiredness and climbed the stairs. On the landing he switched on the nightlight and peeped in to check on both girls. Emily's duvet was already in a heap on the floor, casting a mountainous shadow on the wall. Paul thought of Gina. Why wasn't she here? Here to see stray arms and feet protruding from the bedclothes, or to arrange the vast array of soft toys in their currently required order of merit. Removing Emily's thumb from her rosebud mouth and disentangling Cele's fingers from her mass of dark curls, Paul kissed them both and crept towards the bedroom door. Only then did his foot catch on something between the two beds.

In the dim glow of the nightlight, Paul discerned a check tea-towel, some plastic mugs and a container filled with scraps of paper. Trying to rearrange the jumble of objects as quietly as he could, his attention was drawn to the scraps of paper.

'Girls, you are brilliant!' he whispered, and no longer tired, hurried back to his desk.

*

With Stevie given strict instructions to keep Fiona out of mischief, Jenny welcomed Paul's return to her office. Their greeting, as before, was formal, with Paul as anxious to show Jenny his new ideas as she was to see them. There was now only a short time before Andrew's return.

'I'm afraid they're only rough sketches,' he said, placing the folder on the desk. 'But I'm convinced there's something here that will interest you more than the others.'

Paul watched anxiously as Jenny leafed through pages of numerous drawings and notes. 'From the information you gave me, Miss Sinclair, I'm well aware you've tried the usual gamut of tartan goods and clothing, all of which I appreciate are high quality. But the department stores and shops are already full of them...' He paused for a moment; Jenny had reached what he considered to be Cele and Emily's flash of inspiration. A delicately detailed drawing of a sprig of gorse, set within a shield and tartan border.

'I thought you said these were only rough sketches,' she remarked, picking up the sheet of paper and studying it closely. 'This one clearly isn't, although I confess, I don't quite see the connection to Sinclair's.'

With no intention of telling her that he'd sat up until three in the morning to finish the sketch, Paul replied modestly. 'I – um – got rather carried away with that one. The idea came from your brother's book. Gorse is the badge of the clan Sinclair. It's origin is French... from the Comte St Claire in Normandy.'

Descended from the French – did Andrew know that? He'd never mentioned it before. In fact, Andrew wasn't at all enamoured with the French. She wondered if that was why he'd never spoken of it. Poor Mary, no Scottish laird, merely a French count! Jenny smiled. Paul, oblivious to her amusement, was too busy placing sketches upon her desk.

'It's January now, isn't it? But think of summer...'

Jenny appeared puzzled. 'Summer?'

'Picnics!'

'Picnics?'

'Yes, a range of upmarket picnic and tableware, using the gorse as the main emblem. Of course you can still incorporate the tartan, but make it less heavy for summer. The scope is endless. Start with the fabric; you already have the mills, the looms and the workforce. Go on from there, incorporating it into home wear, household linens, bedding, anything...'

Paul gave a knowing smile. 'We're all well aware that everyone associates Scotland with the thistle, but this is your opportunity to be different... *This* is the House of St Claire!'

'The House of St Claire?' Jenny looked deep into Paul's eyes, trying to read his thoughts. His eyes were blue, just as she'd expected days ago... they were also fired with enthusiasm. 'Go on,' she urged.

'A name that's not only suited to an entirely new range of products,' he continued, placing an even more detailed design of a shield in her hand, 'but also one that goes back to the true origins of the Sinclair family name. Just think of it... gorse-embroidered crisp white linen or cotton could look so fresh for summer. Thistles and tartan might be OK for winter, but they can also be a bit old-fashioned.'

Paul stopped short, wondering if he'd gone too far. Jenny was wearing her tartan suit, adorned by a traditional silver and amethyst thistle brooch. 'I'm sorry, I didn't meant to be rude...'

'That's all right, no offence taken. You've raised a perfectly valid point. However, as our weather is so unpredictable, and the season often short, what happens after summer?'

Paul seemed positively delighted at the prospect of short summers. 'Grouse shooting?'

'Grouse shooting?'

'Yes,' he beamed. 'Now look at these!'

These, Jenny, perceived, examining the pages Paul had given her, were sketches of hampers and accessories. The crisp white linen on his earlier designs made way for soft heather colours and wider bands of tartan, yet there was still the ever-present gorse emblem.

'Are you suggesting we go into the food market?' Jenny asked dubiously. 'Mother and Andrew would never agree to that.'

'No! You send the hampers stocked with non-perishable House of St Claire merchandise to the food companies. They supply the rest, either to retail outlets or the estates themselves who are holding the shoots. It's much too risky to start dealing with food!'

'Thank heavens for that.'

'I'm sorry, Miss Sinclair… you don't like the idea? You should have stopped me earlier…'

Jenny was intrigued. This was a totally different Paul Hadley from the person she'd met little more than a week ago.

'No. I didn't want to stop you, because I think it's a great idea. The potential is enormous. As for the House of St Claire emblem, I think it's beautiful. I'm convinced it's exactly what we need. A complete change of direction for Sinclair's and we must after all move with the times. Your idea of following through the seasons is also excellent,' Jenny added, reminded of her sister-in-law's extravagances of changing the décor of the Edinburgh house, according to the time of year. 'There's so much scope, particularly at Christmas. Women usually want everything to match in the home according to the seasons.'

'I'm glad you said that and not me! Although I have to admit I thought it. I didn't want to offend you twice in one day.'

Paul looked at her, waiting for a reaction, and was relieved to see her smile. At the same time through the window a shaft of wintry sunlight broke through the heavy grey skies, casting golden glints on her hair and in her eyes.

Feeling strangely uncomfortable, Jenny began gathering up papers, her hand brushing accidentally against his as she did so. Paul moved away, sensing her embarrassment, but his eyes never left her face.

Quickly regaining her composure, Jenny returned his gaze. 'Apart from my brother's book was there anything else that inspired you?'

'Yes. Your niece and my daughters!'

'Fiona and the girls?'

'Yes, because ever since last Friday, Celestina and Emily have been playing at having picnics. I found paper shapes of sandwiches and shortbread on their bedroom floor, when I went to tuck them up for the night.'

Jenny laughed. 'And the House of St Claire emerged just like that?'

'Yes. More or less. By the way, how is Fiona?'

As if on cue, Fiona crept round the office door. Paul smiled and held out two neatly folded drawings. 'These are for you. They're from Cele and Emily.'

Fiona looked nervously in her aunt's direction and stepping forward, took the pictures with a quick, 'Thank you,' then, with a whispered, 'I like your hair,' she was gone, retreating behind Stevie's wheelchair.

Paul frowned hard. 'What's wrong with Fiona?'

'I'm afraid I told her not to disturb us.'

'Oh, dear! Then I hope I haven't got her into trouble.' Paul stroked the back of his neck, where his hair had recently curled. Fiona had missed nothing; she'd obviously noticed he'd had a haircut.

Jenny fixed him with a warm smile. 'I'm not a complete dragon, you know. In fact I'm especially fond of Fiona and I'm taking her to see her Grannie – my mother, this weekend. I think the poor child could do with some fresh air in her lungs after being cooped up with me for almost two weeks. She's like me really... adores the wildness of the West Coast - so we can run wild together. In addition to that, Mr

Hadley, I have to confess I have an ulterior motive. If I can get Mother on my side this weekend, then Andrew won't be such a problem. I'll ring you on Monday with a progress report if you like?'

Paul nodded thoughtfully in reply. He'd certainly welcome Morag Sinclair's responses to his suggestions. However, at that precise moment, he could only visualize Jenny and Fiona like two Highland ponies, copper manes blowing in the wind, galloping free along a desolate west coast shore.

CHAPTER EIGHT

On Friday evening Jenny and Fiona left the cloudless blue skies of Edinburgh and headed for the west coast. Fiona chattered incessantly, clutching the drawings Paul had given her from Cele and Emily. Though far from complimentary, illustrating her missing front teeth and red spots on her face, Fiona was delighted with them. They'd also drawn her plaits complete with Sinclair ribbon bows. She couldn't wait to show Grannie and Miss Tandy.

'Are we nearly there?' she asked for the umpteenth time.

'I'm afraid not, Fiona, we've a wee while as yet. Try and sleep for a bit, otherwise you're going to be very tired tomorrow.'

Folding the drawings and placing them carefully in her pocket, Fiona soon nodded off, leaving Jenny to contemplate the coming weekend. Since Paul had first suggested the House of St Claire project, her head had been buzzing with ideas. Now all she had to do was convince her mother to agree with her. With Andrew's imminent return, there was much to discuss in so little time.

Casting a sideways glance at her niece, who was still sleeping, Jenny turned in the direction of the Connel Bridge. Then, as expected, the heavens opened and the rain poured down in dense grey sheets. Across Loch Etive, visibility was virtually nil but to Jenny that didn't matter; from here she knew the road so well. After the next bend in the road, and if the rain clouds cleared for just a moment, she would see the distant lights of Conasg House, home to three generations of Sinclairs.

Fiona stirred as the car came to a halt and three figures stood in the light of the open doorway.

'Hello Grannie,' she said sleepily, while Hamish, the odd-job man and gardener, lifted her gently from the car, 'I've so much to tell you. My new friends…'

'Tell me tomorrow, dear,' Morag said kindly, patting Fiona's cheek. 'It's long past your bedtime. Let Tandy get you some nice warm milk and tuck you up in bed. I'll come and see you in a wee while.'

With Hamish delivering his young charge into Tandy's capable hands, Morag turned to embrace her daughter. 'Jennifer, I'm so glad you could come, yet by the looks of it… you could do with something stronger than warm milk! My dear, you look exhausted. Hurry up into the warm.'

Following her mother through to the sitting room, Jenny saw not the familiar electric fire but blazing logs and coal.

'Tandy thought you might be cold after your journey,' Morag said, as if reading her mind. She unbuttoned the neck of her heavy-knit cardigan, before pouring out two glasses of whisky. 'Personally, I don't feel cold at all… but as Fiona's been so poorly…'

Jenny smiled as she sipped at her glass. The cut crystal sparkled in the firelight and she felt suddenly warmed by the amber liquid. She knew she always looked and felt more tired when she was cold.

Morag, in her usual layers of woollens, needed no additional warming aids, but she did allow herself a nightly tot of whisky – purely on medicinal grounds, she told Tandy. It was her one and only extravagance.

'So, Jennifer… you have some new plans for the business. I'm glad someone has… Andrew seems not to care what happens to us.'

'I don't think that's quite fair, Mother. Andrew is deeply committed to Sinclair's.'

'Hmph! Then why, if is so committed, has he taken himself off to Switzerland for two weeks? How is that going to help the business? I recall at New Year, both you and Andrew talking of a heavy workload and the need to forge ahead.'

'I know, Mother, and these past two weeks – even with Fiona – I've…'

'And that's another thing! How could Andrew even consider going away when Fiona was so poorly? Mind you, I expect that was more Mary's doing. What your poor father would say to such extravagance!'

Putting down her glass, Jenny walked towards the diminutive figure reclining in her father's favourite armchair. Easing herself into a sitting position on the floor, she reached for Morag's pale and wrinkled hand.

'Mother,' she whispered softly, 'we're not going to starve, you know.'

'Maybe not,' sniffed Morag, 'but nevertheless Andrew should still be here!'

Reminded of the fact that her brother had always been Mother's favourite, Jenny sighed wistfully. 'Well… he isn't, so you'll just have to make do with me instead.'

With an uncharacteristic gesture, Morag stroked Jenny's sleek copper hair, where it hung loose about her shoulders. 'You must forgive me, Jennifer… January has been a particularly depressing month so far. Not only have we had rain almost every day, but also I've been trying to clear out your father's study.'

Jenny looked up, startled. Morag hardly ever went into Father's study. She'd always insisted it should remain exactly as it was when he died.

'But you always said…'

'I know,' said Morag, running a finger along the threadbare tapestry of William's chair, 'however, I thought I might start using it for myself. Tandy's always scolding me for cluttering up the dining table and my bedroom with papers and files.'

At the mention of her name, Miss Tandy opened the sitting room door.

'Fiona's all tucked up and nearly asleep,' she announced to Morag before turning to greet Jenny. 'Miss Jennifer, it's so nice to see you again.

I'm sorry I didn't get a chance to welcome you when you arrived. No point in standing round in all that rain.'

Morag, not content to take her companion's word, slipped out of the room to check on her granddaughter for herself.

'Thank you for the fire, Miss Tandy. I must say it was a truly welcoming sight. I was expecting the electric fire.'

'Och! You know what your mother's like. I have to do battle with her over these things occasionally. She says some dreadful things to me at times but having been with her so long, I'm used to her funny little ways. And before she comes back down to have another go at me, I'll away and make your hot water bottle.'

Flora Tandy had indeed been with Morag Sinclair a long while; they'd even gone to school together. To Morag she was simply Tandy, her long-suffering friend and companion. To Jenny she was always Miss Tandy; in turn Jenny was always 'Miss Jennifer'. The two women admired and respected each other.

When Morag reappeared she found Jenny looking through papers in her briefcase. 'So... what's this wonderful new idea you have for Sinclairs. Are you going to show me?'

'Not tonight, if you don't mind, Mother. I'm really tired. I'm also looking forward to sleeping on my own for a change.'

In response to Morag's raised eyebrows, Jenny smiled mischievously.

'I've had Fiona sharing my bed for the past two weeks and it's beginning to play havoc with my beauty sleep.'

'Oh, I see. I thought perhaps you'd seen Cameron...'

'No, I haven't,' Jenny said, snapping her briefcase shut, all laughter disappearing from her eyes. She rose from the settee.

'Goodnight, Mother, if you'll excuse me.'

Kissing her daughter's cheek, Morag returned to William's chair and patted the faded tapestry upholstery. 'Well, William, my dear - I didn't handle that very well, did I?'

*

Snuggled beneath the covers of the ancient double bed, Jenny stretched her toes searching for the hot water bottle. It took ages for the heat to penetrate and only then was she able to wriggle the bottle up with her feet until it was within her grasp. Like a mother with a newborn child, she clasped it to her breast, feeling the warmth spread through the folds of her fleecy pyjamas.

Cameron had always teased her about the nightclothes she took to Conasg House. But the mere slip of eau-de-Nil silk she wore when he was home on leave did nothing to keep her warm. In Cameron's arms there was no need for fleecy pyjamas - no need for anything at all. Drawing her knees into a foetal position, Jenny wept silent tears for the past six years of her life.

Cameron Ross - dashing naval officer and submariner, had literally swept the nineteen-year-old Jennifer Sinclair off her feet at their very first meeting.

'He's a real maiden's dream, the epitome of a romantic hero. Marry him as soon as you can!' her fellow students had urged as she showed off her diamond solitaire… but Jenny hadn't wanted to marry Cameron – not then. She was only in her first year at university. It would be far better to wait until she finished her studies. She'd also promised her parents she would wait until she was twenty-one.

Later, with Cameron away so much, it seemed they'd barely got used to each other again before she was standing alongside all the other naval wives and girlfriends waving goodbye. Which was why, with her parents' help, she'd bought the tiny cottage at East Lothian. Far away from Gare Loch and the Faslane naval base, they not only had a bolt-hole where they could be together, but also the cottage would be near enough to Sinclair's when they did eventually marry.

'A maiden's dream,' Jenny cried into her pillow. 'Well, I was certainly the maiden.' But last year, any time spent with Cameron was more of a nightmare than a dream. He'd become so moody and possessive… Perhaps there'd been more in his sister's warning at Christmas than she realized. In fact only last night, when quite out of the blue, Cameron had phoned asking to meet her, his tone had been bitter and scathing.

'"*I'm sorry, Cameron*,"' he'd mimicked. '"*I'm afraid I can't. I promised to take Fiona to Conasg and there's a business proposition I have to put to Mother.*"'

Unable to believe her ears at his mocking tone and not wanting to disturb Fiona, Jenny was on the point of hanging up on him when she heard him shout.

'Well, bloody well go, then, Jennifer! And to hell with Sinclair's and the whole damn lot of you!'

Closing her eyes, Jenny slept fitfully. In her troubled dreams Cameron's cruel laughter echoed behind her as he chased her down a seemingly endless corridor hung with Sinclair tartan. His pursuit of her was relentless. Terrified and struggling through swathes of fabric and ribbon, she tugged and pulled, desperately seeking escape.

Shaking with fear and Cameron ever closer on her heels, she made a last-ditch effort to escape, pushing her way against a heavy bale of tartan cloth, only to wake with a large feather bolster clutched against her breast. With trembling hands, Jenny switched on the bedside lamp, fixed the bolster back into position and made her way to the dressing table.

Conscious of the tiny beads of perspiration on her forehead, she pushed her tangled hair from her face and, finding a stray elastic band, pulled her hair into a ponytail. It was then she noticed the antique rosewood photo frame: the one that contained her favourite photo of Cameron. Stifling a sob and in the eerie stillness of the room, Jenny removed the photo from its frame and tore it into tiny pieces. From

now on Cameron Ross no longer existed.

CHAPTER NINE

'Come on, Auntie Jen! It's a lovely day, there's porridge and eggs and Grannie says we can go for a walk by the loch and…' Fiona's words came pouring out in an endless stream.

'Fiona! Will you leave your Aunt Jennifer to get dressed in peace?' Morag's voice called from the landing. 'Come along now if we're to go for our walk.'

Fiona bounced off the bed and ran to the window, where she struggled to draw back the heavy chenille curtains. Shafts of watery sunlight came streaming through the window, causing Jenny to blink and shield her eyes.

Hearing Fiona's footsteps on the stairs, muffled conversation in the hallway and the opening and slamming of the front door, Jenny leapt from the bed and made her way to the window. She need not have worried. Grannie and granddaughter were both well wrapped up against the chill of the morning, wearing bonnets, scarves and gloves. They were also half way down the drive and from the spring in their step looked as if they'd been up for hours.

Jenny shivered as her toes touched the gap between carpet and linoleum, and she gazed longingly back at the bed. With the hot water bottle long since cold, and Miss Tandy (according to Fiona) waiting for her in the kitchen, there was only one thing for it; a quick dash to the cavernous bathroom with its ancient plumbing… and breakfast.

'They've already set off on their walk,' Tandy said in her clipped Argyll accent. 'It will do Morag a power of good having you both here for a wee while. That cold she had left her feeling dreadfully low, and she wouldn't hear of me calling for the doctor. As for going to see him… That – so she said – was just a waste of petrol! Now, Miss Jennifer, what can I get you for breakfast?'

Insisting that porridge and tea were more than enough, it wasn't long before Jenny set off in pursuit of her mother. Fiona was right, it was a lovely day. After the heavy rain and low-lying cloud of recent weeks, there was a brilliant, clear blue sky. The sun shone on the snow-covered peaks of Glen Etive, which in turn were reflected in the icy still waters of the loch.

Scanning the shore for signs of movement, Jenny gulped in a deep lungful of cold air and then watched as a narrow funnel of warm breath escaped her lips. In the distance she saw two figures. The eldest walked at a steady pace, while the youngest stopped and started, darting to and from the water's edge like a puppy.

Jenny smiled fondly. In a way Fiona was like a puppy. Her thick hair, this morning tied in bunches, hung below the tartan bonnet like the ears of a cocker spaniel. The young 'puppy' seeing her aunt's approach bounced towards her, arms waving and 'ears' billowing.

'My goodness, Jennifer,' said Morag with a shake of her head, 'does Fiona never stop running about or talking? I feel quite exhausted already and it's not from the walking – I'm quite used to that.'

Jennifer laughed. 'I know what you mean. I have to admit it's been quite an eventful two weeks. Certainly never a dull moment with Fiona around.'

'So I gather. I've heard all about chicken "spots", picnics, the scarecrow from the Wizard of Oz – who wasn't – and two little girls with unusual names. No wonder you couldn't wait to get to bed last night.'

Listening to Fiona's catalogue of events, Jenny was reminded that she still had to tell Morag about her meeting with Paul Hadley and also put forward his ideas.

Later that afternoon, with Tandy occupying Fiona in the kitchen, Morag took Jenny into the study. Formerly William Sinclair's domain, it was here that Morag now chose to keep an eye on the family business. The dark cabinets and desk remained just as they were in William's time, the only difference being that Morag, unlike her husband, appeared dwarfed behind the vast oak desk with its green and gold embossed leather top.

Handing over Paul's folder, Jenny announced boldly. 'It's all in there, just waiting for you, Mother. I hope, in fact… I think you'll be delighted!'

Morag looked up, bemused, noting a new-found radiance on her daughter's face; such a contrast from last night. What on earth could be in the folder that Jenny had clung on to so possessively?

Watching anxiously as Morag lifted each page in turn, Jenny waited for her to reach Paul's exquisitely detailed drawings.

'It's gorse, the Sinclair family emblem,' Jenny explained, her eyes shining. 'Isn't it beautiful? Apparently Conasg means gorse. To think I never knew… I've often wondered why great-grandfather called this house…'

'Of course!' Morag broke in. I remember your father telling me years ago. I wonder why we've never thought of using it before.'

'Quite possibly because everyone associates the thistle with Scottish products. That's what Mr Hadley says, and I'm inclined to agree with him. He suggests using the gorse as the emblem for the House of St Claire and changing our products to suit the seasons.'

During the next hour Paul Hadley's name came up frequently. Morag couldn't fail to notice the eagerness in Jenny's voice as she described his proposals for the House of St Claire, her enthusiastic flow reminiscent of Fiona's excitable torrent earlier in the day.

Jenny paused for a moment, 'I'm sorry, Mother, I haven't given you a chance to think or say anything yet. It's funny, Mr Hadley was exactly the same when he was describing everything to me.'

'I see... so that's something you both have in common, 'E' for enthusiasm.'

In the hallway Fiona took great delight in banging the heavy brass gong heralding the arrival of tea.

'It must be four o'clock,' announced Morag. 'Let's go and see what delights Fiona and Tandy have made for us today.'

Grandmother and aunt watched as Fiona, aided by Tandy, wheeled in the ancient trolley with its carved wooden legs and squeaky castors. It creaked and groaned like some ancient retainer before coming to a halt. Jenny wondered just how many times it had made the same journey along the hallway at Conasg and into the sitting room.

As usual on the top shelf was the impressive Sinclair silver tea-set and underneath, Tandy's special shortbread and the day's selection of dainty finger sandwiches. Less delicate were the scones and jam tarts. No doubt made by Fiona, who had skimped neither on the jam for the tarts, or the sultanas for the scones. Jenny caught Tandy's eye and smiled. Flora Tandy, ever mouse-like, said nothing. She simply handed Morag a plate and began to pour the tea. Watching Fiona distribute the thistle-embroidered napkins, Morag declared matter-of-factly, 'Let's hope this time next year those thistles are replaced by gorse.'

Tandy and Fiona looked at Morag in bewilderment, while Jenny could only stare in disbelief.

'You've decided... already? Don't you need more time to think? I mean, we could discuss it further this evening, if you wish?'

'I do wish,' Morag replied. 'I wish to discuss how soon we can get this project off the ground. I also need to speak to Andrew and there'll be no more jetting off for a while!'

While Fiona was trying to fathom all this talk of flying and getting off the ground, the telephone rang. It was Andrew. The family had just returned home and he was replying to Jenny's message left on his answerphone.

He said little, other than that he was delighted Jenny was staying with Morag until Sunday and it would be perfectly all right to bring Fiona home on Sunday evening.

'Fine, we'll see you tomorrow then, Andrew. I trust the family is well, and no broken bones.'

'What? Oh, no ... no broken bones.' Just broken spirits, Andrew thought to himself, hanging up the phone. He'd almost added that after the events of the past few days, he and the family could do with a holiday but bearing in mind the last time he'd mentioned holidays to his sister, he thought better of it.

*

'And you are sure about the House of St Claire?' Jenny asked, seeking reassurance from her mother, before walking to her car.

'Positive,' Morag replied. 'I suggest you tell Andrew all about it first thing in the morning and then get him to ring me. In the meantime I'll leave it for you to arrange a meeting between Andrew and your Mr Hadley.'

Morag caught the look in Jenny's eye. Had that last remark been an unfortunate turn of phrase? It seemed difficult to tell. Paul Hadley's name had cropped up frequently during the weekend, yet Jennifer said little about him personally, other than mention his two young daughters. It was thinking of her own daughter that filled Morag with renewed hope. Perhaps the House of St Claire was just what Jennifer needed - a sense of purpose maybe? Something to care for, watch over and nurture... like a mother.

'Goodbye, Grannie. Goodbye, Miss Tandy. Bye-bye Hamish,' Fiona called from the car window as Jenny drove slowly away. This time it was the remains of the scones and jam tarts she clutched, a welcome home gesture for her family. 'And you have got my pictures from Cele and Emily, haven't you, Auntie Jenny?'

Jenny nodded and reassured her. The drawings, now somewhat dog-eared, having been passed round the family so many times during the weekend, were folded safely in Jenny's briefcase.

'Would you like me to stop and show you?' Jenny asked, slowing down at the end of the drive.

Fiona was thoughtful as she waved a last farewell to Conasg. 'No, thank you, I think they'll be quite safe there for a while. It's prob'ly better for me to look after these instead.' She held up the plastic container, 'But you won't let me forget my pictures when we get home, will you?'

Jenny made a mental note; she would not forget. But whether or not there would be any jam tarts or scones left to take in with the pictures remained to be seen. All that Argyll fresh air had given Fiona an enormous appetite.

CHAPTER TEN

Delighted to see Fiona again, mother, father and siblings showered her with hugs and kisses. It was as if they were competing with one another. Who cared for her the most; who had missed her the most, whose present did she prefer? Watching Fiona revel in all this attention, Jenny was only too aware of the tense atmosphere pervading the Edinburgh house. What had happened in Switzerland to prompt such a homecoming for the youngest member of the family?

Leaving Fiona to extricate the remaining misshapen jam tarts and scones from the container, Jenny said goodbye. Andrew walked with her to the front door and announced quietly, 'I intend to make an early start at the office tomorrow. There must be plenty to catch up on. I suppose I ought to give Bill Freeman a ring too. I don't expect you had time to visit the trade fair.'

'As a matter of fact I did, Andrew. Let's just say it was extremely beneficial and you'll no longer be requiring Freeman's. Still, we don't want to talk of that now, do we? You're missing out on your jam tarts.'

From the kitchen, over-enthusiastic voices were praising Fiona's grey wedges of pastry, now seriously depleted of jam and sultanas. Even more convinced that something had happened in Switzerland, Jenny reached for her car keys. Now was not the time to enquire, far better to wait until later.

Andrew turned gloomily to his wife. 'Thank goodness Jennifer chose not to stay. For one awful moment I thought she was going to ask about the holiday.'

Mary said nothing and continued on her way upstairs to run Fiona's bath. As far as she was concerned, she didn't ever want to discuss the events of the past two weeks. Their holiday had been an unmitigated disaster.

*

True to his word, Andrew made an early start for the office. His original intention had been to start at eight o'clock, but unable to sleep, he rose early and was behind his desk shortly after seven. To his surprise everything at Sinclair's was in its place, with no hint of a single tyre-track on his precious carpet. Looking into Jenny's office, he saw nothing outstanding: no piles of papers, memos or unanswered mail. In a way he was disappointed, he'd hoped to find something - no matter how small - to criticize. That way there would at least be something he could use as an excuse for the anger and frustration he felt. Reluctantly, there was nothing for it but to check through his emails and wait for his sister to arrive. Why, he puzzled, had she said they no longer needed Bill Freeman?

Making a pot of coffee, Andrew caught sight of the assorted postcards he'd sent to the office. Pinned to the noticeboard, they showed chocolate-box chalets nestling beneath snow-covered mountains and clear blue skies. Who then would have guessed the events that had taken place behind those brightly painted shutters? Foolish though it seemed, shutters like that always reminded him of children's fairy-tale illustrations. Unfortunately, the events of the past two weeks had turned from fairy-tale into nightmare reality.

The week had begun badly enough with Mary's fall, and descended into farce with Mary's obsession to find a suitable partner for Gordon King. Then there had been Catriona and Iain's constant bickering over Gina and Phillipe, the ski-instructor. On reflection, Andrew realized he should have recognized the danger signs from the onset. One always did with hindsight. However, once the wheels were set in motion there was no turning back.

On the last night of the holiday, and still obsessed with Gordon King, Mary had suggested they join Gordon and his mother for dinner. Catriona and Iain were going to a disco organized by the ski-instructors.

'We're far too old for discos, Andrew; let's leave that to the young ones. After all, it is their last night. It will be back to some serious studying for them both next week.'

Initially Andrew was dubious; these 'disco things' sometimes got out of hand. Iain and Catriona seemed positively naïve compared to some of the other youngsters at the hotel, but as Mary had insisted brother and sister must remain together at all times… Not only that, Mary had even suggested that she and Andrew might have an *early night* for once.

That look in his wife's eye was one Andrew didn't see too often. Which was why, deep down he'd always been jealous of Jennifer's relationship with Cameron. In the early days his sister and her fiancé had been so alive with their love. Lately, of course, he reminded himself, all that had changed.

Deep in thought, Andrew stirred his coffee. It had never been quite like that for Mary and himself. Instead, it had been more the expectation of two sets of family friends, one willing their eldest son (and the other their youngest daughter) to make the perfect match. A match they'd both drifted into following a polite and dignified courtship.

Andrew rubbed a hand across his chin. It wasn't that he didn't love Mary - he did. Yet, somehow their relationship (unlike Jenny and Cameron's) seemed to be missing that certain magic spark. Last Friday night in Switzerland he'd hoped Mary could re-ignite that flame.

Sadly for Andrew and Mary, magic was to be in short supply but the sparks were there in abundance, their spell broken by the shrill ringing of the telephone.

'*Monsieur Sinclair? Excusez- moi, mais votre fils – euh – il est…* '

'Andrew? What is it? What's wrong?' Mary cried, watching her husband get out of bed and make a grab for his clothes.

Mary reached for the duvet, anxious to cover her nakedness. Her earlier fleeting boldness giving way to embarrassment. She was no longer twenty years younger, as she'd imagined only moments ago. 'Andrew! Who was on the phone? Why are you getting dressed?'

'It's Iain; he's drunk! That was reception. Iain's been causing a commotion downstairs in the bar and they've called the manager. There's no point in you coming, Mary. I'll deal with it and pay for any damage.'

'Damage! What damage? Where's Catriona – don't say she's drunk too?'

'They didn't say; I expect she just helped Iain back to the hotel after the disco finished. I'll send her up, then perhaps take Iain for a spot of fresh air to sober him up. You go back to bed, dear.' Andrew looked tenderly at his wife, where she stood trying to conceal folds of pink flesh. Yes, she had tried to provide the magic; in fact they both had. Perhaps later there would still be time to rekindle earlier passions.

Long before Andrew found Iain, he heard his son's inebriated shouting coming from a corner of the now empty restaurant. The manager was trying to coax Iain into drinking a cup of strong black coffee.

'Piss off!' Iain declared angrily, pushing the coffee away, where it spilled all over the crisp white table cloth. 'I don't want you bloody coffee! I want Gina! Gina… Gina… Gina…' sang Iain drunkenly, his head resting in the pool of coffee seeping across the white linen.

Andrew gathered the cup and saucer together and passed it to the manager. ' *Je m'excuse patron…* his language – I've never heard my son speak like that before. *Combien pour le – um - damage… est- ce- que beaucoup* broken?' Andrew reached for his wallet.

'It eez of no problem, Monsieur Sinclair. It eez but one broken glass. The glass I can replace, *mais ce n'est pas possible pour moi*... to mend, 'ow you say a broken 'eart?'

Andrew looked up, deeply puzzled, as the manager enlightened him.

'The first broken 'eart eez always the hardest, yes? Especially if it eez broken by the – er – older woman of... shall we say much experience?'

Andrew needed no further explanation; his son's drunken ramblings bore witness to that. Heaving Iain into an upright position, Andrew looked round for Catriona.

'You 'ave lost something, Monsieur Sinclair?'

'My daughter, Catriona. Wasn't she with my son?'

' *Mais non, monsieur, votre fils* he eez alone!'

Filled with panic, Andrew shook his son. 'Iain! Where's Catriona?'

'Gina?' mumbled Iain. 'Where's Gina?'

'No. Not Gina! Catriona. Your sister! Where is she?'

The force of being manhandled by his father as he was pushed into the lift made Iain wince. Why was his father yelling at him, when his head hurt so much and all he wanted to do was sleep? As the lift doors closed and they moved swiftly upwards, Iain felt the earth spinning. Where *was* his sister?

The commotion outside the lift prompted Phyllis King to send her son to investigate. Gordon was surprised to see Andrew full dressed; they'd said goodnight ages ago. Mary stood open-mouthed at the door, watching her husband and Gordon carry Iain to the bathroom. There was no sign of her daughter.

'Where's Catriona,' she asked anxiously. 'Is she drunk too?'

Having at last made sense of Ian's drunken ramblings, Andrew shook his head, 'I'm afraid it's worse than that. It appears Catriona went off with Phillipe to his flat.'

'What! But she's only sixteen! Andrew, you must do something!'

'I intend to – I'm going right away.'

Watching Andrew pick up his padded coat and prepare to leave, Gordon called after him. 'Wait a moment – I'll come with you. You might need some help.'

Quite what help was needed Gordon had no idea. He simply felt that Andrew Sinclair could do with some moral support.

Living life to the full, morals didn't exist in Phillipe Boccard's dictionary of life. Every fortnight he welcomed each planeload of tourists, particularly if they contained fresh, dewy-eyed teenagers just ripe for the picking. So what if he had a reputation and his employers had issued strict warnings? They also knew he was one of their best ski-instructors. Besides, most of the time he adhered to company rules and when he didn't... well, he only bent them a little. Wasn't that what made life more exciting? He'd even said as much, earlier that evening, when he and Gina had plotted together. Neither of them could have realized just how quickly the heat of the disco, plus copious amounts of wine, would affect their chosen victims.

Flushed with euphoria and nervous excitement, Catriona gazed about her. Here she was on the last night of her holiday alone with Phillipe in his apartment. Greedily she accepted the wine he gave her, drinking it in large gulps and offering up her glass for more. Her friends would be so jealous when she described being swept into his arms... and the kisses... oh, the kisses! And if they didn't believe her... she already had the photos as proof of his existence. During the disco she'd even planned how she would persuade her best friend Hazel to return with her at half-term. Money wasn't a problem; she had ample savings in the post office. As for her parents... well, she'd worry about that later. All she wanted to do now was to sink into Phillipe's embrace, just as they did in the films.

Reminded of a scene from her favourite DVD, Catriona stretched nervously on the sofa and waited. In turn Phillipe responded, drawing her into each romantic sequence; ffirst kissing her tenderly and caressing her breasts, before taking her gently by the hand and leading her to the bedroom. With a frisson of anticipation and trying to ignore the effects of the wine, Catriona paused for a moment. What was the next sequence? What happened in the next scene when the dashing hero… Ah, yes! The bed! She sighed dreamily and allowed Phillipe to pull her down beside him. Then, giggling nervously, she found herself naked between the sheets.

In the street outside, running footsteps crunched noisily on snow and ice. Wasn't it funny, Catriona thought, momentarily distracted, how snow creaked in such a strange way when the temperature fell below freezing. Now the creaking continued, but this time indoors even though it wasn't freezing here. Here it was warm and Phillipe – her own wonderful Phillipe – was naked in the bed beside her. Feeling him move towards her, Catriona gasped as his tongue drove hungrily into her mouth and his hand moved swiftly from her breasts to between her legs. She froze; this didn't happen in the film she'd watched with Hazel. And she was sure their hero hadn't smelt of wine and garlic when he… Catriona struggled, not only couldn't she breathe but also she felt sick!

Andrew, hearing his daughter's scream, ran along the corridor to Phillipe's apartment. Surprised to find the door unlocked he entered to find Catriona, clad in only a sheet, being sick on the floor. Phillipe, who had grabbed a bathrobe, tied it nervously about his waist.

'I 'ave done nothing,' he exclaimed. 'I 'ave not touched her!'

'You bloody liar!' Andrew yelled. 'Just look at the state of her! Why, I'll kill you – you bastard!'

Not waiting to give Andrew the opportunity, Gordon pushed him to one side where he landed on the bed near his daughter. Averting his eyes, Andrew looked up just in time to see Gordon striking the retreating Phillipe squarely on the jaw.

Back at the hotel, with Catriona safely installed with her mother, Gordon and Andrew took stock of the situation over a glass of brandy. Nursing bruised knuckles, Gordon asked, 'will you press charges?'

'I'm not sure – what exactly can we prove? Catriona's been swooning over the fellow ever since we got here.'

'So presumably she went willingly to his flat...?'

Andrew gave a rueful shrug. 'I guess so, however as Catriona's in such a state of shock and doesn't want to talk about it... Phillipe swears blind it never got that far but I don't know if I believe him. As for Mary, she says she - er - thinks Catriona's all right, if you know what I mean. Besides, as we're going home tomorrow, do you think it wise to involve the police?'

'From what little I care to remember,' Gordon replied, 'I'd be prepared to say we got there just in time. At least you didn't kill him, Andrew, otherwise the police *would* have been involved.'

'Hmm. And I have you to thank for that, Gordon.' Looking at his own bulging waistline and Gordon's balding head, Andrew gave a wry smile. 'We don't exactly fulfil the picture of two Sir Galahads, do we?'

'Probably not,' Gordon chuckled. 'And this Sir Galahad had better go and check on his mother!'

Andrew sat alone, pondering whether or not to return to Phillipe's flat. What good would it do now? The door would not be left unlocked a second time and Phillipe's face had already taken quite a bruising. He wouldn't look quite so appealing for several weeks, thanks to Gordon's intervention. Perhaps, Andrew considered, he might even think twice before his next attempt at seduction.

A faint smell of cigarette smoke and heavy perfume met Andrew's nostrils. Someone had come into the bar. Without saying a word Gina sat down and studied him carefully. Inhaling deeply on her cigarette, she sent a controlled circle of smoke in his direction. Andrew turned away.

'Your son, he is all right now?' she enquired.

Andrew could only nod in reply. This woman had been responsible for getting his son drunk while that smarmy Lothario... Not wishing to be reminded of it, Andrew got up to leave.

'Don't go,' Gina said, placing her hand on his knee, her voice low and seductive. 'I thought perhaps we could have a drink together...'

'The bar's closed!'

Gina swept Andrew a knowing look beneath her long dark lashes. 'Perhaps, but we do not need the bar, do we?'

Andrew was tired... he was also mildly tempted. All week he'd been listening to Iain drooling over Gina and here she was sitting before him, her hand placed seductively on his knee. Seeing her in such close proximity, she really was strikingly beautiful, her skin glowing and taut and her body inviting. Inviting him – Andrew Sinclair – but to what? Something in Andrew stirred, distant memories of the local minister spouting fire and brimstone. *'Get thee behind me, Satan,'* had been the strident cry from the pulpit. Reminded of his wife waiting for him upstairs, Andrew brushed Gina's hand from his knee and stood up. 'Um - some other time, perhaps.'

*

Now sitting in his office waiting for Jennifer, Andrew couldn't help but wonder what might have happened if he'd gone with Gina. Doubtless he'd never know, but the prospect still haunted him and he felt so ashamed. On the flight back to Edinburgh, all four members of the Sinclair family sat in silence, consumed with guilt. Andrew, because he'd almost succumbed to temptation, Iain for the trouble he'd caused at the hotel, Catriona for allowing herself to be found in such a compromising situation and Mary, not only for nagging Andrew into booking this holiday but also for insisting that they left their youngest child behind. Last night, unable to face any more of his wife's self-recrimination, Andrew couldn't wait to get back to work.

Hearing a car door slam, Andrew rose and went to the window. In the car park below, Stevie was negotiating herself from car to wheelchair. Although he'd never admitted it, it never failed to amaze him how she coped with her disability. Andrew sighed and ran a hand through his thick sandy hair. Why had he been so opposed to his sister employing this young woman as her PA? He supposed it was silly things really: her being called Stevie when her real name was Cressida and...

'With a name like Cressida Stephens,' he'd overheard her say to Jennifer, 'is it any wonder I prefer to be called Stevie? It also drives me mad when people pat me on the head. I always expect them to ask me if I take sugar!'

Andrew made sure he *never* patted Stevie on the head. He also knew she didn't take sugar, but oh, that wretched wheelchair of hers. It left such terrible tyre tracks in his carpet!

'Good morning, Mr Sinclair. Goodness, you're here early. Your holiday must have done you a power of good!'

CHAPTER ELEVEN

Arriving at the office half an hour later, Jenny chose not to ask about Andrew's holiday. The atmosphere in the Edinburgh house the previous evening was warning enough. Instinct told her to tread warily; she had quite a bombshell to drop before Andrew. That in itself would be a shock. To find Paul's plan already had Morag's approval was bound to provoke confrontation.

Jenny placed the bulky folder on Andrew's desk. '*This* is the reason we won't be needing Bill Freeman,' she said softly. 'I suggest you have a good look through it while I deal with the morning's post. Later... perhaps when we stop for coffee... we can discuss it in greater detail.'

Andrew scanned the pages of drawings, noting as he did so the detailed House of St Claire logo. It all seemed so alien. What was Jennifer thinking of? More to the point, who was this Paul Hadley? Someone who'd certainly never worked for Bill Freeman. An hour later, when Jenny popped her head round the door, she was surprised to see Andrew's face devoid of emotion.

'Well... what do you think, or do you need more time?'

'Hmm... although it looks as if you and this – er – Paul Hadley have come up with a plethora of ideas, I can't say I'm that impressed. It's not at all Sinclair's usual style.'

'Precisely! That's the point I've been trying to make these past months, Andrew. Besides, it's a shame you don't approve – because Mother does!'

'She what?' Andrew's eyes flashed angrily. 'You mean to say you've already shown these to Mother?'

'Yes, I took them to Conasg at the weekend.'

'Hmph! You certainly didn't waste any time, going behind my back.'

'That wasn't my intention. My main reason for going to Conasg initially was to give Fiona a break. The poor child had been cooped up in this office for a fortnight. As for wasting time, Andrew, time is the one thing we do *not* have if we are to promote the House of St Claire this year. That's why Mother wants you to ring her this evening.'

'Damn this evening! I'll ring her now,' Andrew said, making a grab for the phone. 'I shall demand to know how she could make a decision like that without consulting me?'

'Quite possibly because you weren't here,' Jenny reminded. 'You were on holiday. Surely you can't have forgotten that already?'

At any other time, Andrew would have responded to his sister's caustic tone. This morning however, he had no choice but to ignore it. If only he could ignore the haunting memories of the holiday so easily.

Spared a further outburst from his sister, Andrew sat in silence as Jenny repeated their mother's request. There was no need to ring now; it would be cheaper this evening. It also meant he would have more time to consider the House of St Claire.

Not one to accept defeat, Andrew turned again to Paul's file. The House of St Claire certainly sounded impressive - as for using the exquisitely executed gorse design as a new logo, even he had to admit there were endless possibilities. What irked him the most was that he'd had no part in its inception, and that only made him resentful.

Listening to Andrew's protestations that evening, Morag Sinclair gave her son short shrift for neglecting the family business. At least someone - namely Jennifer, had Sinclair's interests at heart. Hurt by such a pronouncement, Andrew knew it was pointless trying to remonstrate. Instead he merely agreed that a change of policy might be a good idea.

In truth it hadn't been such a difficult decision to make – once he'd recovered from the initial shock – but he didn't want to admit to

Jennifer that his mind was already springing into overdrive.

Encouraged by yet another positive conversation with her mother, Jenny couldn't wait for her lunch appointment with Paul. How would he react? He would have to meet Andrew too, of course, later that week if possible. In the meantime there was so much to plan.

Sitting at the table she'd reserved in her favourite Italian restaurant, Jenny looked at her watch. No, she wasn't late - they'd said one o'clock and she was always punctual. Nevertheless, not only was she slightly disappointed Paul wasn't here already, but also the waiter was walking towards her, notepad in hand.

'Miss Sinclair, do you wish to order?'

Jenny looked at her watch again and then out of the window. She'd hoped to be back at the office by two o'clock. Surely Paul couldn't have forgotten such an important meeting? 'Luigi, have there been any messages for me – my business appointment, he hasn't telephoned?'

'No, Miss Sinclair, nothing at all.'

'Very well, then,' Jenny said, reaching for a breadstick, 'as it appears I shall be eating alone, if you'll just bring me the ricotta and spinach stuffed pancakes and a glass of white wine...'

'Very well, Miss Sinclair and in the meantime, if your friend arrives, I'll direct him to your table. Perhaps he has been held up in traffic. I'm told it is very bad today.'

Jenny nodded and smiled. Yes, perhaps Paul had been held up in traffic, but if that was the case, couldn't he have telephoned?

In a less happy frame of mind, Jenny finished her meal, drank only half her glass of wine; declined Luigi's suggestion that she try their latest selection of desserts, and prepared to leave the restaurant. If Paul Hadley turned up now, he would have to manage without lunch and simply follow her to the office. That's if she felt like talking to him!

Slamming the outer office door, Jenny brushed past Stevie to her own office.

Stevie looked aghast and called after her, 'Um – Mr Hadley rang, he said he was sorry and-'

'I don't wish to know and I don't want to be disturbed, I have a headache!' Jenny called, slamming her own office door.

Slumped at her desk, Jenny flung open a drawer in search of some paracetamol. She didn't really need them, but in case Stevie should ignore her warning and come into the office, it might at least look convincing. To her dismay it wasn't the headache remedy she came face to face with but a photo of Cameron! Yet another man who had recently let her down.

Staring into what she'd recently decided were Cameron's mocking eyes, she thought of Paul Hadley's eyes - as she'd last seen them - smiling enthusiastically in her direction.

'Men!' she cried in a fit of pique, throwing Cameron's photo in the waste paper basket. 'Who the hell needs them?' Through tear-filled eyes she reached for a tissue and thought of her beloved father. 'You always said I was too trusting, didn't you... and you were right.'

Jenny sniffed and blew her nose. Things wouldn't have seemed that bad if Paul Hadley's ideas hadn't been so good, so fresh and new, but if he was going to be this unreliable and as she'd trusted him so implicitly... She didn't know which was worse. Where did she, or more to the point Sinclair's, go from here?

In Jenny's case it was endeavouring to avoid Andrew as far as possible. Even now she could see him gloating over Mr Hadley's non-appearance, perhaps even rehashing Paul's ideas and taking them along to Bill Freeman with that 'I told you so' look in his eyes. As for her own eyes they were red-rimmed and swollen when Stevie tapped on the office door and ventured forward with some letters to sign.

'Um – I'm sorry to bother you Jenny, as you specifically requested otherwise, but these letters need to be signed today and…'

'And I'm sorry for snapping at you Stevie, blame it on the time of the month.'

'I see, so it wasn't a headache but more a case of PMT?'

Jenny fixed Stevie with a rueful smile, 'Or in this instance PHP.'

'PHP? What's that?'

'Paul Hadley Phobia. To think I'd begun to put so much hope and trust in that man and he couldn't even remember to turn up for a lunch appointment!'

'Oh, he remembered all right,' said Stevie, 'he just couldn't make it and hoped you'd understand. Needless to say he was deeply sorry and I've lost count of the calls he's made in an attempt at offering you an apology. But… as you specifically said you didn't want to be disturbed…'

'Then instead of ringing, why the hell couldn't he just call at the office and explain in person?'

'Quite simply because both his children have chicken pox, his wife is still away on holiday and the neighbour, who usually helps out, is visiting her mother in hospital.'

Jenny clasped a hand to her face. 'Did you say chicken pox? Oh, my God! That can only mean one thing… Fiona… they must have caught it from Fiona!'

'Yes, that's precisely what I thought.'

'Then why didn't you tell me, Stevie?'

'Tell you!' Stevie spun her wheelchair to face Jenny head on. 'I can't believe you've just said that. If you remember I did try, the moment you charged back into the office after lunch, looking like a bull in a china shop. Then, when you said you had a headache and slammed the door in my face…'

'And now I'm left feeling shame-faced. I'm truly sorry, Stevie. You're right, it's not your fault. Blame it on Sinclair pig-headedness.'

'Hmph! Yours I can just about cope with, Jenny. It's your brother's I have problems with. When Andrew's in one of his moods, I wouldn't put it past him to slash the tyres on my wheelchair.'

Jenny forced a smile. 'Well, today, you won't have to worry about that. It won't be your tyres Andrew will be deflating; it will be my ego. I had such high hopes for the House of St Claire. I'd hate for it all to disappear.'

'There's little chance of that,' Stevie added, handing over the pile of letters for signing, 'Mr Sinclair's been working on that all day. The telephone's red-hot, what with phone calls to New York and Geneva.'

'You mean red-hot like my temper?'

'No comment. Anyway, apart from the dreaded PMT, I'm not surprised you're tired and upset. What with looking after Fiona and the office for two weeks, then to have Mr Hadley stand you up… Why don't you go home, forget about Sinclair's, have a nice hot bath and an early night? I'm sure you'll see everything in a different light tomorrow.'

Jenny had already forgotten about Sinclair's, but her thoughts were not on baths and early nights. In her mind's eye she conjured up a vision of Paul trying to cope with Celestina and Emily. Coping with one chicken-pox infected child, namely Fiona, had been bad enough; coping with two must be a nightmare. Holding herself responsible for Paul's current dilemma, Jenny decided there was only one thing for it. She must go and help.

'I don't believe it,' she cried, looking in her diary. By Paul's name there was only a telephone number. How could she be so stupid? She didn't even know where he lived! Racking her brains, she tried to remember all he'd said when he'd first introduced himself. Who had told him about Sinclair's? Alistair – Alistair Jennings, yes, that was it! She must ring him immediately.

'Jenny, darling,' came the smooth response. 'Why haven't I seen you? Are you avoiding me? You promised me lunch ages ago, remember?'

Jenny certainly remembered all right, which was why she preferred to forget! Alistair Jennings gave her the creeps. It had been one thing earlier that afternoon making comparisons between Cameron and Paul Hadley, but Alistair Jennings, with his wandering hands and sexual innuendo, was even worse. She was beginning to wish she'd never rung him. There was only one solution, get rid of him quickly even if it meant agreeing to a lunch date – she could always cancel later – and in the meantime ask for Paul's address. Thankfully, Alistair duly obliged.

CHAPTER TWELVE

Surveying the peeling front door of the large Victorian house, Jenny stood nervously on the doorstep. How would Paul react to her being here, when she'd stubbornly refused his calls all afternoon? Her stomach lurched when she heard the ringing of a distant bell, followed by the sound of hurried footsteps.

The door opened, but it wasn't Paul who stood there. Surely this ageing hippy wasn't his wife? Hadn't Stevie said Mrs Hadley was away?

'I'm looking for Paul Hadley. Have I come to the right house?'

'Why, yes,' came a cheery reply, 'he's just away to the chemist's. I'm sure he'll only be a wee while. Would you care to come in and wait?'

Jenny introduced herself, then with an air of uncertainty followed the unknown woman, clad in a bizarre array of textiles and colours, through the house to a welcoming kitchen.

'I'm Helen Craig, Paul's neighbour,' she said, extending her hand. 'I try to help Paul whenever I can and in turn he helps me with lifts to the hospital. It's a bit too far for me to go on my bike. He would have taken me today of course, only he had a prior business appointment.' Helen Craig looked wistful. 'Poor man, he never got there in the end. The school rang, you see, and he had to fetch the wee bairns home. Quite poorly they look, too, but at least they're sleeping now. As if he doesn't have enough problems already… Anyway, enough of my blethering, how about a nice cup of tea?'

Reaching for the kettle, Helen was aware of Jenny's eyes scanning the general disorder in the house. 'It's in a terrible muddle, isn't it?' she said softly. 'Mind you, you should have seen it before Gina left; it was even worse then.'

82

'Gina?'

'Paul's wife. I feel truly sorry for him, you know – she's hardly ever here and when she is… You've never met her, I take it?'

Seeing Jenny shake her head, Helen continued sadly, 'As for Cele and Emily, well… let's just say Gina wasn't cut out for domesticity, though she does try sometimes, poor dear.'

'How long did you say Mr Hadley would be?' Jenny asked, anxious to change the subject. It didn't seem right discussing people she didn't know.

'Och, not long now. The chemist's isn't far. He would have gone earlier, only he was hoping for a phone call. With me being at the hospital, I couldn't come in before and of course he'd never leave the girls all alone. So you see… we were all in a right pickle and I've still got Mother's laundry to attend to.'

'If you want to go, Helen, I'm more than happy to stay and look after Celestina and Emily. They do know me and I've plenty of time.' Yes, plenty of time thought Jenny, having said goodbye to Helen Craig. Plenty of time to feel guilty about Fiona passing on the chicken pox virus and also *that* phone call – no doubt her phone call, the one Paul had been waiting for!

'Goodness, you do look poorly,' said Jenny, dabbing Cele and Emily with the calamine lotion she'd bought on her way over. 'I'm so sorry, you appear to have caught Fiona's chicken pox. She'll be very upset when I tell her.'

At the mere mention of Fiona's name both girls appeared to brighten. 'How is Fiona?' they asked, almost in unison.

'She's much better, thank you, and delighted with the drawings you sent. She even took them to show her grannie last weekend.'

The girls were impressed, then Cele added softly, 'Our Grannie Hadley is dead but our other grannie – Grannie 'Tino' is in Italy.'

While the girls waited for the calamine lotion to dry, Jenny set to remaking their crumpled beds and quite forgot about Paul. It came as a complete surprise when she heard a key turn in the lock and his voice call, 'Helen, I'm back.'

'Helen's gone home,' Cele shouted down the stairs to her daddy, but…'

Two at a time Paul rushed up the stairs, desperate to know why Helen had left the girls so unexpectedly. In his hands were bottles of Calpol and calamine lotion and pads of cotton wool.

'Miss Sinclair! What are you…?'

Jenny held up her own medical supplies. 'Snap!' she said, fixing him with a smile.

Back in the kitchen, Paul's profuse apologies for his non-appearance at lunchtime were in turn replaced by Jennifer's for inflicting Fiona's germs on the two small children, now happily looking at their picture books.

'Mr Hadley, I can't begin to tell you how embarrassed I am by all this. I hold myself completely responsible. Therefore, I insist you must let me help in any way I can.'

'Well, Helen's been very kind,' said Paul, 'and it won't be so bad if I'm going to be working from home…' he looked anxiously in Jenny's direction. *Would* he be working from home?

'Speaking of work, that's also one of the reasons I'm here. My mother is more than happy for you to proceed with the House of St Claire project and I'm pleased to say Andrew didn't take too much convincing either.'

Paul looked at Jenny in disbelief. It was as if a huge weight had suddenly been lifted from his shoulders. 'Why, that's wonderful! Are you sure?'

'Absolutely positive.'

'So… when do you want me to begin?'

'Well, obviously we need to get this project off the ground as soon as possible. My brother said he'd like to see you tomorrow.'

Paul's heart sank and he raked his fingers through his hair. How could he manage tomorrow with the girls so poorly?

'If you're worried about Cele and Emily, that isn't a problem,' Jenny said, reading his mind, 'I'll happily come and sit with them while you discuss the House of St Claire with Andrew.'

'That's very kind of you, Miss Sinclair, especially as I understand from your PA that you're completely snowed under with work at present.'

Jenny felt herself colour. So that was the excuse Stevie had used, when Paul had been trying to get hold of her. She flicked at an imaginary piece of fluff on her jacket. 'Oh, I'm quite sure I can bring some of it with me. And, as we're going to be working together from now on, can I suggest we drop the Miss Sinclair… please call me Jenny.'

'Only on condition you call me Paul,' he said, making eye contact, before walking to a cabinet in the far corner of the room. 'Somehow I think we should be celebrating but I'm afraid the choice looks pretty dismal from here… unless you like neat vodka or apricot brandy?'

Jenny shook her head. 'Thank you, no – not if I'm driving and especially not on an empty stomach.'

'Then perhaps I can offer you supper, once I've seen to the girls' tea. That's if you don't mind lasagne from the freezer? The choice in there is a bit like the drink's cabinet – limited.'

Smiling, and completely at ease, Jenny found herself helping Paul prepare trays for the children's tea. Then when the girls were settled for the night, she sat down with him at the pine kitchen table. Surprisingly, in the warmth of the cosy yet cluttered kitchen, even supermarket lasagne tasted good after the earlier traumas of the day. And with Paul having found a decent bottle of Chianti Classico tucked away at the back of the cabinet, she allowed herself one small glass.

'To the House of St Claire,' she said, raising her glass in his direction.

'The House of St Claire,' he acknowledged, 'though on reflection perhaps this should have been champagne. I'm sorry I can't oblige. Next time perhaps?'

'Oh, there'll definitely be a next time,' Jenny said, her eyes sparkling with enthusiasm for their new venture, 'and I can assure you the champagne will come later... courtesy of Andrew. Knowing my brother as I do, I can guarantee it will be one of the best!'

One of the best... Paul mused after he'd waved her goodbye. Certainly one of the best things that had happened to him in recent weeks was meeting Jenny Sinclair!

*

The next morning a welcome smell of coffee pervaded the house as Paul relieved Jenny of her laptop and a bag of shopping and helped her off with her coat.

'I'm sorry I won't be there to introduce you to my brother, but I've given Stevie strict instructions to look after you. Andrew's not too bad, really,' said Jenny, attempting reassurance. 'He's just a bit like a mother hen when it comes to Sinclair's. Secretly I think he wishes *he'd* thought of the House of St Claire... still, as we're all working for the same team, it doesn't really matter, does it?'

Jenny studied Paul for the first time since he'd opened the front door. He looked tired and anxious. Here she was chattering on about Andrew and she hadn't even asked about Celestina and Emily.

'You look tired, Paul – did the girls have a bad night?'

'Afraid so. I seemed to be up and down with them all night long. It's the wretched itching; it makes them so uncomfortable.'

'You mustn't worry about them now, I'll take good care of everything here and Stevie knows where to contact me if I'm needed.'

With Paul safely on his way, Jenny went upstairs to check on Emily and Cele. Two blotchy faces peered out from beneath duvets decorated with Spot the Dog motifs – which somehow seemed strangely appropriate. The girls looked flushed and tired.

'You'll need to drink plenty of fluids and get lots of sleep,' Jenny told them kindly, at the same time wondering just when their mother was going to make contact. To date (according to Helen Craig), all Paul's messages to Switzerland asking Gina to call remained unanswered.

Without the constant ringing of the telephone and interruptions from Andrew, Jenny was amazed how quickly she dealt with her backlog of work. Much later, making herself a sandwich and another pot of coffee, she hoped desperately for Paul's sake that Andrew wouldn't be too bombastic. *For Paul's sake*, she mused. With her Sinclair work finished, was there anything she could do for him? The girls had already eaten a light lunch and were sleeping again, but there must be other jobs she could do.

The house, she noticed, was far tidier than before. If she were to help in any way, then it would have to be something quiet. In the utility room her gaze alighted on a basket of clothes, neatly folded and ready for ironing. 'Perfect,' she whispered, securing the ironing board into position and plugging in the iron.

Newly cleaned and descaled, the iron no longer spewed forth sludge. Instead there came a gentle purring sound as steam wafted easily over each freshly laundered garment. Jenny hummed softly to herself, surprised that ironing in the afternoon could be so therapeutic. Her own laundry duties were usually a frenetic exercise performed while watching the ten o'clock news.

Studying the mounting pile of children's clothes ready for the airing cupboard, Jenny reached for the first of Paul's shirts. It had been simply ages since she'd ironed a man's shirt. Now she didn't even know if she could... without thinking of Cameron.

Carefully placing the shirt on the ironing board, she smoothed out the fabric and ran her fingers across each pearl button, checking to see they were all secure. Tears pricked her eyes as she did so and she lifted a newly ironed sleeve to her cheek.

In the early days of their relationship, Cameron would always stroke his hands against her cheek before leaving for the naval base. 'No tears, remember,' he would murmur softly, 'I'll be back soon.' The problem then had been coping with his long absences; now it no longer mattered.

Although the room was warm, Jenny felt a shiver run through her body at the memory of their very last meeting. Cameron's verbal attack on all the Sinclair's had been ferocious. It was true, since the death of her father she'd thrown herself into the family business. They all had, Mother and Andrew too. It was a case of necessity – either that or let Sinclair's go to the wall. No one, least of all Jenny, was going to let that happen. She sighed and whispered softly. 'Six years, Cameron, we had six whole years – yet I'm only just beginning to realize I never really knew you.'

Hearing a faint stirring at the door, Jenny turned to find a small, sleepy figure. It was Emily holding a toy rabbit unceremoniously by the ear. She looked delicate and frail, like a flower fairy from the Cicely M Barker books Jenny enjoyed as a child. Those same treasured books were now in Fiona's possession, yet she still remembered each one. Swallowing hard, Jenny held out her arms and drew Emily towards her. From now on Cele, Emily and Fiona would be her own trio of flower fairies. She would do everything she could to protect them.

'Can I have a drink, please, Jenny?'

'Of course. Tell me what you'd like and I'll bring it right up.'

Returning to bed dragging the rabbit behind her, Emily waited. When

Jenny appeared, she saw she was holding a glass of juice in one hand and several of her daddy's shirts in the other.

'Perhaps you can tell me where the airing cupboard is, Emily, then I can put Daddy's shirts away.'

Drinking thirstily, Emily pointed to the airing cupboard and watched as a jumble of clothes fell at Jenny's feet. There might just be room for the girls' clothes, but not for the shirts she'd ironed so carefully.

With the air of an intruder Jenny sought out Paul and Gina's bedroom. A heavy smell of stale perfume pervaded the air, and make-up and postcards littered the dressing table. She felt strangely uncomfortable. Perhaps she should have squeezed the shirts into the airing cupboard after all.

Anxious to vacate the room as soon as possible, Jenny went straight to the wardrobe, only to discover to her horror it wasn't Paul's. In fact there was no sign of Paul anywhere, not even a solitary tie. Every shelf, rail and hanger was filled to overflowing with women's clothes. Jenny was aghast; even Mary didn't possess such quantities. And the colours! Sheer unadulterated extravagance were the only words to flash through her mind as she stood clasping Paul's shirts to her breast. Shirts that had undoubtedly seen far better days. No wonder Paul had looked so dishevelled at their very first meeting.

Without realizing it, Jenny found herself loathing Gina Hadley. She was all for husbands and wives having their own interests, but it seemed Gina's interests did not extend as far as her husband and two adorable little girls. What kind of woman was she to ignore her husband's phone calls when her children were so poorly? With the intrusive chirp of the telephone, Jenny was to find out sooner than expected.

' *Ciao*! Who is that? Helen, is it you?'

'No, it's Jenny.'

'Jenny! Jenny who? What are you doing in my house?'

Completely taken aback, Jenny replied without thinking. 'I'm helping Paul.'

'How very interesting - and how exactly are you helping Paul?'

Angered by Gina's menacing tone, Jenny replied tersely, 'What do you mean, how am I helping Paul? Here in the house of course.'

'Oh, I see... then you are a cleaner.'

'No, I'm not!' Though her reply was indignant, Jenny knew trying to explain her present situation could prove difficult. Not that Gina was able to see down the phone, but if she could... what would she say to the woman who was standing in *her* bedroom with an armful of Paul's shirts?

A stream of incomprehensible Italian flooded down the line, followed by a venomous, 'So, this is what he gets up to when I am away! He has wasted no time!'

Jenny was alarmed and assumed that Gina had been drinking. No normal person would jump to such ridiculous conclusions. As for the torrent of accusations...

Determined to command attention and take control, Jenny shouted down the phone. 'I don't particularly care what *you* think at the moment, Mrs Hadley, but I can assure you I am *not* having an affair with your husband! If you'll just stop yelling at me for an instant and listen... I am here because your children have been ill. I'm only doing what *you* should be doing; taking care of your family!'

Apart from background laughter, the line remained strangely quiet.

'Mrs Hadley?'

' *Si*... yes, I am still here. *Scusi*... Where is Paul?'

'He has an important business engagement and will be back this evening.'

'And Cele and Emily?'

'They are in bed with chicken-pox. Would you like me to bring them to the phone?'

Gina hesitated, then a voice in the background called out, '*Gina*! *Viens, cherie, nous sommes en retard.* '

'No, it is all right,' Gina said hurriedly. 'I must go. Tell Paul I will ring him... I will come home.'

'Was that Mummy on the phone?'

'Yes,' said Jenny, placing the shirts on the bed and placing her arms round the newly woken Cele. 'She's coming home, isn't that lovely?'

Cele made no comment and Emily appeared requesting drawing paper.

'Daddy keeps it in his study, I'll show you where.'

In Paul's study, Jenny finally discovered where to put his shirts.

'It's all right,' Emily said, sensing her reluctance. She pointed to a pile of cartridge paper. 'Daddy won't mind.'

It wasn't the paper that bothered Jenny so much, it was seeing the room and all it revealed. A narrow camp bed had been pushed against the wall to make way for a single wardrobe and a drawing office desk. Hurrying back to Gina's bedroom, Jenny returned with Paul's shirts. It had been one thing opening Gina's wardrobe door but nothing would induce her to open Paul's. She'd ventured too far into his private life already.

Reaching for two sheets of cartridge paper, Jenny recognized copies of the designs Paul had taken to show Andrew. All neatly laid out on the desk and numbered, she hoped with all her heart that today's meeting with her brother had gone well.

*

The look of elation on Paul's face following the success of his meeting with Andrew Sinclair was short-lived. Cele announced glumly, 'Mummy rang; she's coming home.'

'What was that?' Paul asked, watching the girls rush off to retrieve their latest drawings.

Jenny shifted uneasily. 'Your wife rang earlier and… I have to confess I was quite rude to her. I'm sorry, I owe you an apology.'

'I doubt it,' Paul said bluntly. 'Gina has a knack of upsetting people; that's when she's not putting on her "charm personified" act.' His tone was bitter and resentful. 'What exactly did she say to upset you?'

'Oh, nothing really. Looking back on it, I think she simply caught me at a bad moment.'

'By that I hope you don't mean the girls have been naughty and playing you up?'

'Gracious, no! They've been wonderfully behaved. It's been a real pleasure looking after them. When they're better, I'm hoping you'll let them come and have tea with me and Fiona.'

Paul eyed Jenny suspiciously. 'Only on condition that you tell me what Gina said to you. Please… Jenny?'

'Um… it's quite preposterous really. She accused us of having an affair. Now, tell me, how did the meeting go with Andrew?'

'It went well, really well,' Paul said quickly, anxious to spare Jenny's blushes. 'He's convinced we can all work together on the House of St Claire project *and* get it off the ground asap.'

'Thank heavens for that… and did Andrew tell you what happens next?'

'Next, according to your brother, we go to the factories; discuss materials, design possibilities, production and marketing. The initial objective is to produce a House of St Claire range - albeit small - for the summer. Andrew then wants to be ready to take New York and Geneva by storm.'

'He what? You're joking!'

'Not according to Andrew,' Paul said with a grin. 'He's deadly serious. There's a British week in New York and also Geneva; he wants the

House of St Claire represented at both. He's already pencilled both events in his diary.'

Jenny reached for her laptop. 'Then I'd better get a move on and do some homework, otherwise I shall get left behind by you men.'

'So I can't persuade you to stay and have a drink?' Paul said, holding up a bottle. 'I bought it on the way home. I thought we deserved something special to celebrate the birth of the House of St Claire.'

Jenny hesitated, 'Another time perhaps? Your wife said she was going to ring and if she finds I'm still here… There's a casserole in the oven and I'm sure you'll find both girls will sleep well tonight. No doubt I'll see you at the office.'

With a gentle smile of acknowledgement, Paul watched her go to her car. What a day! Perhaps his luck was changing after all. To begin with Celestina and Emily were looking so much better and there was no knowing where this opening with Sinclair's might lead. Closing the door on the murky winter's evening, Paul was comforted by the welcome smell wafting from the kitchen. For the first time in ages he'd returned to find a decent meal waiting. What a pity, then, that several hours later, Gina should cruelly burst his bubble by ringing to announce her imminent arrival at the airport.

CHAPTER THIRTEEN

In the weeks that followed, life for the Sinclair's slipped back into its usual routine. Andrew, thankful the skiing holiday was no longer mentioned, committed himself wholeheartedly to the House of St Claire. He and Paul made rapid progress by working long hours, which Gina appeared not to mind and Mary compensated for by dividing her time between numerous committees. For Jean and Iain it meant serious studying and for Fiona, the anticipation of an early picnic with Aunt Jennifer when the primroses were in bloom.

As the day approached, Fiona was bitterly disappointed to learn that Cele and Emily were unable to come. The picnic wouldn't be the same without her two new friends. Paul had given no specific reason but instinct told Jenny that Gina was probably being difficult. Things were best left alone.

'Why do you want to go on a boring picnic, when you can come shopping with me for pretty dresses?' Gina had demanded. Her question had been met with silence by both Cele and Emily. Young as they were, both girls knew it was best not to antagonize their mother or provoke disagreements. They had learnt that from their father since Gina's return from her skiing trip.

Initially full of remorse at her extended absence, she'd surprised them all. Remorse, however, soon gave way to boredom, and a phone call from one of her glitterati friends soon rekindled Gina's feelings of wanderlust. The problem was how to approach Paul and tell him she was going away again.

Gina need look no further than the morning's post. The promotional package for the *British Week* trade fairs gave her the opportunity she was waiting for.

'You are going away, Paul?'

'I doubt it, Gina; that's more Andrew's line.'

'This Andrew, you enjoy working with him, yes?'

'Mmm. Strangely enough I do, even though we're like chalk and cheese. I think we make a pretty good team. We owe a great deal to Andrew and Jenny Sinclair - like keeping this house, for instance.' Paul refrained from adding, *and also keeping you in clothes*, but as Gina had been somewhat restless of late, it was probably best to keep quiet.

'Then... why don't we invite them to dinner?' Gina added brightly.

Paul couldn't believe his ears. It had been months since his wife had suggested inviting people to dinner. Perhaps his earlier thoughts had been ill-founded. Gina was a very good cook when she chose to be; the problem was she didn't choose to be very often. Perhaps in a small way, the dinner party could be a gesture of thanks on their behalf. Smiling with satisfaction, he replied, 'I think that's a wonderful idea, Gina. Perhaps you could ring Jenny at the office and arrange a convenient date?'

To Jenny the dinner invitation was like a bolt out of the blue. The one and only conversation she'd had with Gina Hadley was one she chose not to remember. How should she reply? Gina must have remembered their heated exchange of words. She said the first thing that came into her head.

'Well, it's very kind of you, but Andrew and I are extremely busy at the moment – the House of St Claire, you know...'

'Exactly,' cooed Gina. 'This is why we both want you to come - a little thank you to Sinclair's - and of course I never thanked you properly for looking after Celestina and Emily when I was away.'

Jenny was confused. Could this be the same woman she'd spoken to on that cold winter's afternoon? It must be the better weather, she concluded, warming the hearts of her fellow men or in this case, fellow woman.

Surprisingly, Andrew was perfectly accommodating to Gina's offer. Wednesday would be fine, he confirmed; Mary had one of her committee meetings and Catriona could look after Fiona…

'I'm not sure Andrew,' said Jenny. 'Could we not make it an evening when Mary can go with you?'

'Nonsense! Why would Mary want to come? She's not the least bit interested in discussing trade fairs or the business and there's still a great deal Paul and I have to arrange. I was only saying to Alistair Jennings today…

Jenny froze at the very mention of the name. For weeks Alistair had been pestering her for another dinner date to replace the one she'd cancelled. She was now running out of excuses. Andrew had chosen Alistair's company to supply the food for the House of St Claire hampers, and with advertising already under way…

'Very well, I'll tell Mrs Hadley eight o'clock next Wednesday, only please don't forget. I'd rather not go alone.'

'There's little chance of that,' Andrew said, making a note in his diary. 'I'll take the wine and if you can get some flowers for Mrs Hadley…' Watching Jenny walk away, Andrew stretched contentedly in his chair. Having spent so many hours working late at the office, it would be an evening to look forward to and, if he could persuade his sister to chauffeur him on Wednesday, he could have the odd glass or two and maybe even a brandy…

*

When Wednesday came, nothing could have prepared Andrew for the shock of seeing Gina by Paul's side when he opened the door. But if Gina had recognized Andrew, it was certainly well concealed.

As the evening wore on and he was mellowed by fine wine and a full stomach, Andrew could only sing the praises of the excellent meal Gina had prepared. It was one of the rare occasions when she'd surpassed herself. She also couldn't thank Jenny enough for her earlier help, when Cele and Emily were ill.

With Andrew extolling at length the virtues of the home-made soup, pasta and *tartufo*, Jenny and Paul found themselves in quiet conversation. Delighted with the results from the factory, they were in the process of discussing the merits of the new machine (brought in to create the delicate gorse design), when Gina exclaimed, 'Your sister! Jenny is your sister? I thought she was your wife!'

'Gracious, no!' Andrew said, roaring with laughter. He patted Jenny's hand. 'Mary – my wife – is almost twice the size of Jennifer!'

Flushed with embarrassment as Andrew continued to laugh, no doubt aided by copious amounts of wine, Jenny was seriously beginning to wish she hadn't come. For the rest of the evening she felt Gina eyeing her suspiciously whenever she and Paul were in conversation.

Conscious of the atmosphere changing from one of jovial relaxation to one of hostility as the two women studied each other across the table, Paul breathed a sigh of relief when Gina left the room to make coffee. He in turn went to fetch the brandy.

Glaring at Andrew, Jenny excused herself to go to the bathroom. Instinct told her there was trouble brewing. With Andrew so reluctant to leave, she wondered how much longer they would have to remain? Coming back downstairs she heard voices from the kitchen and through the half-open doorway, saw Gina holding a glass of brandy. Taking a large gulp from the glass, Gina smiled provocatively in Paul's direction, placed her brandy on the kitchen table and sidled up to him. Not wishing to draw attention to her presence, Jenny stood frozen to the spot with one hand on the banister rail.

'Paul, darling,' Gina cooed huskily, 'why don't you come to my bed tonight? Wouldn't it be nice to sleep with your little Gina again? It has been such a long time since...'

Gina ran her hand up and down the inside of Paul's thigh. Feeling sickened, Jenny watched as Paul pushed Gina's hand aside and walked away. Gina's dark eyes flashed angrily, then, just as she was making a grab for Paul's arm, she caught sight of Jenny on the stairs. In a moment she stifled her look of rage and donned a simpering smile.

'Men!' she said, shrugging her shoulders. 'They never know what they want do they?' If the smile was sweet, the underlying tone was venomous.

Back in the dining room, Andrew knew what he wanted - another glass of brandy. He hadn't felt this relaxed for weeks and with Gina now sitting by his side and her foot rubbing seductively against his leg, he raised his glass in her direction. Fancy Paul having such a damned attractive wife...

Andrew's obvious delight at Gina's blatant attention was more than Jenny could bear. There was nothing for it other than to insist she take Andrew home. As if rehearsing a school play, she announced woodenly, 'Andrew, I think your wife will be wondering where you are! And as I've an early appointment tomorrow...'

Looking anxiously in Paul's direction, Jenny was desperate for support. Would he take the cue?'

'Why, yes, Andrew and so have we. Aren't we supposed to be making an early start tomorrow... going to the mill to see Duncan?'

They weren't, of course, but Andrew was so confused it didn't matter. Paul's remark had the desired effect. He helped Andrew to his feet and at the same time acknowledged Jenny's grateful look of thanks.

*

'Your behaviour was absolutely disgraceful, Gina! What the hell were you trying to prove in there with Andrew Sinclair?' Paul loaded the dishwasher while Gina sat slumped at the table with yet another brandy, sulking like a spoilt child.

'At least he didn't push me away, like you did.'

'That's a joke, considering you're the one who did the initial pushing.'

'Me! What do you mean? I didn't push you away this evening; I asked if you wanted to…'

''Exactly! " *Darling, why don't you come to my bed tonight?*" ' Paul mimicked Gina's earlier fawning tone, 'What do you think I'm made of, Gina? You turn me out of *our* bedroom with some feeble excuse that you sleep better on your own — I doubt you have that problem when you're away skiing — then ask me if I want to come to your bed like some damned slave. Good grief, you've got a nerve!'

After weeks of trying to conceal the brutal facts, the truth was out at last. Consumed with guilt that he'd raised his voice while the girls were in the house, Paul slammed shut the door of the dishwasher. It was pointless trying to hide his feelings anymore. Things had to come to a head sooner or later and it might as well be now. Gina's ongoing outrageous behaviour was simply the catalyst in their rapidly disintegrating relationship.

If Paul was going to raise his voice, Gina could surely go one better. A verbal torrent of abuse poured forth from her lips — most of which was in Italian. Furious that her husband was ignoring her, Gina continued to yell incoherently.

With an air of calm self-possession, Paul turned and walked away. 'I'd save your breath if I were you Gina. I've heard it all before anyway.'

At that moment Gina threw her empty brandy glass across the room and screamed, this time in English.

'Yes! I do want you out of our bedroom. I want you out of it forever - that means always! Do you understand Paul… *always*? You are so…. so *boring* and I… I *hate* you! Did you hear what I said? I *hate* you!'

'Yes, Gina, I heard you. And I'm sorry you find me so boring. That's possibly because I've always tried to accept my family responsibilities, which is more than you've done in recent years. Still, that's fine by me. At least I know where I stand. I could of course add that I find the way you've completely disregarded your role as wife and mother a total disgrace, but deep down, I think you know that already. And… if you aren't happy here, then I can only suggest you leave.'

'*Don't worry, I shall.*' Gina called, storming to the kitchen door. 'I'd planned to anyway. I already have my ticket!'

Relieved that at least Cele and Emily appeared not to have been disturbed by such a commotion, Paul began sweeping up the broken glass.

That night however, none of them slept well. While Paul and his daughters listened to the slamming and banging of drawers and doors until early morning, Andrew in his inebriated state kept calling for *Jeannie*. At least that's what Mary thought, becoming increasingly irritated by her husband's drunken ramblings. Not only was she disgusted that he had returned home in such a state, but also she couldn't understand why Andrew should keep calling for their ex-neighbour. Jeannie had moved away months ago.

Alone in her tiny cottage Jenny also tossed and turned. Every time she closed her eyes the sordid scene of Gina rubbing her body against Paul's returned to haunt her. By early morning, however, Gina's bags were packed and loaded into a taxi, whereas Andrew surveyed his own (dark grey and puffy), beneath bloodshot eyes in the bathroom mirror.

CHAPTER FOURTEEN

The small green shoots tended so lovingly beneath the apple tree had long since flowered and died, along with the golden carpet of daffodils that had followed closely behind. To Jenny daffodils were always a welcome sign, a true harbinger of spring. Only yesterday evening, leaving the office for the weekend, she'd noticed people looking less grey and sombre. Instead of a huddled retreat into shadowy darkness, they strode confident and erect, taking in all Mother Nature had to offer, even in the heart of Edinburgh. It wouldn't be long before leaves unfurled completely and dappled shade obscured the castle for yet another summer.

Turning on the radio, Jenny heard a band playing 'The Bluebells of Scotland' and was instantly reminded of her mother and Hogmanay. It was one of the few occasions when Morag let her hair down. The transference of thought between bluebells and hair ended with Fiona. The missing front teeth had now grown and the auburn plaits were even thicker and longer. To Cele and Emily they remained a source of fascination. Tireless attempts at creating plaits of their own always ended in disaster.

'It's no use,' Paul had confided to Jenny, 'I can do most things for the girls but plaits... Cele's hair is far too curly and as Emily's is still baby-fine, it's impossible.'

'The girls,' Jenny murmured to herself. 'I wonder how they are.'

It was ages since she'd seen them, and such a pity they'd missed Fiona's picnic. She'd promised to make it up to them, too, but there always seemed so much to occupy her. The House of St Claire had received such a positive response from every quarter. Heartened by its success, Jenny had even succumbed to lunch with Alistair Jennings.

Too late she realized her mistake. Barely a week went by without Alistair's pestering. It always began with an excuse about Sinclair's and ended with an invitation to lunch, dinner or the theatre. At the office Stevie was instructed to take most of Jenny's calls while at home, she preferred to use the answerphone.

'That was "The Bluebells of Scotland" for Flora Macintosh on her eightieth birthday' the radio presenter announced cheerily. 'Well Flora, you'll not be needing a mackintosh today if you're heading off to pick bluebells. There'll be blue skies and sunshine just for you on this sunny Saturday.'

'Blethers!' said Jenny, peering from the kitchen window. 'Not from where I'm standing there isn't. Still, hopefully the weather would improve as the weekend progressed. Were there bluebells out already? Perhaps she should go and investigate.

Conscious of her flashing answering machine, Jenny paused to listen. She recognized Paul's voice immediately.

'Jenny, so sorry to have missed you, but I was wondering if you'd heard from Andrew. There's something I need to check with him urgently. Perhaps you could return my call?'

The remainder of the tape contained the usual assortment of messages. Alistair, still refusing to give up, and Mary and Morag, both enquiring as to Andrew's whereabouts in New York. Like Paul, they were anxious to speak to him.

As far as Jenny was concerned, the fact that Andrew hadn't rung could mean only two things. Either the House of St Claire had been a complete unmitigated disaster, having no success at all on Fifth Avenue – or else it was a roaring success, with Andrew rushed off his feet dealing with prospective customers.

Jenny prayed for the latter and thought it a shame Paul had been unable to go with Andrew, but with Gina still firmly absent from her family – and quite likely to remain so, Andrew had insisted he could cope alone. Jenny picked up the phone to ring Paul…

*

'I'm sorry, are we early?' he asked. 'I thought when you rang yesterday you said three o'clock.' Paul stood at the door with Celestina and Emily holding tightly on to his hands.

'I did,' said Jenny, rubbing flower from her fingers. 'Only Andrew rang me in the wee small hours – presumably forgetting the time difference between here and the States. Then I couldn't get back to sleep and the inevitable happened. I dropped off just as dawn broke and overslept. I've spent the rest of the day trying to catch up.' She gestured to the marble slab on the table, its surface covered with flour and trays of scones waiting to go in the oven.

'I'd say inviting us to tea hasn't made things any easier for you.'

'Nonsense!' Jenny smiled at the two little girls. 'I've been looking forward to seeing you all again. Believe it or not, everything's under control. Mother and Miss Tandy quite despair of me, I always make a mess like this when I'm baking. However, they do say they prefer my scones to Mary's. Then again, that's not too much to my credit is it, when Mary excels at everything else in the kitchen?'

'Ah, but could she run the House of St Claire?' asked Paul.

'I doubt it – speaking of which, great news from Andrew! Just wait until I tell you! Look, why don't you and the girls make yourselves at home? They can play in the garden if they wish. It's quite safe out there, no hidden dangers or prized specimens to worry about.' Opening the back door for them, Jenny turned back to the chaos in the kitchen. 'I'll just clear this up and we can have tea. The scones will be cooked by then and I'll call you when everything's ready.'

Jenny watched as Paul led his daughters outside where they peered into nooks and crannies, examining each bush and flower. Eventually they felt confident enough to leave him and ran off to peer over the wall at the far end of the garden.

'They're still painfully shy,' Jenny said, when she and Paul stepped back into the cosy warmth of the kitchen.

'I'm afraid so. Unfortunately, Gina's behaviour hasn't exactly done wonders for their self-confidence.'

'Have you heard from her lately?'

Paul raked a hand through his hair and sighed. 'Oh, I've had the odd phone call, and she sends the girls postcards now and then. The last one came from Canada.'

'Canada! I thought she'd gone to France. How on earth did she manage to get from France to Canada?'

'Quite easily,' Paul said bitterly. 'She has so-called friends everywhere, and just in case you're wondering, I gather she's done a spot of modelling along the way. Goodness knows, I couldn't support that kind of lifestyle.'

Turning from the oven with a tray of freshly baked scones, Jenny saw that his face was full of hurt and anguish. 'Paul... I'm so sorry...'

'And I'm sorry too. I've no right to bore you with my domestic problems. Let's change the subject, shall we? What's this great news from Andrew?'

Preparing the scones and filling dainty porcelain dishes with golden yellow butter and jewel-red raspberry jam, Jenny told Paul the good news. The reason for Andrew's earlier silence was because the entire St Claire range had taken the American market by storm. The order books were full!

'That's wonderful, Jenny!' Paul said, crossing the room towards her and, without thinking, hugged her warmly. Suddenly aware of their bodily contact, he drew back sharply, looking first at the ceiling and then down at her face. Searching for something to say, he said simply, 'You - er - have flour on your nose.'

Blushing and cursing her pale skin, Jenny rubbed some of the flour away.

'I think you'd better call the girls in for tea. It's all ready for them.'

Cele and Emily ran in from the garden, laughing and giggling, their excited faces flushed with fresh air and new-found adventures. Delighted by the change in their appearance, Jenny showed them the cloakroom where they could wash their hands, then led them back to the table. Without warning Emily became suddenly quiet and whispered something in her sister's ear.

'She doesn't like jam with bits in,' Cele explained, watching her father spooning jam on to Emily's scone.

Jenny fixed Emily with a sympathetic smile. 'No, of course she doesn't. Silly me! I should have remembered. You're just like Fiona. She also doesn't like jam with bits in. Well, that's not a problem, Emily. You come with me to the pantry. I've some wee pots I make for Fiona. I know she won't mind you having one of those.'

Jenny walked to the pantry, aware of the little girl tugging at her father's hand. She wanted her daddy to come too.

'There you are,' Jenny said, pointing to the top shelf full of jams and jellies, 'which one would you prefer; raspberry, bramble or blackcurrant?'

From behind Paul's back a tiny voice whispered, 'Blackcurrant, please 'cos I like Ribena.'

Unable to reach the top shelf, Jenny fetched a small pair of steps and reaching forward located three small jars. Here you are... just the thing. Blackcurrant jelly. No bits, you see.'

At that precise moment, a solitary ray of sunlight pierced the gloom of the pantry doorway and Jenny held the jar up to the light. Now

Emily could see for herself. Coaxed gently by her father, she stepped forward and held out tiny expectant hands. As she did so, dappled afternoon sunlight played on her face and hair, reminding Jenny of a Botticelli angel. An angel she'd seen in the Louvre, during a weekend spent in Paris with Cameron.

Disconcerted by Cameron's untimely appearance in her chain of thought, Jenny took a pace backwards and almost lost her footing.

'Careful!' urged Paul, taking hold of her hands as the steps tilted sideways, before lowering her gently to the floor.

What was probably only seconds seemed to Jenny like an eternity as, for the second time that afternoon, Paul held her close. With the faintest of smiles he whispered softly, 'You know, you look quite different today. I've never seen you in jeans and a sweatshirt before. You're not at all like the Miss Sinclair of our very first meeting.'

Colouring at the memory of that auspicious encounter, Jenny felt her mouth go dry. So much had happened since then. Not only did Sinclair's seem to be moving in the right direction but also her own existence. At least now she felt she had a purpose in life. She was no longer Andrew Sinclair's put-upon little sister or Cameron Ross's long suffering fiancé, she was Jennifer Sinclair... joint founder of the House of St Claire!

With Paul standing so close, and conscious of the warmth of his body, Jenny looked up into his calm, dignified face, convinced he was about to say something significant. Instead it was Emily's voice that broke the pregnant silence.

'Daddy, the butter's ever so yellowy, isn't it? And the blackcurrant jelly is lovely.'

Grateful for the diversion as Emily tucked into her scones, Jenny explained, 'That's because I buy the butter from the farm. It's a luxury I allow myself only at weekends. During the week it's low fat spread which is revolting. Ugh!' She pulled a face, which caused Emily and Cele to burst into ripples of laughter.

Paul smiled too, watching Jenny entertain his daughters. Who would have guessed the slight, trim figure dressed in jeans and sweatshirt was also an astute businesswoman? From where he was sitting there was no reason at all for her to eat low-fat spread; still, at least it had made the girls smile.

Remembering Jenny's earlier antics, Cele and Emily continued to giggle. They'd also noticed the still faint dusting of flour on her nose. They watched, intrigued, as Jenny reached for a silver tea strainer before pouring tea from a blue and white china teapot. They'd never seen a tea strainer before. Their mother's method of making tea was throwing a tea bag in a mug, and drowning it with warm water.

'Thanks, Jenny,' said Paul, taking the cup she offered. 'I have to say you're a tonic for us all. I'd forgotten what Sunday afternoon tea was like.'

'Then you must come again, but I'll make some more jams and jellies first.'

'That would be lovely, but I still don't think it's right taking Fiona's jelly.'

'Nonsense! There's still more than enough for Fiona,' Jenny said, placing assorted jars in a shoe box for Cele and Emily to take home. 'Besides, I shall soon be going to Conasg to pick strawberries. Mother keeps us all well supplied with soft fruits thanks to Hamish.'

'Who's Hamish?'

'Oh, Hamish is like Miss Tandy: he's been with the Sinclair's for years. And very proud of his fruit and vegetable garden and greenhouse, he is too. Which is probably just as well. Mother and even Miss Tandy, have very fixed ideas about serving only seasonal produce at meal times.'

'Hmm. They sound a very interesting trio, the residents of Conasg

House.'

'They are. You must meet them some time.'

Paul fixed Jenny with a wry smile. 'I'd like that, but I don't think I'm quite up to it at the moment. I'd need to prepare myself first. Come along, girls, time to go - and next time we go shopping, remind me to look for jam without bits.'

'I suppose in some ways you could say life is like that,' Jenny said, handing over the shoe box of jam. 'Sometimes clear and smooth... just like the raspberry jelly. Then at other times it can be really fruitful, offering the occasional whole strawberry, like the House of St Claire.'

'And what about marmalade?' enquired Paul, continuing the theme.

'Marmalade? Oh, would you like some marmalade as well? I didn't think the girls liked it.'

'No, they don't. That wasn't what I had in mind. I was thinking more along the lines that just like life, marmalade can be pretty bitter, unpalatable and unpleasant at times.'

Jenny appeared deeply reflective. 'Hmm, in that case I suppose all we can do is discard it and find something to take away the unpleasant taste it leaves behind.'

'I think perhaps you're right; I'll remember that the next time I'm struggling with my supermarket trolley.'

Paul's eyes met hers as two smiling faces gazed up at her adoringly. Jenny took both girls by the hand and walked with them to the front gate. Hugging and kissing them goodbye, she watched Cele run to the car. Emily, meanwhile remained behind, and Jenny kissed her again. Fixed firmly by her father's side, she studied Jenny carefully.

'Aren't you going to kiss my Daddy goodbye?' she said softly.

'I - er -' Jenny hesitated just as Paul bent forward to save her further embarrassment. He brushed his lips gently against her cheek.

'Goodbye, Jenny, and thank you. It's been a truly wonderful

afternoon.'

CHAPTER FIFTEEN

Mary replaced the receiver of the phone. She was triumphant. Shona Munro, secretary of the Arisaid Ladies, had just rung with excellent news: their recent charity lunch (where they'd handed over a five-figure cheque) was featured in the latest edition of the Edinburgh Review. She couldn't wait to tell her husband when he came home from his first day back at Sinclair's.

On the desk in Andrew's office lay the pile of contracts from America plus the usual publicity blurb gathered along the way. It was amazing how many papers you could collect in a week and they all needed to be sorted before he went home this evening. This wasn't going to be easy, as there was still so much to finalize. He'd also promised Mary he would take her to the theatre and leave the House of St Claire at the office for once. Winning American contracts was one thing, he told himself, Sinclair's must now meet the required deadlines.

'You promise me you won't let me down, Andy,' Sol Sutherland had demanded during brunch in New York. If I give you these orders for Saint Clara, you will personally see to it they are delivered on time.'

'You have my word on it, Sol. And yes, I will see to it, personally, but as a family we Sinclair's are *all* involved in the House of *St Claire*.

Andrew had placed special emphasis on the *St Claire* but to no avail; Sol still insisted on referring to the company as Saint Clara! Not to worry, thought Andrew, the contracts were all that mattered.

'Well,' drawled Sol as the waitress placed a huge plate of steak, eggs, hash browns and grits on the table before him, 'I'm glad you are all involved – even old Morag, but in the States we expect commitment, too.'

'Isn't that the same thing?' Andrew asked.

Sol surveyed his brunch. 'Not from where I'm sitting, it isn't, Andy. To begin with... see this plate of steak and eggs?' Sol picked up his knife and stabbed at an egg. The golden orb of yolk split open, sending a stream of yellow in the direction of the steak. 'Well, I'd say the chicken was involved but that Aberdeen Angus was sure as hell committed!'

Andrew had laughed loudly. Sol Sutherland, a short, balding man in his mid-sixties, was an old friend and Andrew's main business contact in New York. Son of a Scottish immigrant father and Jewish mother, he had an uncanny head for business. He was convinced his fellow Americans were all ready and waiting for Saint Clara. They loved all things Scottish, didn't they?

'I sincerely hope they do,' Andrew murmured, checking his watch and placing the contracts in the office safe. As for the numerous photos he'd taken of the House of St Claire's impressive trade stand, he'd leave those for Jenny to peruse at her leisure.

Dropping the pile of photos on his sister's desk, Andrew was already halfway home when he remembered the one photo he'd meant to destroy. It was too late to go back for it now, Mary and the theatre were waiting. Remembering it again during the interval, he turned to his wife and said softly.

'Mary... about the British week in Geneva, I've been thinking...'

'Oh, Andrew! You're barely home five minutes and you talk of going away again!'

'No, that's just it, I'm not. Anyway, the Geneva trip isn't until the autumn.'

'Then why discuss it now?' Mary said tersely.

'I thought Jenny could go – she could represent Sinclair's. She's got friends there, hasn't she? She also speaks the language, which is more than I can. Pidgin French is OK if you're on holiday, but business-wise I'm not much good.'

'Well… you could always borrow a book or a language course from the library or else go to evening classes, isn't that what you tell the children to do?'

'Gracious, Mary! Don't you think I've enough to do already? You're always complaining that I spend too much time at the office at it is.'

'So I do, Andrew, but I'm only teasing, my dear. And I think it would be perfect to send Jenny. As you say, she still has friends in Geneva. They might not have seen each other in a while, but I know they keep in touch by phone and email. Perhaps Paul could go too, as he missed out on the New York trip?'

'Sounds even better,' Andrew replied. 'I'll discuss it with Jenny in the morning.'

*

Jenny was sifting through her emails when Andrew appeared in her office.

'I'm pleased to see you looking better, Andrew. At least you seem to be getting over the jet lag. Luckily, you won't have the same problem when you go to Geneva, it's such a short flight.'

'I'm not going to Geneva… you are.'

'What?'

'I thought it would be better if you went to represent the House of St Claire. I discussed it with Mary last night and she agrees with me.'

'Oh, does she, indeed?'

'Well… you do speak the language better than me and know Geneva pretty well. Just think you can even catch up with your friend – the one married to that scientist-boffin laddie.'

'You mean Moira MacCulloch, at least she was until she married Helmut, and for your information he's a physicist.'

'That's it - Moira!' Andrew said brightly, 'You're still in contact with her, aren't you?'

'Yes… but…'

'Good, that's settled then, you can go and stay with her.'

'Just a minute, Andrew! Moira might be a very good friend but I can't just impose myself on her after all these years. I shall be going out to work for Sinclair's while I'm in Geneva – if I go to Geneva. For that I shall need a decent hotel room, not a flat teeming with children and a mad scientist!'

'I thought you said he was a physicist,' Andrew teased. 'OK, pick yourself a decent hotel, and don't forget to tell Paul so he can give Gina the details… in case she needs to contact him.'

'What has this to do with Paul and Gina? I thought she left ages ago?'

'She did, but apparently she wants to spend some time with the children. Paul tells me she's coming home for a while, which means he's free to go with you to Switzerland. It's really quite convenient when you think of it.'

Jenny didn't want to think of it, not at all! When had Gina announced her intention to return? Paul certainly hadn't mentioned it, but she'd seen so little of him recently. Was that because he and Gina were to be reconciled?

*

Some weeks later, hunting for her passport and Moira's telephone number, Jenny felt a sickening in her stomach. What did Paul think of the whole idea, and why hadn't he rung? It was all very well Andrew saying everything had been arranged, but had Paul been given any choice in the matter? If he and Gina were back together as man and wife, then the last thing he probably wanted to do was head off to Geneva with Andrew Sinclair's sister!

*

Paul looked anxiously in Jenny's direction. She'd been strangely quiet from the moment they checked in at the airport. Yet Andrew had assured him, repeatedly, that she'd raised no objections to his presence on this trip. Somehow Paul wasn't convinced. He discerned a distinct atmosphere as they sat side by side on the aircraft. The situation wasn't improved when they appeared to be wedged together by an overlarge woman who'd taken up occupancy in the aisle seat next to Paul.

'Perhaps we can persuade her to move as the plane's only half full,' he whispered in Jenny's ear. No sooner had the words been spoken than an airport bus pulled up alongside the plane and hurriedly deposited a delegation of Japanese. Delayed by their connecting flight, they were en route for the United Nations in Geneva. Jenny groaned as cameras and duty-free bags were stashed in every available inch of space, and every seat was filled.

When the eighteen stone of *beached whale* by Paul's side flopped back heavily in her seat, he found himself propelled even further in Jenny's direction. 'I'm so sorry about this,' he murmured. 'At least we're not complete strangers.'

'Nor are we heading to New York, thankfully,' she said softly.

Moments later, grateful for the diversion when the cabin crew appeared with welcoming tea and coffee, Jenny considered Paul's last remark. No, they weren't complete strangers but how well would she get to know him during the coming week?

Paul meanwhile, was pondering Jenny's broken engagement. He'd noticed months ago she no longer wore her engagement ring, yet it wasn't in his nature to ask the reason why. He knew only too well what it was like having to cope with people prying into your private life.

Coping was one thing Paul excelled at. He'd had experience of that in vast quantities, particularly following Gina's turbulent exit after that never to be forgotten dinner with Andrew and Jenny. Now she was back and he was fed up with the day-to-day uncertainties and the constant speculation of friends and neighbours. For the moment he'd agreed to Gina moving back, solely to keep the peace for the sake of Cele and Emily, but on his return Gina had assured him she would be moving into a flat of her own. Quite where, Paul had no idea. As for who would be paying for it…

'*Au Grand Passage, s'il vous plait,*' Jenny called to the taxi driver. Paul climbed in beside her and the taxi wove its way through the maze of early morning rush-hour traffic.

'So this is Geneva,' he said. 'I thought the traffic in Edinburgh was chaotic. This is horrendous!'

Drivers tooted their horns and there was much gesticulation of arms as the taxi driver deviated from lane to lane across the bridge.

'*That* was the Pont du Mont Blanc,' Jenny informed him. 'I always hated crossing that bridge, even when I was simply a passenger. It was bad enough in those days, now it's even worse!'

Paul noticed the smile on her face as he grabbed for the strap to stop him sliding across the seat. He was relieved to see her looking more relaxed. At breakfast there'd been no sign of the anxious young woman he'd had as travelling companion yesterday evening. Instead, there was the Jennifer Sinclair that he'd come to admire, business like and efficient and all ready to go. Orange juice, croissant and coffee were hurriedly dispensed with and the next thing he knew, she was hailing a taxi to the Rue du Rhone and one of Geneva's prestigious department stores.

'*Mademoiselle Sinclair, bienvenue a Geneve.* I trust your stay will be a happy and successful one. I think you will find we have everything in order for the House of St Claire.'

'I do hope so, Monsieur Arnaud. My brother had tremendous success at the British Fair in New York. I am hoping to return with similar results.'

'You can be sure at Grand Passage we will not let you down, *Mademoiselle Sinclair*. Come, I will show you. You and *Monsieur Hadley*. *Suivez- moi, s'il vous plaît.* '

Guy Arnaud led the way, closely followed by Paul and Jenny. Large posters proclaimed *British Week* and Union Jacks hung everywhere. On the third floor they even came face to face with a red London bus!

'How on earth…?' Paul asked.

'Ah, that is our little secret, Monsieur Hadley.' Guy Arnaud smiled and touched the side of his nose.

Paul couldn't believe his eyes. He'd been to trade fairs before but nothing as impressive as this. Wherever he looked there were pockets of the British Isles stretching from the furthest corners of the West Country to the north of Scotland, Ireland and the Shetland Isles. In the food hall, traditional cheeses, bacon and sausages sat temptingly on marble slabs, while a rosy-faced man in blue and white apron, and sporting a straw boater, balanced jars of Marmite and Oxo cubes.

As if reading his mind, Jenny declared, 'In case you're wondering, pork sausages, bacon, Marmite, Oxo cubes and last but not least, Cadbury's chocolate, were the most requested items amongst ex-pats when I was living here.'

'You're joking?'

'No, absolutely serious. If anyone wanted to come and stay with us, that was their entry permit to the flat. We always knew when people had visitors from home by the smell of sizzling sausages and bacon.' With all this talk of food, and wishing she'd had more than a croissant for breakfast, Jenny moved swiftly on.

The muted sound of bagpipes heralded their *arrival* in Scotland. As expected, there was a plethora of tartan and thistles, exactly as Paul had predicted months before. The whisky distilleries were there too, just as they'd been in America, and there - in all its splendour - was the House of St Claire!

Inspired by the Isle of Skye distillery display (that he'd seen and much admired in New York), Andrew had commissioned a studio to replicate scenes from Scottish life throughout the seasons. The result was a delightful tableau showing to full advantage every range of St Claire merchandise. To complete the picture, and against a backdrop of misty mountains and purple heather, hung the shield of St Claire.

Jenny stopped and stared. A lump rose in her throat and she wanted to cry. She remembered Paul's original folder of designs and his so-called 'rough sketch'. In recent months she'd witness the transformation of Sinclair's from a staid family business into the iconic House of St Claire. She'd also seen, and examined in great detail, Andrew's photos from New York. Yet somehow this was different; this was truly special. Her mother had even described this new addition to the business as 'Jenny's baby'. Was this what giving birth felt like?

In a moment all the pain, frustration and anxieties of the past year appeared to float into the mists as Jenny surveyed her *child*. No birth could have taken place in a more enchanting setting. Paul took a clean white handkerchief from his pocket.

'Here,' he said softly, 'I think you've something in your eye.'

Jenny blinked and turned towards him. 'I'm sorry, you must think me terribly silly. I had no idea it could look so perfect. Don't *you* think it looks beautiful?'

Paul swallowed hard and dabbed at her eyes. 'Yes, I do, extremely beautiful, as are you, Jenny. And as for being silly… you're not silly at all; you are perfectly lovely.'

CHAPTER SIXTEEN

Pressing the button marked *'troisieme etage'*, Jenny felt the lift surge and groan on its way. Years ago, when still a student, she'd lived here in the same apartment block with Moira. Then the flats had appeared modern and new; now they seemed dated and shabby. The familiar smell of Gitanes cigarettes permeated the lift shaft and memories of her earlier arrival came flooding back. Moira, who at the time was working as a secretary for CERN, had rung Jenny excitedly.

'Jenny, I know you're looking for something for your year out – why don't you come to Geneva? I've just seen a notice on the board here… an American couple looking for a mother's help. Would you like me to ring them?'

At the time the conversation had been extremely one-sided. Moira would see to everything. Jenny could lodge with her and as she already knew a colleague of the American physicist…

'Just get yourself over here,' Moira had insisted, and Jenny had duly obeyed.

That was years ago, before university, before Cameron, before everything… Jenny rang the doorbell and waited.

'Jenny! Just look at you! You look gorgeous. Och! You haven't changed a bit, unlike me!'

Moira flung out her arms and enveloped her friend in a warm embrace. Jenny knew she couldn't say the same of Moira. Her friend had developed a considerable amount of padding since they'd last seen each other, the result of three bonny children in rapid succession.

Released from Moira's arms, Jenny handed over her parcel. Howls of delight burst forth as Moira unwrapped the bacon, sausages and chocolate.

'You remembered,' she sighed in gratitude. 'Just like the old times.'

'How could I forget? I thought I'd be refused entry otherwise. I was only saying to Paul…'

'Oh, yes, Paul – where is he? You haven't left him waiting outside, have you?' Moira peered into the empty corridor… 'I thought you were going to bring him.'

'He – um – said he didn't want to intrude, but I suspect he was simply being polite… the prospect of two women chattering all night about the good old days… Anyway, he wanted to ring his children.'

'He's married, then?'

'You could say that,' said Jenny, anxious to change the subject. 'It's very quiet, Moira – aren't the children here?'

'No, children's gymnastic class. Helmut's on his way to fetch them. So make the most of a few minutes' respite.'

'How is Helmut?'

Moira's face shone. 'Just the same. He's still my gentle giant and I love him to bits. So that's one in the eye for the folk back home, who said it would never last!'

Jenny recalled the atmosphere of abject disapproval in the small Scottish community when Moira MacCulloch had announced her intention to marry a foreigner!

'They're just a load of contemptuous bigots!' Moira had announced tearfully. 'Anyway, it doesn't matter, we shall be staying on in Geneva after we're married. At least there we won't be treated like outcasts.'

Geneva boasted a true cosmopolitan society where people from all nations lived and worked alongside one another without fear of disapproval. They even boasted a Scottish society of ex-pats who had welcomed Helmut with open arms. Helmut, with his red hair and red beard could have stepped straight from the pages of Rob Roy. A true

Highlander if ever there was one (even if it was only through marriage), he was immensely proud of his Scottish connections and the name of MacCulloch - Son of the Boar. It was such a pity Moira's parents were never there to witness their son-in-law's transformation from German into Scot.

Through the closed front door, Moira recognised the sound of the lift stirring into life.

'Someday I expect that lift to give up the ghost completely. I only hope I'm not in it when it does. Helmut keeps telling the *concierge*, who in turn tell the *regie*, but as usual nothing happens. The only thing they're good at is increasing the rent!'

I did notice it was looking a little bit shabby in the foyer,' Jenny remarked. 'Not at all like it used to be when M and Mme Sablon were in charge.'

'Ah, Mme Sablon. She was a sweetie, wasn't she? Especially when letting us use the laundry room, even though it wasn't our turn. Luckily, I have my own washing machine now... an absolute necessity with my wee clan.'

As if on cue, two sandy-haired boys tumbled through the door and a flaxen-haired girl sat cradled in her father's arms.

'Jenny! Why, it is good to see you again,' said Helmut, in his deep, soft voice. You are looking well, I think. Why have you left it so long to come and see us?'

'Pressure of work, I'm afraid, Helmut. Although now I'm back I do wish I hadn't left it so long.'

'Ah, but in places the city is much changed with drugs and graffiti... I expect you noticed?'

Jenny nodded, but wasn't it a sign of the times? What city didn't have similar problems these days?

The boys, rushing past Jenny to the kitchen for a drink, called loudly,

'Wow! Sausages and bacon, Dad... and Cadbury's chocolate!'

At the mention of chocolate, the small girl wriggled free from her father's arms and ran to the kitchen.

'Two squares each,' Moira said fiercely, 'and then only after you've washed your grubby hands and come and said hello to Jenny.'

Hearing the children groan, Helmut broke in. 'Let's not forget our manners, shall we? Jenny is our guest. Do as your mother says and then come and say hello.'

Minutes later, three obedient children stood before Jenny and recited in unison, 'Thank you for the chocolate and sausages.'

'There, that's better,' Helmut said, winking in Jenny's direction, 'so let me introduce you to my bairns.'

Jenny bit her lip, trying not to smile, as Helmut proudly introduced each child in turn, while instructing them to shake hands with their mother's *very* special friend, who'd come all the way from Scotland.

With the formalities over and the chocolate distributed, Wilhem-Duncan, Johan-Angus and Gisela-Morag, disappeared along the hallway. Helmut was running their bath.

'I know,' said Moira smiling, 'it's quite a mouthful to remember, isn't it? Helmut and I almost came to blows over their names. I wanted German names – almost in defiance of my parents' disapproval of my marriage – and Helmut wanted Scottish, in the hope of appeasing them. So we ended up with Will, Joe and Gila. I suppose you could say it's a compromise of sorts.'

Conscious of the sound of splashing coming from the bathroom, Jenny heard Gila's small voice plead. 'I want Jenny to bath me, then she can tell me about Scotland and where Mummy used to live.'

'Not a problem,' said Jenny, 'I'd be delighted.' She took off her jacket and was about to place it on the back of a chair when Moira intervened.

'Hold on a mo. That beautiful jacket of yours deserves a coat hanger, and putting out of harm's way. While I'm at it, I'll also find you something to protect your skirt and that lovely silk blouse. Once Gila and the boys get splashing about in the bathroom, it's worse than a wet day on Glencoe in there!'

Paul meanwhile, sat alone at the hotel. He'd rung Gina, who'd been unusually civil, and in turn spoken to both Celestina and Emily. Later, he'd also telephoned Andrew with the day's progress report, and even suggested they take on more staff.

The next morning at breakfast, Paul waited for Jenny to check through the emails on her iPad. 'I rang Andrew last night, as you suggested,' he said. 'Needless to say he's delighted that the House of St Claire has received such positive response. In turn he asked me to remind you about the guest list for the Sinclair Christmas party. He said perhaps you could email him.'

'Christmas! You are joking! As for sending emails, I've more than enough to deal with already. We've also got two more days at Grand Passage, then I have to make sure everything is dismantled and shipped back safely to Edinburgh.'

Paul fixed her with a wry smile. 'You'll have your work cut out for you there. I wasn't aware there was a shipping route out of Lake Geneva.'

'Don't be so pedantic or I might get my own back!'

'Meaning?'

'Meaning I might take you to the Cochon d'Or and make you eat frog's legs and snails.'

'You wouldn't dare!'

'No, you're right, I wouldn't,' Jenny agreed, 'I think it's a disgusting practice. I'll take you for a *raclette* instead and show you some of my old haunts.'

Watching her switch off her iPad, Paul pondered her invitation. What on earth was a *raclette* and which animal - or part of the animal - did it come from?

At the end of the week, walking across the Pont du Mt Blance to the old town, Paul repeated his question out loud.

Jenny grinned wickedly. 'Ah! You'll have to wait and see, although I will give you a clue – it certainly isn't in anyway related to a haggis.'

'Jennifer Sinclair! Unlike you, I might not have pure Scottish blood running through my veins, but even I never fell for that old chestnut about " *the poor wee haggis, with his short hairy legs, running aboot the misty glens, only to be hunted doon by some dreaded Sassenach with a twelve bore shotgun*".'

Jenny stopped in her tracks.

'What's wrong? Was it something I said?' Paul queried.

'No, your Dr Finlay impression was spot on, and I was about to tell you that you don't need a twelve bore shotgun for a *raclette*, but it's the Cochon d'Or. It's gone! It's not there anymore!'

Disappointed, they searched for another restaurant close by, but to Jenny it wasn't the same. Paul however, enjoyed the novelty of watching cheese melting on the *raclette* machine.

'The girls would love this and think it enormous fun,' he said, scraping the oozing cheese onto his plate to have with hot skinned potatoes and assorted pickles.

'Then we must look for a portable machine to take back with us. I'm sure Grand Passage have them in their homeware department.'

After the warmth of the restaurant, the cold night air caught them both by surprise. Without thinking Jenny huddled close against Paul's side.

'It must be the Bise,' she said, taking his arm, 'It's a bitter north wind and cuts right through you. The only cure for that is a *chocolat Danoise* or a brandy. Come on, I'll race you back to the hotel; it's way too cold to walk round the lake now.'

Paul watched in amusement as she scooped up spoonfuls of chocolate-laced whipped cream, below which was a steaming cup of hot chocolate.

'I don't know how you can, Jenny, not after all that *raclette* and *tarte aux pommes*.'

'Perhaps if you were to try it... It's just the thing to beat the cold.' She held the spoon in his direction.

Paul leaned forward and, holding her hand to steady the spoon, opened his mouth. Their eyes met across the table and Jenny drew back. 'Perhaps not,' she said, feeling colour flood her cheeks, 'you'd probably find it too sickly; best stick to your coffee and brandy.'

Walking Jenny back to her room, Paul contemplated their last night in this amazing city. Tomorrow it would be back to Edinburgh and... what? Gina being charming with her obsequious smile or Gina the snarling tigress, pacing the floor like a caged animal. Neither prospect appealed to him. He turned to look at Jenny, who was not only warmed by the success of the past week, but also extolling the virtues of *chocolat Danoise* for keeping out the cold.

With Jenny by his side, Paul felt anything but cold. Struggling to keep his tone casual, he thanked her for the *raclette* and arranged a time for breakfast. Then, watching her take the key-card for her room from her handbag, he could contain himself no longer. He had to say something... do something. Opting for the latter, he reached forward and drew her into his arms.

'Jenny...' he murmured, his lips seeking hers.

Swept into his embrace, Jenny found herself curiously unresisting. This moment was so predictable. It was why she'd been wary of this trip from the very beginning, and also why she'd not taken Paul to see Moira. Every time they'd found themselves alone together, and even during this evening's meal in the noisy and crowded restaurant, their body language had said it all.

Now, she was utterly helpless, while her heart said one thing and her conscience another. Her mind was in turmoil and Paul was whispering in her ear... something about the magical week they'd spent together and this being their last night... before going home.

Going home to what? Jenny puzzled, aware of Paul taking key card from her hand, opening her bedroom door and guiding her gently inside. In her case it meant returning home alone to her cottage, in Paul's case it was going home to his daughters and... Gina.

Gina! From the wonderful sense of wellbeing locked in Paul's arms, Jenny felt panic rise inexorably in her breast. In her mind's eye she saw Gina Hadley on the night she and Andrew had gone to dinner, saw her scarlet fingernails encircling Paul's inner thigh and... She shuddered and pulled away from his embrace.

'Jenny? What's wrong? I thought that you... I mean we...'

'So did I,' said Jenny as tears pricked her eyelids. 'But aren't you forgetting something... your wife?'

'How could I forget?' Paul said bitterly. 'That's what I was planning to tell you. Gina's leaving when I get back to Edinburgh. She says she's moving into a flat. I was hoping that might make it easy for us to be together... that's if you do want us to be together?'

'Yes, I do,' Jenny said, tears brimming in her eyes. 'However, I hardly think *easy* is the right word, Paul. Regardless of where Gina goes, she'll still be your wife... there's also the girls to consider.'

'But Celestina and Emily adore you! You only have to see the way they look at you. They'd be delighted if we all spent more time together.'

'Exactly, and can you imagine Gina's reaction to that? Gracious! I can still remember her outburst when the girls had chicken pox, let alone the way she looked at me when she realized I *wasn't* Andrew's wife. Even you describe her actions as completely unpredictable. I'm truly sorry, Paul, I can't risk putting the House of St Claire in jeopardy.'

Jenny turned away sadly, only to feel his hands on her shoulders. 'The House of St Claire – is that all that matters to you?'

'No, it isn't. It's been a lovely week Paul, and I've really enjoyed working with you; being with you…'

'But?'

'I don't think now is the right time to discuss our feelings.'

'Do we need to discuss them? Don't we know already how we feel about each other? This past week I've wanted you so much, Jenny. I thought you felt the same…'

'I do,' she whispered, lowering her eyes, unable to look at his face so full of longing, 'but as I've said already, it's not that easy, is it?'

'It is from where I'm standing,' he said huskily, cupping her face in his hands.

Feeling his lips on hers once more, Jenny knew it would be so simple to let her earlier defences drop. Exactly like Paul, she'd fought against these feelings all week. Mellowed by the fine wine they'd shared earlier in the evening, the welcoming ambience of her hotel room with its exquisite furnishings, subdued lighting and king-size bed, she knew she only had to whisper the words 'please stay.' Instead, summoning all her will power, she pushed him away and forced herself to think of Cameron.

'I'm so sorry, Paul, but while you are still married to Gina and I'm married to…'

Paul looked at her aghast. ' *You* are married?'

'According to me ex-fiancé, I am. That's why Cameron broke off our engagement. He accused me of being married to Sinclair's.'

'Of course you're not! You're simply committed to the family business and I have absolutely no intention of letting that drive a wedge between us, Jenny. Believe me, I do understand. I might not be a Sinclair, but…'

'And I believe you too, Paul, but that wedge is already there. Until we know what's going to happen with both the House of St Claire and Gina… Perhaps after Christmas…?'

The very thought of Christmas filled Paul with horror. Last year's had been a nightmare, and as for this one… he hardly dared think about it. Dejected, he looked at his watch. It was midnight, wasn't that what Shakespeare called the bewitching hour? There was nothing bewitching about the prospect of yet another Christmas spent with Gina, but if he and the girls could spend even the remotest part with Jenny…

'Yes, perhaps after Christmas,' he repeated, turning away and making his way to the door. 'And as it's so late and we have to make an early start in the morning… I'll see you at breakfast. Goodnight, Jenny… sleep well.'

Hearing the door close, and desperate to call him back, Jenny knew it was futile. Had they been any other couple they would have been declaring their love for each other, their naked bodies entwined and their passion rising. Only they weren't any other couple, were they? Like the lyrics from one of her favourite songs they were 'lost and alone'. Paul lost in a loveless marriage, while she was alone - mourning the loss of six years of her life spent with Cameron. If only she wasn't quite so far away from home. If only she had someone to confide in…

*

Half an hour later, Moira sat on the bed cradling Jenny in her arms like a child, trying to decipher through the heartrending sobs why she'd been called at such a late hour.

'It's all right Jenny, I'm here now. You go ahead and have a jolly good cry.'

'B-but Helmut and the children… won't they be wondering…'

'Och! Don't you fret about Helmut and the bairns. Once my family are in bed they don't sleep like logs, they sleep like Scots pine!'

Jenny smiled through her tears and sat up. 'I'm sorry, I've made your shoulder all wet. Let me get you a towel.'

'There's no need for a towel, but if that state of the art contraption is a hairdryer, I'd be grateful for that.'

Moira directed a warm blast of air onto her soggy shoulder. 'You see, it works all the time,' she said with a grin.

'Wherever did you get such an innovative idea?'

'My dear, when you've had three children in rapid succession, you come up with all sorts of tricks. Otherwise you'd be changing your clothes umpteen times a day. Now, as I managed to get past the night porter and into these opulent surroundings, looking like a Michelin man, would you like me to stay awhile longer? I suspect what you'd really like to talk about is Paul.'

'How did you know, when you haven't even met him?'

'Quite possibly, because I sensed you *didn't* want me to meet him. Och, I know you made some excuse about his children, but I do have eyes, Jenny. The look on your face the other evening when you came to see us was a real giveaway. Every time his name came up in the conversation... Dare I ask, are you in love with him?'

'Yes, I think I am,' said Jenny, watching Moira step out of her padded ski suit to reveal red and white spotted pyjamas. 'At the same time I know I shouldn't be, because he's married. Tonight, when he came back with me to my room and he...'

Moira looked anxiously about the room. Jenny looked as if she was about to cry again. What had happened when Paul was here? Because, unless she was mistaken, the bed all neatly turned down with chocolates and a single red rose on the pillow, looked as if it hadn't been slept in. And until she'd arrived, it probably hadn't even been sat upon either.

'How can my feelings for Paul be so strong,' Jenny began through her tears, 'when this past week's been the first time Paul and I have been properly alone together? Yet I spent six years with Cameron and… Oh, Moira, I'm so frightened of committing myself to anyone again.'

Removing the rose from the pillow, Moira placed the chocolates in Jenny's hand and reached for a box of tissues. 'Right,' she said, 'now that we have all we need for a jolly good chin-wag, I suggest we do just what we used to do when we were carefree and single.'

'What's that?'

'Snuggle down under a duvet, talk about men, put the world to rights, switch on the TV, watch the late-night movie and gorge ourselves on chocolate.'

Jenny forced a smile, 'We can hardly gorge ourselves on this little box of chocolates. Although… as I haven't touched the others they've been leaving all week - I was taking them back for Fiona…'

Five minutes later, the two friends sat snuggled beneath a duvet, munching chocolates and pouring out their souls. The only difference being that Moira did most of the munching and Jenny did the talking.

When Jenny paused to dab at her eyes with a tissue, Moira broke in softly. 'I'm not going to tell you what to do, as you have to decide that for yourself. I also suspect you're sick to the back teeth of people telling you that you'll soon get over Cameron.'

'But I really thought I loved him, only now I'm not so sure.'

'Hmm, well… I suppose everyone has a different perception of the word "love". After all these years, I still adore Helmut – love him to my very soul, in fact. When we're together it's magic and when we're apart it's gut-wrenching. I'd be totally gob-smacked if he ever walked out of my life.'

'Like the way Cameron walked out of mine?'

'And was that gut-wrenching?'

'N-no, looking back on it, I don't suppose it was, not in the way you describe. I was just so hurt by what he told me and the look of utter contempt on his face when he said it.'

'So... why exactly did that bastard walk out on you?'

'Because I wouldn't set a date for our wedding. The time never seemed right somehow. First there were my studies - then when Father died and Mother needed my support... It was imperative that we all threw ourselves into keeping Sinclair's afloat. That's what Cameron refused to accept or understand. He even accused me of being *married* to Sinclair's!'

Moira reached for Jenny's hand. 'Look, for what it's worth, I don't think you would ever have married Cameron Ross – even if you'd waited a million years. The "time" as you called it would never have been right; whereas with Paul...'

At the mention of the name Jenny looked up, her red-rimmed eyes in her pale, tired face framed by a curtain of sleek strawberry blonde-hair.

'Oh, I'm so jealous of your gorgeous hair,' Moira said, tugging at her own mousey curls. 'Do you know I'm even going grey in places. I reckon it won't be long before my hair looks like a Brillo pad left on the sink for too long.'

'Nonsense, your hair's very pretty. When I was small I always wanted curly hair.'

'And now... you want Paul?'

'Yes, but this evening when we almost...' Jenny blushed, 'and as I've only known him for about nine months.'

'Hmph! And we all know what can happen in nine months.'

Jenny glanced fleetingly at Moira's generous stomach. 'You're not, are you?'

'No, more's the pity. I just look permanently pregnant that's all. Which is why you'd better finish off the last of the chocolates while I give you my take on all this. The way I see it, you spent six years with Cameron and never felt the time was right to marry him… and yet you spend one week here in Geneva with Paul and you're head over heels in love with him.'

'Yes, but I pushed him away, Moira. If only you'd seen the haunted look in his eyes. Yet, earlier this evening, during dinner, when he smiled and held my hand in his, it was like hands joined together in prayer… like a wonderful dream come true…'

'Whew!' Whistled Moira, now in need of a tissue herself, 'Trust you to be so poetic, I talk of gut-wrenching and gob-smacked and you talk about prayers and dreams. Speaking of which, hadn't we both get some sleep? I'll need to be away and up at the crack of the sparrow to see my wee clan off to school and work, and you'll be heading home to Edinburgh.'

CHAPTER SEVENTEEN

Waking from another night of troubled sleep, Jenny turned and looked at her bedside clock. It was barely five o'clock. She'd hardly slept since returning from Geneva and last night was no exception. Knowing it was pointless trying to go back to sleep, she considered her options: have her shower and a leisurely breakfast, go into the office early or else avoid all the rush-hour traffic and take advantage of the almost empty Edinburgh streets. This way she could weigh up the House of Sinclair's competition in the run up to Christmas.

Opting for the latter, she found herself in the centre of town. With her thoughts still on Paul and *that night* in Geneva, she walked towards the kerb.

'Jenny! Jenny Sinclair!' A hand reached out and clutched at her shoulder.

In a daze, Jenny turned to see Helen Craig, whose bike lay at the kerbside, wheels spinning, while a white van accelerated away.

'Goodness! You gave me a fright,' Helen said, leading Jenny to the safety of a shop doorway. 'For one minute I thought you were about to step in front of that delivery van. Luckily, there's not much traffic about yet, so he was able to avoid you.'

Jenny looked about her in a state of confusion. 'I can't begin to imagine what happened, Helen. I suppose my mind must have been elsewhere. I simply didn't see him.'

'Hmm, from the expression on your face, when I saw you from across the road, you looked as if you'd seen a ghost.'

Helen's choice of words couldn't have been more appropriate. All week Jenny had felt haunted by events of the past year. She shivered and regarded Helen standing by her side in her usual array of rainbow-coloured garments. Her appearance was somehow strangely comforting and reassuring.

'I'm not surprised you're shivering,' Helen scolded, taking her by the hand. 'That suit you're wearing – beautiful as it is, might be all right in a nice warm office but it's hardly suitable for such a cold morning. Dare I ask, what's brought you into Princes Street at such an early hour?'

'I heard there were some particularly impressive window displays. I thought I ought to see them for myself, before the streets get too crowded with early Christmas shoppers. Find out what Sinclair's competition is up to.'

'I don't know,' replied Helen, straightening her bike and rummaging in the basket on the handlebars for a brightly knitted shawl, 'you out and about in the early morning and Paul working away into the wee small hours, all for the sake of inspiration.'

'Paul?'

'Yes, my dear, talk about dedication to business. His light has been on most mornings at half-past two. When I asked him about it, he said almost the same as you. I gather the Geneva trip was a huge success?'

Curiously unresisting, Jenny was grateful for the comforting warmth of the shawl Helen was draping about her shoulders. 'And in case you're wondering Jenny, my dear, I'm not a nosy old busybody, spying on Paul, it's my bladder you see… I always seem to need the loo at that time in the morning. I see Paul's light from my window.'

Troubled by all this talk of Paul and Geneva and fearful of giving her true feelings away, Jenny said hurriedly, 'Look, Helen, I really must dash – get the ideas from some of these window displays down on paper. Perhaps we could have lunch one day?'

'I've a better idea,' came the reply, 'why not come and have tea with me instead? As for the shawl, don't worry about it. I took it along to

Mother this morning - I always check on her first thing. As usual she told me not to mollycoddle her and sent me away with a flea in my ear.'

Listening to Helen's delightful laughter as she mounted her bike, Jenny noticed her blue and white striped leg warmers, made presumably from the cut-off sleeves of some long-discarded sweater. 'Hmm,' she murmured quietly to herself. No doubt Helen Craig would get on extremely well with both Flora Tandy and Morag Sinclair!

*

Recalling that Paul had mentioned the Sinclair Christmas party during their time in Geneva, Jenny was not unduly surprised to find a memo on her desk from Andrew. As with previous years, Morag wanted their proposed guest lists asap! It had always been Sinclair custom to hold the annual staff dinner-dance at a nearby Edinburgh hotel, but this year was to be extra-special. Even Morag was thrilled at the prospect of the House of St Claire's first Christmas. In recent years she'd only attended the dinner; this year she and Tandy would be stopping over. She'd already told Andrew to book extra rooms, saying it should be a night to remember; she might even let her hair down!

Jenny compiled her own list and took it to Andrew's office where she found his, already complete and ready to send to their mother. She scanned the two lists of names. For the most part they were identical save for two additions which left her with mixed emotions.

Naturally Paul's name should appear on both lists but seeing 'Mr and Mrs Paul Hadley' written in Andrew's bold script caused her to question the reason why. Was Andrew merely being polite, not wishing to offend Paul by including Gina's name - or did Andrew know something that his sister was unaware of?

Paul had not only spoken of Gina's return as being purely to see the children, but also of her intention to move into a flat of her own. Perhaps, if she were to take up Helen's invitation to tea, she might discover more. In the meantime she was equally unhappy with the second addition on Andrew's list: Alistair Jennings! Christmas spirit and goodwill to all men apart, she would do her utmost to avoid him.

'Ooh, I love the shawl,' Stevie quipped, wheeling herself into the office. 'Is this the equivalent of Dior's New Look for the House of St Claire?'

'No, it isn't,' Jenny said, not wishing to be reminded of her narrow escape with

white-van-man, 'I hadn't realized quite how cold it was this morning and borrowed this from a friend. I intend to return it next week.'

Stevie fingered the garish crochet-edged knitted squares and grinned. 'Phew! Thank heavens for that. Heaven knows what your brother's going to say when he sees you, although I suspect something along the lines of *lowering the tone...*'

At that precise moment, Andrew strode into the office.

'Jenny, you haven't forgotten that Mother needs your list for the... 'Good God! What *is* that you're wearing?'

Stevie spun her wheelchair to hide her face and took out her handkerchief to suppress her giggles.

'It's a sample, Andrew. I thought we might use it for next season.' Jenny winked in Stevie's direction. 'Don't you like it?'

'No, I don't! I think it's bloody awful. It looks like something from a jumble sale! If you think...'

Unable to keep up the charade, Jenny's face broke into a grin. Surprisingly for once, Andrew did not share her sense of humour.

'If that's your idea of a joke, Jennifer, I don't find it very funny!'

Watching him leave the office, followed by the slamming of a door, Jenny heard Stevie declare, 'Gracious! What's eating him? When you were in Switzerland, he was like a dog with two tails.'

'Then perhaps I'd better go away again.'

Pondering the very prospect, particularly if it involved Paul going with her, Jenny received an unexpected phone call from her sister-in-law with a surprise invitation to lunch. Mary wanted to meet her at the Caledonian Hotel.

Later, preparing to leave the office, Jenny whispered in Stevie's ear, 'Whatever you do, don't tell Andrew I'm meeting Mary for lunch, just in case it has anything to do with his foul temper this morning. Far better to tell him I've gone Christmas shopping. He'd have a fit if he knew we were eating at the Pompadour.'

Mary sat at a corner, looking unusually tired and ashen-faced, not what you'd expect from someone sitting in such opulent surroundings and with the prospect of a superb meal ahead. Eating surprisingly little, she picked at her food like a sparrow. Jenny was amazed. Andrew's wife usually attacked her meals with refined gusto.

'Is there anything wrong, Mary? The whitebait – is it not to your taste today?'

Mary looked up from where she'd been subconsciously decapitating a tiny silver fish on her plate. On one side there was already a small pile of heads, yet Jenny knew only too well her sister-in-law always ate her whitebait whole.

Without warning Mary's eyes filled with tears. 'It's Andrew,' she blurted out, 'I think he's having an affair.'

'*What*? I don't believe it!'

Mary's shock pronouncement and Jenny's gasped response were swallowed up by the music playing in the background. Mary sat with fork poised, ready to sever another head.

Shifting uneasily, Jenny could only think of her extremely staid brother. 'Andrew…having an affair,' she said in hushed tones. 'Surely not. Do you have any proof?'

'No, not really. Let's just say it's women's intuition.' Mary placed her fork to one side and reached for a handkerchief. 'You see... he's different.'

'Different? In what way?'

Jenny waited patiently for an explanation. When it came she wished she hadn't asked.

Checking to make sure no one else was within earshot, Mary continued, her face crimson with embarrassment. 'When we're alone together... in bed... he's different; he wants to do things we've never...'

'It's all right, Mary, don't say any more, I think I understand,' Jenny reached for her sister-in-law's hand. In truth, she didn't really, but the very thought of Andrew and Mary in bed together... It was one thing, teenagers finding it repugnant to think of their parents making love, but when it came to your brother's wife about to divulge...

Mary clung on to Jenny's hand. 'What am I going to do? You're the only person I can talk to. I daren't mention it to Shona as it would be all round the Arisaid Ladies' committee in days. I thought... as Andrew's your brother and you work together... you might know what's going on.'

Jenny shook her head. 'All I know is that Andrew's in the office every day and things are pretty manic at the moment, what with Christmas approaching and the House of St Claire is taking up so much of our time.'

'Yes, I am aware of that and as Andrew's been working such long hours... and before you say anything, I can confirm that. He always rings me before he leaves for home, and I recognize the chimes of father-in-law's old clock in the office.'

Frowning, Jenny considered the prospect of Andrew having an affair. Like herself, he did have to work late on occasions, but not to the extent Mary was implying. Other than his foul mood this morning, nothing else seemed out of the ordinary.

As if reading her mind, Mary broke into Jenny's train of thought. 'There's also the perfume, you see – sometimes he smells of a very heavy perfume. He got so angry when I asked him about it this morning and insisted it was his new aftershave.'

'And does he have a new aftershave?'

'Yes, I've even seen it on the bathroom shelf, only it doesn't smell the same. When Andrew comes home after working late, it always smells so sweet and sickly.'

Something in Jenny's head stirred at that moment. What was it Stevie had said only that morning? Andrew behaving like a dog with two tails when she and Paul had been in Geneva! Her mind went into overdrive. Gina wore a heavy, sickly perfume. Jenny remembered it vividly. She also remembered Gina practically devouring Andrew across the dining table. But Andrew and Gina together – *never*!

With the seed of doubt sown, an icy chill ran through Jenny's veins. But how to reassure her sister-in-law... that was the problem.

'Look, Mary, I'm sure there's nothing to worry about. Perfumes and aftershaves can smell differently on each individual. Remember the Christmas Mother bought us both the same scent, yet the fragrance was different on both of us?'

Mary was deeply reflective. Yes, she did remember. Perhaps she was reading too much into Andrew's actions of late and if, while Andrew was in New York and under the outrageous Sol Sutherland's influence, they'd taken in some blue movies... well, that might explain things. She nodded and smiled weakly in Jenny's direction.

Anxious to finish her meal and return to the office, Jenny kissed Mary goodbye. 'Thanks for lunch, now off you go and don't worry. We'll meet again soon. My treat next time, don't forget, but it will have to be somewhere less grand.'

Back in the office, Jenny's earlier suspicions made an unwelcome return. From now on she determined to keep a surreptitious watch over her brother. No one, not even Stevie, must suspect a thing. Managing to evade all Stevie's questions relating to lunchtime, she made some excuse about Mary planning a Christmas surprise for Andrew. Crossing her fingers, Jenny hoped and prayed it wasn't going to be the other way round!

'OK,' said Stevie, 'if you won't tell me about Andrew's surprise, you can at least tell me where you got that hideous shawl.'

Disappointed to learn it was on loan from Paul's neighbour, Stevie continued, 'Oh! I thought you'd bought it from the bag lady; she tried to sell me something equally revolting the other day.'

Jenny wasn't interested in the bag lady who appeared to spend half her time accosting people on the square at lunch time, and the other half loitering in the chemist's on the corner, she was far more interested in her brother.

In the days that followed, she left her office door open, keeping a watchful eye on Andrew and listening out for any suspicious phone calls. She also made the excuse that with Christmas fast approaching, not to mention organizing the seating plan for Sinclair's dinner-dance, it was far easier for Stevie to wheel her chair in and out of the office.

Andrew accepted this without comment and work continued as before, until late one Thursday afternoon. Answering what Jenny had taken to be a routine phone, call her brother's face had altered dramatically. Even from this distance he appeared embarrassed and uncomfortable. Jenny quickly picked up a file and made her way to his office, where almost immediately Andrew hung up his phone with an abrupt. 'No! Definitely not tonight – Monday at eight-thirty.'

'Problems, Andrew?'

'What? Oh, no, just someone at the golf club wanting a game.'

Jenny bit her lip and, about to return to her office, suspected Andrew was playing a different sort of game. 'By the way,' she called back. 'How's Mary? I thought she was looking rather strained the last time I saw her. I got the impression she was worried about you... working all these late nights. You're not overdoing things, are you, Andrew?'

'Of course not! I have to work late, Jenny! You of all people should know that...all these new products to launch...' His gaze rested on the House of St Claire folder she was holding.

'Yes, I do, Andrew, and I'm sorry to be the cause of your problems.'

'What makes you think that?'

'Well... I suppose if I hadn't introduced you to Paul Hadley, you wouldn't be working all these late nights.'

The meaning of her statement was twofold, but leaving Andrew to ponder his own interpretation, Jenny made a discrete exit.

CHAPTER EIGHTEEN

Saturday and Sunday were what Jenny had come to call 'marmalade days'. Days of decision making and problem-solving when, if nothing went right, she only had herself to blame. The phrase had sprung from all those months ago when Paul and the girls had come for tea.

Turning away from the rain-spattered window, she studied the two boxes on the dining table. One to be filed away and the other discarded. The former contained her personal collection of papers, newspaper cuttings and photos relating to the House of St Claire, and the latter an assortment of letters, postcards, theatre tickets and programmes, all connected to the six years she'd spent with Cameron.

With firm resolve she took one last look at them, before hurrying outside to deposit them in the recycling box at the far end of the garden. At that moment a gust of wind, heavy with driving rain, lashed against her back, long before she had time to reach the shelter of her kitchen. Soaked to the skin, she filled the kettle before hurrying upstairs for a change of clothing. Ten minutes later, dressed in warm leggings and an overlarge Arran sweater, she drew the curtains on the miserable weather and picked up her tea tray. Taking it to the fire, she nestled against a pile of floor cushions and poured out the fragrant rose pouch tea into a fine china cup.

'Mmm, roses and warm summer days,' she sighed nostalgically, her gaze falling on a rose-patterned photograph album on a shelf in the alcove.

Curious as to its contents, Jenny turned over page after page of photos encased in yellowing cellophane. Her reaction was one of both joy and sorrow. The photos had all been taken at Conasg House, before her father had succumbed to what he called 'the indignity of a wheelchair'.

Though tear-filled eyes she recalled those wonderful days. It had been such an idyllic time. A carefree summer when she'd walked the shores of Loch Etive, run barefoot through deer-hair grass, laughed in unison with the tumbling brooks that cascaded down the hillside and then, utterly exhausted, spent endless hours just talking and arguing playfully with her father in the gardens at Conasg.

There a tapestry of rhododendrons had created their own Impressionist painting against a backdrop of clear blue skies. Clear like the jelly favoured by Fiona and Emily, as opposed to the unpleasant and lumpy, bitter marmalade Andrew preferred, or the heavy and depressing clouds she'd so recently shut out.

Andrew, she mused. What would he be doing today? Certainly not playing golf! Today's rain had been relentless and the damp chill that accompanied it pervaded to the very marrow. No doubt Andrew would be assuming the role of dutiful husband and father. Carving the Sunday roast, reading the newspapers with Fiona on his lap, helping Catriona and Iain with their homework and later discussing the forthcoming week's activities with Mary before they said goodnight.

Jenny felt sickened. Time and time again she'd tried to dispel from her mind the picture of her sister-in-law at the Pompadour, struggling through her tears and whispering, 'When we're in bed together, he's different...'

'Poor Mary,' whispered Jenny, as she closed the photo album and turned her thoughts to Andrew's clandestine meeting. Hadn't he said eight-thirty on Monday evening, which was now little more than twenty-four hours away!

More convinced than ever that Gina was responsible for this current distress, Jenny tried to fathom why. What was Gina's relationship to her brother? Was she his mistress, and if so, how long had it been going on? No doubt in other circles the words tart, whore and bit on the side would come into play. Jenny shuddered, contemplating the mere connotations of these words in addition to her own thoughts on the word play: play as in relation to enjoying oneself or play as in the local amateur dramatics group. Either way, Paul and Gina Hadley featured prominently. They'd both entered centre stage and whether or not Gina was merely *playing* with Andrew, she was determined to find out. As for the other stage direction that sprang to mind *exit stage left*, that could only relate to Cameron. In the course of this current marmalade weekend, he'd made a definitive exit via the back door and recycling bin!

Early on Monday morning Jenny weighed up the situation. Firstly, she would have to make sure she acted normally throughout the day. Later, however, there would be the problem of what to do once she left the office at five-thirty. It was important not to arouse Andrew's suspicions. Perhaps if she were to ring Helen Craig?

*

Sprightly footsteps clipped down the hallway and the door was thrown open to reveal Helen Craig looking like a liquorice allsort! Gone was the familiar woollen hat and red hair and in its place a neat black bob even Mrs Bertie Bassett would be proud of. Horizontal stripes began at Helen's neck and continued to her ankles in layers of pink, white, brown and orange, all interleaved with black. Only the flat blue aniseed-flavoured *sweet* was missing.

Jenny greeted her with a warm smile. 'Thanks for inviting me Helen, and also for the loan of the shawl.'

'Och! Away with you,' said Helen, 'it's nothing; I've been hoping you would ring. As for the shawl, you could have kept it. Although, I suspect it's not really your cup of tea.' Helen eyed Jenny's neatly cut tailored suit and continued, 'From what I've seen of your wardrobe, you only wear two or three shades at a time. Unlike me, who goes for the whole caboosh.'

Helen chuckled loudly, her merry laughter seeming to bounce off the weird collection of furniture and ornaments filling the hallway. No wonder Cele and Emily adored spending time here, Jenny thought, following Helen into the warmth of the sitting room.

'Now come and sit yourself down by the fire, kick off your shoes and make yourself at home,' Helen insisted. 'You must be fair worn out.'

Too tired to argue, Jenny removed her high heels and wriggled her toes in a multi-coloured rag rug. 'Gosh! I haven't seen one of these in years. Did you make it?'

'Aye, like most of the things here, if you hadn't already guessed.' Helen waved her arm to encompass the array of brightly patterned rugs, blankets and runners. 'My grannie taught me to knit and sew when I was a wee lassie. Times were hard and Mother had to work, so nothing was ever wasted. The trouble is if you've been brought up in that way, the habit sort of sticks – not like some people I could mention!'

Jenny thought immediately of Mary, but as Helen didn't know Mary or Andrew… she presumed this could only be a reference to Gina.

Hearing the kettle sing out from the kitchen, Helen busied herself making a large pot of tea, and returned pushing a heavily laden trolley.

'Goodness! How many people are you expecting?'

'Just you my dear, just you,' Helen said, lifting the teapot.

Declining another slice of Dundee cake, Jenny patted her stomach. She'd eaten far too much, despite protestations from her hostess that she'd eaten barely enough to keep a sparrow alive.

'I can understand why Cele and Emily love coming here, Helen. Everywhere is so warm, welcoming and homely.'

'Thank you, my dear. And I really enjoy having them. They're such dear wee souls. I shall miss them terribly when they go. It won't be the same without them.'

Jenny sat up with a jolt. 'Go! Go where? I didn't know they were leaving, Paul never said.'

'Oh, not Paul, just Gina and the girls. She's threatened to take them away if Paul doesn't buy her a flat in Edinburgh. She even mentioned taking them back to Italy to live with her parents.'

'She can't. That's outrageous! Paul won't let her... will he?'

Jenny looked to Helen for reassurance. What would Paul do without his two cherished daughters? He'd given up his career to remain at home with them; they were his whole life. Of course he now had the House of St Claire, but that was completely different...

'Hmph! She can and she will, if she's a mind to, but as I said to Paul, it's all blethers! It's simply Gina trying to get her own way. I've seen it so many times before.' Helen began stacking plates and teacups back onto the trolley, her usually twinkly eyes filled with anger and concern. 'There's no way Paul can buy her a flat... not unless he sells the house, and I know he doesn't want that. No, my dear, the best we can hope for is that Gina's latest boyfriend comes up with the goods... Then, she'll simply pack up her bags and go. Once and for all, I hope, for Paul's sake. If only you knew the half of it...'

Jenny's ears pricked up at the mention of the words, *latest boyfriend*? Could that be Andrew? There was so much she wanted to ask Helen, particularly as she did want to know 'the half of it', but how to begin...

'Erm... What about this new boyfriend of Gina's... has she known him long?'

Helen smoothed her recently dyed black hair and gave a wry smile. She certainly saw plenty of him when Paul was in Geneva, because I was the one who did all the babysitting. As for the boyfriend... shall we say he's not what she usually goes for?

He's no spring chicken this one, in fact he's more like an old broiler, though I only saw him the once, when he brought her back very late one night. He's certainly going to have his work cut out for him keeping up with Gina Dintino!'

'Gina who?'

'Dintino. That's her professional name, the one they always quote in those celebrity magazines. Didn't you know?'

Jenny shook her head. There was obviously so much she didn't know, and there was still Andrew's eight-thirty appointment to deal with. At any other time she would have found it faintly amusing to hear her brother described as an old broiler. This evening, it all seemed so sad and pathetic.

Waving goodbye and heading back to the office, Jenny's mind was in turmoil. It wouldn't be only Paul and Helen who'd be heartbroken to see Celestina and Emily taken away; she would too. As for Fiona... she'd be utterly devastated. Doubtless her niece would expect her aunt to do everything within her power to prevent that from happening. For the moment, however, that would have to wait. First she must deal with Andrew...

Apart from the security lights Sinclair's appeared to be deserted, but there in the car park was Andrew's sleek BMW with its personalized number plate and distinctive cream leather upholstery. The same car Helen had mentioned, while steering her own set of wheels back to the kitchen. Up on the second floor a light shone in Andrew's office. Jenny breathed a sigh of relief. At least he'd had the presence of mind to draw the blinds.

*

Reaching for her handbag, Jenny stepped from the car. Already her throat had gone quite dry and her hands felt clammy. Bracing herself, she took a deep breath and whispered to the enveloping darkness, 'I must remain perfectly calm and behave as normal... nothing must seem out of the ordinary.'

'This is normal!' a tiny voice echoed in her head as she walked along the dimly lit corridor towards the stairs. She never used the lift at night in case it got stuck - as it had once before – and as it was imperative to make as little noise as possible...

With each step Jenny's heart began to pound, and the dull thumping in her chest and ears appeared to echo in the stairwell. Surely Andrew and Gina could hear it too, or was it just a figment of her imagination? One thing she hadn't imagined was Gina's presence. The heavy scent of her perfume in the air was proof enough.

Lifting her white-knuckled hand from the banister rail, Jenny held it to her face and grimaced. Even the banister rails were impregnated with the same cloying perfume. Small wonder Mary's earlier suspicions had been aroused.

In Andrew's office, Gina finished her whisky and watched Andrew walk to the now familiar cupboard. Unlocking the door, he reached in for a heavy tartan rug, which he placed upon his treasured carpet.

'And what is that for?' Gina teased.

'I thought we could... well, you know...'

Gina sidled up to Andrew and stroked his cheek. 'But you said we would discuss my flat; you promised me you would look at the estate agent's details and give me a cheque for the deposit.'

'I will, Gina, later... but can't we just...?' Andrew reached out, grabbing Gina around the waist. He drew her roughly towards him.

Gina flashed her dark eyes and shook her curls brazenly in his face. 'My goodness, Andrew, how desperate you are. Just as you were in New York, my darling. Am I to understand by such a display that Mary has not been performing her wifely duties to your satisfaction?'

At the mention of his wife's name, Andrew was momentarily overcome with guilt. For a brief moment he hesitated as Gina's mocking eyes searched his face. Sensing that she'd perhaps spoken out of turn, Gina swiftly remedied the situation. Reaching for Andrew's hand, she slid it sensuously under her short skirt until it reached her buttocks.

Touching bare flesh, Andrew let out a gasp. 'But you're not wearing...'

Moving his hand between her thighs, Gina tossed back her head and laughed, her body writhing seductively against Andrew's. 'Why so shocked, my darling? I'm only following Scottish tradition. Aren't you pleased I am wearing nothing under my kilt!'

Beads of perspiration broke out on Andrew's forehead. 'Your kilt! What you're wearing can hardly be described as a kilt! There's barely half a metre of fabric in your skirt. Do you have any idea how much material goes into a kilt?'

'No,' Gina pouted, 'and I don't much care either, I'm far too interested in other things.' Wriggling away from Andrew's grasp, she smoothed down the woollen boucle fabric of her skirt and moved towards the desk and the estates agent's brochures. Andrew meanwhile gazed longingly at the tartan rug. He'd been waiting all weekend for this moment. Gina met his gaze and read his thoughts.

'No! Not the rug,' she said, beckoning him nearer. 'Here...here on the desk.'

'But...'

'But what, Andrew? Come now, don't be a spoilsport. I never had to persuade you in New York.'

Andrew felt himself going hot under the collar at the memory, and also of Mary's reaction on his return when he'd tried to...

'Oh, what the...?' he sighed, seeing Gina's firm buttocks spread-eagled across his desk.

Loosening his trousers and bending over to enter her, Andrew's eyes alighted on the estate agent's details and all thoughts of passion deserted him.

'Bloody hell, Gina! I said a *small* flat, not something that looks like a Hollywood Palace!'

With Gina still wedged beneath him, Andrew reached angrily for the pages containing photos of penthouse flats and luxury apartments.

'You've got to be joking! I can't afford a place like that!'

Gina wriggled sideways, her face set in a deep scowl, 'In that case, Paul will just have to sell the house!'

'That's hardly fair...'

'Fair? *Fair*! And have you been fair with me, Andrew, considering what you promised me in New York...? Why, only last week, when you couldn't get enough of me, you even suggested I went to the estate agents to find a flat where we could be together...'

With his trousers round his ankles, Andrew felt strangely vulnerable.

'In view of the circumstances, Gina...' he began, unaware of his office door opening quietly.

'In view of the circumstances, from where I'm standing,' Jenny's voice echoed, 'I would suggest you have some explaining to do.'

'Jenny! What the hell...! I thought you left ages ago.' Andrew made a frantic grab at his trousers, panic and guilt written all over his face.

'I did – but I forgot a file for tomorrow's meeting. As it's so urgent I thought I'd come back for it.'

At that moment, Andrew looked like a frightened schoolboy caught smoking in the dorm. His clothes and hair were dishevelled and his face was a profusion of pink. Gina, meanwhile was tucking her blouse into what Jenny presumed to be her skirt. No doubt Mother and Miss Tandy would describe it as a belt!

Clutching the property papers, Andrew announced feebly, 'I was - er - helping Gina to choose a flat.'

'Oh, I see,' said Jenny with a sardonic smile. 'And I suppose when I came in you were about to give her the key to the door!'

Not waiting for Andrew's reaction, Jenny clutched her file tightly to her breast and fled hurriedly down the stairs into the late November night.

Behind her she could hear Andrew calling her name and Gina's screams. Whether Gina's hysterical ravings were directed at Andrew or herself, she wasn't sure. She had no intention of finding out. She'd seen enough and said enough. Now all she wanted was to go home.

CHAPTER NINETEEN

Leaving Sinclair's car park with her heart still pounding, Jenny couldn't wait to get on to the open road where she could relax and take stock of the situation.

'Just concentrate on the DVLC,' she told herself, 'don't let you mind wander.'

Like a mantra she kept repeating the same phrase over and over again. It was her way of describing her route home to friends who questioned the sanity of such a long journey: Dual carriageway, Village, Lane and Cottage.

Moments before exiting the dual carriageway, she noticed a car approaching from behind at breakneck speed. Passing her, it came to an abrupt stop on the road ahead. Braking hard, and with a squeal of brakes, the driver slammed the car into reverse, only to be halted by the tooting of horns and flashing headlights from behind.

'Stupid idiot!' Jenny muttered, switching on her CD player. 'If you've missed your turning you go ahead to the next one. You don't reverse back down the dual carriageway!'

With the strains of Schubert's 'Trout Quintet' echoing softly in the car, Jenny breathed a sigh of relief when her own headlights picked out the village signpost. There remained only the lane and the narrow driveway to her cottage.

Knowing the end of the CD signalled the approach to the little-used lane, she allowed her thoughts to turn away from the sickening scene she'd witnessed earlier. Far better to concentrate more on a soothing cup of drinking chocolate, a hot water bottle and bed. It therefore came as a complete surprise to discover in her rear-view mirror that she was being followed.

With every minute the pursuing car came closer, it's lights flashing angrily, until Jenny found herself blinded by pure terror and headlamps on full beam. Panicking, she accelerated hard and swung the wheel sharply; never had the lane seemed so full of twists and turns and never was she more relieved to discern the welcoming silhouette of her cottage roof.

With a squeal of tyres, and narrowly missing the gatepost, Jenny slammed on her brakes, sending a shower of gravel ricocheting against the garage door. Then, grabbing her handbag and briefcase, she ran for the safety of the porch.

'Keys! Keys! Where are the damn keys?' she cried, as a beam of headlights swept across the hedgerow at the bottom of the lane and an icy tremor trickled down her spine. With trembling fingers Jenny forced the key into the lock but with her hands shaking so much, the door handle simply wouldn't budge.

At that moment the sound of metal hitting her gatepost and wheels skidding on gravel filled her whole being with terror. 'Turn, damn you!' she cried, pushing so hard that she jerked open the door and found herself in a heap on the floor.

'Oh, thank God!' she sighed, turning to slam the door shut. But relief soon gave way to renewed terror when she saw a man's foot wedged in the doorway and felt strong arms firmly grip her shoulders. Opening her mouth to scream, she emitted one ear-piercing shriek before her mouth was clamped tightly shut.

'Jennifer, for Christ's sake shut up! It's me, do you hear, it's me Andrew – your brother! I'm not some bloody rapist!'

'Andrew…? *Andrew*! What the hell do you think you were *doing* back there? You gave me the fright of my life. Do you mean to say it was *you* driving like a maniac and scaring me half to death?'

'I'm sorry, but I needed to talk to you.'

'Talk to me? *Talk to me*! All I can say to that, Andrew Sinclair, is that you picked a bloody stupid way of doing it!'

'I know, I realize that now, but at the time… Look, I've said I'm sorry, Jenny, so will you please move away from the door and let me in? It's either that or stay where we are and wait to see if the people, who also live in this Godforsaken place, have done the neighbourly thing and called the police.'

'You don't think they have, do you?' Jenny said, rising to her feet with Andrew's help, before he stooped down to retrieve all her scattered papers and passed them over.

Jenny clasped them to her breast. 'So… what was it you needed to talk about?'

'My God! Isn't it obvious? I want to talk to you about this evening. But first would you mind if I poured myself a drink? I certainly need it; in fact I think we both do.'

Motioning him to the decanter on the sideboard, Jenny watched and waited as her brother poured two large whiskies. He looked and felt distinctly uncomfortable. Where to begin…

'Erm… how much do you know, Jennifer?'

'Let's just say until this evening it was purely speculation.'

'So you weren't at the office by accident? I guessed as much… Then when, may I ask, did you begin to… er… speculate?'

'The day I had lunch with Mary and she told me she suspected you of having an affair.'

Andrew groaned at the very mention of his wife's name. He took a deep gulp of his drink. 'Mary knows? Oh, dear God!'

'No, she doesn't know for certain, she was merely guessing. I told her it wasn't possible you'd do such a thing - that you'd betray both your wife and family. I also told her she was probably imagining it.'

Despite the underlying tone of sarcasm, Andrew seemed relieved, until Jenny announced. 'However, it was from that moment I decided to keep an eye on you.'

'You mean spy on me!'

'Call it what you like, Andrew, but I didn't want to see you make a fool of yourself with Gina. You do realize you're just one of many to join her list of conquests? When you embarked on your sordid little affair, did you have no feelings at all for Mary and your family, let alone Paul and his two girls?'

'Oh, come on Jennifer, you know as well as I do Paul and Gina's marriage broke down long ago. You can't accuse me of splitting up the family home.'

'That's precisely where you're wrong! Did you know Gina was threatening to take the children away from Paul – even leaving them with her parents in Italy – if he doesn't comply with her wishes and sell the house? Doesn't that split up the family home?'

Andrew looked sheepish. 'Well… she did mention something of the sort, and I remember thinking at the time it didn't seem particularly fair to Paul, so…'

'So?' Jenny demanded.

'So… I just happened to mention that I might be able to help her find a flat.'

'And you think that was being fair to Paul? Well, I don't – I call it downright stupidity!'

How long they sat and talked, Jenny didn't know, but it came as a relief to hear Andrew agree, albeit reluctantly, to sever the relationship with Gina once and for all.

'Please believe me,' he begged, 'I've already tried to finish with her once before but she's like a drug… you have no idea.'

Jenny watched her brother bury his head in his hands. 'Just like a drug,' he repeated softly. 'You try it once – just for kicks – then get swept along by the excitement and euphoria of it all. Before you know it, you're hooked.'

'Hmm. Well, I hardly think we can get you a place at the Arisaid Ladies' Drug Rehab unit, Andrew. With Mary as president and Shona Munroe as secretary…'

'I don't find that at all funny,' Andrew grunted.

'It wasn't meant to be… so now can you tell me, why Gina? Was it because she's Paul's wife or did you see her as a challenge?'

Andrew shook his head and fixed Jenny with a wry smile. 'No, hand on heart, Paul had absolutely nothing to do with it. When I first met Gina Dintino, I didn't even know Paul. Gina and I first met in Switzerland and later at the British Fair in New York.'

Jenny turned to face him, her expression one of incredulity. Had she heard correctly? She'd always known the skiing holiday had been a disaster and Iain had been infatuated with an older woman. If that woman was Gina… And what about the trade fair in New York, had Andrew and Gina planned that in advance…?

'Before you ask,' said Andrew, 'New York was *not* planned. Gina had been in Canada when she was offered a job in New York. Quite by chance we found ourselves invited to the same reception. Gina said it must have been fate.'

Declining to comment, Jenny had a vague recollection of the New York photos. Yes, she had seen a group of women on one of them, but the significance of such a meeting had never registered. She frowned; something was bothering her. Something Helen had said earlier that evening.

'And what about Geneva?' she asked, 'Whose idea was it to send Paul with me to…'

Andrew hung his head. 'Gina's, I'm afraid. She said with Paul away there was less chance of him finding out. Also, with you in Switzerland... it would be easier for me to tell Mary I was working late.'

'Oh, Andrew! How could you? Don't you see it wasn't fate at all? You fell into Gina's lap just like a ripe plum!'

Slumped in the armchair, nursing another glass of whisky, Andrew knew he'd been a complete and utter fool; he'd also begun to realize the relationship couldn't last. This evening, when Gina had produced the list of expensive flats, he'd suddenly begun to panic. Not wishing to admit it, he was almost grateful for his sister's intervention, even if it did mean being discovered with his trousers down!

Momentarily checking his trousers, Andrew stood up to adjust his waistband. In doing so he caught a sweep of headlights from the window and heard footsteps on gravel.

Jenny heard them too. She looked at him aghast. 'That can't be Gina, can it?'

'No, I made sure I sent her home in a taxi. She doesn't know where you live, does she?'

'No, but Paul does...'

Preparing to face up to the inevitable, Andrew opened the door. To his relief it wasn't Paul standing in the porch but a young policeman.

'Good evening, sir, sorry to trouble you, but someone reported hearing a young lady scream. I was wondering if you...'

'That was me, officer,' Jenny interrupted, stepping forward and directing the young man to the sitting room. 'A bat flew out of the porch as I was opening the door. It gave me such a fright and my brother told me I'd probably disturbed the whole neighbourhood. I can only apologize for wasting your time.'

'That's all right miss; we have to check these things out, you know. Can't be too careful these days.'

Making his way back to the front door, the young officer turned to face Andrew. He'd already noticed the photo of Jenny, Andrew and the family on the sideboard so presumed all was above board. At the same time however, he'd also seen the half-empty whisky decanter and smelt alcohol on Andrew's breath. 'I take it you won't be driving again tonight, sir… as you've been drinking?'

Once again Jenny came to Andrew's rescue. She gestured to the piles of papers and her briefcase. 'No, he won't, officer. I'm afraid we got somewhat carried away celebrating a new contract. In fact, just before you arrived, I'd even suggested to my brother that he ring his wife and tell her he was stopping over with me.'

'Phew! That was quick thinking, Jennifer. I owe you a favour.'

'Hmm, I might hold you to that, sometime. Meanwhile I suggest you do ring your wife, no doubt she's already worrying where you are and imagining all sorts of things.'

Knowing exactly what was meant by 'all sorts of things', Andrew reached for his mobile.

'I'll speak to her too, if you like,' Jenny whispered. 'Just tell her we lost complete track of time discussing Sinclair's and drinking too much malt.'

'Good idea, and if you tell her I'm in no condition to drive and I'm stopping over, maybe we'll both convince her.'

*

The next morning Andrew surveyed his car. The damage was extensive.

'I shouldn't worry about it too much if I were you,' Jenny said, slipping her arm into his. Cars and gate posts can be mended, broken marriages hardly ever.'

'Yes, so they can,' Andrew said, deeply reflective. 'You're right as usual Jennifer, just as you were about the House of St Claire. And, regardless of what happened last night, I am glad that Paul walked into our lives.

157

Now if only Gina would make her exit...'

Waving goodbye, Jenny echoed her brother's parting comment and thought longingly of Paul.

CHAPTER TWENTY

Stevie breezed chirpily into Jenny's office with the morning's post. 'Is Mr Sinclair moving house?'

'Moving? No... not that I'm aware of. What made you think that?'

'Only that there's a pile of details from estate agents on his desk.'

Jenny froze. Was the enquiry purely innocent, or did Stevie suspect something? 'Oh, those,' she said, desperate to keep her tone casual. 'I think they're for a business contact Andrew met in the States. He plans to spend some time in Edinburgh, but doesn't fancy being stuck in a hotel for months. Andrew suggested renting.'

Stevie gave a low whistle. 'Hmm. Well, I'd certainly like to meet him - that's if he's not already married. Anyone who can afford a property in the Royal Mile must be loaded!'

Desperate to change the subject, Jenny turned to examine the bulky envelope on her desk. Recognising Morag's handwriting, she opened it immediately.

'As you can see my mother hasn't wasted any time,' she said, extending the list in Stevie's direction. 'It's confirmation of the guest list for Sinclair's Christmas party, all signed and sealed with her approval. Can I suggest you put everything else on hold, Stevie? Send out the invitations asap, then contact the hotel with provisional numbers.'

'Speaking of wasting time,' Stevie said, returning the list to its envelope, 'that new GP of mine certainly hasn't wasted any. I've already received my appointment to see the specialist at the hospital. I'm afraid it means having to take a whole morning off work for tests and X-rays. Will that be OK?'

'Of course! You know you don't even have to ask. This new doctor...

what exactly did he say when you saw him?'

Stevie emitted a deep sigh and shrugged her shoulders. 'Not much other than suggesting I see the specialist again. Apparently there's some new treatment I could try... physiotherapy and different painkillers, as the others upset me so much. I know it's never going to be a case of "take up your bed and walk, Stevie" and that I'm stuck with this wheelchair and crutches for the best part of my life... but you never know, do you?'

For a moment Jenny forgot all about Andrew and Gina and turned her attention to her loyal PA and friend. 'Is the pain still bad?' she asked, regarding the wistful gaze of Stevie's china-blue eyes framed by close-cropped dark brown hair.

'Oh, you know what it's like, Jenny. Some days are OK... and on the others I could quite cheerfully take myself off to Holyrood Park and jump off Arthur's Seat - that's if I could jump! Perhaps I should change that to wheel myself off the highest point.'

Jenny placed a comforting hand on Stevie's shoulder. 'Then promise me you won't do anything of the sort – at least not until after you've organized Sinclair's Christmas bash. Seriously, though, *no more* cancelled hospital appointments and take advantage of the fact you've got a nice new GP. Do I make myself clear, Miss Stephens?'

Stevie spun her wheelchair to face her boss head on. She grinned and gave a mock salute. 'Yes, ma'am!'

'Good! So... now as my brother's just arrived, I'd better go and have a word with him. He mentioned having a disco as well as a band this year.'

Andrew was in the process of flicking through all the property papers when Jenny entered his office. His face filled with alarm. 'Jenny... if you've come about last...?'

'Don't worry, I haven't, I merely wanted to suggest you got rid of those estate agent's details. Stevie thought you were moving. I told her you were looking for a friend. I also think it might be an idea to open a window.'

Andrew nodded and reached for his waste paper basket. There was no need for explanation. Even he had noticed the distinct underlying smell of Gina's cloying perfume.

The sudden gust of cold November air took them both by surprise. Leaning from the window, Jenny breathed in deeply, sensing the distinctive smell of autumn days that heralded bonfires in the garden and tea in front of the fire.

Satisfied that Gina's presence had evaporated like some ghostly spirit, she closed the window. As she did so she noticed a gentle flurry of leaves from the trees, and the familiar shadowy outline of Edinburgh castle reappeared through skeletal branches.

'Everything all right at home?' she asked softly.

Andrew, having decided to go home for a change of clothes before coming to the office, had been dreading awkward questions from Mary and the children. His relief when none came was palpable. Iain, however, couldn't resist the opportunity of teasing his father about having to stay with Auntie Jen as a result of over imbibing.

Watching Andrew pour himself another cup of black coffee, he reminded his father of the previous weekend when he'd reprimanded both Iain (and his friend Callum) of drinking more beer and lager than was good for them.

'Fancy not being able to hold your drink, Dad!' he'd joked, to which Andrew had merely responded with a grunt.

'Yes, everything's fine, thank you, Jennifer. Looks as if you did a good job of convincing Mary we'd overdone it with the malt. In fact she was more interested in telling me about last night's committee meeting of the Arisaid Ladies. Oh, and yes, I'm to ask you what you'll be wearing to the Sinclair dinner-dance. She and Catriona both want to know.'

Jenny smiled to herself. Thank goodness for Mary; at least she could be relied upon. Any suspicions of her husband's infidelity were soon forgotten if there was a new dress to buy...Pushing his waste paper basket and its incriminating evidence out of sight, Andrew fidgeted with his fountain pen and blotter. 'Um - about last night... I think I owe you a great deal.'

'Let's just forget it,' Jenny said, 'or at least try to – as long as it's over. No inquests, no recriminations.'

'Oh, it's over. You have no fear of that. I've been a bloody fool! I realize that now. When I returned home this morning and saw Mary and the children having breakfast together, I couldn't help but think of Paul and his two girls. When I recall what you said – that Gina actually threatened to take Cele and Emily away from him if he didn't sell the house... What kind of mother could do such a thing?'

'Not a very nice one,' Jenny replied, watching Andrew reach for his handkerchief and blow his nose hard, 'And certainly not one worth losing sleep over.'

'I know. The only problem is... while I'm prepared to forget all about Gina, will she be prepared to forget all about me?'

'In time perhaps.' Jenny cast her mind back to the company's dinner-dance guest list, already approved by their mother. 'However, you might have to wait until after the Sinclair dinner. You've obviously forgotten... you invited Gina as well as Paul!'

'You don't think she will come?' Andrew buried his head in his hands, recalling Gina's volatile display of histrionics the previous evening. There was no telling what she might do.

Anxious to get on with the day's work, Jenny added brightly. 'Don't forget the dance is still several weeks away. We can only hope by that time something – or someone – will have diverted Gina's attention elsewhere. Now, if I don't get a move on, there won't be time for me to go shopping for my dress and I shall end up like Cinderella with nothing to wear!'

Swallowing hard, Andrew watched her go. Their father would have been so proud of his only daughter. No matter where she went or whatever she wore, there was no danger of Jennifer looking like Cinderella. She was a truly wonderful ambassador for the House of St Claire. How strange that in all the years they'd spent together as older brother and little sister, the past twenty-four hours has somehow drawn them even closer together.

CHAPTER TWENTY ONE

Jenny brought Stevie's wheelchair to a halt in front of yet another shop window. Despite her promise to Mary of finding something to wear, her search had been in vain. Repeated phone calls from both Mary and Catriona had done nothing to improve the situation. Announcing that they'd already found their dresses, they advised Jennifer to find something quickly - before there was nothing left to choose from!

'The problem is, they're all too fancy and a bit OTT for my liking,' said Jenny, eyeing the window display with its froth of lace and frills. 'Look at them, Stevie. I'd be like the fairy on top of the Christmas tree in most of those.'

Stevie chuckled. 'They're not like the fairy we had on *our* Christmas tree. Mum made ours an elaborate satin and lace dress and trimmed the wings with silver tinsel, only she forgot to make it any knickers. I took great delight in telling everyone who called that our fairy had a bare bum!'

'Cressida Stephens! What a frightful child you must have been. If I'd known I would never have employed you.'

Happy to have something to laugh about, particularly after the Gina-Andrew debacle, Jenny turned the wheelchair in the direction of Princes Street. Almost immediately she bumped into an elderly woman laden with bags of shopping.

Listening to Jenny's apologies, the old woman smiled sympathetically in Stevie's direction and began picking up her scattered shopping.

'Och, dinner yae trouble yerself,' she said, first making eye contact with Jenny before patting Stevie on the head. 'Poor wee thing,' she whispered, 'it's so sad, isn't it?'

Watching the woman walk away, Stevie didn't know whether to laugh or cry. Why was it, just because you were in a wheelchair, people thought you were completely brain-dead? Seemingly unaware of her friend's sensitivity, Jenny proceeded to push the chair through the milling crowds.

'Lunch, I think, before we die of starvation. I refuse to look at another frock until we've had something to eat.'

'Sorry to be the cause of so much aggro,' Stevie said as Jenny negotiated the busy restaurant and tutting diners while trying to find a suitable table.

Eventually a kindly waitress intervened, directed them to a corner table and brought them each a menu. Stevie breathed a sigh of relief. 'That makes a change. They normally presume I can't read either and ask my mother for my order. It really is like that radio programme... *Does He Take Sugar?* Sometimes I get so cross.'

'As you did when that woman patted you on the head?'

Stevie shifted uneasily in her chair. 'So you did notice. Was it that obvious, Jenny?'

'No... it's only because you're my dearest friend and I know you so well. I sensed at the time you were angry and thought it best to simply get away.'

'Thanks, boss!' Stevie said, sniffing back a tear. 'Now let's eat shall we, so we can carry on dress-hunting.'

For Stevie finding something to wear wasn't a problem. It was a simple choice of black evening trousers and a patterned silk blouse. The muscle wastage in her legs meant she only ever wore trousers plus brightly coloured tops to lighten her sallow complexion. She reminded Jenny of her one big mistake, just after she'd been taken on at Sinclair's. At her first company dinner, she'd worn black from top to toe.

'Gracious, I must have looked like a black widow spider all ready to pounce from my wheelchair; small wonder no one asked me to dance!'

'No… probably not a good choice,' Jenny agreed, 'especially as black widow spiders kill their mates. Speaking of which - dancing and mates, don't forget to ask that young man of yours to the Christmas do.'

Stevie toyed with the bowl of sugar cubes on the table. 'Um - I can't do that… I hardly know him. Besides he's not my young man, he's my nurse. Well, not my nurse exactly… but one of the guys from the physiotherapy department.'

'Oh, I see,' said Jenny, convinced that Stevie was blushing. 'But I thought you said he'd taken you to the theatre a couple of times?'

'Only because his friend couldn't go at the last minute. I expect he feels sorry for me 'cos I make such a fool of myself struggling with these new exercises. Now, are we going to find you something to wear or stay here discussing my love-li..?'

Paying the bill and making their way to the dress department, Jenny pondered those last few words. Stevie had almost said love-life! So… her suspicions were well founded after all. The athletic young man she'd seen on more than one occasion waiting outside the office had more than just a clinical interest in her PA. Warmed by such a prospect, she tackled the rails of silk, taffeta and velvet.

'Any idea what you're looking for?' asked Stevie, scanning the rails for herself.

'Not particularly, but as Mary's wearing black taffeta and Catriona's wearing cream lace a` la Kate Middleton, I suppose I'd better try and avoid something similar.'

'What about velvet?'

Jenny paused with her hand on an ottoman silk dress. 'I suppose it's a possibility. I haven't had a velvet dress for years, though Mother always dressed me in velvet at Christmas when I was small. I do, however, like this ottoman silk.'

'Yes, it's OK,' Stevie said, half-heartedly, 'but it's also black. Didn't you say Mary was wearing black? Why not try this one instead? You've certainly got the colouring and figure for it.'

This one, Jenny discerned, was a bias-cut, deep-emerald velvet evening gown. At first glance she wasn't so sure, thinking it was strapless – she loathed strapless dresses of any description. Then she realized that although there was no right shoulder to the dress, the left side had a wide shoulder strap, which followed the diagonal line across the bodice and down to the hemline.

Stevie waited in anticipation outside the changing room. As expected, Jenny looked stunning. With her ivory complexion and sleek strawberry-blonde hair, the dress not only fitted and hung beautifully, it also showed off her figure and colouring to perfection.

'Wow! Alistair's simply going to love you in that!' said Stevie. 'You can forget all about that ottoman thingy – and why do they call it ottoman silk? I thought an ottoman was an upholstered seat. You certainly don't need any upholstering, Jenny!'

'Thank you for that, Cressida! There was me thinking I'd found the perfect dress and you go and spoil it all by mentioning Alistair Jennings. Besides, I thought he hadn't replied to his invitation.'

'He hadn't, until this morning. His reply came in the same post as Mrs Hadley's.'

'What! But Paul told me Gina couldn't come.'

'Apparently not. According to her note a last-minute change of plan means she can come after all. Now what about that dress? Please say you're going to have it.'

The sheer magic Jenny had felt when trying on *that dress* dissipated rapidly. If only Stevie hadn't mentioned Gina and Alistair. And why had Gina changed her mind? Not wishing to draw attention to the fact, she turned her thoughts elsewhere. 'You – um – don't think the dress is too... well, you know...?'

'No, I don't! Even though I'm not sure what you mean by '*you know*'. How can a beautiful classically-cut evening dress be too much – unlike that hideous garment over there! Now that really is too much – or should that be too little?'

Jenny followed Stevie's gaze to where a red satin evening dress graced a nearby mannequin. At least she supposed it was meant to be an evening dress, with its plunging neckline and the front skirt slit from hip to hemline. Stepping to one side, she noticed the back view was slightly more modest. There the hemline dipped into a small fish-tail effect.

Stevie watched Jenny's eyes register disapproval while her own eyes widened in amazement at the price-tag. 'Tell me, Jenny,' she whispered as an aside, 'How can they charge so much for so little? If you want my opinion, apart from the price, it looks like something you'd wear to the Vicars and Tarts disco they're holding at our local community centre!'

The sombre-faced, blue-rinsed assistant (blessed with an acute sense of hearing), raised only an eyebrow while packing the emerald green velvet between several layers of tissue. Even if she agreed with the comments, having worked in this department for more than forty years she remembered the key word *discretion*. Instead, handing over the neatly boxed garment, she said softly, 'Could I suggest madam looks in the next department? We've recently taken delivery of some delightful new lingerie... ideal for such a dress as yours. Sometimes VPLs can be a bit frumpy, but I can assure you ours are exquisite. You won't get any of those unsightly lines.'

'What on earth are VPLs?' Stevie hissed, placing the box on her lap while Jenny wheeled her in the direction of French knickers, camisoles and suspender belts.

'Smooth-fitting briefs made for wearing under figure hugging garments. I think the VPL stands for visible panty line. The idea is you don't get tell-tale knicker lines across your bottom. I wear them all the time under trousers or pencil slim skirts.'

'Ah! So that's your secret. No wonder Alistair told Andrew that he thought you had a pert *derriere.*'

'He what! When?'

'When you were in Geneva. Alistair called at the office in the hope of taking you to dinner one evening. He went out to lunch with Andrew instead... I overheard part of their conversation when they were leaving the office. Mind you, I don't think your brother was very impressed.'

'Neither am I! Oh, don't look so glum, Stevie. You've only backed up my earlier impressions of Alistair Jennings.'

'So, you won't be giving me my marching orders – that's if I could march?'

'Definitely not!' Jenny replied, preparing once more to do battle with Princes Street. 'You're probably the only person I can trust and rely on.'

Returning to the office Jenny pondered the problem of Gina. Should she tell Andrew now or wait until later? What good would it do at this stage? Besides, knowing Gina, she could quite easily change her mind again, meaning Andrew would have worried in vain. No, she decided, it was best to say nothing at all. Nearer the date, if she thought there were going to be problems, she would tell him then.

For the moment at least, Andrew and his family appeared to be settled, and with no further lunchtime invitations from Mary, Jenny presumed all was well. These days her sister-in-law was more concerned with organizing a family trip to the Christmas pantomime. A trip, which to Fiona's delight included her special friends Cele and Emily.

Retrieving the box containing her evening dress, Jenny prepared to leave the office and waited for Stevie to switch off her computer and head for the cloakroom. Helping her into her padded jacket, she said, 'Stevie...that pretty lace underwear you were admiring earlier, why don't you also treat yourself…? You don't have to restrict yourself to cotton knickers and sports bras.'

'I know,' Stevie acknowledged. 'I was only thinking the same thing five minutes ago. The only trouble is I'd have a hell of a job getting them on.'

'What do you mean, the camisoles or the French knickers?'

'Neither,' Stevie grinned, lifting a trouser leg. 'I'd simply have the devil of a job trying to hook suspenders on to my pop socks!'

*

Still smiling to herself, and giving silent thanks for Stevie's enduring friendship and delightful sense of humour, Jenny locked her front door and made her way upstairs. As she'd done earlier in the evening, she ran her fingers lightly over the emerald velvet gown and resisted the temptation, yet again, to try it on. She was too tired now; all she wanted was a warm bath and bed, but perhaps at the weekend… Closing the wardrobe door, she considered the expense of today's purchases. Had she been too extravagant? No doubt her mother and Miss Tandy might think so, but with the addition of assorted accessories, she could also wear the same dress for Christmas, New Year and even Burns Night.

Burn's Night! That was at least two months away yet, according to Flora Tandy, Morag was already making plans for Burn's night celebrations at Conasg House! Goodness, *Sinclair's dinner- dance*, *Christmas, New Year* and *Burn's Night*, Jenny thought as she lay submerged beneath a layer of sweet-smelling bath foam; there was so much to look forward to.

Relaxed and recovering from her arduous shopping expedition, her gaze took in the range of gorse-decorated bottles and containers gracing the bathroom shelves. They were yet another of Paul's ideas and one they'd been able to get into production quickly, made easier by the unanimous decision to keep the packaging simple. With Christmas fast approaching, it was proving to be an extremely popular line.

'Brilliant! Cut down the packaging and we cut down the costs,' Andrew had declared, before sending Jennifer and Stevie away to test and sample a wonderful range of fragrances. Thankfully, that experience had been far more pleasant than today, struggling with a wheelchair through swarms of harassed shoppers. Reminded of the one strict criterion (as far as the House of St Claire bath range was concerned), Gina Hadley took an uninvited seat on Jenny's train of thought. Nothing, she'd decided, must smell heavy or cloying or even vaguely reminiscent of those scents favoured by that dreadful woman!

Thoughts of Gina, however, turned invariably to thoughts of Paul, causing a now familiar stirring in Jenny's breast. To her dismay since that night in Geneva, and every time she and Paul had found themselves alone at the office, she'd been overwhelmed by inexorable panic.

Willing Gina and Paul to alight at the next station in her mind, Jenny forced herself to think of something else. 'Think of Stevie,' a tiny voice whispered in her head. 'Think of the fun-side of today's shopping trip and how she made you laugh. Think of that sumptuous emerald velvet...'

Stepping from the water and reaching for her bath-robe, Jenny did exactly that and for several moments it worked. Unfortunately, thoughts of one evening dress turned to thoughts of another when she dislodged a scarlet satin heart from the hook on the bathroom door. Placed there by Cameron, it not only brought back painful memories of their relationship, but also reminded her of Gina's scarlet lipstick and that awful red satin dress she'd seen today. What was it Stevie had said? "How can you pay so much for so little?"

Now, *that* really was extravagant, Jenny told herself switching off the bathroom light, who exactly would be foolish enough to pay *so* much for *so* little?

CHAPTER TWENTY TWO

'Andrew, sorry to disturb you. I was wondering if you could give this your seal of approval? It's the seating plan for the Sinclair dinner. Stevie's had to make some last minute adjustments, but I think for the most part it's satisfactory.' Jenny placed the revised plan on Andrew's desk.

His eyes scanned the table layout, noting the diplomatically placed circular tables, each seating ten guests. Last year they had been rectangular, prompting disgruntled comments of 'being stuck on the end'. Andrew scrutinized the Sinclair table.

'You were in danger of being outnumbered by females,' Jenny enlightened, until Mother suggested inviting Dr McAllister, and Mary thought it might be a good idea if Callum, Iain's friend, came along to escort Catriona.

Andrew glanced back at his computer screen, where a table of figures flashed repeatedly.

'I haven't got time to read the name of each guest at every table, Jenny, and I'm sure Stevie's been her usual efficient self. Perhaps if you simply reel off who's sitting on our table and who's in the immediate vicinity?'

'Well… apart from us Sinclairs – that is you, Mary, Catriona, Iain, Morag and myself, there's Miss Tandy, Alex McCallister, Duncan and Callum. I think you'll find that makes ten.'

Andrew frowned hard. 'And do you think that's fair on Paul? I know Duncan's worked flat-out to get everything off the production line and into the stores, but it's Paul's initial designs that have made this year such a huge success. I'm surprised, Jennifer. I thought you of all people would have wanted Paul on our table. Surely Duncan could sit at the adjoining table?'

'Yes... he could, and you're right, Mother and I both intended for Paul to be sitting with us but...'

'But?'

'I thought it better if Paul sat there... next to Gina.'

For a moment Andrew looked as if he was about to explode. His face went puce and his eyes widened in alarm as he made a grab for the table plan. 'Gina! You've got to be joking! I thought you said she wasn't coming. Even Paul told me she was going to be away.'

'She was, but apparently she's changed her mind. She sent a letter of acceptance and even rang Stevie to make sure it had arrived.' About to add, 'you know Gina' Jenny bit her lip. Instead she reached across the desk to retrieve Stevie's neatly executed seating plan.

Andrew looked panic-stricken, his earlier flushed cheeks now a deathly white. 'Oh, my God! What are we going to do, Jennifer? What the hell do you think she's playing at?'

Making her way to the cabinet, where she knew Andrew kept a bottle of whisky, Jenny poured him a glass of his favourite malt and made sure there was no danger of them being disturbed. Stevie was now going through the Sinclair Christmas card list.

'Hmm, well... at the moment, other than drinking that whisky, I suggest you do nothing. Just behave as normal. At least Gina won't be on *our* table. As for what she's playing at, we can only hope she'll be playing at being the dutiful wife for once. Who knows, she might even have a conscience after all. Perhaps she thinks being by Paul's side, it will save him from further embarrassment.'

Secretly both brother and sister thought this highly unlikely, but with the dance only days away, Jenny realized there was little she could do other than make Andrew a very strong cup of black coffee!

Five minutes later, returning with the coffee and removing the whisky tumbler, she added thoughtfully. 'What if… when I see Paul - we've a meeting arranged for tomorrow - I explain the seating arrangement. I'll try and think of an appropriate excuse between now and then. I'm sure he'll understand.'

'Wait a minute!' Andrew cried, the whisky having hit the spot. 'I've got another idea. Where's that seating plan?'

Once more with the plan spread out across his desk, Andrew turned to Jenny with a satisfied smile. 'Got it! All we have to do is move Alistair Jennings from that table to this one, where Paul and Gina are sitting. Alistair and Paul have known each other for ages. That way it won't look so odd.'

Jenny bit her lip. Andrew's suggestion certainly made sense but having Alistair in such close proximity to the Sinclair family table… 'I suppose it is a possibility, but as you're fully aware, I don't much care for Alistair - and that's putting it politely. Oh, I know his marketing of the House of St Claire hampers was superb, particularly those for the glorious twelfth, he just makes my flesh creep that's all.' Jenny gave a shudder, 'As for the last time he took me to dinner - an invitation I was deeply reluctant to accept, he was like an octopus with hands everywhere.'

Dejected by Jenny's response, Andrew sat in silence. It had seemed such a good idea, the perfect solution in fact. Alistair, who was always so full of himself, would probably keep Gina entertained for most of the evening and thus reduce the risk of her straying towards the Sinclair table. If only he could convince Jennifer… 'Um – we don't really want Gina upsetting Mother or Mary, do we? And if Alistair's octopus hands are busy elsewhere…'

'Oh, all right,' Jenny agreed, making a mental note that Andrew hadn't included himself in the *upsetting*. 'I'll tell Stevie to make the necessary alterations. Only *please* don't forget I have absolutely no desire to be in close proximity to Alistair Jennings. While I'm happy to help you out, Andrew, I shall expect you to do the same!'

'Of course, of course!' Reaching out, Andrew gave his sister a hug. 'I really appreciate this, you know. I'll also try and make it up to you some time.'

'There'll be no "try" about it, Andrew Sinclair,' Jenny teased, amused by his brotherly show of affection, 'Just make sure you do!'

Stevie listened patiently to yet more alterations. Hers was not to reason why; yet she knew Jenny loathed Alistair. He didn't exactly make Stevie's flesh creep but lately, she'd had the distinct feeling there was an ulterior motive behind Alistair's frequent visits to the office. What was he trying to prove? More to the point, what was he after? Her immediate thought was that he was hoping to wheedle his way into Andrew's good books and perhaps a place on Sinclair's board. Failing that and far, far worse was that he had serious designs on Jenny!

'Heaven forbid!' she muttered to herself, with the photocopier whirring away in the background and her imagination giving rise to flights of fancy. Yes, she had done as instructed with the revised seating arrangements. Alistair *would* be sitting at the adjoining table – but with his back to the Sinclairs! That way she could sit him next to Gina Hadley, whom she also didn't much care for, thus making it possible for Paul to be facing in Jenny's direction

Later, her mother would accuse her of playing with fire. Stevie, as usual, saw it differently. Jenny deserved some happiness in her life. She'd wasted six years of it on the moody and self-obsessed Cameron Ross, spent endless hours working tirelessly for Sinclair's, and with Paul perhaps she… OK, so Paul was married to Gina, Stevie conceded, helping her mother peel vegetables, but in name only if recent rumours were to be believed. She'd even heard whisperings of a divorce. Why then, argued Stevie, couldn't Jenny and Paul be just good friends?

'Because,' insisted her mother. 'I don't think being good friends is going to be enough for either of them – Jennifer or Mr Hadley – and you'd best not interfere, Cressida.'

*

Stevie felt disheartened. She should have known better than to discuss the situation with her mother. Still, she had kept one thing from her. Gina might be sitting on one side of Paul but Stevie would be sitting on the other! There, from her vantage point, she hoped to gauge the atmosphere between Jenny and Paul. Apart from their first frosty encounter, they got on well together and she remained convinced something had happened between them in Geneva. It showed in the way Paul looked at Jenny whenever he came to the office; and though not one to gamble, Stevie would have bet her entire Christmas bonus that Paul Hadley didn't make Jennifer's flesh creep.

*

'What a relief. That meeting went better than I imagined,' said Paul as they left the buyer's office. 'Just think – an entire window given over to the House of St Claire. What a perfect start to New Year!'

Jenny was also thrilled at the prospect. She couldn't wait to tell her mother and Andrew, especially as Morag would be arriving in a few days with Miss Tandy. Andrew had offered to go and fetch them, but his offer had been declined. Instead, Morag had insisted that the dust sheets be taken off the Bentley. It was about time it was taken out for a run, and what better than the journey from Argyll to Edinburgh? With Hamish behind the wheel, driving at a leisurely pace, she would at least see some of the scenery. When Andrew drove, she told him, the countryside simply whizzed by like some speeded-up film. Small wonder he'd crashed his car into his sister's gatepost!

'Do you have time for lunch, Paul?' Jenny ventured, thinking it would be far easier to explain about the dance over lunch as opposed to standing outside the buyer's office.

Paul appeared to hesitate; they hadn't lunched together in ages. Prior to that week in Geneva, working lunches had been a familiar practice; since then... Since then what? Neither of them had spoken of it - it was like an unseen barrier between them. Perhaps this was the opportunity he'd been waiting for. Lunch together might help put things right – give him a proper chance to explain his feelings towards her.

Paul studied her face; her ivory complexion and such gentle questioning eyes. If only he could reach out and hold her again, feel her respond as before. Now was not the place, however. He daren't risk upsetting her again.

'Lunch sounds like a great idea, Jenny, but only if I'm paying. You see I have an ulterior motive. Don't look so worried. I need your help in choosing something for Celestina and Emily. I've promised them new dresses for Christmas and they've told me they must look their best when going to the pantomime... As you're used to buying clothes for Fiona, I hoped you might be able to help me.'

Relieved, Jenny followed him to the restaurant where she prepared to broach the subject of the forthcoming dinner. If Andrew had been shocked to learn of Gina's intention to attend, Paul was mortified. 'But she told me she was going away! She couldn't be bothered to attend some silly company Christmas dinner!' The words escaped from his lips before he realized whose company Gina had been referring to.

'Sorry, Jenny, I shouldn't have spoken like that about Sinclair's.'

'You didn't, you merely repeated Gina's opinion. I dare say it's one we've all shared over the years. Some company dinners - even Sinclair's, can be a bit of a bore. I just hoped... we just hoped,' she added quickly, 'this year would be special.'

Noticing her slip of the tongue, Paul reached for her hand across the table. 'Let's hope it will be. The House of St Claire has much to celebrate.'

Making their way to the children's dress department, Jenny recognized the assistant who'd served her on the previous shopping trip with Stevie. She graced Jenny and Paul with a sweeping smile before continuing on her way to lunch. There her friend from the lingerie department was already waiting.

'Someone you know?' asked Paul, staring in disbelief at the blue rinse.

'Not really. According to Mary, she's the company stalwart and has been working here since the year dot. Sadly, she's a dying breed, nothing's too much trouble - not like this one.' Jenny nodded in the direction of the young assistant whose attention they were trying to attract.

'Thanks, Jenny,' Paul said, almost an hour later. 'I had no idea I was going to take up so much of your time. I'm extremely grateful and it's such a huge weight off my mind. The colour will be simply perfect for them both.'

He smoothed his hands against one of the midnight-blue velvet dresses.

'I confess I wasn't so sure about the colour at first but the broderie anglaise trim on the neck and sleeves makes a pretty contrast. As you say if Fiona's dress is bottle green, we can't have them all dressed identically, can we?'

Jenny fixed him with a warm smile. 'I don't know, I'm sure Fiona would love it, though I'm not sure Mary would approve of three little girls in blue a` la Gilbert and Sullivan.'

'Or green?' Paul offered.

'Or green... and definitely not red,' Jenny said, her attention drawn through the archway to the women's dress department and the red satin dress, still on display.

Paul followed her gaze. 'Definitely not red,' he repeated in a low voice. My goodness! Isn't that dress hideous? I can't imagine anyone wanting to buy that.'

'Mmm. Stevie and I said exactly the same when we here the other day. As for the price…'

With both dresses wrapped, Paul was only too grateful of Jenny's offer to keep them at the cottage until Christmas, thus avoiding the temptation for the girls to go Christmas present hunting. Back in Princes Street he handed over the bag and bent and kissed Jenny quickly on the cheek.

'Thank you,' he murmured, 'you have no idea how much I…'

'Looks as if you've had a successful shopping trip,' a voice called out.

Turning, Jenny and Paul came face to face with the two assistants they'd seen earlier.

'I'm sure your little girls will simply adore their dresses,' said the blue rinse. 'I saw you looking at the delightful velvets and taffetas. You do know that you can remove the broderie anglaise trim for washing?'

Jenny nodded and was about to remark that she had noticed when the assistant turned her attention to Paul. 'And did madam show you our exquisite range of lingerie? As I said to her the other day, it's exactly what's needed to go under that beautiful dress of hers. The perfect Christmas present, if you ask me,' she added, winking at Paul.

Not waiting to hear more, Jenny took Paul by the arm and led him away. Fortunately for her, he hadn't noticed that she was blushing. Instead he roared with laughter, watching the blue rinse and her friend totter back inside the store.

'Do you know, Jenny, I'm convinced they've been drinking. No doubt a pre-Christmas tipple in the wine bar across the street. What was that she was saying?'

'Oh, nothing important. Look, if you don't mind, I'd better dash. Stevie needs me to sign the company Christmas cards. Let me know when you want the dresses and thank you for being so understanding about the seating plan.'

With that she was gone, disappearing amongst the bustle of afternoon shoppers, leaving Paul to ponder the past few hours: their earlier business meeting, lunch and the successful hunt for Cele and Emily's dresses. Later, waiting outside the girl's school, realization dawned.

'You fool,' Paul Hadley, he told himself. 'No wonder Jenny was so anxious to get away, that woman thought Jenny was your wife! She'd probably seen you lunching together, shopping together and...'

Remembering how he'd even kissed Jenny goodbye, Paul's imagination went into overdrive. How wonderful it would be going home to Jenny. Preparing dinner together, they would discuss the day's events at Sinclair's, and later help Celestina and Emily get ready for bed...

A flurry of children appeared at the school gates to be met by mothers with welcoming arms. Paul's arms were just as welcoming as he listened to the animated conversations taking place. Talk of Mary and Joseph, donkeys and shepherds filled the air, filling him with a sense of panic. He might have bought the girls their dresses but as for the children's nativity play and Christmas itself... would Gina be in attendance?

'Are you sure Cele is coming?' he asked as Emily sat with her nose pressed against the car window looking out for her sister.

'Yes, but first she's got to see her teacher. It's about angels.'

Five minutes later the last trickle of children and mothers with pushchairs appeared in the playground. At the rear, holding the hand of a young classroom helper, was Cele. Paul could tell she'd been crying.

'I'm very sorry, Mr Hadley, Cele appears to be very upset. It's about the school nativity play.'

Stepping from the car Paul took his daughter in his arms and murmured kindly, 'Cele, darling, won't you tell Daddy what's wrong?'

'Mrs Edwards won't let me be an angel. She says my hair's too dark and curly! I can only be an angel if I've got hair like Morag Frazer.'

'Hmm, well I'm afraid not everyone can have fair hair,' Paul consoled, lifting Cele into the car. Perhaps you can be something else instead? There must be lots of other parts you can play.'

Cele stuck out her bottom lip. 'Mrs Edwards says I can be the innkeeper's wife... but I don't want to be.'

'Why is that?' Paul asked, dreading the reply.

'Because Darren Henderson is playing the innkeeper and he smells!'

Switching on the ignition, Paul emitted a long drawn-out sigh. 'This' he said quietly under his breath, 'is going to be one of those evenings.' Instead of going home to the tranquil scene he'd imagined earlier, there was not only Gina to contend with but also a distraught innkeeper's wife.

For some reason known only to herself, and before Paul had left to fetch the girls, Gina had stormed out of the house announcing there was a tin of ravioli in the cupboard and fish fingers in the freezer!

Later, removing his jacket, Paul hung it on the bathroom door, rolled up his shirt sleeves and ran the girls' bath, adding two large capfuls of sweet-smelling bath gel to the water. He watched as the thick layer of bubbles rose slowly to the surface and parted them to check the temperature, noting as he did so the deep rose-coloured water. For the second time that afternoon he found himself thinking of Jenny. What was it she'd said way back in the summer when she'd held rose-tinted jars of fruit jelly and spoken of angels... something about marmalade days?

Paul's own would-be angel stood at the bathroom door with the remnants of ravioli and dry tears on her cheeks.

'Better now?' he coaxed, helping her into the bath. Cele sniffed and nodded and waited for her daddy to lift Emily in beside her. In doing so, he caught site of the official manila envelope he'd stuffed hurriedly into his jacket pocket.

The contents of the letter stated quite categorically that Gina was agreeable to a divorce. The problem was that that had been last week, when Gina was calm and co-operative and could be reasoned with. Now, given today's state of mind, anything could happen. Not only that, before the first court hearing they would have to face the Sinclair dinner together – as man and wife.

Emily piled bubbles on to her head and announced brightly, 'Look, Daddy, look Cele, I'm a Mr Frosty ice cream.'

Cele for once was not amused; instead she looked up at Paul and declared. 'Anyway, I'm having a *new* teacher, 'cos Mrs Edwards is having a baby like Mary and Joseph and she's got to leave school *really soon*. Hooray!'

'I 'spect that's 'cos it's a long way to Bethlehem,' Emily said, piling yet more bubbles on her head.

Swallowing hard, Paul smiled at them both and reached for a towel from the radiator.

CHAPTER TWENTY THREE

With the tables cleared and the band playing, Andrew allowed himself a moment to relax and survey the proceedings. He glanced only briefly at Gina who, with her back to him, sat in animated conversation with Alistair Jennings. Breathing a sigh of relief, he caught Paul's eye. Andrew smiled and nodded acknowledgement. He'd been dreading coming face to face with Paul and Gina, yet their arrival had passed without incident. Paul had paused only briefly to speak to Morag and introduce Gina before joining Alistair at their table.

Once out of earshot, Morag and Flora Tandy found themselves discussing Gina's dress – or what little there was of it. The red satin frock with its plunging neckline and deeply revealing side split, which only days before had shocked Stevie to the core, was now tightly moulded over Gina's curvaceous body. Paul had disliked it on sight, but had refrained from voicing his opinion. He knew from bitter experience it was best to remain silent. Tonight was not a good time to provoke Gina. For the moment she appeared calm and was certainly enjoying the attention of Alistair and the other male guests at their table. As at the airport almost a year ago, female sympathies lay with Paul. He, meanwhile, was secretly grateful to have the down to earth Stevie sitting by his side.

'Wow! You actually know Gina Dintino!' gasped Callum, listening to Iain boasting at great length about last January's skiing trip. 'I was only reading about her in last week's…'

Choosing to forget the embarrassing scenario when he'd got horribly drunk, Iain had also forgotten the reason for inviting Callum this evening. His friend was supposed to be Catriona's escort.

Mary and Catriona were *not* amused. As for coming face to face with Gina Dintino, nothing could have prepared them for the shock to discover she was Paul's wife! Whenever Andrew had mentioned Mrs Hadley, he'd never said she was that dreadful woman from their ill-fated skiing trip. The questions now racing through Mary's head would have to wait; Andrew reached for Mary's arm and led her onto the dance floor.

Enthusing about the latest piece of Sinclair machinery, Duncan McIntyre sensed Flora Tandy wasn't particularly interested and turned to face Jenny instead.

'You must come and see it some time, it's really quite amazing. I expect there's no time before Christmas but in the New Year perhaps?'

Jenny wasn't listening; her attention was elsewhere. She was watching Gina leaning heavily on Alistair's shoulder. Having whispered something in his ear, she gave a deep throaty laugh and held her glass in his direction to be filled. Paul's quiet entreaties to ' *take it easy* ' were ignored.

'I don't want to take it easy, I want to dance! But you don't want to dance, do you Paul?'

Gina addressed the entire table. 'My husband is such a bore, not like Alistair. We've had some great times together, haven't we, darling?'

For once not so sure of himself, Alistair looked about the table, where fellow guests sipped their drinks uncomfortably and averted their eyes.

Jenny watched as Alistair withdrew from Gina's grasp, anxiety written all over his face.

Keen to avoid confrontation with Paul, he called across to the neighbouring table. 'Jenny, why don't you come and join us? Perhaps you might be able to persuade Paul on to the dance floor?'

All eyes from the top table were now on Jenny. She met her mother's gaze, and was surprised to hear her announce. 'Yes, you go and dance with Mr Hadley, my dear – forget about us oldies. Who knows, I might even take to the floor myself later, that's if Duncan and Alex ever stop talking about machinery and golf!'

Allowing herself to be led by Paul through the group of people already dancing, Jenny stood in the middle of the floor. Gina glared at her angrily, drained her glass and sidled onto Alistair's lap.

'So sorry to drag you away from your family,' Paul said, slipping an arm around her waist, 'perhaps it's just as well the band are playing a slow waltz; I'm afraid I'm not much of a Fred Astaire or a John Travolta when it comes to dancing.'

Jenny smiled, remembering Callum's earlier gyrations on the dance floor with Catriona. The band's attempt at playing Stevie Wonder's 'Woman in Red' had been a bad choice. Callum had failed to impress both Catriona and Gina. Trying one fancy step too many he'd simply skidded across the parquet floor on his bottom. Catriona had been deeply embarrassed and Gina had simply roared with laughter.

'Quite frankly I was only too glad to get away,' Jenny replied. 'Duncan's very sweet but I'm afraid I can't quite share his enthusiasm for every piece of equipment we purchase for Sinclair's.'

'Mmm. I know what you mean. Duncan's a prime example of man's love of machinery, but he does tend to go into every nut and bolt – or should that be microchip? Still, he's a very personable fellow and as Andrew was saying only last week, it's largely thanks to Duncan the House of St Claire products got into the stores in time for Christmas.'

Jenny smiled and nodded in agreement. When Paul's eyes met hers she relaxed in his arms while their feet moved in rhythm to the music. All too soon however, the magic was broken. The last strains of the waltz faded away and once again they stood apart, only inches away from Mary and Andrew.

Delighted that the evening was going so well, the bandleader beamed broadly and made his way to the edge of the stage. 'Ladies and gentlemen, moving on from our earlier rendition of "Woman in Red" we shall now play Chris de Burgh's "Lady in Red" and... as I see we have our own lady in red here tonight, perhaps we could ask her to lead the way in the ladies' excuse me...?'

All eyes were on Gina as she unfolded herself from Alistair's lap and made her way across the floor. Initially thinking Gina was planning to reclaim her husband, Jenny could only watch in horror as she made a bee-line for Andrew. Andrew's face filled with horror and grasping Mary's arm, he remained frozen to the spot.

In desperation, Jenny turned to Paul. 'I don't care how you do it,' she hissed, 'just get Gina out of here and away from Andrew - now!'

Looking from Jenny to Andrew and then to Gina, Paul recognized in his wife's triumphant glow and Andrew's state of panic yet another case of betrayal. With time of the essence it was useless pondering where or when, or even for how long, for Jenny's sake he must act quickly.

Halting Gina's progress, he reached out and took her firmly by the arm. 'Gina, my love, how delightful that you should want to dance with your husband. Shall we lead the way?' So saying, Paul nodded to the bandleader to strike up the opening bars.

What seemed like an eternity to Jenny and Andrew, was in fact only moments - yet it was long enough for Mary to recognize a familiar scent. The same heavy perfume she'd recognized on Andrew's shirts...

Twisting away from her husband's grasp, Mary turned her attention to her sister-in-law. She wanted an explanation... what had Jenny been keeping from her?'

Fully aware that a showdown with Mary was inevitable, but not now and not in full view of her mother and all their invited guests, Jenny took the only available means of escape. Under the watchful eyes of Morag, Miss Tandy and Stevie, Jennifer Sinclair invited a bemused

Alistair Jennings to dance.

She shuddered as warm, clammy hands clasped her body tightly, until she was barely able to breathe. Sickened by the way Alistair held her way too close for comfort Jenny realized the disastrous mistake she'd made. Dancing with Alistair was not the same as dancing with Paul. To begin with, Alistair had been drinking heavily and he also reeked of Gina's perfume. As for the way he kept running his hands up and down her buttocks... if only she could break free... First she must wait for Gina and Paul to leave the dance floor.

Horrified, Jenny caught a glimpse of red satin at the far end of the dance floor. Surely the Hadley's weren't still here? Couples were beginning to change partners again and panic rose inexorably in her breast – what would happen now? Briefly Paul's eyes met hers but they showed no flicker of emotion.

Stony-faced and tight-lipped, Paul led his wife into the cold December night, where she tried to extricate herself from his grasp.

'Paul, let me go! What are you doing? Where are we going?'

'*We* are going home, Gina!'

'But they're playing that song for me! I wanted to dance with A...'

Opening the car door, Paul forced her inside. 'I know.... You wanted to dance with Andrew. But this is one time, Gina, when you are *not* having your own way. I refuse to be made a fool of, particularly in front of the Sinclair's and their guests.' Paul fastened Gina's seat belt as she continued to struggle from the car.

'You're hurting me - let me get out or I'll scream!'

Closing the passenger door and running round to the driver's seat, Paul continued, 'Oh, you can scream all you like, Gina. As for hurting, I suggest you sit still, then the seat belt won't cut into you. You could also try covering up some of that bare flesh. Quite frankly, in that dress you look like a common...!'

Sickened and disgusted, Paul watched Gina clasp the bodice of her dress to cover a bare breast. She then tried pulling the material to cover her exposed thighs. Angrily she glared in Paul's direction, but he said nothing and stopped only briefly at the exit from the car park. There he reached into the rear of the car for a travel rug and threw it across her lap.

The journey home was spent in silence, which from experience he knew to be the calm before the storm. Offering up silent thanks for Helen, who'd offered to have the girls for a sleepover, he knew that at least Cele and Emily would be spared the ensuing vitriolic scene.

Gina, still swathed in the travel rug, emerged from the car docile as a lamb. Once indoors, however, she turned on her husband like a wild animal ready for the kill. Her dark eyes flashed as torrents of abuse poured forth from her cruel and twisted scarlet-pained mouth.

Weary from so many months of her unpredictable behaviour, Paul stood quietly by the fireplace. He'd decided on the way home he wasn't going to be drawn into yet another of her screaming tantrums. Everything that needed to be said had been gone through already; their marriage was at the point of no return.

Furious at failing to draw Paul into verbal combat, Gina changed tactics by loudly proclaiming her liaisons with Alistair and Andrew, but to no avail; Paul would not be provoked. It was only when Jenny's name was mentioned that she discerned a flicker of emotion in his face.

'Rant and rave all you like, Gina, this time I refuse point-blank to subject myself to one of your slanging matches.' Paul's voice remained calm and unemotional as he continued coolly, 'You spoke earlier of being hurt, physically hurt, but you've only yourself to blame wearing that ridiculous dress…'

Having discarded the rug, Gina picked it up again and covered herself as if she were naked. Warily she slumped into an armchair and waited for Paul to continue, convinced he was going to say something she didn't really want to hear.

'And as for being hurt, have you thought of the pain you've caused everyone, Gina? The emotional hurt to the children and myself and even the people I've worked with; decent people without whom we wouldn't even have this house. No, of course you haven't, you've been far too busy thinking of yourself and having a good time at everyone's expense!'

Gina slid even deeper into the armchair. She'd never seen her husband like this before. He seemed so cold and distant... almost alien. Usually she never had any trouble provoking him into argument. An argument that would add fuel to her next tirade, leaving her to delight in the way he always gave in to her. This time however, there was no such response.

Reaching into his breast pocket, Paul drew out his wallet and removing his driving licence and personal papers, placed it on the mantelpiece.

'In there, Gina, you'll find more than enough for where you intend to go. Take what you need, as I understand you've already decided against spending Christmas with us. And if you haven't yet made your usual excuses to Cele and Emily, I shall tell them you've had to visit your parents in Italy. There's no point in spoiling their Christmas further. For your information, I now intend to return to the hotel to make my apologies to the Sinclairs. When I get back, I expect to find you gone. Do I make myself perfectly clear?'

Panic-stricken, Gina stared after him in disbelief. Her mouth felt dry as she opened it to speak. Paul *couldn't* leave her... Not like this! No! He couldn't possibly walk out on her.

'Aren't you even going to say goodbye?' she called, her voice catching in her throat.

With his hand on the door, Paul stopped and turned slowly to face her.

'Gina, I appear to have spent the best part of our married life saying goodbye to you. I'm sure I don't need to say it again. Let's use your phrase, shall we...? *Ciao*, darling!'

*

Returning to the hotel, Paul was surprised to find many of the older guests departing or in the process of saying goodbye, leaving the younger ones heading for the disco. Morag, perceptive as ever, decided she'd had enough excitement for one night and summoned Tandy, who'd been dancing with Alex McAllister, to accompany her to their room.

'No doubt Andrew and Mary – and Jennifer too, if she can free herself from the clutches of that Alistair fellow – will see to the rest of our guests,' Morag said tersely.

'What about Miss Stephens?' Tandy asked, glancing in Stevie's direction. 'Do you think she needs help getting back to her room? Such a shame her young man couldn't come this evening. Miss Jennifer tells me he's on duty at the hospital tonight. Poor thing, she looks quite lost and all alone at that table.'

'Knowing Miss Stephens, I'd say she's only too glad to be sitting in that wheelchair. At least she's been spared the likes of Duncan trampling over her feet all night. She's also an extremely capable young woman but if it makes you feel any better, then I suggest you go and ask if she needs any assistance. Meanwhile, I'm away to my bed.'

Stevie, acknowledging Morag's departure and touched by Flora Tandy's concern, expressed her thanks, saying she intended to remain a little longer; she enjoyed watching people dance.

'I expect she'll go away feeling sorry for me,' Stevie told herself. She had no intention of divulging the real reason for her staying put. Jenny, much to her dismay, had been dancing with Alistair for ages – or at least Alistair had been monopolizing her for ages. Stevie was therefore waiting for Paul's return. She hoped to see them dancing again ; they made such a lovely couple – but where was Paul?

Like Jenny, Stevie's eyes were constantly on the door, watching as each cool gust of air from the corridor heralded the entrance or departure of a guest. Moment later, she only had to look at Jenny's face to know that Paul had arrived. Without warning, Alistair found himself alone on the dance floor. Much to his annoyance, he saw Jenny hurry to Paul's side and lead him to an empty table in the corner.

'Well…' she asked, 'did you get her home safely?'

'Oh, I did more than that, Jenny. I told her to leave… Gina wasn't planning to stay with us for Christmas, anyway. I don't think you or Andrew need worry anymore.'

Registering the note of solemn finality in his voice, Jenny sat down and whispered, 'Thank God. I'm *so* grateful, Paul.'

'You don't have to be. In fact, I can only apologize for the trouble she's caused.'

Paul glanced in Andrew and Mary's direction. There was a distinct frostiness between husband and wife. 'I can only hope, and here I speak from experience, that Mary has a forgiving nature.'

'You knew?' Jenny gasped, when Paul sat down beside her, 'you knew about Andrew and Gina?'

'Not exactly. Let's just say I had my suspicions. You get used to recognizing the signs. It wasn't until tonight that…'

Tears welled in Jenny's eyes. 'I'm sorry… so very sorry. I know Andrew bitterly regrets betraying your trust and friendship.'

'Then tell him not to worry; if it hadn't been Andrew it would have been someone else. As if you hadn't already guessed she and Alistair… though quite who was the hunter and the hunted, I've no idea.'

Unaware he was the current topic of conversation, Alistair was already making his way across the room, determined to lay claim to Jennifer again. How dare she leave him looking like an idiot in the middle of the dance floor, and why was she closeted in that cosy corner with Paul? Not looking where he was going, Alistair found his way barred by Stevie. Seconds later she ran her wheelchair deliberately over his foot and rammed him against the table.

Ignoring Alistair's cry of pain, Paul drew Jenny gently towards him; he caressed her fingers and looked earnestly into her eyes.

'Jenny, there's so much I want to say to you, I simply don't know where to begin; added to which this isn't the right place. Perhaps next week we...'

'Damned woman!' Alistair muttered, limping to their side. 'I'm sure she did that deliberately. Don't know what the hell she's playing at with that bloody wheelchair of hers!'

He froze when he saw the intimate exchange of glances between man and woman and, as if that wasn't enough, Paul made no attempt at releasing Jenny's hands from his grasp.

'Ah, Jenny, my sweet, there you are. Sorry to break up your little tete-a-tete, but you can't leave a fellow standing on the dance floor like that. Not good for my reputation, you know.'

Choosing to remain seated, Jenny bit her lip hard. The temptation to remind Alistair about his reputation was almost too much. Nothing would induce her to return to his lecherous grasp.

Sensing defeat in one quarter, Alistair turned his attention to Paul.

'Got Gina home all right, did you? She's a wild one that wife of yours, not like our sweet Miss Sinclair here.'

Alistair leered lasciviously at Jenny, disappointed that Paul didn't rise to the bait. 'Very well, as I can't persuade you to finish our dance, perhaps you'll save me the last waltz? That's if Paul will let you, for unless I'm very much mistaken he wants you all to himself.'

Not knowing how to respond, Jenny watched as Alistair rubbed at his bruised foot and ankle. Thinking that he was about to go and leave them in peace, she was totally unprepared for what followed.

Without warning, Alistair gave Paul a hearty slap on the back followed by a jovial, 'Good on you, Paul old chap! Looks like you've beaten me to it, but don't forget it was me who first introduced you to Jenny and your meal ticket...'

Casting her mind back to last January and the trade fair, when she'd first met Paul, Jenny frowned hard. Alistair hadn't introduced them; Paul had been alone when he...

By now, and sensing a glimmer of revenge, Alistair turned his attention back to Jenny. 'That's right, my dear... our friend Paul here came to me looking all lost and forlorn, desperate for work. It was me who delivered him into your arms, or should that be the other way round now? He's obviously taken heed of what I said.'

'Whatever do you mean?' Jenny snapped.

'Well... I told Paul you were a real soft touch and from where I'm standing, I'd say he's already found that out for himself. Aren't I right Paul? You've already got your feet under the Sinclair table, who knows... tonight - if you play your cards right, and with your wife conveniently out of the way, it could be more than your feet in Jennifer Sinclair's bed!'

Stunned, Jenny looked at Paul. She was waiting for some show of denial on his part but none was forthcoming. Had Alistair been telling the truth? Was that all she'd been – a real soft touch and Paul's passport to security?

Calmly Jenny released her hand from Paul's grasp and rose from her chair, showing no sign of emotion to either man: Alistair, who made no secret of his designs on her, and Paul who had played on her trust.

'If you'll both excuse me, I really must go and see to Stevie. She's looking very tired and also appears to be having problems with her wheelchair.'

'Come back soon, and don't forget the last waltz,' Alistair called.

Swallowing hard and choking back tears, Jenny forced herself to walk slowly in Stevie's direction. She had to behave as if nothing had upset her. 'Last waltz indeed! Who the hell does he think he is?'

'Pardon?' Stevie said raising an eyebrow. 'I didn't quite catch that. Are you OK, Jenny? You look dreadful. It's not your feet coming back to life after all Duncan's earlier trampling?'

Jenny forced a flicker of a smile. 'No, not Duncan's clod-hoper feet, but you could say I feel well and truly trodden on. Look, I don't feel like staying here any longer. Andrew and Mary can see to the final farewells. Are you coming too?'

Stevie hesitated, she wasn't ready to leave. What had happened in that far corner? One moment it seemed Paul and Jenny were getting on so well and the next... that idiot Alistair had to go and spoil things. It was a pity she'd only managed to bruise his foot and not put him out of action completely. 'What about the last waltz?' she asked feebly. 'Won't you even stay for that?'

'Stevie, as I consider you a true friend, I'm too polite to tell you what you can do with the last waltz! However, if Alistair asks for me you have my permission to tell him to go to hell!'

Dumbstruck, Stevie watched Jenny's eyes fill with tears before she turned on her heels and left the room. Deeply concerned as to whom was responsible for making her cry, Stevie's gaze scanned the room. It could only be one of two people: Paul, who was looking distinctly ill at ease, or the loathsome Alistair, returning from the bar with two large glasses of wine. He proffered one in Paul's direction with a loud, 'Cheers, m 'dears, and here's to absent friends.'

Stevie reached dejectedly for her own glass of wine. What an evening! What a truly awful evening it had turned out to be, especially when she'd had such high hopes.

'Damn you, Gina Hadley!' she hissed under her breath. 'This is all your bloody fault. As for you, Alistair, what a pity I wasn't driving a double-decker bus instead of a wheelchair. Then you wouldn't be looking quite so smug.'

In desperation, swinging round to have a closer look at Paul and the obsequious Alistair, Stevie caught her elbow against the sugar bowl left behind when the waiter brought the coffee.

'Damn,' she cried, watching the silver bowl resound solidly against her glass before sending a pool of deep red wine trickling into a drift of sugar. 'That's all I need!'

Mopping up the wine as best she could, Stevie surveyed the unsightly stain as it seeped into the white damask cloth. From there she ran her forefinger into the residue of unsullied sugar. White against red, she mused; white, like Jenny's ashen face as she'd fled the room and red for Gina's ridiculous dress.

CHAPTER TWENTY FOUR

In her hotel room, Jenny sat at the dressing table and faced her sorrowful reflection in the mirror.

'You fool, Jennifer Sinclair. You complete and utter fool! How could you let yourself be taken in by such a man?'

With fresh tears brimming in her eyes, she remembered her first meeting with Paul. Had his dishevelled appearance been a ploy to make her feel sorry for him? And what about Gina, had that also been part of the same plan, with Paul actually encouraging his wife to make a pass at Andrew? Surely not, right from the start (particularly as a result of the chicken pox affair), he'd made no secret of the deepening chasm in his marriage. Added to which he'd always given the impression of being sincere and honest. As for that night in Geneva, when she'd almost succumbed to Paul's entreaties... Jenny shuddered at the very thought, tears streaming down her face. The more she tried to think about events of the past year, the more confused she became.

'No!' she cried aloud, reaching for a tissue and dabbing at her eyes. Andrew had assured her the Geneva trip was purely Gina's idea – Paul had taken no part in it.

Now she wasn't so sure. Spying the complimentary basket of travel-sized St Claire products in front of her, she picked it up and threw it across the room in the direction of a champagne bottle. 'You and your damned clever ideas, Paul Hadley, how I wish I'd never met you!'

Unzipping her dress, Jenny noticed a bottle of bath gel wedged precariously between two champagne flutes. Walking over to retrieve it, she dislodged a gift card edged in Sinclair colours.

Smiling ruefully, she read her brother's message, written earlier in the day.

'Jennifer, Let's drink to the House of St Claire and a wonderful year. Many thanks for all your help, not only with Sinclair's but also you know what. Enjoy the evening. Love, Andrew. '

How typical of Andrew, Jenny thought bitterly, and how simple it was. Just send you sister a bottle of champagne to ease your guilty conscience. But would Mary be won over so easily? If Mary hadn't suspected until this evening the full extent of Andrew's affair, she would certainly know by now.

'Poor Mary,' murmured Jenny, struggling with the champagne cork. She filled her glass to the brim and returned to the dressing table with the bottle. 'Here's to you, Jennifer Sinclair,' she said, eyeing her reflection, 'what was it your dear brother wrote on his card...? "A wonderful year"!'

Had it been a wonderful year? It certainly should have been; it had often seemed that way as they went from store to store. In fact, at every stop the House of St Claire was received with high acclaim, and Paul's name greeted with glowing accolades.

'And here's to you, *Mr Paul Hadley...*' she said, draining her glass and pausing to refill it, 'who would have guessed that you could be so cruel?'

*

In his inebriated state, Alistair was certain of Jenny's return. Paul however, was of a different opinion. He'd seen Jenny approach Stevie, witnessed their brief conversation, and watched her leave the banqueting suite. Furious with Alistair for coming out with such a comment, he was even angrier with himself for not denying it. What made it worse was that he couldn't ever recall Alistair describing Jenny as 'a soft touch'.

Paul raked his fingers through his hair. Knowing Alistair's reputation, it was possible, but even if he had said it, last January he'd been at such a low ebb in his life and since then… Since then, Paul told himself, his life had been transformed. Problems with Gina apart, he'd not only met Jenny, but also had been partly responsible for the House of St Claire's inception. With a vastly improved work situation and his two precious daughters settled at school, there'd been no need to dwell in the past.

Alistair wandered off drunkenly in search of more wine, leaving Paul with only one thought in mind. He must find Jenny and he must find her quickly. He had to explain – that's if she would listen, and also apologize for any offence caused. With firm resolve he placed his glass on the table and stood up. There had been no ulterior motive behind his friendship with Jenny. Surely she would see that?

'Stevie, where's Jenny? It's imperative that I speak to her.' Paul, looking tired and drawn, waited for a reply.

Tracing her finger in the spilt sugar, Stevie deliberated for several moments. Jenny might have said, 'Tell Alistair to go to hell,' there'd been no mention of Paul. Nevertheless, she must err on the side of caution. After all, Jenny was her boss.

'Stevie, please!' Paul urged. 'I must speak to her. There's been a terrible misunderstanding. If it's not resolved tonight then… it may all be too late.'

Moved by the desperation in his voice, Stevie motioned Paul to sit by her side. She was getting a crick in her neck looking up at him and she didn't want to shout. Besides, Alistair, having procured yet another bottle of wine, was searching for a drinking partner.

'Oh, no!' Paul groaned. 'Not him again! This is all *his* fault. Alistair and his big mouth!'

'He's got big feet too,' Stevie said with a smile, recalling the incident with her wheelchair.

'Hmm. As I don't think you'll be able to get away with that twice, will you *please* tell me where I can find Jenny?'

Stevie knew she had to act quickly. To her dismay Alistair had already spotted Paul and was weaving his way across the floor. Without explanation she dropped her handbag and watched bemused as the contents scattered at Paul's feet.

'It's more than my job's worth to give you Jenny's room number,' she said furtively 'but as *her* room is *next* to mine – when I do see her I'll tell her you're anxious to speak to her.'

Giving Paul a knowing look, she continued, 'Before you go, do you think you could help me with my bag and just check to see if my room key is still there? As Jenny very kindly booked me a room on the ground floor - next to the fire escape, in case of emergencies, I don't want to disturb her when I go trundling past, do I?'

Paul frowned. What was wrong with Stevie? Why did she keep looking first at him and then at her open handbag? He gave a broad grin. The penny had dropped at last, or at least the key fob had… right into his hand. No, Stevie couldn't possibly give him Jenny's room number, but she could give him her own! And twice she'd already mentioned Jenny was in the room next door!

'Stevie, you're an angel,' Paul said, kissing her on the cheek. He tucked the key back in her handbag and murmured, 'Wish me luck!'

'That's right, I'm an angel on wheels, and I wish you all the luck in the world, Paul. Now, where's that Alistair Jennings? Let's see if he's ready for a second onslaught from my wheels.'

Paul didn't wait to find out; he was already setting off for the ground floor bedrooms in the adjoining annexe.

*

In her room at the far end of the corridor, Jenny sat with unfocused eyes, a half-empty bottle of champagne by her side and a scattering of St Claire products at her feet. In the street outside a car horn tooted noisily. She rose and walked to the window.

Late-night revellers from the Sinclair dance waved and shouted their farewells to each other. Glad that someone had enjoyed themselves, Jenny closed the curtains and, catching sight of her reflection, discovered she not only felt awful, she looked awful too.

Slumped on the dressing table stool, she tugged first at her hair and then at her unzipped dress, shaking it free from her shoulder. Forcing her mouth into a sultry pout, she frowned. There was something about her newly tousled appearance that just wasn't right.

'No, Jennifer, you just haven't got it. You'll have to try harder than that, if you want to emulate Gina Hadley!'

With a wistful sigh, she reached for Andrew's card. 'A wonderful year,' she repeated. 'Hmph!' Andrew might have thought so, but from her own point of view it had been extremely tiring. Her pale, wan face and eyes, red from her tears and heavy with exhaustion, bore witness to the fact. Unlike Andrew, she hadn't even had a holiday this year... but, she brightened, she did at least have the remains of his champagne!

'That's it! That's just what I need. Another glass of champagne, and perhaps some colour in my cheeks.'

Having re-filled her glass, Jenny tipped out the contents of her make-up bag. Only last week, when she'd treated herself to her usual beauty products, hadn't she been given a free gift bag containing a bright red lipstick and black mascara? Humming the tune of 'Woman in Red' while clumsily applying several coats of lipstick and mascara, she was startled by a knock at the door.

'Jenny, it's Paul,' a muffled voice pleaded. ' *Please*, I must talk to you.'

' *No!* ' she called back, moving to the door. 'Go away! Go home to your wife, Paul. Compare notes on how you've made complete and utter fools of the Sinclairs.'

'Jenny! It isn't like that. You have to let me explain! If working together on the House of St Claire means anything to you – anything at all – then you must let me in.'

Spying the remains of the champagne, Jenny gave a curious smile. Yes, the House of St Claire. Why not invite Paul to join her in a toast to its success and her stupidity?

Aghast at her appearance, when she eventually let him in Paul remained rooted to the spot. It was only when he heard footsteps echoing at the far end of the corridor that he found his voice and stepped across the threshold.

'Jenny! What have you been doing to yourself?'

Ignoring his question and closing the door behind him, she walked unsteadily towards the champagne and waved the bottle in front of him. 'Here you are, you see, you're just in time for a drink.'

Watching her fetch the empty glass and fill it to the brim, Paul could only stare in amazement.

'Oops! It's a little bit full,' Jenny giggled, passing over the champagne, 'but you don't mind, do you? The Hadley's believe in doing things to excess. Cheers!'

'Jenny, please! This isn't you at all. Why are you behaving like this?'

'Behaving like what?' she said, and grabbed at the remains of her own drink before slumping down on the bed and kicking off her shoes.

Taking in her unusual state of disarray, her tousled hair, clumsily applied lipstick and smudged mascara, Paul shook his head sadly. Any moment now, her dress was in danger of slipping even further, exposing even more of her underwear, and should she really be drinking any more champagne?'

'Be careful of your dress!' he warned, as Jenny slipped sideways, spilling the contents of her glass on the bed's satin throw. Hurriedly reaching for a box of tissues, Paul passed them in her direction, only to have Jenny push them away.

'I don't need them and I don't need my dress either because I'm going to bed. Besides, as you probably don't like my dress, then it really doesn't matter if I take it off...'

Paul moved slowly towards her. 'Jenny... I think it's a beautiful dress...'

'No, you don't! For a start the neckline's not low enough, is it? As for the colour, don't you think it's boring, shouldn't it be red and shouldn't it be split to the thighs? So saying, Jenny hitched the hem of her dress well above her knees and dropped the bodice to reveal her new set of black silk lingerie.

Stunned, Paul took her firmly by the shoulders.

'Stop it! Jenny, stop this! You don't know what you're doing!'

Struggling against him, she fell back on to the bed where she lay quiet and still against the pillows. Paul sat down beside her and with trembling fingers raised the bodice back into place. Aware of her turning on her side, he buried his head in his hands. This was all his fault, he thought sorrowfully – he had reduced her to this.

In desperation, Paul reached for his still full glass and swallowed deeply. Instinct told him he should leave now, before the situation got out of hand. But how could he leave her when she wasn't in a fit state to be left?

Feeling a hand on his arm, Paul watched in silence as Jenny took his glass, drank the remainder, and then slipped seductively out of her dress.

'Come along,' she whispered, holding out her arms. 'Isn't this what you want, Paul? I'm a real soft touch, you know. Why don't you give me your hand, then you can feel for yourself. You don't really want to go home to your wife, do you? Won't I do for tonight? Just think you can tell Gina you made it a Sinclair double!'

Mention of Gina caused Paul to snap, and grabbing Jenny by the shoulders he shook her angrily. 'Stop it, do you hear! Gina might act like a whore, but I will *not* have you behaving like one! For your information I have *never* thought you a soft touch. I can't even remember Alistair saying it in the first place - that's if he ever did, but if you'd rather believe him than me…'

Rising dejectedly from the bed Paul walked towards the door. 'You're right, Jenny, I do want you… but not like this. I want you because I love you, but you probably won't believe that either. In which case, I'd better leave…'

Reaching for the door handle, Paul heard a muffled cry behind him. Turning, he saw her face filled with tears.

'Please don't go,' she sobbed. 'I don't want you to leave. I'm so sorry… but Gina and Andrew and then Alistair….'

'Hush,' he whispered, hurrying back to take her in his arms. 'It's all right. Everything will be all right, you'll see.'

*

Long before dawn broke through the heavy December darkness, Paul eased himself from the armchair and fumbled for his jacket. From the dim glow of the bedside lamp he watched Jenny sleeping peacefully, her tears long since dry and all trace of the vulgar make-up gone. Cradling her in his arms earlier, she could have been a child; then he'd wanted nothing more than to console her and hold her protectively in his arms until she fell asleep.

As she slept, Paul studied the dim outline of their surroundings. Jenny's dress lay in a heap on the floor amidst a scattering of St Claire toiletries. There was even an empty champagne bottle. Shifting uneasily, he wondered how he could leave without disturbing her.

Jenny stirred. The room felt suddenly cold and her head was beginning to throb. Shivering, she puzzled why she was on the bed, covered by only a throw, and not between the duvet where it would be cosy and warm. And why was she still in her underclothes? She would never sleep in her underwear and certainly not her expensive new black silk.

'I'm cold,' she murmured, sensing another's presence, and feeling a strong pair of arms lift her gently beneath the covers, urged softly, 'Please stay, please stay and keep me warm... Cameron...'

Saying nothing, Paul held her in his arms. If Jenny's thoughts were of her ex-fiancé, then she must be thinking she was with Cameron. Kissing her gently and caressing her face and hair, he realized it would be oh, so easy to pretend he was Cameron, especially as he wanted her so much.

Angry with himself for even thinking this way, Paul moved to the edge of the bed, but felt a restraining hand on his shoulder. A whispered voice pleaded with him, 'Don't leave me.'

'Jenny, I really shouldn't stay... it's not Cameron, it's Paul.'

'I know... and it's because you're not Cameron that I want you to stay. Cameron was so... he said such cruel things...' Stifling a sob, Jenny reached out and drew him into her arms.

After weeks of longing, and the thought of holding her close all too much, Paul undressed and slipped into the bed beside her.

CHAPTER TWENTY FIVE

Christmas lunch at Conasg House was a sombre affair. In true matriarchal fashion, Morag took her place at the head of the table. She surveyed each member of the family: Mary, looking deeply unhappy, sat next to her subdued husband; Catriona and Iain were casting each other furtive glances and Jenny was looking decidedly tired and strained. Only Fiona remained unchanged.

Andrew in turn regarded his mother fearfully, expecting her at any moment to raise the subject of the dance. So far she'd said nothing, which was strange. Usually she and Tandy would spend hours having a post-dinner-dance discussion. They would then praise or criticize everything from the food, flowers and table settings, to the band and even the clothes people had worn. It was a standing family joke. Morag and Tandy were like hawk and mouse on such occasions, vying with each other in their opinions.

No one need wonder what they'd thought of Gina's dress. Their expressions alone had made that clear. And, prior to her discovery of her husband's infidelity, even Mary had voiced her thoughts openly while declaring her sympathy for Paul.

'That poor man,' she'd repeated over and over again, 'and those poor children of his. I'm so glad Fiona suggested we take them with us to the pantomime, Andrew. Can you imagine what it's like having a mother like that!'

At the time, and choosing not to imagine, Andrew had simply shaken his head and taken a deep gulp of wine.

On Christmas Eve, however, Mary had taken a less than benevolent view towards Cele and Emily when Fiona raised the subject of the pantomime.

With the family preparing to go to church, it was a wonder the whole household hadn't heard Mary and Andrew arguing. Only the celebration of Midnight Mass had drawn a veil over hostilities. Even now, with the natural flow of conversation resuming, Andrew still felt uneasy.

Fiona meanwhile, chatted merrily away to her grandmother and aunt, reminiscing about her chicken 'spots' and their summer picnics. It was inevitable therefore that the names of Celestina and Emily – and even Paul, should crop up time and time again.

At the mere mention of his name Jenny felt herself blush and reached for a glass of water. Since that fateful night of the dance she'd been unable to face him, not even to hand over the girls' dresses. She'd made some excuse to Stevie and left them with a note in her office.

Puzzled, Stevie had simply followed instructions and the dresses were duly handed over. In return Paul (also looking decidedly subdued) left a small package for Jenny which as yet remained unopened in her room upstairs. Anxious to change the subject she thought asking Fiona about the forthcoming pantomime was a safer option.

Fiona's eyes widened in anticipation and in one breath she announced, 'It's going to be Cinderella and she has a wicked stepmother and a fairy godmother and goes to a ball and wears a pretty dress. There's also a glass slipper and a handsome prince and I'm going to wear a pretty dress too... only mine is that lovely green like Auntie Jenny's and Cele and Emily's dresses are dark blue like the sky at night; I 'spect Cinderella's dress will be white or gold.'

'Not red, then?' Iain asked sarcastically, joining in the conversation. From beneath the table Catriona kicked his ankle hard. Mary and Andrew glared in his direction and sat, daggers drawn.

'No, of course not, silly! Red's a horrid colour!'

Glaring at her brother, who was pulling a face at her, Fiona continued angrily. 'Only nasty step-mothers wear red, or sometimes wicked witches with frizzly black hair and big red mouths.'

'Sounds like someone we know,' muttered Iain beneath his breath, this time keeping his ankles well out of reach.

'But I wear red sometimes, Fiona, particularly at Christmas. You've always liked my red Paisley shawl,' Mary reminded her youngest daughter.

'Yes, but you're different, you're a kind mummy and you love me.'

With all eyes directed on Fiona, Mary produced a lace-trimmed handkerchief from her pocket and blew her nose. Even the stoic Morag gulped back a tear.

Aware of her new-found attention, Fiona addressed her audience. 'My mummy's a nice mummy, she lets me have my friends to tea and we're all going to the pantomime! But I can't go to Cele and Emily's house 'cos their mummy's a whore and anyway,' sighed Fiona, 'she's gone away again.' Puzzled, Fiona turned to face her grandmother. 'What is a whore, Grannie, is it a type of horse?'

'*Fiona!*' gasped Mary. 'Go and wash your mouth out with soap and water this instant!'

While Iain refrained from saying, *well, it is something you mount*, Fiona stared at her mother in disbelief; her lovely mummy – who only moments ago she'd described as loving and kind. Her eyes welled with tears as she climbed down from the table and made to leave the room.

'Just a moment,' said Morag, holding out a hand to her granddaughter. 'Now, Fiona, you come and sit on Grannie's knee and tell me all about it. I expect there's been a wee bit of a misunderstanding here, that's all.'

'L-last night, I heard Daddy talking to Mummy about fetching Cele and Emily for the pantomime,' Fiona began through tear-filled sobs. 'W-when I asked if I could go with him, Mummy said no, but she did say they could come back here for tea after Cinderella.'

Here, Fiona looked at her mother, wondering if it was safe to continue. 'Then... much later, I heard Mummy and Daddy shouting. They thought I was in bed, but I listened at the door and Mummy said she didn't want me going with Daddy to see his whore. I *only* wondered what it was Grannie, I didn't know it was rude.'

'Goodness!' declared Tandy. 'Is that the time? If we don't all hurry away to the drawing room, we shall miss the Queen's speech. Shall I go and switch on the television?'

Andrew coughed and wiped his scarlet face with his napkin before placing it on the table, while Mary sat folding and unfolding hers on her lap.

'What a good idea,' replied Morag, thankful for the diversion. 'We mustn't forget Her Majesty. Fiona, be a good girl. Run along and put Grannie's footstool in front of her chair, will you, dear?'

Fiona hesitated, she was still thinking about her mother's angry outburst. 'It's all right, dear, I'm sure Mummy didn't mean what she said about the soap and water. Let's just say what you overheard wasn't very polite and it's best not to say it ever again.' So saying, Morag left the dining room without uttering another word and the rest of the family followed in silent procession.

Boxing Day, unlike Christmas day, began in a more relaxed fashion. Jenny woke to the smell of kippers and Fiona bouncing all over the bed.

'Daddy says you're a lazybones, Auntie Jennie. He was up ages ago and has even had his breakfast.'

'I know, I can smell it. How your father can eat kippers for breakfast never ceases to amaze me. Is everyone up, then?'

'Everyone 'cept Iain. He wasn't very nice when I tried to wake him up.' Fiona turned to the door for fear of being overheard. 'He even said something rude,' she whispered softly, 'not the same thing I heard Mummy say, but I don't think Grannie would like it.'

Jenny, amused by her niece's wide-eyed innocence, laughed good-naturedly.

'Well... I expect Iain didn't take kindly to being bounced upon, like Tigger from Winnie the Pooh. Now, perhaps you can tell me what's for breakfast - apart from kippers - and also what everyone is planning to do today?'

'Mummy and Daddy are going for a walk. Miss Tandy's going to teach Catriona how to crochet, so I thought I'd go with you and Grannie to the grave.'

It had been Morag's suggestion to visit William Sinclair's grave, following their return to Conasg House after Midnight Mass. 'We'll slip out quietly on Boxing Day morning,' she'd said, unaware that they'd have Fiona for company.

Jenny and Morag stood each with their thoughts, in silent contemplation, while a cold wind stirred wayward tufts of grass spared from the final autumn mowing. Fiona, sensing the solemnity of the occasion, remained at the far end of the churchyard searching for treasures. On a recent visit, when she'd found a skeleton of a leaf, Hamish had shown her how to press it between the pages of an old gardening book.

'The wee lassie has come back with her own skeleton from the churchyard!' Hamish had announced with a chuckle. Tandy, who'd quickly dispensed him from her kitchen with a broom, was unable to share his macabre sense of humour.

Watched by Morag, Jenny placed three freshly picked sprigs on her father's grave: one each of gorse, purple heather and rosemary. The rosemary from the herb garden at Conasg was for remembrance. The heather and the solitary sprig of gorse she'd found in a secluded spot were from the amenity land close by. When her father was alive they'd often walked there, arm in arm together.

Jenny felt a pang of guilt and remorse. Until she met Paul, the only association with the yellow gorse was her father. Now, touching the golden-yellow flowers, she kept seeing Paul's face. The face that had been so full of enthusiasm, when he'd first shown her the beautifully detailed emblem for the House of St Claire.

Perceiving Jenny's desire to be alone, Morag joined Fiona on the main footpath. Kneeling by the headstone, Jenny traced the writing with her finger. 'Oh, Father, if only you hadn't died when you did, if only you hadn't been taken from us. I need you to help me... will you... can you?'

Shutting her eyes, she tried to visualize the last time she'd seen her father, remembering how he'd waved from the window as she'd reversed her car towards Conasg's main gates. Had he known then that he was so close to leaving them... so close to his final breath? Through a haze of tears, the picture became blurred and a distant squeal of delight from Fiona caused the memory to fade completely. Tiny footsteps sounded on gravel and a solitary tear falling on the gorse glinted in the wintry sunlight.

'Look! Auntie Jenny, look, I've found a lucky stone.'

Fiona's face was radiant. She held up her latest treasure - a small stone with a hole in it.

'I'm sorry,' said Morag breathlessly, following her in pursuit. 'I tried to stop her interrupting your special time with your father. She was a bit too quick for me today, I'm afraid. I must be getting old.'

'Nonsense, Mother! You're not getting old – why you've more energy than most of us put together.'

'By most of us, I take it you're not including Iain. I sincerely hope that boy has shifted from his bed.'

Jenny laughed. 'No, I'm not including Iain. Let's hope he has made a move by now, either that or been driven from it by Miss Tandy's singing and the Hoover!'

Turning to take Morag by the arm, Jenny became filled with concern. Had she just imagined it or was her mother looking unusually tired? There was however, nothing wrong with her eyesight. Even from the far end of the churchyard she'd not missed Jenny's *conversation* with her father.

Fiona reverted to her earlier habit of running round them in circles.

'A lucky stone, a lucky stone,' she sang, opening her fingers slowly and peering into the palm of her hand. 'Grannie... do you think this is like the stone Coinneach Oddar found?'

'Gracious, child! What a memory you have. Fancy you remembering the Brahan Seer.'

Puzzled, Jenny enquired. 'Who or what is the Brahan Seer. I don't recall you mentioning that before.'

'Coinneach Oddar,' Morag explained. 'He lived in the seventeenth century and was famous for his Highland prophecies. Folks say he fell asleep on a hillside and when he woke up he was clutching a stone with a hole in it.'

'A stone just like mine?' Fiona broke in, holding hers up to the sky.

'And like Coinneach Oddar, can you see the truth and the future in your stone?' asked Morag, her voice gently teasing.

'No,' Fiona said sadly, 'but I can see the sun. Still,' she said after a pause, 'I 'spect that's 'cos this stone is special too. You can't see the future but you can wish for it!' Cheered by her own response, she darted off along the footpath, leaving mother and daughter to continue arm in arm.

Hearing Fiona chattering away merrily to herself, Jenny smiled fondly.

'Talk about old head on young shoulders. No doubt she's making her own wishes for the future.'

'I expect so,' acknowledged Morag with a deep sigh, 'and what would you wish for the future, Jennifer, my dear?'

Completely taken aback, Jenny became flustered and shrugged her shoulders.

'At this precise moment, Mother, I don't honestly know.'

Returning to Conasg in a pensive mood, they saw Mary and Andrew walking ahead of them. Hand in hand they appeared deep in conversation.

'Thank heavens for that,' murmured Morag. 'Well, that's one of my wishes granted. Fiona's stone must be lucky after all!'

In the hallway Tandy stood waiting to greet them and take their coats. I'm glad you're all safely home,' she said. 'They say we're in for some awful weather. Aye, the weather is about to change and we're in for some snow. In fact, I've just heard on the radio there's been a dreadful avalanche.'

'Not here in Scotland?' Jenny asked, already dreading the drive home.

'Och, no. I think that nice young man on the radio said the Italian Alps.'

*

Not wishing to be bounced on again by Fiona, Jenny made a point of rising early next morning. She knew even before drawing back the curtains that it would be as Miss Tandy predicted. There was a perfect stillness about the landscape. A stillness only associated with heavy falls of snow. Ben Cruachan, completely enveloped in a mantle of white, was like a scene from *The Snow Queen*. Perhaps later, to give Mary and Andrew more time alone together, she would read Fiona the story of Kay and Gerda.

Before then no doubt would be the mandatory building of a snowman. Even Iain would get up for that if it meant being able to bombard his sisters with snowballs. That could only happen, however, after the ceremonial placing of Hamish's old gardening hat, two pieces of coal, a carrot and a row of small pebbles. The latter, far better for the snowman's mouth than last year's donation of Hamish's old set of false teeth!

'In that case,' Jenny told herself, imitating Flora Tandy, 'you'd best be getting a decent breakfast inside you, Miss Jennifer!' and she determined to eat hers before the dreadful smell of kippers pervaded the entire house.

Tying back the curtains, she heard whistling in the drive and looked down to see the paper boy struggling through the snow back to his bike, propped against heavy wrought iron gates. Today there'd been no cycling up to the impressive oak front door and aiming at the letterbox!

Morag would be pleased; she hated newspapers with chewed up edges.

In the kitchen, alone and ashen-faced, Flora Tandy stood stirring the porridge. 'Och, Miss Jennifer,' she cried, 'there's been a terrible accident.' She pointed to the front page of the newspaper. 'Those poor wee lassies... it is their mother, isn't it?'

'Wee lassies, Miss Tandy? I'm afraid I don't understand.'

'Fiona's friends. Mr Hadley's wife? Isn't Dintino her professional name?'

Jenny sat down slowly on the hard kitchen stool and picked up the paper. The stark black headline – 'THEY WERE WARNED NOT TO GO!' – glared out at her. '*Yet another party of skiers refusing to heed avalanche warnings chose to ski off-piste...*' ran the story.

Hurriedly scanning the paragraphs searching for Gina's name, Jenny was sure there had to be a mistake. The accident had happened in the Italian Alps and although Gina was Italian, there must be other Italians with the same surname. Would she really have left her children at Christmas? Fiona had been quite vocal in talking about '*nasty mummies*' but could Gina be that cruel?

Jenny's eyes rested on the third paragraph '... *a party of eight experienced skiers... three killed, two injured and three still missing... a search party out looking for survivors...* 'Miss Tandy had not been mistaken. Gina, described as model and socialite, was one of the two skiers found injured and airlifted to hospital.

'Oh, thank God, she's been found,' Jenny whispered.

Flora Tandy, surprised at such benevolence, continued stirring the porridge.

Running along the hallway to the study, the only thought in Jenny's mind was to ring Paul. He would need help... and if she left straight away... It was only when she heard the dialling tone she was reminded of the fact they hadn't seen each other since that fateful night of the dance.

Jenny shuddered at the memory. She'd not only drunk too much, but also her behaviour had been completely out of character. Waking alone the next morning, recalling only too well what had happened... she also remembered hearing Paul say that he loved her. Was that true – or was it simply the champagne and their uncontrollable passion in the heat of the moment?

In the gloom of the ice-cold study with its heavy chenille curtains still drawn against the chill of early morning, Jenny felt a wave of panic sweep over her. What would she say to Paul – even if he did pick up the phone... wouldn't it be better to hang up instead?

Numbed by shock and cold and transfixed by a large painting of Princes Street hanging above the fireplace, Jenny discerned an exasperated voice at the end of the line.

'Hello! Hello?'

Wanting to say so much, all that came out was a feeble, 'Paul... it's me, I've just seen the papers. I was wondering...'

'Jenny? Thank God it's someone I know! I've been inundated with phone calls from Gina's friends and the Press. I even considered taking the phone of the hook, but in case the hospital...'

'Is there any news from Italy?'

'None, other that she's still in intensive care.'

From down the line Jenny heard the ring of a doorbell and a man's muffled voice.

'Jenny,' Paul continued, his voice desperate, 'I'm so sorry, I have to go... it's the taxi.'

'The taxi?'

'The taxi to take me to the airport. I managed to get a seat on the next plane to Milan. I didn't feel like driving myself in all this snow.'

Reminded of the weather, Jenny pulled back the study curtains. The brilliant white dazzled her eyes. Her reason for ringing was to offer help – to leave immediately, how could she in such conditions?

'I was wondering if you needed any help, but as I'm at Conasg and there's so much snow... it could take me ages to get to Edinburgh.'

'It's kind of you Jenny and if you could give Helen a ring, I'm sure she'd appreciate it. The girls are staying with her until I get back.'

A distant car horn appeared to be tooting impatiently. 'What? Oh, yes. All right,' she replied, 'I'll ring Helen, have a... safe trip.' She'd stopped herself just in time from saying the word *good*. In current circumstances it seemed highly inappropriate. 'And Paul – thank you for the present.'

Replacing the receiver, Jenny looked up to see Morag wrapped in layers of thermals and woollens. She seemed surprised to find her daughter in the study so early in the morning.

'I'm sorry, my dear. I didn't mean to startle you. I merely wanted to sort through some paperwork for Andrew to take back to the office.'

Morag walked towards the desk, where she placed a bulky pile of papers before fastening the curtains with their heavy gold tassels.

'Do you feel all right, Jennifer? You look quite pale. Perhaps it's the cold, let me switch on the fire.' Stooping low, Morag flicked the switch on an ancient brown socket and a thin, feeble red twist of heat shone dimly from the hearth.

'It's not the cold, Mother, its shock. I've just been on the phone to Paul Hadley. His wife was one of the survivors in yesterday's avalanche in the Alps. I can't stop thinking about Emily and Cele.'

Morag was tight-lipped, as if waiting for further information. 'Well...' she said tersely, 'and what is the situation regarding Miss Dintino?'

'She's in intensive care,' Jenny began, thinking it strange how Morag almost refused to acknowledge Gina as Paul's wife. 'Paul's on his way to the airport to catch a flight to Milan and the girls are with his neighbour.'

'I see. So I suppose as a Christian I should be sorry for the woman. However, if she'd been doing her duty as a mother, *none* of this would have happened.'

Jenny presumed the emphasis on the word 'none' also included Andrew and Gina's affair. Please God her mother wasn't going to ask *her* for the all the sordid details!

Saved by a discreet tapping on the study door, Jenny discerned the welcome smell of coffee. Tandy stood on the threshold, carrying a tray. 'I thought you could both do with this, shall I leave it on the desk? And... Miss Jennifer, Hamish said to tell you they are clearing the road. It should be open again in a couple of hours.'

Jennifer fixed her with a grateful smile. 'Thank you, Miss Tandy.'

Moments later she passed her mother a cup of coffee and added quietly, 'If you don't mind, I'd rather leave today instead of tomorrow. In the meantime... can I suggest you hide all the newspapers from Andrew and Mary? Tell them they haven't arrived yet because of the snow. They'll find out sooner or later of course...'

Nodding in understanding, Morag made her way quickly to the

kitchen to issue instructions to her companion. 'And you'd best make sure you've none of your silly magazines lying around either. They always appear to document Miss Dintino's exploits in words and pictures!'

Flora Tandy looked up, horror struck. Until today she'd no idea Morag knew of her weakness for such publications. Much as she enjoyed Morag's company and living at Conasg, the magazines she favoured, with their celebrity interviews and photos of exotic locations and lifestyles, were her only form of escapism. Not for those beautiful suntanned creatures was there one bar of an electric fire and plain arrowroot biscuits!

Tandy frowned, watching Morag turn on her heels and head back to the study. How did Morag know about these magazines anyway? Not only that, how did she know that Gina had featured so prominently... unless of course she'd read them too?

Alone in her room Jenny packed her suitcase and gathered together the smaller items left on the dressing table. Only one thing remained - the present from Paul. The present she'd thanked him for, yet still hadn't opened. For that she felt guilty. Only once during Christmas did she get as far as untying the simple gold ribbon, then courage had failed her.

Unlike Pandora, Jenny was afraid, not because of its hidden contents but because it served only to remind her of the moments spent in his embrace; moments when humiliation and anger had turned to a shared and almost desperate entwining of their two naked bodies. Later, on that same fateful morning, unable to respond to Paul's gentle questioning, she'd listened to his murmured apologies, let him depart without explanation, and shed silent tears.

Even now, with fresh tears pricking her eyelids, there could be no escape from her feelings. Prior to reaching the height of their passion, they'd both declared their love for each other, with Jenny saying she couldn't bear to be the other woman in his life and Paul mentioning divorce.

Divorce! It sounded so final, yet according to Paul it was what Gina wanted; what she'd demanded in fact. She was already looking forward to *la vita nuova*.

'*La vita nuova*,' Jenny repeated softly, what of Gina's new life now? How bad were her injuries? Would she be expecting Paul to care for her? She'd made so many demands on him in the past and as she was still his wife…

Jenny gave a strangled cry. Much as she loved Paul, she must try and suppress her feelings and think of something else instead.

'Think of Celestina and Emily,' she said, slipping her thumbnail beneath the Sellotape, they're the ones who need you the most… until Gina and Paul come home…'

The narrow package in Jenny's trembling fingers revealed a slim black box and a letter.

My dear Jenny

I am writing this letter as I fear – by not returning my calls – you are avoiding me.

If I've hurt you I can only apologize, but I beg you to give me a chance to explain.

After what's happened between us, we must talk. Even you must realize it's something we can't discuss on the phone. Have lunch with me, one day before Christmas, please!

If however, you feel that's impossible, then I shall try to understand. As you know my contract with Sinclair's terminates at New Year. If I don't hear from you by then, I shall assume you no longer wish to speak to me and I shall endeavour to keep out of your way – seeing Andrew if there are any outstanding problem with the House of St Claire. Please don't let things end like this. I love you, Jenny. Will you ring me?

Paul

Examining the date of the letter, she saw it had been written within days of the dance. Later, when she'd been too embarrassed to face him (or even speak to him on the phone), Stevie, angry and exasperated with her boss's feeble excuses, had wheeled herself into the office like Boadicea on her chariot. Placing the small package on Jenny's desk, she'd passed on Paul's impassioned instructions. 'He says to open it now! Don't wait until Christmas!'

Conscious that Paul's request had been ignored, Stevie turned away, trying hard to conceal her impatience and despair. As a consequence, the atmosphere throughout the day had worsened. Never had Jenny and Stevie been so hostile, and their farewells at the end of the evening so coolly polite.

CHAPTER TWENTY SIX

'Jenny! How kind of you to come; Paul was deeply touched, especially as it meant leaving your family at Christmas.' Helen Craig took Jenny's coat and led her through to the sitting room.

Pausing at the foot of the stairs, she held a finger to her lips. 'I think the girls are asleep at last. It's been a terrible time for them; you wouldn't believe the amount of people they've had ringing at their door. Those *dreadful* tabloid newspapers! Mind you, I soon got rid of them once Paul had left.'

'How is he? Have you heard from him?'

'No, not yet, my dear, which makes the waiting even worse. Celestina and Emily are like startled rabbits every time the phone rings. They didn't really want to go to bed, but I insisted. I told them you were coming and you'd read them a story. I hope you don't mind?' Helen looked in Jenny's direction. 'I gather you're very good at it. They still remember how you looked after them when they had chicken pox.'

Jenny sighed wistfully. 'Yes, I seem to have developed quite a reputation for looking after other people's children. Do you think I should go up now?'

'Let's leave them for a while, shall we? If they wake then of course you must go up. Can't break our promises, can we? Now, let me get you something to eat, you must be starving.'

Helen produced the familiar tea-trolley laden with food, but despite Helen urging her to eat, Jenny wasn't hungry. The food only stuck in her throat. Like Cele and Emily, the not knowing and waiting was all too much to bear. 'I'm sorry, Helen, I'm not really hungry, I expect I'm still recovering from eating too much at Christmas.'

'Never mind, perhaps later, when you've got over your long journey. I gather you had quite a bit of snow on the west coast. What were the roads like?'

Describing the road and weather conditions, Jenny was glad to be sitting in the warmth and comfort of Helen's sitting room. She wanted desperately to ask about Paul and Gina, but where to begin was the problem. The last time she was here Helen had spoken of Gina's latest man friend. At the time she'd been convinced Helen didn't know his identity, but had she learnt about him since? Perhaps Paul, or even Gina, had mentioned Andrew and the connection with Sinclair's?

An assortment of clocks all set at different times ticked and whirred away, creating a hypnotic effect. Jenny dozed momentarily, only to be woken by the shrill ringing of the phone. Helen leapt from her chair to pluck at the receiver.

'Hello? Paul! Thank goodness you've arrived safely. Yes, the girls are fine. They're sleeping at the moment and Jenny's here too. Where are you calling from?'

There was a pause and Jenny strained to hear the one-sided conversation.

'I'm sorry, Paul, the line's so bad, I can barely hear you. Perhaps if I ring you back? Give me the number quickly in case we get cut off.' Helen reached for a pen. 'Damn!' she said looking at Jenny. 'Trust me to pick a pen that doesn't work. I don't suppose…'

Reaching into her handbag, Jenny produced Paul's present; a slender gold-nibbed fountain pen in Sinclair colours. She watched anxiously as Helen wrote down the number and redialled. He answered immediately.

Most of Helen's replies were monosyllables until she mentioned the children. 'Yes, as I said, the girls are fine, so please don't worry. They're sleeping at the moment and I also got rid of those dreadful reporters; I was only saying to Jenny… would you like a word?'

Beckoned to the phone, Jenny took the receiver, not knowing what to say. Thankfully Paul did most of the talking, explaining the situation at the hospital.

'Promise me you'll ring if there's anything I can do,' Jenny said, before replacing the receiver. Turning back to Helen, she shook her head.

'Oh, dear! Is she...?'

'No, she's still on a life support-machine but the first scan showed extensive brain damage. The result of the injuries sustained in the accident.'

'Can they do anything?'

'They're not sure. They plan to do another scan tomorrow and Paul will see the doctor. He'll try and ring about lunchtime so he can speak to Cele and Emily. It all sounds very serious.'

Helen looked towards the stairs, half-expecting movement, but there was none. 'Those poor wee scraps,' she said, 'as if they haven't had enough to contend with already.'

'Can I go up and see the girls? I promise not to wake them.'

Jenny stood in the doorway of Helen's bedroom and saw the dark, curly hair of the unwilling innkeeper's wife entwined with that that of the angelic Emily.

Cele's arms were wrapped protectively around her younger sister as they lay in the Jacobean style double bed, completely enveloped by a patchwork quilt in autumn colours.

'I always let them sleep in my bed when they stay,' whispered Helen, leading Jenny back downstairs. 'They get frightened if they're not together. When I see them curled up like that under the quilt they remind me of Babes in the Wood under a carpet of leaves.'

Jenny supposed there was a similarity, particularly with the autumn-coloured squares of fabric made from Helen's long since discarded clothes and remnants of material. She chose not to mention the other similarity that sprang to mind at the mention of Babes in the Wood (children being abandoned, following the death of their parents), or Fiona's recent naïve remark about nasty mothers leaving their children. She yawned and put a hand to her mouth.

'Och, look at you,' said Helen. 'You're fair worn out! Now I'm not going to take no for an answer. You are going to stay here tonight, Jenny Sinclair!'

'But...'

'There's to be no buts about it, and in case you're wondering, there's plenty of room in this old house, and I can lend you a nightdress. First of all though, I'm going to make us some supper. You must build up your strength for tomorrow.'

'Tomorrow?'

'Aye, I have a feeling when Paul rings he's going to be in dire need of you.'

Jenny lay in bed filled with a deep sense of foreboding. Staring at the plain wooden cross on the opposite wall, something told her she should be praying. The difficulty being, the simple act of prayer that she usually found so comforting had completely eluded her since the night of the dance.

How would Paul be needing her, and was Gina so badly injured there was no hope? There were so many unanswered questions. Heavy with sleep, Jenny closed her eyes and waited for morning.

Unlike Fiona, Cele and Emily were late sleepers and quiet risers. Jenny awoke in unfamiliar surroundings to the sound of Helen humming 'Onward Christian Soldiers' as she attacked the dusting. Every item of china, glass, wood and brass was lovingly picked up, dusted with a flourish of brightly coloured sheepskin, and replaced carefully.

'I'm determined to keep myself busy,' Helen said. 'I've a feeling we've a long wait until lunchtime.'

'Then you must let me do something,' Jenny insisted, spreading honey on to thick wholemeal toast. A vivid china orange with dark green leaves rested in the middle of the table. She found her attention drawn by its garish colours compared to the gloomy weather outside.

'There's homemade marmalade in there; the leaves form the lid and you just lift it off,' Helen instructed, dusting the ears of a china spaniel guarding the hearth.

'I'm afraid I don't much care for marmalade - unlike my brother, Andrew, who always goes for those with the thickest, darkest peel.'

The spaniel was returned to its resting place with a heavy thud. Helen said nothing, but from her tightly pursed lips, Jenny presumed that she knew all about Andrew, and what he'd recently gone for! Thinking it best not to mention Andrew again, Jenny watched as Helen rose from the hearth and moved towards the table.

'In that case,' she said, 'I'll away with this to the pantry. The girls don't like marmalade either.'

Marmalade days, Jenny thought, seeing the orange disappear into a stripped pine cupboard. There had been plenty of those recently!

Leaving the house with Helen's old-fashioned wicker basket and a shopping list, Jenny cast a cursory glimpse towards Paul's front door. There was no sign of reporters or photographers today, but how lovely it would be if the door were to open and she'd find him standing there.

The curtains, she noticed, were also still drawn. Had Helen left them that way deliberately - or would she go in once the girls were up and Jenny returned with the shopping?

Perhaps there'll be no need, Jenny thought, feeling a shiver run down her spine. In Latin countries, didn't they still keep curtains drawn in times of sorrow? Gina was, after all, Italian. There was also something else she vaguely recalled about Italian law, but for the moment it escaped her. She must concentrate on shopping for lunch instead.

Finding the shop Helen had suggested, Jenny crossed off each item on the reverse of the used envelope she'd been given. Her pen moved silently and effortlessly. This morning in panic she'd hunted for it everywhere, only to find it by her breakfast plate. She'd quite forgotten Helen had used it to write down Paul's number – how ironic.

She remembered the pen from their week in Geneva. They'd noticed it – or at least Paul had, in the window of an upmarket boutique. It was the type you used to see years ago in all the reputable stationers, now sadly replaced by plastic biros and felt tips.

'Gracious! A St Claire pen,' Paul had teased, recognizing the familiar Sinclair colours. 'Our fame must be spreading, Jenny!'

Knowing that she always used a fountain pen, she could only presume Paul had returned to the shop later when he was on his own.

Celestina and Emily sat at the breakfast table finishing off their breakfast. Helen was wiping the remains of egg yolk from Cele's chin and Emily toyed with the remaining two bread and butter soldiers on her plate.

'There you are,' said Helen with a smile, hearing the door open. 'I told you Jenny had only gone shopping for our lunch. Now will you believe me, and perhaps, Emily, you'll finish your soldiers?'

Jenny was warmed to see the girls' faces light up when she entered the kitchen. 'Perhaps those soldiers will disappear if they have this on them?' She placed a jar of bramble jelly in front of Emily, unscrewed the lid and scooped a spoonful onto her plate.

Emily beamed. 'Did you really stay the night?'

'Yes, I saw you both under your blanket of leaves and I heard Helen snore!'

The girls giggled when Jenny pretended to be Helen snoring loudly. From the kitchen sink, Helen gave her a thumbs-up sign, and gulped back a tear. It had been weeks since she'd heard the girls laugh like that.

Cele became suddenly thoughtful. 'Helen's bed isn't really made of leaves, is it?'

'No,' Jennifer replied, 'But with the heavy carved woodwork and that lovely quilt, it did remind me of the pantomime Fiona and I saw last year. It was about two children who slept under a bed of leaves…'

'Will you tell it to us?' Cele asked. 'And will you help me with my letters, please? Daddy says I should practice my "d"s and "b"s.'

Sometime later Cele produced a large sheet of b's and 'd's and Emily tried writing out her own name in large letters.

'I'm glad I have Grannie Hadley's name and not Grannie 'Tino's,' she said, concentrating hard on the curly tail of the 'y'. I don't like writing letters… drawing is best.'

Jenny passed Emily a large sheet of drawing paper and crayons and continued with her own writing. A brief note to enclose with a pretty card for her mother (and Miss Tandy) by way of thanks for Christmas, plus her apologies at leaving earlier than planned. Later, having popped upstairs to ring Stevie on her mobile, not only to avoid being overheard but also to collect her thoughts before Paul rang again, she found a few moments to copy down the text hanging beneath the wooden cross in her room.

When lunch was ready, there was no Fiona to bang the gong summoning them to the table, only Helen clapping her hands. Briskly rounding them up like stray sheep, she sent the girls off to wash their hands and eyed the array of clocks nervously. Paul had told her he'd ring at lunchtime. She only hoped for the girls' sake that he would ring after and not during.

When the phone rang Cele and Emily ran to it eagerly.

'That's right,' said Helen, 'you speak to your daddy, then let Jenny have a word while you come and help me with the dishes. I've this amazing washing up liquid that makes the most enormous bubbles.

Let's see who can make the biggest.'

Helen motioned to Jenny to close the door behind her; and watched by two curious little girls, she squeezed a vast quantity of thick green liquid into the washing up bowl.

Celestina and Emily stood wide-eyed as Helen whisked the water frantically with her hands to produce copious amounts of lather. Moments later, they watched transfixed, as she clasped thumb and forefinger together and blew hard.

Opening the door, Jenny saw both girls cupping snowball-sized bubbles. Goodness! Was it only the other day she'd seen Catriona and Iain hurling snowballs at each other? It seemed like an eternity ago. Helen looked up with questioning eyes. Jenny swallowed and shook her head.

'Your Daddy's coming home; he's asked me to meet him at the airport.'

A shower of bubbles filled the air as the girls clapped their hands and danced about the kitchen. They did not see Helen wipe away her tears.

*

From the window of the taxi, Paul stared with unseeing eyes at the heavy grey skies and swirling mists sweeping across the tarmac at Milan airport. First reports had indicated flight delays because of fog.

'Please God, let them be wrong,' he said, taking his suitcase from the puzzled driver. He couldn't bear to be parted from his children for a moment longer.

' *Signore*?'

'What? Oh…nothing. *Grazie*.'

In bewilderment the taxi driver examined the handful of euros Paul thrust into his outstretched palm. ' *Grazie Signore!*' he called, but Paul was already out of earshot, running towards the main entrance.

Relieved to be allocated a window seat and ignoring his fellow passengers, Paul closed his eyes. It was only when the plane was above cloud level and the bright rays of morning sunlight pierced his eyelids that he opened them again. In the seat in front of him an American couple were chattering excitedly about the magnificent view they could expect once they flew over the Alps.

Feeling a tremor run through his body, Paul forced himself to look from the window at the mountainous spectacle below. There, row after row of crested peaks newly dusted with snow, glowed with a rosy hue.

'Say! Just look how the sun has painted it all pink,' the American said to his travelling companion.

'Yeah, sort of welcoming... yet at the same time truly awesome,' came the reply.

'Welcoming,' thought Paul with a shudder. Had Gina found it 'welcoming'?

Shielding his eyes from the sun-dazzled peaks, he scanned the mountains and snow-fields still in shadow. Smooth and white, they reminded him of the starched cotton sheets covering Gina's body at the hospital. Momentarily trying to shut out the picture from his mind, he closed his eyes again. It was no good. The scene, like Gina's poor battered body when they had found her, was frozen.

'She was one of the lucky ones, Signor Hadley,' the junior doctor had beamed just after Paul arrived. 'They managed to find your wife within the first hour... so there is a chance.'

Later, of course, with the arrival of the neurosurgeon and the junior doctor dismissed with a flea in his ear, there was a different prognosis. Grim-faced, Paul sat amidst a tangle of machines, tubes and wires by Gina's bedside. In anguish and disbelief he'd watched both his wife and the afternoon sun fade away.

Waiting for Paul at the airport, Jenny studied the milling crowds. Her heart leapt when she saw him. For the moment at least, she would forget all about the night of the dance.

Looking haggard and drawn, Paul stood motionless at the exit barrier, while Jenny walked slowly towards him. She wasn't even sure if he'd seen her.

'Paul,' she whispered, taking his arm.

He said nothing until they reached the car park and she put her key in the ignition.

'Can we sit here for five minutes? Much as I want to see them, I don't think I'm quite ready to face the girls just yet.' He groaned softly and placed his head in his hands.

Jenny placed a reassuring hand on his arm. 'Would it help to talk about it... tell me what happened?'

'It was awful, simply awful! She looked so... all those machines, all those wires. When I first arrived some idiot said there was hope, but you only had to look at her to see...' Paul choked back a sob and reached for Jenny's hand. Then, taking a deep breath, he continued.

'She'd sustained such horrific injuries... the brain was damaged, you see. It was irreparable and the monitor line was... They told me I'd have to take the decision to switch off the machine. I couldn't do it, Jenny... not at first... and then...'

'And then?' Jenny repeated, feeling his grip on her hand even tighter.

'They showed me the results of a second scan, which only confirmed what they'd said earlier; irreparable brain damage. Not only did I agree to them switching off the machine but also I now have Gina's family accusing me of killing her.'

'Killing her! But why? How?'

'Because I gave my permission. You can in Italy, you know, as long as the brain is dead.'

Jenny bit her lip hard. It all came back to her now. The death of Ayrton Senna - the Brazilian racing driver, he'd been critically injured during the Italian Grand Prix several years ago. His family had been faced with the same agonizing decision.

'So...what happens now?'

'I go back in a couple of days to arrange the funeral and Cele and Emily must come with me. Gina's family are insisting on it, even though half of them have never seen the girls before.'

'Aren't they too young to cope with that... the funeral, I mean... plus meeting people they hardly know?'

'Of course they are but in the circumstances I don't have much choice. Not only that, I also have to tell them that Gina is dead. Whether or not they'll understand the full implications of the situation remains to be seen. They know about going to heaven when you die. As for how they'll react when they see their mother's coffin...'

'Oh, Paul, you make it sound so awful'

'I'm sorry, Jenny. That's the way I feel at the moment. Just think in a couple of months the shops will be full of Easter eggs... that's if they're not already! We'll be telling the children stories about the Easter bunny and wondering why they look so puzzled at scenes from the crucifixion. Besides...'

'Besides what?' Jenny whispered, dreading the reply.

'As Gina's parents have said they want her buried in Italy, I have a horrid feeling they're also planning to make some claim on their grandchildren. Unfortunately, my Italian isn't that brilliant but I overheard part of a conversation with Gina's mother and...'

'You don't honestly think they would do such a thing?'

Paul sighed, dejected. 'I don't know, Jenny. Quite frankly I don't know what to think anymore.'

Without warning, and filled with a deep sense of longing and desperation, Paul reached out and drew her into his arms. 'Jenny... the night of the dance... why didn't you reply to my calls?'

Not waiting for a reply, Paul kissed her firmly on the mouth and in the confined space of the car they clung to each other, both unable to speak and oblivious to the car pulling alongside. It was only when they heard a car tooting and muffled cheering from its passengers, they drew apart. In an instant Jenny switched on the ignition and they made their exit from the car park.

*

A few days later and quite by chance, Jenny found herself parked alongside the same battered Cortina. She spied a solitary ski boot wedged in the corner of the rear seat.

'Oh, well,' she remarked, eyeing the empty lager cans strewn on the car's floor. 'I expect whoever the boot belongs to will survive without it!'

The journey to the airport had been fraught. Paul looked numb and grey like the weather, while his daughters appeared totally bewildered. Travelling in torrential rain, they'd discovered there'd been an accident on the motorway holding up all the traffic. By the time they reached the airport their flight was already being called.

Jenny, desperate to find something for the girls to take on the flight if only to remember her by, left them briefly. She still couldn't come to terms with the fact that she might never see them again. Could their grandparents really fight Paul for custody? Surely they were only bluffing?

Leaving Paul to check in the luggage, she hurried towards a kiosk selling soft toys and, snatching up two rabbits with long floppy ears, fumbled in her purse for the money.

'Keep the change – or put it in the charity box,' she called to the astonished assistant and ran back to where Paul was frantically searching for her. To her dismay he and the girls were already heading for passport control. Thrusting the furry animals towards two bewildered and tired-looking faces, she turned to Paul as a man in uniform stepped forward.

'Hurry along, sir, you're holding up the queue.'

Amidst much murmuring from onlookers, Paul reached out, grabbed Jenny by the shoulders and for the second time that week kissed her full on the mouth. Then he was gone.

Numbed and with silent tears coursing down her cheeks, she watched the back of his head as the tragically forlorn trio were ushered through the barrier. A short while later, a lonely wretched figure with aching heart, watched the Alitalia plane taxi down the runway into the enveloping mist.

Clutching their new toys, Cele and Emily cried too. They didn't like airports – people always cried at airports. It was barely a year since they'd been at this airport saying goodbye to their mother and now they were on this large aeroplane flying through the clouds…

This journey, so their Daddy had explained, was to bid their mummy a last farewell. On either side of him Paul felt tiny hands reaching reassuringly for his. With a determined set of jaw, he forced a smile and closed his mind to the harrowing days that lay ahead.

CHAPTER TWENTY SEVEN

'I like your pen. It's very House of St Claire, isn't it?' Stevie was watching Jenny sign the day's correspondence.

'Thank you. I must say it does write beautifully. In case you're wondering, it was a present from Paul... the box you kept pestering me to open.' Jenny smiled and handed back the letters.

Stevie did her best to hide her disappointment. She'd been hoping the box contained jewellery, not a pen. Although she had to admit, it was a very nice one. 'Has Paul rung again?' she asked.

Jenny screwed the cap back on the pen. 'Yes, he phoned last night. He's coming back the day after tomorrow and I shall be going to meet him. He has some legal business to attend to first.'

And what about Cele and Emily... are they coming too?'

Jenny shook her head sadly. 'I don't know, he didn't say...'

'Well, I think it's disgraceful!' Stevie broke in. 'They can't take the girls away from Paul just like that... can they?'

'If you don't mind, I'd rather not think about it; the whole situation is all too depressing as it is. Let's wait and see, shall we?'

Stevie wheeled herself from the office, leaving Jenny alone with her thoughts. If Cele and Emily didn't come back, what was she going to tell Fiona? Mary had been on the phone constantly. Fiona was distraught at losing her friends. Not even the prospect of a trip to Conasg for Burn's Night celebrations consoled her.

Burn's Night! Jenny had quite forgotten all about it. What with events leading up to Christmas, not to mention the reason why Yuletide festivities had been curtailed. Now Morag was summoning them all to Conasg to let their hair down. She was planning quite a gathering.

Andrew was already complaining about going. There was too much to do in the office, he argued – meetings to organize and business trips to arrange. And with Paul away it meant an even busier workload. At least this year Mary hadn't suggested a skiing holiday.

'We must go, Andrew,' Jenny declared. 'We can't let Mother down. You know how much she loves Burn's Night at Conasg. Let's face it, Christmas wasn't exactly a roaring success.'

Andrew turned in Jenny's direction. There was no need to say more, her look said it all.

'You've heard from Paul, I expect? How did the funeral go?' Andrew mumbled the last five words. He felt duty bound to ask, but the last thing he wanted to discuss was Gina's funeral. It had been bad enough trying to evade the issue last weekend. On one side he had Fiona pestering him for news of Celestina and Emily, and on the other Mary throwing him furtive glances.

Giving the barest details of the funeral, Jenny assured Andrew that Paul had every intention to 'knuckle down to business' on his return.

'You needn't worry about Paul, he's totally committed to St Claire. I think it also helped when I told him that it was a unanimous decision on our part to renew his contract.'

His sister's words 'totally committed' reminded Andrew of his meeting with Sol Sutherland in New York. This time it was his train of thoughts that chugged into motion. Picking up Gina along the way, Andrew remembered every stop en route. It had been an exciting and perilous journey, yet deep in his heart he always feared it would end in disaster.

Studying the arrivals board, Jenny watched the letters and numbers click into place. With each passing moment they moved slowly upwards until at last she recognized Paul's flight. A surge of relief swept through her body. Like the prophets of doom, the morning papers had been full of disasters: plane crashes, earthquakes and floods. It was true what they said – everything appeared to come in threes.

Before leaving for the airport she'd emptied her bag and discovered three pieces of paper. The same pieces of paper she'd picked up while staying with Helen and the girls. Like Burn's night, they too had been forgotten. One was a drawing, the other a child's letter and the third, the text Jenny had copied using Paul's pen.

Three pieces of paper, Jenny pondered, each with three possible courses of action; to show them to Paul, to keep them until the appropriate time; or simply throw them away. The first two she'd folded neatly and put in her desk drawer, the third she put back in her handbag.

Waiting for Paul to clear passport control and customs, she studied the words of Cardinal Newman once more.

May he support us all the day long
till the shades lengthen, and the evening comes,
and the busy world is hushed,
and the fever of life is over,
and our work is done!
Then in His mercy may He give us
a safe lodging, and a holy rest,
and peace at last.

Wiping a tear from her eye, she thought perhaps she could give the text to Paul. It would be a great deal more comforting than Emily's picture of Gina, bloodied and broken in a pile of snow, or Cele's short note, ' *mummy i hop you get detter soon,* ' Poor Cele, she still needed help with her 'b's and 'd's.

From out of nowhere two floppy-eared rabbits dropped into Jenny's lap. She looked up in surprise as Cele and Emily hugged her tightly and warm tears fell on shiny button eyes and pink felt noses.

'How? What happened?' she gasped as Paul lifted her from her seat and into his arms.

Driving from the airport with the girls asleep in the back of the car, Jenny asked him again. 'I still can't believe it. What happened, I thought you said...? Didn't Gina's family make any claim on the girls after all?'

Paul gave a sardonic smile. 'Oh, yes, they tried very hard at first, initially making a huge fuss of the girls, pulling them this way and that, but it was all a ploy. They saw it as a way of trying to extract more money out of me... as if Gina didn't take enough!'

Paul thought bitterly of the night he'd taken Gina home from the Sinclair dance; having left his wallet for her on the mantelpiece, he hadn't expected to find on his return that she'd taken every penny and even emptied Cele and Emily's money boxes.

Jenny looked in her rear view mirror, 'Poor things, no wonder they're so exhausted.'

Turning to check for himself, Paul smiled to see the girls and their rabbits securely belted in together. 'You know, I don't think they slept the whole time we were away. There was always so much noise. Gina's parents' flat was on the corner of a busy street and they're such an excitable family. I'm convinced Cele and Emily thought they were arguing all the time.'

'Poor Gina,' Jenny said softly, 'no wonder she wanted to get away from it all in the first place.'

Paul hesitated. 'You're very forgiving, Jenny... especially after all the pain Gina caused your family.'

'Perhaps... but the dead can't defend themselves, can they? Anyway, Mary and Andrew appear to have called a truce. Christmas, as you can imagine, was somewhat strained and thankfully they've decided against taking a skiing holiday this year. We've all been summoned to Conasg instead…'

To deflect attention away from Gina when the girls eventually stirred, Jenny told Paul of her mother's plans for Burn's night. He found it hard to think of Morag Sinclair letting her hair down.

He'd met her only briefly of course, and then not in the most auspicious of circumstances.

'Don't be fooled by her outwardly fragile appearance,' Jenny told him as she pulled up outside the familiar Victorian house. 'There's great strength and determination in that steely gaze of Mother's – in case you hadn't noticed.'

Paul nodded, he certainly had noticed on the night of the dance. He also hoped never to cross swords with Morag Sinclair!

'Won't you come in for coffee, Jenny? I know the girls would love to tell you about…'

Jenny hesitated, torn between her heart and work. She wanted so much to stay, on the other hand Helen was also waiting…

'If you don't mind, Paul, I'd better get back to the office. Besides, Helen's is anxious to welcome you home. She's been making casseroles and pies for the past twenty-four hours!'

'Then… will you have lunch with me one day? I think we've some unfinished business to discuss.'

Jenny felt herself go both hot and cold at the thought. By 'business' she sensed Paul was *not* talking about his renewed contract. 'Yes, of course,' she said hastily, 'but it will have to be after Burn's night, I'm afraid. In the meantime, I'm sure we'll see each other at the office. I warn you, Andrew has heaps of work already lined up, but don't let him bully you!'

Kissing both girls goodbye, she nodded in the direction of the garden path and smiled. Helen Craig came running towards them with arms outstretched, a welcoming splash of colour in an otherwise dreary day.

CHAPTER TWENTY EIGHT

At Conasg House, Andrew sat at the breakfast table removing bones from his kipper with surgical precision. Tandy appeared with fresh toast and scanned the room for Jenny.

'Oh! Is Miss Jennifer still not down for breakfast? I thought I heard her on the landing. I know she doesn't much care for kippers so I was wondering about scrambled eggs... Fiona dear, will you go and ask your Aunt Jennifer...?'

Fiona was gone in a flash, while Morag sat contentedly reading the morning paper. The previous evening's celebrations had gone exceedingly well. She couldn't have wished for a better Burn's Night supper, and Alex McAllister had brought with him a superb malt whisky. She would look forward to this evening's 'wee dram' with pleasure.

'Boo!' shouted Fiona on entering Jenny's bedroom, and was disappointed to find the bed empty. Hearing a noise in the nearby bathroom, she went to investigate, peeped in and promptly ran downstairs.

'Auntie Jen's being sick and it looks horrid. Yuk!'

'Fiona!' Mary looked up from where she was spreading butter thickly on to her toast. 'Really, dear, do you have to? What a thing to say! People are trying to eat their breakfast.'

Fiona's announcement appeared not to bother Andrew. He lifted his second kipper on to his plate and deftly removed the backbone.

'Well, it certainly can't have been the food,' Mary continued, 'Jenny ate so little last night. Why, she only picked at her supper and had hardly anything to drink.'

Unlike you, my dear, thought Morag, watching her daughter-in-law tuck into a hearty breakfast. 'Tandy, please go and see if Jennifer needs any help. Tell her to stay in bed and I'll be up later.' Morag folded her newspaper. The crossword would have to wait.

Knocking on the bathroom door, Tandy found Jenny rinsing her mouth with water. Her face was ghostly pale and she was shivering.

'I'm sorry to be so late for breakfast, Miss Tandy. Tell them I'll be down in a minute.'

'By the look of you, Miss Jennifer, I don't think so. Your mother says you are *not* to come down and I'm to help you to your bed.'

Like a child Jenny allowed herself to be led back to bed where Miss Tandy plumped up pillows and smoothed sheets. Somehow she didn't have the strength to resist.

'There, now, I'll draw the curtains and you can sleep. It's not a very nice day to look at, is it?'

Silently Jenny agreed. Prompted by the smell of kippers wafting up the stair-well, she'd seen the view from the window only briefly before dashing to the bathroom. It was a typical Conasg winter's day. The rain fell down in sheets and the cloud hung heavy over Ben Cruachen and the loch. Jenny closed her eyes and slept.

How long she slept she wasn't sure. It was only when she sensed the smell of lily-of-the-valley that she realized her mother was in the room. Morag sat on the bed studying her daughter's pallid face.

'My goodness! Tandy was right. You poor thing, you do look quite green about the gills. Have you any idea what caused it?'

'I suppose it could have been something I ate last night, or maybe a bug I picked up from somewhere... All I know is that Miss Tandy has made me so comfortable I hardly feel like getting up at all.'

'Then don't,' Morag said kindly. 'I suggest you have the day in bed and, if you don't feel any better when you return to Edinburgh, make an appointment to see Alex McAllister. You've been looking a bit peaky of late and could probably do with a tonic. I shall also have a word with Andrew, he's probably been driving you too hard.'

Morag pulled the covers up to her daughter's chin. Like Tandy she too was unable to resist the urge to tuck Jenny in, just as they did with Fiona.

'Something she ate, indeed,' Morag said tartly, going back downstairs to join the others for morning coffee. 'All the food served at Conasg is locally sourced and fresh; you'll find none of your supermarket heat-and-serve rubbish here!'

Andrew looked up from his chair, wondering what all the fuss was about.

'I trust that's not my crossword you're doing, Andrew?'

Duly reprimanded, Andrew laid down his mother's paper and turned his attention to Fiona's jigsaw instead.

*

Sponging her face, Jenny returned to her own rose-decorated bedroom. Everyone had been extremely kind at Conasg and taken such good care of her, but she was so relieved to be home. There was nothing worse than being sick in someone else's house, even if that someone was your mother.

'Make sure you drink plenty of fluid,' Morag had insisted. 'You mustn't let yourself become dehydrated.'

The words echoed in Jenny's ears. The problem was she didn't know what to drink. She'd been sick after her last cup of coffee and prior to that the tea she'd tried earlier had tasted so bitter.

Catching sight of her ghostly appearance in the mirror, she unhooked her bathrobe from the bedroom door and went downstairs. Perhaps, if she was lucky, she might find the remains of the lemon barley she kept for Fiona.

With barely a drop left, Jenny dropped the plastic bottle in the bin with a sigh. There must be something else she could try. On the shelf below the jams, she found the box of fruit teas Stevie had bought her for Christmas. They'd sounded so peculiar at the time: blackberry, raspberry, rosehip and numerous varieties of mixed fruit and spices. Which one should she try?

Deliberating over the brightly decorated sachets, she recalled Emily standing in exactly the same spot, deciding on her jam without bits. Pouring boiling water into her cup, Jenny smiled fondly at the memory of two little girls tucking into scones and jam.

Almost immediately a strong smell of raspberries filled the air and Jenny clasped her hand to her mouth. There was no time to get to the bathroom. Instead she grabbed a bucket from under the kitchen sink and made straight for the back door and into the garden.

After ten minutes of feeling sick and standing in the early morning drizzle, she soon began to shiver just as she had at Conasg and hurried back to the kitchen. There, rubbing briskly at her arms and shoulders in an attempt to get warm, she found - not for the first time in recent days, the pressure against her breasts felt strangely uncomfortable.

Puzzled, she reached for the offending cup of raspberry tea and poured it down the sink. How long was this queasiness going to continue? It was only when alarm bells began ringing in her head that she began looking about the kitchen for a calendar.

'Damn,' she muttered, looking at Emily's delightful offering of a paper plate decorated with pasta shapes and a tiny calendar stuck on two strands of red wool, That's no good, it's still only January... I need last year's.

Searching frantically in the kitchen drawer, she found what she was looking for. When was the dance and when had she last had a period? Sometimes towards the end of November was all she could remember.

Since Cameron had broken off their engagement there was no need… and with the Andrew/Gina/Conasg dramas, she hadn't given the missed period a thought.

Working backward from New Year's Eve, Jenny counted the days to the dance.

'Oh, my God! It can't be… I can't be, it's not possible!'

The words of Vera Baxter – one of her mother's elderly friends and local gossip – rang in her ears. Following the discovery that the deputy head girl of the local academy was pregnant, Vera had proclaimed to all and sundry, 'Only good girls get pregnant. Bad ones don't, you see. They know how to look after themselves!'

Giving a low moan, Jenny sat slumped at the kitchen table. If she, Jennifer Sinclair, was pregnant with Paul Hadley's child, was that good or bad?

*

'Hello. Welcome back,' said Stevie, looking up from her desk. 'How was Burn's Night? Andrew told me you had a stomach upset. What was it, the haggis or the whisky?'

Jenny declined to comment. Her mind was already racing back to early morning. She'd been sick again and forced herself to go for a walk before leaving for the office. If nothing else it had at least put some colour in her cheeks.

Being absent from the office meant there was a backlog of emails and paperwork needing her urgent attention, thus enabling her to avoid Stevie each time she appeared with a cup of coffee. The mere smell of the coffee machine turned her stomach and as for drinking it… Not taking too much notice, Stevie put Jenny's unusual behaviour down to sheer conscientiousness. Unlike Andrew, Jenny was hardly ever away from the office, and she hadn't had a holiday in ages.

Friday, apart from being the end of the week, was significant in two ways. It was the day Stevie fed and watered the office plants before the weekend, and also the day she and Jenny indulged in Danish pastries or cream cakes. Having seen to all the plants in the outer offices, Stevie called in on Jenny, Danish pastries in one hand and Baby Bio for the plants in the other.

'Mmm, just smell these, Jenny… almond, our favourite. It's just as well I asked Maggie in the bakers to save them. One of the chaps at Freeman's has a birthday today and he wanted the…'

Her words petered out as Jenny made a dash for the door, sending the Baby Bio flying. Retrieving the bottle of plant food and manoeuvring her wheelchair to the plant stand, Stevie examined the contents.

What on earth had happened to Jenny's plants? They looked incredibly sickly – a bit like her boss, and all this in only a week! OK, so it was only early February and daylight hours were still short, but last weekend everything had been positively blooming in this plant trough. She'd even told her mother about the magnificent display of caladiums.

Now sad and wilted, they looked nothing like the *angel's wings* loved by Fiona, nor did the weeping fig resemble the healthy plant Stevie had been nurturing ever since her arrival at Sinclair's. Stevie could have wept herself. These plants were her children, and like children they had suddenly become very sick. Who or what was the culprit? She determined to find out.

Stevie perceived there were two immediate possibilities: the dreaded wine weevil or Daphne the new cleaner. She shook her head, probably not the latter. She'd even teased Daphne and threatened to run her over with her wheelchair if she so much as added a drop of water to any of the plants. Frowning, Stevie scooped up the pot containing the 'rosebud' caladium and peered at the layer of brown sludge at its base. This was no vine weevil damage… this was coffee! On closer examination of all the plant troughs, she discovered pints of it!

Just how many cups of coffee had she taken into Jenny during the past week and how many had been poured onto these plants? If Jenny hadn't wanted any coffee, then why not say so? Why try to pretend otherwise? She watched as Jenny made her way back to her desk, her face a sickly yellow.

'Good grief! You do look rough, Jenny. Are you sure you're better?'

'I thought I was, but it's this stupid tummy bug, I just can't shake it off.'

'Then why not see your doctor… even if it does mean offending your mother. You could have a dose of food poisoning, in which case you're going to need some proper medicine.'

Jenny felt herself go cold. There was no medicine for her condition and quite how she was going to remedy the situation – let alone tell her mother, she had no idea. For the moment her only concern was to get rid of the offending Danish pastry glistening on its white, shiny plate!

'Stevie, your luck's in,' she said picking up the plate. 'Thanks to my misfortune it's double Danish for you today, unless you want to ring that lovely young man of yours and join him for a coffee or an early lunch…?'

In bewilderment Stevie found herself almost forced from the office, once more in possession of Danish pastries and a bottle of plant food.

*

At the weekend, in between bouts of sickness, Jenny studied the calendar again. Marking the date of the dance and this time counting forwards, she concluded she must be at least seven weeks pregnant. She needed to buy a pregnancy testing kit. However, not this weekend and not from the local chemists. It would have to wait until Monday and the anonymity of an Edinburgh chemist's.

It seemed an eternity to wait with no one to confide in. Even then, with confirmation of the result, whom could she tell? She could hardly tell Mary and Andrew. And Paul - what about Paul? She sensed that she'd already upset him. Her decision not to join him in taking the girls to the cinema hadn't gone down at all well. Cele and Emily had been so looking forward to seeing her again. Paul had been quite brusque with her on the phone, reminding her that it had been her suggestion in the first place that they all went to see the film *Frozen*.

Frozen, Jenny thought to herself. At this precise moment she not only felt frozen with fear and uncertainty about her pregnancy, but also she was desperately sad that she'd let both Paul and the girls down. Having already taken Fiona to see the same film at New Year, it had seemed the ideal choice of outing for Cele and Emily, now that they appeared more settled. How could she possibly explain to them the reason for her non-appearance? The very thought of sitting amongst hordes of people with buckets of popcorn and trays of nachos smothered in sauce, was enough to turn her stomach. As for telling Paul that she was expecting his child… She trembled at the prospect. He'd barely had a chance to recover from the shock of Gina's death and near financial ruin as a result of her extravagant lifestyle. No, now was not the time. Reminded of the song from the film, she so wanted to see again, Jenny began humming the tune to *Let it Go*.

Yes, she told herself, let it go for the moment and think of something else instead. In this instance the *something else* turned into positive thoughts of her brother for once, Andrew's timely intervention with the bank manager on Paul's behalf. For that, and with a new contract in his pocket, Paul was able to move on. Expressing his deepest thanks, Paul had told Andrew that despite several offers of work from other companies, Sinclair's and the House of St Claire would always come first.

Jenny was also grateful. She'd already heard through the grapevine there were more offers of work coming Paul's way, and she was happy for him. However, when she discovered Hendry and Co. had been in touch with him, she had become distinctly uneasy. Bruce Hendry and his father were well respected locally, but as for Bruce's sister, Marina... the nickname 'man-eater Marina' fitted her perfectly. It had been bad enough for Jenny seeing Paul and Marina lunching together before she discovered she was pregnant; now she felt even worse. Still, in two weeks' time she was due to have lunch with Paul herself. That meant two weeks in which to decide what to tell him.

When Monday lunchtime came, Jenny waited for Stevie to leave the office before setting off in the opposite direction. Like an undercover agent she skirted the far end of the square, anxious to avoid meeting anyone she knew. Eventually she arrived at the small corner chemist's.

Inside, to her relief, she found only one other customer, an elderly woman extolling the virtues of the purchase she held in her hand... a box of bicarbonate of soda.

'Aye' she said, looking at the array of fancy packaging on the shelves, 'you can keep all yon' modern pills and potions, for I'm a tellin' you there's nuthin' better for indigestion than this. One big burp and you're better,' she added crudely, waving the box of bicarb in the air. Then, as if to prove her point, she belched loudly.

At any other time Jenny might have found the old woman amusing, only she realized 'one big burp' wasn't going to make *her stomach* any better. Nor was the other old-fashioned remedy favoured by kitchen-sink dramas - a hot bath and a bottle of gin!

'So sorry about that,' the assistant whispered politely. Meg can be a bit - well, you know, at times, but we're all used to her now.'

'She's a regular, then?'

'Och, yes! She comes in practically every day. Hardly ever buys anything, mind you. She just likes looking at the shelves. Mr Frazer thinks she knows our stock better than we do ourselves. He assures us she's perfectly harmless and simply lonely... Now, how can I help?'

Jenny was relieved to leave the shop. Normally she would have welcomed such a friendly and helpful assistant but today was different. Why hadn't she realized there'd be so many pregnancy testing-kits to choose from? She'd come here for anonymity and ended up with an agony aunt.

Clutching the small rectangular package and hurrying back in the direction of Sinclair's she passed a greengrocer's, where bunches of bright yellow bananas caught her eye. Like golden crescents they hung against a backdrop of lush artificial grass and garish posters advertising fruit from the Cape. Once in the office, she put the fruit on her desk and slipped the chemist's bag in her drawer.

Stevie eyed her with a puzzled frown. 'Didn't you hear me say I was going for the chemist's for my 'horsepills'? I could have saved you a journey.'

Jenny felt her cheeks colour. Yes, she had heard Stevie mention she was going to collect her prescription but in the circumstances... Not wishing to arouse suspicion she muttered something incoherent and held up the bunch of bananas. 'Here,' she said, breaking one off, 'have a banana. They looked so tempting and reminded me of summer. I simply couldn't resist them.'

Stevie declined with a shake of her head and watched Jenny peel back the yellow fibrous skin. This was Jenny in a new dimension. Jenny who'd never so much as brought an apple into the office, tucking into bananas, pouring cups of coffee furtively into the plants and trying to conceal packages from the chemist's. And why, Stevie thought (recognizing the logo on the bag), use the chemist's at the far end of the square when the nearest was just around the corner?

Shrugging her shoulders, Jenny said a little too brightly for Stevie's liking, 'Well, if you change your mind, you can always have one later.

Now, are you going to tell me all about your weekend with Charles?'

'He prefers to be called Charlie and - um- actually I didn't see him at the weekend.'

'Oh, but I thought…'

'So did I, Jenny, but little did I realize when Charlie Stuart said about us meeting up with some of his friends, it meant an activity weekend.'

'What sort of activities?'

'Rambling, rock climbing, badminton, table tennis and darts.'

Jenny studied Stevie's downcast face. 'But you're brilliant at darts and table tennis; you even won that tournament last year and…'

'I know,' Stevie interrupted, 'and Charlie said while the others rambled he would have pushed me along.'

'Then why didn't you let him?'

'I'm not sure. I suppose it's because I think he's such a nice chap and I can't see why he wants to bother with a cripple like me.' Stevie looked down at the smooth white tyres of her wheelchair. 'Let's face it, I'm hardly equipped for…'

'Rubbish,' Jenny snapped, glad to take her mind taken off her own problems. 'Cressida Stephens, you are not a cripple and I will not have you behaving like one! Hasn't it occurred to you that Charles – sorry Charlie, wants to be with you because he's fond of you. Correction – very fond of you, taking into account that beautiful bouquet of flowers he sent you last week.'

'So…' enquired Jenny, giving her a hug, 'when are you going to see Charlie again?'

'I'm not.'

'*What*?'

'I told him I thought it would be best if we didn't…'

'Then you must be mad!'

'I know,' Stevie sniffed, 'but in the circumstances it seemed the only way. Now can I please have a banana? Like you, I think I could also do with some edible sunshine.'

CHAPTER TWENTY NINE

At home and alone, Jenny took the pregnancy kit to the bathroom, studied the enclosed leaflet, followed the instructions and waited. The almost instant result was as she'd suspected. She was pregnant with Paul's child and the next step presumably, was to see a doctor.

'Dr McAllister's office, how may I help you?'

'It's Miss Sinclair. I'd like to make an appointment.'

'I'm afraid Dr McAllister's fully booked this week. I can fit you in next Tuesday.'

Next Tuesday! That was another eight days away, Jenny thought, contemplating the clipped and ultra-efficient tone of Dr McAllister's receptionist.

'Miss Sinclair, are you still there? Will next Tuesday at ten be all right?'

'What? Oh, yes. I'd merely been hoping for something sooner… we're very busy at the moment.'

'May I have your Christian name and date of birth, please, Miss Sinclair?'

Jenny duly obliged, remembering that Morag, despite living so far away, was like her daughter and daughter-in-law, also Alex McAllister's patient.

'Then I'm not surprised you're so busy, the shops are full of the House of St Claire range now, aren't they? I was only saying to my fiancé we must put some on our wedding present list.'

Registering the change of tone in Miss Super-Efficient's voice, Jenny groaned inwardly. This woman would probably read her notes, know she was Morag Sinclair's unmarried daughter and even type the letter to the gynaecologist. Why hadn't she thought of this before picking up the phone? Heavens! This was going to be worse than she thought.

*

The clock struck the quarter-hour. Having waited until nine o'clock to ring the surgery, she would be late for work again, which meant more lame excuses. The only saving grace was that for the past few mornings she hadn't been sick. A sure sign, according to the book she'd bought, that her pregnancy was progressing normally.

Andrew eyed both the clock and Jenny's flushed appearance.

'I had a phone call from Mother last night. She's coming to Edinburgh to see the accountant. She wants to get a few things sorted before the end of the financial year catches up with us.'

'Andrew... it's only February.'

'I'm perfectly aware of that Jennifer, but you know Mother. She also mentioned something about her summer wardrobe. Mary says that probably means leaving off her thermals!'

Morag had indeed mentioned her summer wardrobe to her son, and also Flora Tandy. But her retort, 'I need to go to Edinburgh to keep them all on their toes. I'll not have them thinking I'm sitting here waiting to die!' had only aroused suspicion.

Who'd mentioned dying? Tandy certainly hadn't. She'd been reading her magazine – the one that used to feature Gina so regularly. She'd half expected Morag to voice her usual disapproval of such things. Instead, when Morag had picked up the same magazine, she'd simply flicked through the pages, pausing only briefly to admire the twin set and tweeds of some dowager duchess in the 'Welcome to my Home' feature.

Morag looked tired, but it was more than Tandy dared mention. The last time she'd enquired after Morag's health, she'd almost had her head bitten off. She'd later been informed about the so-called appointment with the accountant, and also thought she'd overheard a low and whispered conversation with Alex McAllister.

Munching her way through another banana, Jenny remembered that Andrew hadn't told her exactly when Morag was coming.

'A week Friday,' he called back. 'As usual she's invited herself and Tandy to tea at your place on Sunday. She says you make better scones than Mary!'

Stevie smiled; she was looking forward to seeing Morag again. Something told her that in the dim and distant past Morag Sinclair must have been quite a girl!

Jenny was dropping yet another banana skin in the bin when her phone rang, 'Please can you answer that for me, Stevie? I must just pop to the loo.'

With an air of bewilderment, Stevie took down the message and placed it on Jenny's desk, next to yet another bunch of bananas. Like her boss, she too had been doing some calculations. After all, you couldn't work with someone for all this time and not know when something was wrong. The hazy puzzle in Stevie's mind was beginning to fit together and, if her assumptions were correct, then she held herself partly responsible.

Indirectly she'd given Jenny's room number to Paul, and while not aware of him entering her room, she'd certainly heard him leave. It was a night when her back had been playing up and combined with the uncomfortable hotel bed, even strong painkillers hadn't helped. Contemplating events of the past few weeks, Stevie considered not only the introduction of bananas as a daily addition to Jenny's diet but also her frequent visits to the loo.

So… if Jenny was pregnant had she told Paul… and what was his reaction? Was that why Jenny looked as if she'd been crying the other day? Come to think of it, neither Paul nor the girls had been mentioned for quite a while. Hearing approaching footsteps, Stevie had a quick peep in Jenny's diary. Yes, just as she'd thought, Jenny was supposed to be having lunch with Paul at the same time as...

Doing her best to sound nonchalant, Stevie turned her wheelchair in the direction of her own office. 'Regarding the phone call, Jenny, it was a message about an appointment. I've left it on your desk, only I think if you check your diary, you'll see it's when you're supposed to be meeting Paul.'

Jenny frowned hard, what appointment? Other than meeting Paul... She picked up the piece of paper.

'*Dr McAllister's receptionist says if you don't want to wait until next Tuesday, he'll see you tomorrow after surgery @ 12 o'clock - can you please confirm?*'

Jenny's relief was palpable; she wouldn't have to wait until next week after all. Of course it meant cancelling her lunch date with Paul, but Stevie could tell him she was still suffering with tummy problems – which in a way was partly true, wasn't it? It would also give her more time to think about what she should tell him with regard to the baby.

*

'Jennifer, it's lovely to see you; I always say I never see enough of you Sinclair ladies... but as you're always so fit and healthy...'

Alex McAllister extended his hand and showed her to a chair. He was a kindly man with thinning grey hair, twinkling eyes and the softest of voices. What her mother always referred to as a 'real bedside manner' only today Jenny wished he hadn't, it only made the situation more difficult.

'Now,' said Alex, fixing her with concerned eyes, 'What appears to be the problem?'

'The problem, though I'm not sure if that's the right word, is that I'm pregnant.'

There was no flicker of emotion in Alex's face as he lay down his pen. Recalling post-dinner conversations with Morag at the Sinclair Christmas dance, and also Burn's Night at Conasg House, there'd been no man in Jennifer Sinclair's life since her broken engagement.

'I see,' he said, raising one eyebrow slightly. 'So... if you don't actually see it as a problem, how do you feel about being pregnant? Are you happy or sad? And what about the father?'

'To begin with the father doesn't know I'm pregnant. I'm not even sure if I should tell him. As for being happy or sad, I haven't come here to ask for an abortion if that's what you were thinking.'

'I wasn't,' Alex said, passing Jenny a box of tissues. From the tears brimming down her cheeks, she certainly didn't give the appearance of being overjoyed. Still, pregnancy was a very emotional time.

'I'm so sorry,' Jenny sniffed, reaching for a tissue, 'This is all so very difficult, Alex, you being a long-time friend of the Sinclairs *and* the family doctor.'

'There's no need to apologize, Jennifer, blame it on the hormones we doctors are forever talking about, and please don't worry - patient confidentiality and all that. You have a jolly good cry and when you're feeling better I'll examine you. In the meantime I'll just make a few notes. When was your last period and do - um - any particular days spring to mind of when you might have conceived?'

There was only one day that sprang to mind as far as Jenny was concerned – or should that be night? One night out of three hundred and sixty-five and she just happened to find herself pregnant as a result. Should she divulge that information to Alex or should she simply pretend she couldn't remember?

Opting for the latter, she went through the due process of an examination, heard Alex say that he would be referring her to a gynaecologist, rearranged her clothes and joined him at his desk.

'Right then,' he said, 'unless you've anything else you want to discuss with me now, why don't you come back to see me in a couple of weeks and perhaps in the meantime talk things over with the father. Unplanned pregnancies are always a bit of a shock but I'm sure in a few weeks' time, both you and your partner will be feeling differently.'

Jenny hardly dared think of a few weeks' time. As for 'a bit of a shock' she was still coming to terms with the shock of seeing Paul lunching with Marina Hendry!

Deciding against returning to the office, Jenny stopped in the square where a watery pool of sunlight – heralding another spring, bathed one of the benches in a pale golden glow. Sitting down she searched in her handbag for a proper handkerchief. Her nose felt quite sore from constant rubbing with Alex's paper tissues. Blowing her nose hard and dabbing again at her eyes, she didn't take too much notice of the old woman shuffling down the path towards her.

Sitting down amidst much wheezing and puffing, the old woman spread out an assorted collection of carrier bags and peered at her with rheumy eyes. 'What's up, lassie? Got yerself in the family way and he will nae marry you?'

Completely taken aback, Jenny sat open-mouthed, how could a complete stranger know she was pregnant?

'Och, dinnae ye fret now, being in the club's nae problem these days, you know. They're all at it round my way. As my old mother used to say, "it ain't no picnic but worse things happen at sea." ' The old woman rummaged in a bag, belched, adjusted her hat, struggled to her feet and ambled on her way.

Puzzling as to where she'd seen this strange creature before, Jenny remembered the day she'd gone to the chemist's... old Meg! The old lady who spent most of her days studying the shelves, until she knew all the stock. Presumably she'd seen Jenny with her purchase and, spying her now - sitting on this bench with red-rimmed eyes, presumed the worst.

In one way, old Meg was right, worse things did happen at sea. Cameron had lost two of his closest friends at sea in a naval accident, which was why she always worried about him whenever he was away on manoeuvres. Now it was her who would be doing the manoeuvring… combining her career with motherhood.

Through misted eyes, Jenny watched a sparrow pecking amongst the leaves, revealing a clump of brightly coloured crocuses. After weeks of gloomy weather, spring was coming at last. Spring and a time for new growth, she thought, feeling a stirring in her breast. She had something wonderful growing within her… Paul's baby, but whether or not she should tell him, she was still undecided.

Two days later, relieved to be home, Jenny kicked off her shoes and unbuttoned her waistband. So far the past week had simply dragged by and during the afternoon her pencil-slim skirt had become increasingly uncomfortable. Looking in her wardrobe, she searched for something less restrictive and loose, while contemplating matters needing her mother's urgent attention.

Morag, she knew from experience, would be in the office at eight-thirty sharp. As for the weekend, and entertaining her mother to tea, apart from tomorrow's shopping trip and making the scones on Sunday morning, everything was under control. This evening she could relax, perhaps look through some mother and baby magazines and even do some more knitting. Last night she'd surprised herself by completing the back of a baby's matinee jacket. Tonight she might tackle the two fronts.

Holding her handiwork into the air, she wanted to proclaim to the four walls the words she'd always longed to say, 'I'm pregnant! I'm going to have a baby!' Instead of looking after other people's children she would now have one of her own and Stevie would be so pleased for her.

Only she couldn't tell Stevie, could she? This was something she must keep to herself for the moment, which also meant hiding her knitting and the baby magazines under her bed.

Crawling out from under the bed, anxious to climb into it instead - she was feeling so tired, Jenny remembered she still hadn't prepared her shopping list.

Best do it now she thought, gazing longingly at the bed; you don't want to be late for tomorrow's meeting and subject yourself to Andrew's irritating comment, 'Well, if you didn't live in the sticks you wouldn't be late...'

Smiling to herself, recalling Fiona's first bewildered response to this expression, 'Why does Auntie Jenny live in the sticks? Is she like Eeyore from *Winnie- the- Pooh*?' Jenny made her way downstairs to the kitchen. Were there any jars of *jam without bits* left?

With the uneven stone-flagged floor icy against her feet, she stood on tiptoe to examine the top shelves of the pantry. It was no good, she simply couldn't reach and rather than the sensible option - fetching a pair of steps - she reached for a kitchen chair instead. Yawning sleepily, pleased to find what she was looking for, Jenny held a jar in one hand and steadied herself against the chair with the other. Moments later, she felt the chair tilt backwards, only this time with no Paul to break her fall, she found herself in a heap on the floor; dazed, shivering and cold.

*

As expected the following morning, Morag was the first to arrive. Hamish, having exchanged his role of gardener and handyman to that of chauffeur, had delivered her at eight-thirty sharp. Duly dismissed, Tandy was then taken to have coffee with a distant relation.

From behind her desk Stevie watched bemused. Morag Sinclair's hawk-eyed gaze scanned the office for any sign of change. Not one to miss anything, Morag nodded approvingly at the new photo of Mary and the children gracing Andrew's desk. Presuming she would still find her husband's photo on Jenny's, she was taken completely aback to find William Sinclair obscured by a bunch of bananas!

'If it's not too impertinent a question, Miss Stephens, what is a bunch of bananas doing in Jennifer's filing tray? Surely they have nothing to do with the House of St Claire?'

'No,' Stevie said with a smile. 'Jenny's simply into bananas these days. Slow release energy and sunshine she says…'

'Does she indeed,' Morag replied, eyeing Stevie suspiciously.

Later, with everyone assembled in the boardroom, Morag pronounced her delight with the developments of the past year and suggested they all stop for coffee.

'Jennifer, my dear,' she began, pouring a wee dram into her cup. 'You look a bit peaky – are you all right?'

'Yes, I'm fine thank you, Mother. It's just my back; I foolishly fell off a chair.'

'Did you indeed, and what were you doing perched precariously on a chair in the first place?'

'Hunting for raspberry jelly for Fiona. You know she doesn't like jam with bits.'

'Hmph! Did anyone ever tell you, you spoil that youngest grandchild of mine?'

'That's rich coming from you, Mother,' Andrew retorted. 'Fiona tells me you're taking her to lunch tomorrow at MacDonald's!'

Stevie, coming in with a fresh pot of coffee, thought it highly amusing to think of Morag in a burger bar with not a china cup in sight. She whispered in Jenny's ear, 'Paul's on the phone again. He wants to know if you've recovered enough to have lunch with him next week?'

'Tell him yes,' replied Jenny, anxious to avoid mention of Paul in front of her mother. Trying to suppress the familiar stirring in her stomach whenever she thought of him, she knew she'd have to face him sooner or later.

With the meeting drawing to a satisfactory conclusion, Hamish returned with Miss Tandy and drove the two women to their favourite Edinburgh hotel for lunch.

Away from the hubbub of yuppies and what Catriona called Gothic and Grunge, they were at liberty to eat what Morag called 'proper food' and watch the comings and goings of ladies impeccably dressed in their finest tweeds, twin sets and pearls. There was also just the faintest chance of hearing the latest gossip.

'Will you be wanting to go and look for your summer wardrobe directly after lunch?' enquired Tandy.

'No,' Morag said. 'I have to see the bank manager first.'

'Blethers! You don't have to lie to me, Morag Sinclair. Bank manager indeed! You are going to see Alex McAllister about these dizzy spells you keep having.'

Morag dropped her knife and fork when Tandy continued boldly. 'Och! You Sinclair women, you think you can keep your secrets from everyone, but you can't keep them from me. I know you all only too well.'

'Whatever do you mean?'

'What I mean,' said Tandy, making sure no one was within earshot, 'is that you are worried about your health, Mary and Andrew have been having problems with their marriage, and as for Miss Jennifer…'

'What about Jennifer?'

'Och, come on, isn't it obvious? As her mother, you of all people should know that. Your daughter is pregnant!'

Morag's hands gripped the table. So her worst suspicions were confirmed. 'Well, Flora Tandy, as you seem to be such an old witch, perhaps you'll be so kind to tell me the name of the father?'

'Isn't that also obvious? It can't be that dreadful Alistair Jennings, who has hands like an octopus, so it can only be that nice Mr Hadley. Didn't you see the way they looked at each other when they were dancing? You might be having dizzy spells, Morag Sinclair, but you're most certainly not blind!'

Morag sat with pursed lips and dabbed at her mouth with a napkin. Never had Tandy been so outspoken. She was right, though. She had noticed her daughter and Paul together. She'd also been gravely concerned for Jennifer's welfare. At the time Paul was still married to Gina – albeit in name only - and there'd also been that dreadful scene at the dance when Gina was making a beeline for Andrew. It hadn't taken much to guess what had been going on there!

'So...' Morag began quietly, 'what do you suggest I do about it? I hardly think I can turn to Jennifer and say, My dear, I know you're pregnant so please will you let me help?'

'No... probably not,' said Tandy, 'so I suggest for the moment you do nothing.'

In a rare show of affection, Flora reached across the table and patted Morag's hand. 'Aye, I'd say do nothing, at least until you've got yourself sorted out with Dr McAllister this afternoon. Then, as you're all getting together for dinner this evening, perhaps you'll be in a far better position to judge the situation.'

*

Once more sitting at the head of the dining table, Morag studied her immediate family: Andrew at the far end of the table and Mary, with her eldest children on one side of her, and Jenny, Fiona and Flora Tandy on the other.

Casting a furtive glance in Tandy's direction, Morag turned her gaze back to Andrew. Although his waistline had begun to thicken, he was becoming more and more like his father as he got older; he even had the tell-tale white streaks appearing at his temple.

Morag swallowed hard. In his younger days her husband had been such a fine figure of a man. It still pained her to think of him wasting away before her very eyes. Why was life so cruel?

If what Alex McAllister had told her that very afternoon was correct, there would be no such wasting away for Morag. It would be one fell swoop if she didn't heed his advice, and then gone - just like that, snuffed out like a candle! With a shudder Morag tore her bread roll in half.

Mary Sinclair, unaware of her mother-in-law's secret torment, served the soup with an air of satisfaction. As usual she had surpassed herself. The table was laid with the finest House of St Claire linen and the crystal and silver sparkled and shone in the candlelight. She smiled lovingly at her husband. It was, she told herself, just like old times. Although if she was to be perfectly honest, weren't certain aspects of their relationship even better than before? Mary felt two blobs of colour rise in her cheeks.

That, observed Morag, was at least one thing less for her to worry about, but what of her daughter? Jennifer's face was still strained from the morning. How badly had she hurt her back? Compared to Mary she looked painfully thin, but not for much longer, Morag reminded herself. And as for how to broach the subject of Jennifer's pregnancy, she had no idea.

CHAPTER THIRTY

Bathed in dappled early spring sunlight, Jenny stretched contentedly in bed.

'Mmm, Saturday,' she said with a sigh of satisfaction. The cottage was tidy. The shopping was done and she could have an utterly lazy day all to herself for once.

Filled with a sense of wellbeing, she reached for a magazine and lay back against freshly plumped-up pillows. As the sun rose higher and its rays stronger, rosy patterns danced on the walls and ceiling. From the corner of her eye she caught sight of yesterday's list of things to do. How satisfying to know each and every item had been ticked off. Tomorrow, all she had to do was prepare tea for the family.

Half an hour later, and ignoring the dull pain in her back, Jenny eased herself from the bed, opened the windows wide and breathed in the soft morning air. If the forecast was good, she might even potter in the garden for a while. Miss Tandy always enjoyed wandering round this garden, and there were already magnificent clumps of *tete- a- tete* daffodils to show her. A true herald of spring blooming in East Lothian.

Blooming. What a wonderful word Jenny thought, placing a hand gently on her stomach... blooming just like me, isn't that how they describe mothers to be? Now that wretched morning sickness is behind me, and apart from this stupid niggle in my back, I feel fantastic!

With her mind on the tiny miracle growing inside her; her very own baby to love, cherish and nurture, Jenny felt as if she was walking on air as she made her way back to the bed. She flung back the duvet and froze, poised with her hand in mid-air. All sense of euphoria and wellbeing deserting her, and filled with panic, she rang Alex McAllister's home number.

Relieved to find that he was not on the golf course, Jenny described the tell-tale stain on the sheet that filled her heart with dread. Alex McAllister's voice was as calm and reassuring as ever.

'I shouldn't worry unduly, Jennifer. It is very common with first pregnancies. Have you been doing anything too energetic to upset things?'

'Well, I have been doing some early spring cleaning; Mother's in Edinburgh – did you know? She's coming for tea tomorrow.'

Alex declined to comment. What was it he'd said to Jenny about patient confidentiality? He'd not mentioned to Morag that he'd seen her daughter, and he certainly wasn't going to tell Jennifer that he'd seen Morag.

'Then of course there was the other night... when I fell off the chair,' Jenny continued.

'You did what?' Alex's voice filled with concern. It was some time before he spoke again. 'Jennifer... if you're not expecting your mother until tomorrow, can I suggest you take yourself back to bed and stay there. Hopefully, things will soon settle down, but if not please don't hesitate to call. I'll give you my mobile number, just in case.'

Not wanting to think about the '*just in case*' Jenny did as she was told, filling the seemingly endless hours looking at pregnancy guides, finishing off the tiny matinee jacket and planning the nursery. The box-room, next to her bedroom, she already decided would make the ideal nursery, and when a bigger room was needed, she would simply transform the guest-room at the far end of the landing. But, she mused, laying aside her knitting, what would she choose... pink candy stripe or pale blue gingham?

Definitely not roses, she thought smiling. Her own bedroom was already full of them: roses on the curtains, roses on the walls, roses on the exquisite bed linen. Cameron had even teased her about them, saying it was like something from *Sleeping Beauty*, minus the thorns. He'd also said that, whether she liked it or not, he'd have the room redecorated the moment they were married.

Letting her imagination run away with her, Jenny wondered if Paul would have expressed so strong an opinion. She also wondered what he would choose by way of redecoration, because sooner or later the roses would have to go. The *blooms* were certainly looking tired and faded in places. A bit like me, she thought, yawning and snuggling beneath the covers again, trying hard not to think how wonderful it would be lying here cradled in Paul's arms.

Having drifted into a fitful and troubled sleep where she was pushing a pram through skeins of knitting wool that twisted and wound about her, Jenny woke with a start. In her dreams Paul was waiting with arms outstretched for her and the baby. Now, with the fading hours of daylight, she found herself tangled in a mass of bedding, knitting wool and magazines.

'Too much sleep, that's your trouble, Jennifer Sinclair,' she said, addressing her flushed reflection in the mirror. 'Look at the state of you!'

Deciding on a shower and maybe a brisk walk to clear her aching head, Jenny recalled Alex McAllister's words of advice. Perhaps a brisk walk wasn't the most sensible option, and by the time she had her shower it would be almost dark. Why not have supper on a tray and listen to the classic serial on Radio Four instead?

Dismayed that her favourite shower gel smelt unusually sickly and sweet, Jenny reached down to study the label. Surely the company hadn't changed the formula, and why had the colour suddenly changed from green to red? In a daze, she clutched at her stomach and slumped to the floor of the shower cubicle.

Much later, wrapped in her bathrobe, Jenny wept deep uncontrollable sobs, not only for the acute despair at her loss but also the pain that racked her body. Reaching out for a fresh white towel, she rolled it into a bundle, drew it close and rocked it in her arms as if visualizing her own precious baby, complete with rosebud mouth and fine copper curls. Her own precious baby that was no longer there…

Ringing Dr McAllister, Jenny forgot all about Morag's impending visit. All she wanted to do was drown her sorrows in an endless sleep. What was it Cameron had said about her bedroom – *Sleeping Beauty* without the thorns? Oh, the thorns are there, she thought, rising to her feet and fetching the bottle of paracetamol from the bathroom. They were there piercing her very heart and soul. With tears coursing down her cheeks, she returned to her bedroom in a daze. With luck and just like *Sleeping Beauty*, she would go to her bed surrounded with roses and sleep for a hundred years.

*

With scones and a Victoria sponge to prepare, Jenny tried in vain to focus on the tasks in hand. How many tablets had she taken before falling into a dreamless slumber? Should she ring Alex McAllister again? And how was she going to cope with her guests?

At three o'clock Fiona came bounding through the open front door, gave Jenny what she called a 'right-tight hug, because I love you Auntie Jenny,' and insisted on taking Miss Tandy into the garden immediately. There were daffodils to see, she called excitedly, plus her own promised plot where she hoped to plant some bulbs and seeds of her own.

'But first I must wait for the soil to become warmer,' Fiona explained to her elderly companion.

Jenny smiled when Fiona patted the rich brown soil with the palm of her hand. Sadly, it was not yet warm.

Looking jaded and drawn, Morag ignored the garden for once and chose to remain indoors by the fire instead. Turning from the window, Jenny was surprised to see her mother rubbing her chest.

'Jennifer, dear, I don't suppose you have any bicarbonate of soda? I didn't like to say anything in front of Fiona for fear of upsetting her, but I've had the most dreadful indigestion since eating that burger and fries yesterday. Andrew and Mary did warn me beforehand, it wouldn't be like Tandy's cooking, but the child was so looking forward to our outing together.'

Recalling old Meg's comments about bicarb, Jenny shook her head.

'I'm afraid not, Mother, but I do have something slightly more modern I'm sure will do the trick. Why not go and rest on my bed, where I'm sure you'll be far more comfortable?'

Surprised that Morag allowed herself to be led upstairs without a murmur, Jenny rearranged the pillows. 'If it is indigestion, then you're probably better sitting up. There, is that better, Mother? Now, let's see about that bottle of ...'

On her return Jenny was alarmed to see Morag looking so ill and in an obvious state of distress. Running towards the stairs, she called back, 'I'm going to ring Dr McAllister and also fetch Miss Tandy.'

'I'd rather you didn't, Jennifer. You know how Flora fusses - and I can't abide fuss. However, if you could get me a bowl... I'm sorry but I think I'm going to be sick!'

'Oh, my goodness!' Tandy cried in alarm, when Jenny beckoned her indoors. 'It must be her heart. I was only saying to her yesterday...'

'Her heart? What's wrong with Mother's heart?

With no time to explain, Flora Tandy followed Jenny to the bottom of the stairs and came to an abrupt halt. From overhead she heard a resounding thump and feared the worst. Morag Sinclair, having fallen from the bed while reaching for the bowl, spied a tiny white matinee coat and a mother and baby magazine, before she lost consciousness.

*

Following the paramedics wheeling the stretcher into the ambulance, Jenny reached for her mother's hand and heard her whisper feebly. 'Will you please tell Flora and Fiona to stop crying. I am not going to die!'

Flora Tandy dabbed at her eyes. In little more than forty-eight hours, Morag had twice used her Christian name. Her old friend was either mellowing with age or else she was going to…

'No!' she declared under her breath. 'Morag Sinclair! You've always had your own way, ever since I have known you. I refuse to let you die first!'

*

Alex McAllister sat by Morag's bed and watched her open her eyes.

'Morag, my friend,' he said softly, 'you are one very lucky lady.'

'Meaning I'm lucky to be alive?'

'No… meaning I'd just finished my game of golf, so was able to come rushing to your bedside.'

Morag fixed him with a weak smile. 'Alex McCallister, my husband always said you were a rogue. And there was me thinking you were concerned for my health.'

'Ah, but I am. Which is why, when I deem the time is right for you to return to Conasg House, I want you to promise me you will follow *all* my instructions. I also think it would be a good idea if Jennifer went with you.'

Something in the way Alex spoke Jennifer's name prompted Morag to wriggle up on her elbows. 'Alex… I want you to tell me… is Jennifer pregnant?'

'Morag Sinclair! You of all people should know better than that. Fancy asking me about one of my patients…'

'She might be your patient, Alex, but she's also my daughter and I have reason to believe Jennifer is expecting a baby!'

'Was,' Alex said reluctantly, with a shake of his head. He reached out and patted Morag's hand, aware of a single tear running down her cheek.

*

'Flora Tandy! Will you please stop fussing. How many more times must I tell you? I've come back to Conasg to recuperate, not die!'

Watching her companion retreat with an armful of cushions and yet another rug, Morag turned to her daughter. 'Gracious, if she's not careful she'll kill me by suffocation!'

'Don't be too hard on her, Mother. She's been fraught with worry about you.'

'I know, dear,' Morag sighed, 'but the last thing I need right now is to be treated like an invalid. I simply want to forget all about that silly heart business and talk about a holiday instead.'

Bemused, Jenny sat down at her mother's bedside. Holiday – what holiday? Was Morag planning a trip somewhere to convalesce, and did she want Jenny to go with her as travelling companion and nurse, leaving Miss Tandy behind?

'I wasn't aware you were planning a holiday, Mother. Is this something you've discussed with Alex McCallister or Andrew?'

'Yes… and no,' Morag replied with a twinkle in her eye. 'I'm not going on holiday, Jennifer. You are. Andrew is arranging it all.'

'What? I don't understand. Why is Andrew…?'

'Because we all agree you could do with a well-earned break. I also thing you have some serious soul searching to do. You've not been very well lately, have you?'

Aware of her mother's penetrating gaze, Jenny lowered her eyes. How much did she know?

'How did you… when did you…' Jenny began.

Morag held out a hand, 'Hush, my dear. I don't really know for certain, do I? Let's just say it was an old woman's intuition.'

Gulping back tears, Jenny rested her head against her mother's shoulder.

'Cameron hurt me so much, you know. He even accused me of being married to Sinclair's and said such cruel things about the family. After he broke off our engagement, there were times when I simply didn't know what to do. When the House of St Claire came into being I was filled with such a new sense of purpose, even telling myself that's all I ever wanted until... until I became pregnant...'

'Ssh,' Morag whispered, stroking Jenny's hair. 'In a way, perhaps Cameron was right. After your father died we all expected far too much of you. Look at how you helped Mary when Fiona was born. In fact, not only when she was a baby but also the past seven years! As for Andrew...'

'You mustn't be too hard on Andrew. It wasn't easy for him, either, after Father died.'

Morag gave a snort and reached for her handkerchief. 'The trouble with you, Jennifer, is that you're sometimes way too soft and sweet-natured for you own good, which is why I think the time has come for you to lay a few ghosts.'

'Ghosts? I don't have any ghosts.'

'Don't you? Well, I can think of two for a start, namely Cameron Ross and Gina Dintino.'

'But Cameron's not dead!'

'Maybe not, and much as I dislike the way he treated you, I wouldn't wish that on him just yet. Anyway, enough talk of Cameron. Aren't you going to ask me where I'm going to send you?'

'Even if I don't want to go away?' Jennifer pleaded.

'Of course you will,' Morag grinned triumphant. 'You've always loved

Venice.'

'Venice! I haven't been to Venice since I went with Moira.'

'Precisely… and you've never stopped talking about the place and wanting to go back. All those wonderful paintings, churches and art treasures.'

'Yes, but Moira went to Switzerland and married Helmut…'

'And you got yourself engaged to Cameron, who wouldn't even recognize a decent picture if he saw one!'

'Mother! You said you didn't want to talk about Cameron.'

'Quite so,' Morag acknowledged, 'let's talk about your holiday first, then I suggest you go and have a rest. Perhaps you could also ask Flora to bring me in some tea? Tell her she can stay if she's quiet, and can even bring in one of those awful magazines of hers. Though I can't abide them myself, you know.'

Smiling to herself, Jenny left the room. Her mother was obviously getting better!

CHAPTER THIRTY ONE

The office felt strangely empty and quiet. Stevie was used to Andrew darting in and out, but it was very unusual for Jenny to be absent for days at a time. Then there was yesterday's phone call announcing her intention to have a short holiday.

'Going anywhere nice?'

'Italy,' Jenny had replied, leaving Stevie even more confused. When anyone mentioned Italy, she thought first of Gina and then Paul. 'What about Paul?' she reminded. 'You haven't forgotten your lunch appointment, have you? You've already cancelled twice.'

Reassured that this time Jenny would be ringing Paul herself, Stevie turned her attention to the sad-looking caladiums. Now, completely drained of coffee and dosed with Baby-Bio, they still looked pretty sickly. Should she resort to drastic action, cut them right back in the hope they'd spring into new growth, or else call it a day - drop them in the bin and send them to the great garden centre in the sky? Taking some comfort that at least the weeping fig had perked up, Stevie was still conscious of an awful smell in the office.

'Got you!' she said, reaching down for a bunch of bananas behind Jenny's desk.

Pondering how best to deal with this pile of blackened, mushy fruit, she heard a voice announce. 'Goodness! They don't look too healthy.'

'Paul! What are you doing here?'

'Having lunch with Jenny, remember? Third time lucky by my reckoning. By the way, where is everyone? The place is like a morgue.'

'Jenny's not here. Didn't she ring you? She said she would. Morag's had a slight heart attack and...'

Regretting his earlier choice of words, Paul looked anxiously about the office. 'Gosh! I'm sorry, I had no idea. Morag's not d...'

'No, she isn't,' Steve added quickly, 'but Jenny's been looking after her at Conasg. I'm surprised Andrew never told you. Weren't you supposed to be meeting up last week?'

'Yes, we were, but for once it was me who cancelled. Marina Hendry rang me with a business proposition, which seemed too good to refuse.'

'And was it?' Stevie asked cynically. 'Too good to refuse, I mean?'

'Actually, no... Wait a minute, Stevie! What are you implying?'

'Well, you know what they say about Marina Hendry? They don't call her "Man-eater Marina" for nothing.'

'Are you serious! You don't honestly think Marina's got designs on me?'

'Not me necessarily, but I know Jenny thinks so.'

Paul couldn't believe his ears. 'You've got to be joking... me and Marina Hendry! Wait a minute, is this why Jenny keeps putting off having lunch with me. Making all those excuses and...'

'They're not all excuses, Jenny really did have tummy troubles,' Stevie said, springing to her boss's defence, which in a way was partly true, wasn't it?

'I'm not surprised,' Paul added, conscious of both the sight and smell of the bananas, 'if that's what she's been eating.' His gaze took in the sickly caladiums and slowly recovering weeping fig. 'And, if you don't mind my saying so, everything in here is looking pretty unhealthy at the moment. Even you don't look your usual perky self.'

'That's probably because I've been worried about Jenny and Morag,' Stevie replied. She omitted to mention how much she was not only missing Charlie Stuart. but also bitterly regretting turning down his latest invitations to dinner and the theatre.

Paul's face brightened. 'Stevie... as you look like a poor lost soul, all alone in this office, how about joining another lost soul for lunch?'

'That sounds like a great idea, the only problem is my wheelchair and getting into some of the restaurants. If it's OK with you, and because it's such a nice day, would you mind if we got some baguettes and fresh fruit tarts from the deli, and ate al fresco in the square?'

Paul nodded in agreement. Fresh air seemed like a good idea. Hopefully, it would also clear his head. He'd been in such a dilemma as to what do about Jenny just lately. Perhaps he could even ask Stevie's advice, for unless he was mistaken, she was also keeping something from him. It wasn't just Marina Hendry who'd brought about such a change; Jenny was far too intelligent a woman for that.

Once in the square, Paul manoeuvred Stevie's wheelchair into dappled sunlight, applied the brakes, sat down beside her on the adjoining bench and looked earnestly into her eyes.

'OK, Miss Stephens, before I hand over this vastly expensive lunch, and as you're my prisoner, I demand that you tell me what's going on. What have I done to upset Jenny?'

'Um… well you never sent her any flowers for Valentine's Day.'

'You're quite right, I didn't, which I'll admit was extremely remiss of me. Then again, do you think flowers would have made any difference? I get the distinct impression Jenny's been trying to avoid me. Did she say she expected flowers from me?'

'No… I just thought as you'd been getting on so well together…'

'So did I,' Paul murmured sadly. 'And I'd do anything to put things right between us. Any suggestions… apart from flowers?'

Stevie shook her head; she was getting out of her depth. It wasn't up to her to tell him Jenny was going away on holiday – or that she thought Jenny was pregnant. Relieved to hear a clock striking the hour, she handed Paul the empty food wrappers and motioned to a nearby bin.

'Right, Sir Galahad, if you'll just see to the recycling, then you can return me, and my steely charger, to Sinclair's main entrance.'

'Certainly, m'lady,' Paul grinned, and gave Stevie a sweeping bow.

Once more outside Sinclair's, Stevie studied Paul's unhappy face. Gone was the earlier cheeriness, and she could only assume he was thinking of Jenny. 'Thanks for your company,' he said, bending to kiss her on the cheek, 'I really appreciated it. And next time when I see Jenny... if I see Jenny... I promise I'll take her some flowers.'

Watching him turn and walk away, Stevie felt utterly helpless. She would have given anything to run after Paul and tell him about Jenny and the baby, but how could she, confined to this heap of rubber and metal?

'Paul!' she cried out in desperation. 'Please, you don't understand – Jenny she...'

Stopping by his car, Paul tried to work out what Stevie was saying. If it wasn't for all the traffic... Instinct told him to return to Stevie's side, where he was convinced he caught the words '*love* you'.

Sniffing back tears, Stevie grasped his hand. 'Please don't give up on Jenny,' she begged. 'She loves you... I know she loves you.'

Stooping to kiss her cheek once more, and unused to seeing Stevie so upset, Paul decided to make sure she was safely installed back in her office. Waiting for the lift, neither of them were aware of the tall, athletic figure waiting in the shadows.

'Yes, Mother, I understand. *Yes*, I will tell her as soon as she's back from lunch, but as I'm not long back myself...'

Hearing Andrew's exasperated voice along the corridor, Stevie and Paul exchanged enquiring glances.

'Stevie! Thank heavens! My mother's been plaguing me for the past twenty minutes. Will you *please* ring her?'

Stevie shot Paul a puzzled glance, excused herself and left the two men alone.

'Andrew,' Paul began, placing a hand on his shoulder. 'I'm so sorry. I've only just heard about your mother. Stevie tells me she's on the mend…'

'Yes, and don't I know it! When Mary and I went to Conasg to see if we could help she sent me away with a list as long as your arm. There's even a letter for you somewhere. Now let me see…' Andrew rummaged through a pile of papers in his briefcase and pulled out a slim white envelope.

'Now if you'll excuse me, I have to go out again. I'm already late for my next appointment. Just remind Stevie to ring my mother or my life won't be worth living.'

Andrew smiled as he closed his briefcase and headed for the door. 'Don't worry,' he called back. 'Morag won't eat you!'

Paul was leaning against the desk studying the contents of the letter when Stevie reappeared. 'The mystery deepens,' he said, frowning. Morag Sinclair has summoned me to Conasg House. She says it's urgent. What do you make of that?'

Stevie shook her head, she was equally mystified by all that was going on at Conasg.

Leaving Paul to make arrangements with Helen Craig to look after Celestina and Emily, Stevie headed off in the direction of Jenny's office with a can of air-freshener. She was determined, once and for all, to get rid of the smell of rotting bananas.

'Charlie! What are you doing here?' she gasped, finding her way barred. 'I thought I told you it was better if we didn't see each other again.'

'Aye, I know, and until about an hour ago I thought I might be able to change your mind.'

'An hour ago? What happened an hour ago?'

'An hour ago, I just happened to see you in the park with your new boyfriend.'

'You mean Paul? But I thought you knew about Paul. He's...'

'Obviously I didn't, Stevie, but I have to admit he's a handsome-looking guy. I can't blame you for falling for him.'

'You can't?' Stevie asked, incredulous.

'Why, no. Compared to me, he's far better looking. He also has a great deal more hair than I have.'

Stevie studied Charlie's receding hairline and nodded thoughtfully.

'And what about his eyes... don't you think he's got nice eyes?'

'From where I was standing, I didn't notice his eyes, but at least - unlike me - he doesn't wear John Lennon style glasses.'

'Then of course there's his teeth,' Stevie said, suppressing a smile. She remembered how, on their very first date, Charlie had described the loss of his two front teeth in a rugby scrum.

Pushing his tongue against his teeth, just to make sure they were still there, Charlie heard Stevie giggle. 'Hey! What is this,' he cried. 'Do you intend to go through all my physical attributes – or should I say lack of them?'

Moving her wheelchair to where Charlie sat slumped against her desk plucking petals from the large bouquet of flowers in his hands, Stevie ran her hand over his closely cropped hair.

'Charlie Stuart,' she said softly, 'I think you've got lovely hair, lovely eyes and a perfectly lovely smile. And yes, you are right about Paul, I do think he's smashing, but he's simply a very good friend.'

'But I saw him kiss you - twice - and you said you loved him... outside the office when he brought you back from the park.'

Stevie thought long and hard. 'No, I didn't! I said *she loves you*. I don't love Paul Hadley, you silly! Which is just as well really, as he's madly in love with Jenny... my boss.'

Charlie laid down the flowers and grasped Stevie's hand. 'Then why did you say you didn't want to see me anymore? I thought we were getting along great together.'

'We were… but I thought it wasn't fair on you and your friends being lumbered with a pathetic invalid like me.'

'Och! Blethers, Stevie! If you're an invalid then I must be a haggis! Why, you've got more energy and personality than hundreds of people I know.'

Releasing her hand from his, Stevie ran her fingers over the white-walled tyres of her wheelchair. That's kind of you to say so, Charlie, but aren't you forgetting one thing… my legs?'

'No, dammit, I'm not, 'cos I'll be your legs, Stevie. Besides, what with your legs, my hair, eyes and teeth, between us we'll make a bonnie couple!'

Hearing her laugh, Charlie grinned a toothy smile and, stooping forward, kissed Stevie full on the mouth.

'You know something,' she giggled, 'I don't think you should be comparing yourself to a haggis. According to those wee furry creatures in tourist shop windows, they have far more hair than you!'

*

At Conasg House, Tandy ushered Paul into the study with a gracious smile. 'Morag will be with you in a moment,' she said kindly. 'I'll just go and make some coffee.'

It was a large room, Paul noted, with dark oak panels that smelt strongly of beeswax. Books lined the walls and sombre green drapes hung heavily at the casement windows. Alone in the room, he walked to the fireplace and, lost in thought, studied the large painting hanging above the solid oak mantelpiece.

Although the scene was set in Princes Street at the turn of the twentieth century, Paul's thoughts turned to Jenny and the day they met in Princes Street to buy Cele and Emily their Christmas party frocks. The day the slightly inebriated shop assistant had talked about underwear. Paul felt a stirring in his body; doubtless that was the underwear Jenny was wearing on the night he went to her hotel room…

'You are admiring Mr Stone's picture, I see,' said Morag, quietly entering the room. 'He's recreated the atmosphere perfectly. Extremely clever for a contemporary painter, don't you think? He used to live locally, but went south of the border several years ago. Such a shame, I only hope wherever he is now, he's much appreciated.'

Paul nodded in agreement and stepped back to admire the horse-drawn carriages and dimly lit streets. 'It reminds me very much of Atkinson Grimshaw…'

Morag's face brightened, pleased that Paul had not only admired the painting but also appeared to know something about art. Then, why shouldn't he, considering his exquisite work for the House of St Claire. 'So… you're a Grimshaw fan too, are you, Mr Hadley? How nice.'

Convinced that Morag hadn't invited him here to talk about art, Paul watched her take her place at the desk that had once belonged to her husband. In her hand she held a bulky brown envelope. Brown envelopes, Paul thought warily. He'd taken a distinct dislike to brown envelopes in recent months. The earlier ones had contained divorce papers from Gina's solicitor and endless bills that she'd accumulated, and the most recent, numerous official documents relating to her death. He must make sure everything was dealt with, once and for all, on his return to Edinburgh.

Paul's gaze fell on Morag, now dwarfed behind the uncluttered desk. Apart from the thick brown envelope there was only a row of pens nestling in a shiny brass inkstand, a leather bound sheet of virgin blotting paper and two photographs in antique silver frames. Morag motioned Paul to a chair.

'Mr Hadley, while I must thank you for answering my summons at such short notice, I also owe you an apology. I'm afraid I haven't spoken to you since the death of your – er – wife. It must have been a very painful time for you and the children. I understand from Mary the girls are well; they had tea with Fiona last week?'

'Yes, quite well, thank you, Mrs Sinclair. Mary has been very kind and Fiona's company has helped the girls immeasurably.'

'Good. I'm pleased to hear it. It's reassuring to know the family is able to do something in return. We owe you a great deal, Mr Hadley. Without you injecting new life into Sinclair's….'

Overcome with embarrassment, Paul still felt sure this wasn't why he'd been summoned to Conasg - and it was a summons, wasn't it? Only moments ago, Morag had used the very word. How was she expecting him to respond?

Following Morag's gaze in the direction of one of the photographs, a photo of Jenny on her graduation day, Paul knew he would have to mention the woman he'd come to admire and love so desperately

'I might have come up with the idea for the House of St Claire but without Jenny's doggedness and tireless determination to move Sinclair's forward, I doubt if things would have happened as quickly as they did.'

'Perhaps not,' acknowledged Morag, thinking of other "things" that had also happened quickly. She was now extremely anxious to bring Jennifer into the conversation, 'and I well recall my daughter's faith in you, when she first brought me your drawings. By the way… have you seen much of Jennifer lately, Mr Hadley?'

'Unfortunately no, not since Gina…' Paul bit his lip. He'd been determined not to mention Gina again. He was already convinced Morag knew of her son's affair, and as for what happened on the night of the dinner-dance… Besides, Morag was asking him about Jenny.

'Er - like Mary and Fiona,' he added, 'Jenny has also been an enormous help with Celestina and Emily, and the girls adore her.

They were so disappointed when she didn't join us on our cinema trip because of her stomach upset. Then, when she couldn't have lunch with me for the same reason... How is Jennifer now? Is she better? Is she here?'

Paul waited anxiously, wondering what else Morag was expecting him to say. This tiny sparrow of a woman, dwarfed behind the vast oak desk, sat tapping her fingers against the mysterious brown envelope and its bulky contents. What was it Andrew had said? 'Don't worry, she won't eat you!'

Morag rose from her chair and made her way round the desk until she was facing him. For what she was about to say, she needed to look straight into his eyes.

'In answer to your question... no, Jennifer isn't here. In fact I've sent her away for a rest and I want you to go to Italy to accompany her home.'

Paul's mind was in turmoil at the very mention of Italy. The last time he'd gone to Italy was for Gina's funeral. Why then, would Morag send Jenny so far away simply to recover from a stomach upset? Turning his attention back to the painting above the fireplace, he recalled that in Victorian England it was quite common for people to go to sanatoriums in Italy and Switzerland if they were really ill. Presumably Jenny had been well enough to travel abroad on her own, but was she now so ill that she needed someone to bring her home?

Numbed, he turned back to face Morag. 'I'm truly sorry, I had no idea Jenny was so unwell. Stevie led me to believe it was just a tummy upset.'

'Hmm, and I would imagine that's what my daughter wanted us all to believe. Forgive me, Mr Hadley, but I have to be very blunt with you. From what you've just said and from the look on your face, am I right in thinking you didn't know that Jennifer was pregnant?'

'Pregnant? Jennifer is pregnant but when...?'

'I would imagine only you know the answer to that... as I'm assuming the baby was yours?'

'Actually, I was going to ask *when* did Jenny tell you that she was pregnant?' Paul interrupted. 'she's said nothing to me.'

'She didn't. I found out quite by accident and had my suspicions confirmed the weekend I myself was taken poorly and ended up in hospital. By then, unfortunately, Jennifer had suffered a miscarriage...'

Paul sat with his head buried in his hands, unable to believe his ears. In one breath Morag and told him Jenny was pregnant and the next... that she'd had a miscarriage. Why hadn't Jenny said anything to him about this? Was that why she'd been avoiding him? And now that she was far from home, and presumably all alone with no one to talk to...it was all too awful to comprehend.

'I honestly had no knowledge of this,' he said at length. 'And in view of my wife's recent death, perhaps I shouldn't even be saying this Mrs Sinclair, but I love and respect Jennifer. I would *never* do anything to hurt her. Though, I'm still confused as to why she's in Italy...'

'Of course you are, I should have explained before. I sent Jennifer to Venice, not only because it's a city she fell in love with when she and her friend Moira were students, but also because I thought it seemed the perfect place to lay her ghosts to rest.'

Paul was about to query the word 'ghosts' when they were interrupted by the gentle tapping on the door. Flora Tandy entered with a tray of coffee and chocolate biscuits. Morag regarded her with a wry smile. Flora was taking liberties. Chocolate biscuits was it now, instead of the usual arrowroot?

'Now where were we,' Morag asked, once Tandy had left the room.

'Laying ghosts, I believe,' Paul said with a frown.

'Ah, yes. So we were. And the way I see it is that Jenny has three. The first is her ex-fiancé, the second is your wife and the third has no name…'

'What has Gina got to do with Jenny? Since Gina's death I've hardly seen Jenny!'

'Precisely. And that's why you see. Knowing what you and your little girls were going through, how could she burden you with the news that she was expecting your child?'

'That wouldn't have been a burden. I would have supported her and the baby, only I can't now - can I? If there is no baby…'

Morag watched Paul's face fill with renewed concern. 'Oh, I think you can, because the way I see it, the child she lost… who sadly has no name, is the third ghost. For that Jennifer's going to need you by her side.'

Wishing he could leave that very minute and head straight to the airport, Paul knew only too well it wasn't going to be that easy. How could he leave the girls at such short notice? Sensing his dilemma, Morag broke in kindly. 'If you're worried about Celestina and Emily, would it help if I were to tell you that Stevie has everything under control?'

'Stevie? How?'

'Well, perhaps it's better to say that Stevie has arranged everything with Helen Craig - is that her name? And then of course Mary has also offered to have the girls to stay. Fiona's so very excited, she's already making plans…'

At any other time Paul would have been furious with people organizing his life without prior warning, but this was different. He wanted Jenny to be part of his life. He sighed and managed a weak smile in Morag's direction. 'Well, it looks as if you've thought of everything.'

'Let's just put it down to Sinclair efficiency, shall we Mr Hadley?'

'I do wish you'd call me Paul.'

'Then you must call me Morag,' she urged, handing over the brown envelope containing his airline tickets and hotel booking. 'Stevie, as I've already mentioned, has made all the necessary preparations for Celestina and Emily, but I left all the travel arrangements to Andrew. He likes to do things in style. He also assures me the hotel will be ideal for – shall we say a happy reunion? It's off the Riva degli Schiavoni, do you know it?'

'I'm afraid I don't. I don't know Venice at all. Gina's family came from Abruzzi. But at least I can speak some of the language.'

With a distinct twinkle in her eyes, Morag held out her hand. 'Then I'll wish you bon voyage and good luck, Paul, and give my love to my daughter.'

CHAPTER THIRTY TWO

As the plane circled over the lagoon, Jenny began to have misgivings. She should never have agreed to this trip. On the one hand, she felt guilty at leaving her mother and on the other, she was still coming to terms with grief. Her mind was in turmoil. One moment she'd been dealing with the shock discovery that she was pregnant; the next secretly delighting in the prospect of motherhood - planning a nursery and knitting tiny garments - only for the short-lived joy to be replaced by loss, pain and despair. No, coming to Venice was not a good idea.

Turning her thoughts back to her last appointment with Dr McAllister, Jenny recalled how Alex had assured her that Morag was not only well enough to be left but also that she, Jennifer Sinclair, was a perfectly healthy young woman. Providing she didn't go around falling off chairs in the middle of the night, there was absolutely no reason why she couldn't have lots of babies.

I don't need lots of babies, Jenny had told herself while she was packing her suitcase. I'd be perfectly happy with one. I simply don't want to spend the rest of my life alone. Paul, according to rumour, now had Marina Hendry hanging on his every word; Andrew had Mary and the children and her mother had Flora Tandy. Not to mention Hamish, Jenny thought with a smile, as even Hamish had taken to coming into Conasg House more frequently. Fussing and clucking like an old mother hen, he'd even offered to help with the housework and cooking. In the end Miss Tandy had been practically driven to despair, and Jenny had been driven to pack her suitcase.

With the plane touching down on the tarmac, Jenny found herself swept along the aircraft with the melee of post-carnival tourists and elegantly tailored business-men.

'Please,' she wanted to say to the stewardess, 'can't I simply remain on board and fly back with you to Edinburgh?'

Instead the stewardess flashed a brilliant smile in her direction, revealing exquisite dentistry, and with a 'Welcome to Venice Madam, enjoy your stay,' Jenny alighted on Venetian soil.

In the Arrivals hall a young woman stood holding a placard bearing the name ' *Miss Gennifur Sinclair.* ' Jenny paused and looked inside the envelope she'd been given by Andrew when he'd taken her to the airport.

'All the information you need is in there,' he'd told her, giving her a hug goodbye. 'There'll be someone to meet you at the airport in Venice and they'll take you by car from the mainland to pick up a water taxi. Now off you go. Don't worry about Sinclairs and enjoy yourself!'

Hmph! That's probably easier said than done, Andrew! Jenny thought, stopping in front of the placard bearer.

'Ah! Signorina Sinclair, I am Francesa Vitti - you follow me pliz. I am to take you to where my brother wait with water taxi, si?'

Without warning, the young woman picked up Jennifer's suitcase and was gone. True to her word Jenny was transported from the mainland to where a row of water taxis were waiting on the edge of the canal. A blast of diesel fumes met her nostrils and Francesca turned and waved, 'Come Signorina Sinclair, Giovanni is waiting, 'e will take you.'

Giovanni grinned and reached forward. With one hand grabbing hold of Jenny's arm, he swept both herself and her suitcase on board, while Francesca paid off the driver of the taxi cab and also leapt onboard.

Breathing in deeply as Giovanni manoeuvred his way from the busy quayside and directed his boat at a steady pace across the lagoon, Jenny watched as the refreshing breeze caught at the young man's curls. He looked little more than a boy, yet was presumably old enough to hold a water taxi licence.

Arriving at the hotel, Francesca appeared somewhat agitated and, running towards a short, balding man with a large moustache, she snatched a violin case from his grasp and sped away.

'Signorina Sinclair,' the man beamed in greeting. 'Welcome to our 'otel. You must excuse my daughter, Francesca. She play in orchestra and is late for rehearsal. Come. This way if you pliz. *Giovanni, bagaglio!* '

With Giovanni duly obliging, Jenny was ushered from a lift along pale marble corridors and windows hung with turquoise silk. At length her suitcase was placed outside a polished mahogany door and Signor Vitti drew a large key from his pocket. Jenny stood open mouthed as the door swung open.

Signor Vitti registered the look of shock on her face. 'But you do not like, Miss Sinclair?'

'Oh, I like very much,' Jenny replied stepping across the threshold, but I think there must be a mistake – this room can't be for me.'

'Ah, but it is, signorina. It eez no mistake. Your brother, Andrew say 'e want the best room for you. You are very special sister – si? Like you this room is very special. It once belong to the *marchesa* and while you are in Venice… it belong to you. Now, would you like some tea?'

'Si, Signor Vitti,' Jenny said, fixing him with a warm smile, 'tea would be wonderful.'

Watching him scurry away, Jenny sat on the bed and laughed for the first time in weeks. Here in this magnificent hotel, that had once been a *palazzio* no less, she was sitting in the *marchesa's* bedroom waiting not for her lover, fine wines or sweetmeats, but a tray of tea!

Roused from a deep slumber by the sound of foghorns echoing across the lagoon, Jenny climbed from the bed and walked barefoot to the window. How strange the cool marble felt beneath her feet, such a contrast from the deep pile at Sinclair's and the berber rugs of her cottage.

The windows, she discovered, were still shuttered from her arrival. She had declined Signor Vitti's offer to open them, saying she would prefer to rest before dinner.

'Si, that eez good, Signorina Sinclair - *riposari*. Eet eez better you rest after the travelling, give you appetite for dinner. Your brother 'e say you must eat, and my wife Carla make the best pasta in Venice.'

Yes on both counts, thought Jenny some time later. Carla Vitti did make the most wonderful pasta, and despite Andrew's words ringing in her head, she was able to eat very little. Since she'd lost the baby, her appetite had simply deserted her. What hadn't however, was her desire to retrace her footsteps from the earlier trip she'd made with Moira.

Sensing rain and taking her raincoat from the panelled wardrobe of polished mahogany and gilt, Jenny avoided using the lift. Instead she slipped quietly down the stairs to the side entrance where Giovanni had moored the taxi. Water lapped effortlessly at the brightly painted mooring posts, and in the background she heard Signor Vitti extolling the virtue of his wife's pasta to some unseen guests.

Initially criss-crossing her way through a maze of darkened alleyways and myriad narrow bridges, Jenny was pleased to leave the hotel and St Mark's Square behind her. It was only when delicious smells wafted forth from behind closed shutters, accompanied by the sound of laughter, excited chatter and, even in this magical city, the noise of television, that she began to feel completely and utterly alone. What would her family be doing now? Andrew and Mary, Mother and Miss Tandy and even Paul and the girls, how she missed them all.

Reminding herself that she'd only been here a day and Andrew had insisted she spent a whole week here, Jenny stared about her with unseeing eyes. What was it her mother had said when they'd been closeted together? 'You need a complete break, Jennifer, my dear. You also need to lay your ghosts to rest...'

Jennifer shivered and tightened the belt of her raincoat. The way the sea mist was sweeping across the lagoon was itself almost ghostly. Turning round, she decided to return to the hotel. It might have been enormous fun getting lost when she was with Moira but tonight, standing here on her own, it wasn't the same. Besides, she needed to be in the right frame of mind when dealing with *her* ghosts. Perhaps tomorrow...

*

In the Edinburgh house, where Mary was anything but alone, there was a great deal of excitement. Fiona, freshly bathed and her hair newly plaited in thick coils, jumped up and down at the bedroom window. She ran to where Celestina and Emily were waiting to be dressed by Mary and Catriona.

'I can see Hamish and the car, and Grannie is there too! You see! I told you she promised she would come.'

'Fiona! Will you stop bouncing about like that. Your ribbons have already come undone once. Now, be a good girl, go and find the new shoes and tights we bought for Cele and Emily while Catriona sees to their dresses and I go and welcome Grannie and Miss Tandy.'

In the hallway, Andrew was helping his mother with her coat. Apart from looking a trifle thinner, Morag's eyes sparkled with excitement.

'Do stop worrying, Andrew! Alex McCallister says there's a good few years left in me yet and I've really been looking forward to this outing.'

'I know... but do you not think you'll find it all too tiring Mother, particularly after the journey you've just had?'

'For goodness' sake, Andrew!' Mary scolded, 'stop fussing and take your mother and Miss Tandy into the drawing room. She *will* be tired if you leave her standing there in the hallway like that.'

Mary bent and kissed her mother-in-law, taking in the delicate smell of lily-of-the-valley. Morag's hair, she observed, was newly permed. She was also wearing a brand new tweed suit.

'Are the girls ready?' Morag enquired, aware of much giggling coming from the upstairs landing.

'Almost,' replied Catriona, 'and they're also terribly excited. Fiona's been standing at the window since lunchtime and all three girls hardly slept a wink last night.'

Mary cast a cursory look in the direction of the stairs and whispered in Morag's ear. 'Despite all the noise they're making now, I'd better warn you, Cele and Emily can be a little bit quiet and withdrawn at times. They're still getting over… well, you know.'

Morag nodded in understanding, 'And what of Mr Had… I mean Paul. Have you heard from him yet?'

'Yes, he telephoned Andrew to say his flight was delayed, due to fog in Venice and not here for once.'

'That makes a change, I suppose. Right then, as I'm hoping Paul will soon be setting off to do what he has to do, is my trio of little girls ready to set out with me?' Morag looked at her watch. 'Don't forget we also have to fetch Miss Stephens.'

Fiona led Cele and Emily downstairs, where they stood nervously at the drawing room door.

'Hello, Grannie,' said Fiona, skipping forward. Seeing Morag's knees draped in a tartan rug she stopped short, a worried look upon her face.

'We are still going, aren't we? You're not poorly again, are you?'

'Of course we're still going, Fiona,' Morag said, smiling and holding out her arms. 'When your Grannie makes a promise she keeps it! Although I think your Daddy thinks I'm totally incapable of taking three wee girls out to tea. And look how Miss Tandy has bundled me up in this rug. I feel like a parcel, though I doubt if I'd fit through the letterbox!'

Fiona's eyes opened wide, trying to think of her Grannie being pushed through the letterbox. Then, she remembered something else. She leant forward and whispered in Morag's ear, while everyone looked on.

'No, it's all right, Fiona, I haven't forgotten. You don't have to worry,' Morag whispered in reply. 'Now Celestina and Emily, are you going to come and introduce yourselves? I don't want to get you two pretty girls mixed up, do I?'

Mary and Catriona watched from the doorway, as Hamish helped Morag into the front passenger seat of the Bentley and three excited little girls scrambled into the back. Andrew meanwhile assisted Miss Tandy into his BMW and checked the boot. He needed to make sure there was enough space for Stevie's wheelchair.

'How I'd love to be tucked in a corner to see them all arrive,' Mary said, turning to her eldest daughter. 'Can you just imagine? I expect your father is glad he's only acting as chauffeur and won't have to stay with them for the entire afternoon!'

Catriona gave a wistful smile. 'I think it's lovely, all this plotting and planning on Gran's behalf for Auntie Jen. It's *so* romantic. I do hope it all turns out right in Venice. Do you think it will?'

'Absolutely,' said Mary, closing the front door. 'If not, your Grandmother will want to know why! As for romance Catriona, don't worry, you're still only young. There'll be plenty of romance left in the world for you.'

Mary took hold of her daughter's hand, sensing that each of them had been thinking back to last year's fateful skiing holiday; wasn't that where all this had begun? Initially with Gina at the airport, and later Catriona's narrow escape from the clutches of that awful skiing instructor.

Putting on a brave face, Mary announced brightly. 'I can't promise you a tea as grand as the girls and Grannie will be having this afternoon, but with Iain playing rugby, we can at least share a pot of Earl Grey without his rude comments about smoky dishwater. I've also made us some smoked salmon sandwiches and eclairs, so if you'll just slice the lemon and find the House of St Claire napkins...'

A bemused silence fell as the party of six - comprising an elderly lady leading three small girls, followed by her equally elderly companion pushing a young woman in a wheelchair, were led to their table by the head waiter.

Soft murmurings of approval emitted from the onlookers as the children, dressed in velvet with white lace tights and black patent shoes, took their places at the table. Morag acknowledged her audience with a gracious smile; she was already beginning to enjoy this.

'Are you quite comfortable there, Miss Stephens?' Flora Tandy pushed Stevie's chair nearer the table. 'Will you be needing a rug?'

'Of course she doesn't, Flora!' said Morag, 'and don't you dare go asking me if she takes sugar or there'll be no cream cakes for you!'

When Morag winked at Stevie, Fiona began to giggle. She knew how her grannie loved to tease. As if on cue, Cele and Emily giggled too. They were beginning to like Fiona's grandma. Perhaps she wasn't quite so frightening after all, and hadn't Fiona said they could share her? With Grannie Hadley dead and Grannie 'Tino so far away, it would be nice to have a grandma again.

'Young man!' Morag called to the waiter. 'We will have out tea now, if you please. That will be five cream teas... no make that six,' she said, looking at Flora with a mischievous twinkle in her eye.

The waiter walked away only to be summoned back immediately. Morag's clear, clipped voice echoed across the room and all eyes turned in her direction. What was it Fiona had whispered to her only moments before they left? 'Oh, yes! And please can you make that special jam with our cream teas. We would like jam without bits.'

CHAPTER THIRTY THREE

Francesca knocked gently at the bedroom door and entered with the tray. Jenny stirred sleepily and watched the tall, slim figure draw back heavy silk brocade drapes.

'Shall I open the shutters, *signorina*? Last night's fog has disappeared and it will be a beautiful day, I think.'

Jenny nodded, watching Francesca fix the curtains in place with large silken tassels. She also surveyed the contents of her breakfast tray: fresh rolls, assorted cheeses and cooked meat, fruit juice and tea. Apart from a snack on the plane, a minute portion of pasta yesterday evening and a piece of fruit, she'd eaten practically nothing for the past few days. Could she even stomach breakfast? Probably not, she concluded. First she must lay her ghosts to rest, and only when that was completed would she be able to entertain the prospect of food.

'Signorina Sinclair, I excuse myself. When you arrive, I leave you quickly with Giovanni and my father – I 'ad orchestra practice with my violin. Today I do not so... if I can 'elp you... take you sightseeing?'

'Thank you Francesca, that's very kind of you, but I've already decided where I'm going today. I intend to visit the Frari's Basillica and La Fosca.'

Francesca might think it an odd choice, the sharp contrast between the ornate Frari and the small church on the island of Torcello, but Jenny had her reasons.

'My father 'e say you must eat,' Francesca advised, turning to leave, 'and my mother is very worried – you eat so leetle.'

'Please tell your parents not to worry, Francesca. Tonight I will eat, I promise.'

Watching her go, Jenny's gaze took in the opulence of the *marchesa's* bedroom. Trust Andrew! she thought. All this luxury is simply wasted on me.

Running her hands along the crisp white linen sheets, her fingers reached up to trace the carved wooden and gilded bed posts.

'Yes, pure unadulterated luxury,' she whispered, studying the pleated silk canopy above the bed. 'I doubt very much if the *marchesa* got much sleep in this room!'

With her thoughts winging away to Paul and the night of the dance, Jenny felt her cheeks redden. She turned on her side and clutched at her pillow, trying desperately to remember the sequence of events that night. 'Or should that be morning?' she murmured into lace-edged linen. 'Oh, Paul, if only you were here now, if only things could have been different. This bed isn't made for one… it's made for making love… made for making babies.'

With a stifled sob, Jenny forced herself to get up. Lack of food was presumably beginning to play tricks on her. If she had a shower first, then perhaps she might feel like eating something. On the other hand, she must also leave the hotel soon if she was to reach Torcello before the tourists arrived.

*

Hopelessly lost, Paul was beginning to regret not taking a water taxi directly to the hotel. He'd been so sure that with his knowledge of Italian streets and the language he could find his way easily enough. Venice, he discovered to his dismay, was not Abruzzi. Convinced Jenny would have left the hotel already, he faced the prospect of waiting a whole day before he caught up with her.

I should have telephoned, he thought, wheeling his suitcase into yet another blind alley, but as Andrew had assured him it was probably better to surprise Jenny… Initially, it had seemed such a good idea leaving early in the morning. Now… with the sun rising ever higher in the sky he was not so sure.

'Oh, Jenny,' he sighed, 'where are you? Will I ever find you?'

Hearing his plea, an elderly woman scrubbing white stone steps looked up with kind, questioning eyes. ' *Signore?*'

In desperation, Paul showed her Andrew's instructions containing the name of the hotel.

'*Sì.*' she cried, with a toothless grin, and pointed ahead of her. '*Si – dritto attraverso la piazza a poi a destre.*'

When Paul repeated her instructions, the old lady nodded and grinned enthusiastically, leaving him to wonder if dentists were in short supply in Venice. Then he ran as he'd never run before, straight on and to the right, only to discover he'd been near the hotel all along. He'd simply been going round in circles.

The hotel was almost empty, with a lone waiter clearing the remains of the breakfast buffet and laying the tables for lunch.

'La Signorina Sinclair?' Paul enquired.

With a shrug of his shoulders, the young man pointed in the direction of the enclosed courtyard. Paul's spirits lifted. Did that mean Jenny was there? Sadly, he discovered the courtyard was almost empty. There was only a young woman, seated in the shade, playing Schubert's string quintet in C major. She looked up at his approach and laid down her violin. '*Signore?*'

'*Scusi, la Signorina Sinclair, per favore.*'

'Ah, *sì*, she 'as gone.'

'Gone? Gone where – *dove?* You mean left the hotel for good?' Paul's heart sank. Could Jenny have left so soon and decided not to stay in the hotel after all? Had she been making her way back to the airport, while he was making his way here? It was all too much to contemplate.

Wheeling his suitcase to a bench, Paul sat down dejectedly. Seconds later the young woman was smiling and walking towards him.

'No, signore, she 'as not left; she 'as gone for sightseeing. Signorina Sinclair tell me she go to the Frari and Torcello. Per'aps is best you try Torcello. But she must be very 'ungry, signore, she eat nothing for days. I think she only cry.'

Francesca remembered collecting Jenny's breakfast tray. La signorina was sitting on the bed with red rimed eyes, clutching a box of tissues, while her breakfast tray remained untouched.

'*Grazie*,' said Paul, relieved that he wasn't too late, after all. 'Is it OK if I leave my case here?'

'*Prego, signore*,' called Francesca, returning to her violin, watching Paul disappear almost as suddenly as he'd arrived.

*

Approaching the island on the water-bus, Jenny cast her mind back to the time she and Moira had fallen in love with Torcello's isolation in the middle of the lagoon. Earlier, having both marvelled at Titian's *Assumption* in the Frari, they too had taken a water bus before making their way to the delightful octagonal church of Santa Fosca. Standing together in silence, admiring its melancholy beauty, both young women had been lost for words.

This morning Jenny was glad she was the only person heading for Santa Fosca. The other tourists, who'd alighted with her, were heading for Sainte Marie de Genetrix. Those remaining on board would presumably be heading for Murano and Burano in their search of glass and lace.

Glass and lace were the last things on Jenny's mind as she tied a black silk scarf around her head and slipped quietly into the welcoming stillness beyond. How strange to think that many years ago, someone had described Santa Fosca as looking more like an Alpine refuge than a church. More than anything else at that moment, Jenny *was* seeking refuge.

Also appropriate were the two large mosaics, one representing the Last Judgement and the other of the Madonna. The first reminded her of the sad, tragic Gina and how, only months ago, Gina had been judged by the Sinclairs at a time that had been difficult for them all. As for the second mosaic, Jenny directed her gaze to the tear-stained face of the Madonna. The Madonna who appeared to be looking straight at her with gentle hands raised in blessing. Stepping forward Jenny lit a candle, knelt and prayed for the first time in weeks. Unlike the Madonna, Jenny had never got to hold her child… yet she still had to bid it goodbye…

A scraping of chairs behind her told her she was no longer alone. It was a couple from the same water bus. The woman talked noisily, pointing up at the cupola and the man, feigning interest, flicked noisily through his guide book. Through misted eyes, Jenny watched her candle burn slowly away and left the building with heavy heart.

Once outside in the cool freshness of morning, she became suddenly dizzy and overcome with hunger with Francesca's earlier words 'You must eat' echoing in her head.

'Yes, I know and I will,' Jenny whispered as if in reply, recalling the untouched breakfast tray. But did she want to eat here alone on Torcello? Wouldn't it be better to return to the seclusion of the hotel instead?

Deciding on the latter, Jenny was about to head back for the approaching water-bus when she remembered the bridge. The same bridge, from all those years ago, when she'd been here with Moira. Devoid of parapets, it spanned the narrow expanse of water with an air of simplistic solitude. Then, with their heads filled with romantic notions of what life had in store for them, they'd found a small clump of wild flowers, scattered petals into the water below, and made a wish.

Today there were no such flowers. It was still too early in the year. Nevertheless, even without flowers, she could still renew that wish of finding true happiness.

Clutching a small bouquet of pink rosebuds and stepping from the shadows, Paul watched Jenny's progress as if in slow motion. He'd walked across that same bridge only moments ago, thinking to himself how dangerous it would be if someone were to miss their footing and fall into the water. Alarmed to see Jenny looking so thin, haunted, and dazed (almost as if she wasn't aware of her surroundings), he realized she was heading straight for the edge of the parapet. His blood ran cold in his veins.

Sensing it was too dangerous to call out, and running across the grass before leaping onto the bridge to grab her arm before she fell, Paul drew Jenny towards him. She looked at him as if in a dream.

'Paul? Paul! What are you doing here?'

'At the moment,' he said nervously, 'trying to stop us both from falling in the water. Whatever you do, don't look down and don't move, just let me get my balance.'

'What?'

Seconds later, still clinging onto her, Paul steadied himself and edged her onto safer ground. Only then did Jenny realize how perilously close they'd been to danger.

'But how did I get here? I don't remember coming this far. I was in the church and the Madonna was crying and holding out her arms and I was saying goodbye to our baby...'

Fresh tears filled Jenny's eyes as Paul loosened the headscarf from her neck, stroked her hair and brushed away a tear with his thumb.

'I'm so sorry... so sorry about the baby, Jenny. I've only just found out. Why didn't you tell me?'

Unable to meet his gaze, Jenny whispered, 'Who told you?'

'Your mother. In fact it was her idea that I come and take you home. She made Andrew see to all the arrangements. I was so worried about you. In fact, we've all been besides ourselves with worry.'

'We?'

'Yes, me, Morag, Miss Tandy, not to mention Old Hamish, Mary and...'

Jenny gasped and broke away from his embrace. 'You mean they all know about the baby... they know everything?'

'No, don't worry,' Paul said, fixing her with a reassuring smile. 'They can't know everything, can they?' He lifted her face to look into her soulful eyes. 'Jenny, I love you, you do see that don't you? The night of the dance... it wasn't exactly the ideal way to conceive a child, was it?'

Her voice was barely audible as she looked down at the blue-grey water flowing away under the bridge. 'Perhaps not... but I wanted the baby... our baby... so much. After the miscarriage I suddenly felt as if I had nothing, when everyone else... Mary and Andrew, you and the girls - even Mother has Miss Tandy, though I suspect Dr McCallister would put all that down to hormones.'

Paul smiled and brushed his lips gently against her cheek. 'Hormones apart, you have me, if you want me, not to mention Fiona, Cele and Emily and of course we mustn't forget Stevie. She's also been frantic with worry.'

'Stevie! Is she in on this conspiracy too?'

'I'm afraid so,' Paul said, bending down to retrieve the rosebuds that he'd thrown to the ground earlier. 'Gracious! She gave me a right ticking off for not sending you flowers on Valentine's Day.'

Jenny took the flowers and, carefully removing a single bloom, tossed it lovingly into the water. 'For the baby,' she said softly.

Paul thought for a moment, then slowly removed a stem for himself. 'For Gina, ' he murmured.

There was no need to explain. Jenny knew that without Gina she and Paul would never have met. In silence, standing alone on the bridge, they watched the two rosebuds drifting slowly away, while high in the sky above them, wispy clouds parted like curtains revealing a golden ray of sunshine.

'As a little bird from your hotel tells me you have been neglecting yourself when it comes to food,' said Paul, taking her arm, 'we are not leaving Torcello until you've had something to eat and after that...'

'After that?' Jenny said, tilting her head to look at him.

'I thought we could go to Burano or Murano to buy Stevie a wedding present.'

'What? But Stevie's not even engaged!'

'There I have to correct you, Miss Sinclair.'

'You mean Stevie and Charlie... when? Are you sure?'

'Positive,' Paul grinned. 'Andrew told me just before I caught my flight. It seems he came back from lunch the other day and found Charlie Stuart on one knee proposing to your PA.'

'That's wonderful! I can't wait to congratulate them both. How soon can we return to Edinburgh? I wonder if there's a flight...?'

Paul looked up in mock alarm, stopping outside a nearby restaurant. 'Not so fast, Jennifer Sinclair. I've been given strict instructions to keep you here for a few days longer.'

Finishing their lunch, Paul gestured to the waiter for the bill, then reached for Jenny's hand and held it to his lips.

'I've been thinking, perhaps we could go to Burano and Murano tomorrow, instead? Andrew just happened to mention something about a certain *marchesa's* bedroom. I wonder if you'd care to show it to me...?'

A flush of colour dusted Jenny's cheeks as the waiter brought the bill.

'*Luna di miele*? ' he enquired with a smile.

No, thought Paul, no honeymoon on this trip... but one day soon, I hope.

CHAPTER THIRTY FOUR

With memories of Paul's Edinburgh house and Jennifer's cottage long behind them, Jenny stood in the doorway of Paul's studio. It had been the right decision to move to this house after all. Here, not only had they begun a new life together, but also it meant Paul had a proper place to work.

Jenny watched him now, taking comfort from his very being as he sketched away in earnest. Gone was the strained and anxious-looking Paul she'd first met ten years ago and in his place, a man completely at peace with himself. Overcome with a surge of contentment, Jenny watched the dappled late afternoon sunshine dance on Paul's head, picking out the stray silver hairs at his temples and the fine laughter-lines around his eyes. Sensing her presence, he looked up to greet her.

'Everything OK?' he enquired softly.

'Yes, fine – it's just so quiet without the girls. Would you mind if I sit here for a while? I promise not to disturb you.'

'Of course. I won't be a moment. I'm just finishing off this sketch.'

Listening to the soft scratching of pencil on paper, Jenny thought fondly of Celestina and Emily. Now old enough to go to school summer camp, they had both grown in confidence in recent years. Cele of course remained the ever-protective older sister, but Emily was no longer the shy, nervous child Jenny remembered.

Aware of Paul laying down his pencil, Jenny asked, 'What's that, a new idea for the House of St Claire?'

'Mmm. Come over here and tell me what you think of it.'

'What is it supposed to be?'

Paul pulled Jenny onto his lap and caressed her cheek. 'What does it look like?'

She frowned, surprised at what she saw. Paul had never designed anything like this before for Sinclair's.

'Well... it looks like a tartan pram, with the House of St Claire emblem on the side.'

'And what do you think of it?'

For a moment, Jenny said nothing; she didn't want to hurt his feelings, yet for the first time ever she thought the design to be in appalling taste.

Paul, looking deeply solemn, waited patiently for her reply. 'I take it you don't like it.'

'No, darling, I'm afraid I don't. Isn't it a bit over the top?'

'I see, so you won't be wanting a pram like that for our baby, then?'

Turning to face Paul, Jenny saw that he was smiling at her.

'H-how long have you known,' she said, looking back at the drawing of the pram.

'Oh, Jenny!' Paul said, drawing her closer in his arms. 'I live with you and work with you, we've been married for eight years and you think I don't know everything about you. I've been waiting for weeks for you to tell me about the baby... why haven't you?'

Jenny's eyes filled with tears as she clung to him. 'Because I wanted to make sure. We've had so many false alarms, I just couldn't bear to disappoint you again.'

Comforted by the warmth of his embrace, she thought back to all her previous miscarriages and the dark empty nights she'd lain in his arms, totally bereft, as they'd mourned the loss of yet another baby.

'Well, take it from me, this is no false alarm,' Paul said confidently, tearing up his drawing. 'and as our baby is going to need a proper pram, I'd better get cracking on a decent design worthy of our son and the House of St Claire. In the meantime, Mrs Hadley, may I suggest you go and ring your mother?'

Watching her walk into the hallway with a spring in her step, Paul emitted a sigh and turned to the familiar painting of Princes Street hanging on the wall above his desk. Morag had given it to him only last month as a birthday present.

'You take it,' she'd insisted, when Jenny left the room to bring in his birthday cake. 'I want you to have it - I know it reminds you of Jenny and a special time in your relationship and hopefully you can....'

Reluctantly he'd accepted the gift, offered with her frail and wrinkled hands, and then noticed the twinkle in her eye.

'Morag,' he'd asked, quizzically. Hopefully I can what?'

'Give me a photograph of your son to hang in its place alongside those of my other grandchildren.'

Smiling, Paul had kissed her on the cheek and murmured softly, 'Bless you, Morag. You're just as perceptive as ever, I see. Don't worry, I shall make sure you get your photograph.'